THE
SURVIVORS

ALSO BY JANE HARPER

The Dry

Force of Nature

The Lost Man

THE
SURVIVORS

JANE HARPER

FLATIRON
BOOKS
NEW YORK

THE SURVIVORS. Copyright © 2020 by Jane Harper. All rights reserved. Printed in the United States of America. For information, address Flatiron Books, 120 Broadway, New York, NY 10271.

www.flatironbooks.com

Designed by Omar Chapa

The Library of Congress Cataloging-in-Publication Data is available upon request.

ISBN 978-1-250-23242-7 (hardcover)
ISBN 978-1-250-81795-2 (signed edition)
ISBN 978-1-250-79336-2 (international, sold outside the U.S., subject to rights availability)
ISBN 978-1-250-23241-0 (ebook)

Our books may be purchased in bulk for promotional, educational, or business use. Please contact your local bookseller or the Macmillan Corporate and Premium Sales Department at 1-800-221-7945, extension 5442, or by email at MacmillanSpecialMarkets@macmillan.com.

Originally published in Australia in 2020 by Pan Macmillan Australia Pty Ltd

First U.S. Edition: 2021
First Signed Edition: 2021
First International Edition: 2021

10 9 8 7 6 5 4 3 2 1

For Charlotte and Ted

THE
SURVIVORS

PROLOGUE

She could—almost—have been one of The Survivors.

Standing there, outlined by the weak light, her back turned and the salt water lapping at her feet. Then she moved. Just a small shift in weight and the in-out of breath, but enough to break the illusion before it was fully formed.

She was still looking away, focused on something he couldn't make out in the dark. Somewhere, a wave broke and the sea surged, fresh and cold against his own legs as it fizzed white around her bare calves. He watched as she reached down with her free hand and gathered her skirt hem above her knees. The air was filled with a fine haze and her T-shirt clung to her back and her waist.

The sea swelled again, and this time the drag of the undertow was strong enough that he took a step toward her. She didn't notice. Her face was tilted down, the silver chain of her necklace glinting against her collarbone as she leaned forward to examine something in the water. She dropped her skirt hem as the tide rushed out again, and lifted a hand to sweep aside her ponytail, which had fallen over one shoulder. It was heavy from the sea spray. A single strand of hair had caught in the corner of her mouth and she brushed it free, her fingertips running across her lips. A tightness spread across his chest and shoulders.

If you're going to do it—

The thought whispered beneath the rush of a wave. The undertow pulled again. He fought it, briefly, then took another step.

She heard him now, or sensed him at least. Some disruption in the natural rhythm flowing around her.

If you're going to do it—

She looked up. He sucked in a breath of salt-soaked air.

Do it now.

1

Kieran hoped the numbness would set in soon. The ocean's icy burn usually mellowed into something more neutral, but as the minutes ticked by he still felt cold. He braced himself as a fresh wave broke against his skin.

The water wasn't even too bad, he told himself. Not at the tail end of summer with the afternoon sun doing its best to take the edge off. Definitely goose bumps rather than hypothermia. Kieran knew he had personally described water far colder than this as "nice." Only ever here in Tasmania, though, where sea temperatures surrounding the small island state were relative.

Sydney—the voice in Kieran's head sounded suspiciously like his brother's—*has made you soft.*

Maybe. But the real problem was that instead of slicing out through the blue with breath expanding in his chest and the water roaring past his ears and nothing but hundreds of kilometers of rolling sea separating him from the next-nearest landmass, he was standing perfectly still, waist-deep, three meters from the beach.

His daughter lay milk-drunk against his bare chest, cocooned in a dry towel, a tiny sun hat shielding her eyes as she dozed. At three months old, Audrey was growing heavy now. He shifted her weight and, ignoring the mild ache in his shoulders and the cold against his legs, looked out at the horizon and let her sleep on.

Audrey was not the only one out for the count. On the beach, Kieran could see his girlfriend lying flat on her back, fully clothed, one arm flung over her eyes and her mouth slack. Mia's head was resting on a rolled-up towel with her hair splayed out in a long, dark fan against the sand. She could sleep anywhere these days, as could he.

There was almost no one else around. A teenage couple he hadn't recognized had wandered by earlier, hand in hand and barefoot, and further along the sand a young woman had been beachcombing at the shoreline since they'd arrived. At the height of summer holidaymakers outnumbered Evelyn Bay's nine-hundred-strong population by two to one, but now they had mostly left, their real lives calling them back to the mainland and beyond.

"Hey!"

A familiar voice made Kieran turn. The man was emerging from one of the small side paths that connected a row of weathered beach houses to the sand. He was grinning as he hoisted a battered backpack higher on his shoulder. At his feet loped a large dog of undetermined breed, whose size and shaggy gold-brown hair made him look disconcertingly similar to his owner.

Kieran waded out of the water and met Ash McDonald on the sand, turning so Ash could see the baby on his chest.

"Bloody hell." Ash used a callused finger to pull back a corner of the towel and leaned his unshaven face in to look at Audrey.

"Well, she's too pretty to be yours, mate, but congratulations all the same." He straightened and winked at Mia, who had roused herself now, brushing the sand from her skirt as she walked over to join them. "Just kidding. She's beautiful."

"Thanks, Ash." Mia smothered a yawn as he kissed her cheek, and reached down to pat his dog. "Hello, Shifty."

Ash nodded at Kieran's wet shorts. "How's the water?"

"Nice enough."

"Reliving the good old days, eh?"

Kieran smiled. "Rather be swimming."

Kieran couldn't count how many hours he and Ash had spent as teenagers standing up to their waists in the ocean for recovery the day after a football game, waiting for the frigid water to work its alleged magic. A lot.

Ash had been a summer face floating around Evelyn Bay on and off for years, but at fifteen he'd become a full-time fixture when his parents' divorce propelled his mother back to her hometown.

Kieran hadn't known too much about him, other than he was from a mining town in the west of the state so hardened that their local football team played on gravel, not grass. Given that, Kieran probably shouldn't have been as surprised as he was when the new guy showed up at training and, for the first time in his life, Kieran wasn't automatically winning the speed drills, his goal accuracy ranking was at risk, and on-field maneuvers that had gone unchallenged for years were now aggressively contested. He had wasted a few weeks feeling pissed off, then hit the gym and the oval even harder, only to feel pissed off again when he ran into Ash doing exactly the same.

It had been midway through the season when Kieran had arrived late to the beach and waded out only to find himself accidentally standing next to Ash. Not willing to be the one to move, Kieran had crossed his arms and stared hard at the sea. They'd stood side by side in silence for the whole session. Somewhere invisible to the north lay mainland Australia, to the far south, Antarctica. In front of them, nothing, all the way to the horizon.

"Set more personal bests this month than I did the whole of last year at my old club."

Ash's voice had caught Kieran by surprise. He had glanced over at the other boy, who was sometimes a shade stronger or a second faster or a beat quicker to react, and sometimes wasn't. Ash didn't take his eyes off the water as he spoke again.

"Been good, actually."

And bloody hell, Kieran had realized with a mix of annoyance and dawning appreciation, the bloke was right. It *had* been good. Kieran had never been better than when he was racing around after this dickhead. The coach had called time and Kieran had watched as Ash started to wade back to the beach. He had opened his mouth.

"Hey, wait a sec."

Ash had. And from then on, that was pretty much it.

Neither played footy too often anymore, but nearly a decade and a half down the line, Kieran was at least as fit as he had been then, and his job as a sports physiotherapist meant it was now his turn to encourage people to stand in freezing salt water. Ash seemed about the same too, Kieran thought. His landscaping business had given him the look of gnarled good health that came from throwing around bags of soil and wrestling downed trees.

"When'd you get back?" Ash set his backpack down on the sand, and Kieran heard the dull metal clang of gardening tools inside.

"Couple of hours ago."

Kieran and Mia had stayed only as long as was polite in his parents' house before making an excuse to get out for some fresh air. He could still see their back veranda from where he stood, only a white wooden fence separating their property from the beach. Kieran thought about having to head back inside and felt faintly claustrophobic.

"How's your dad doing?" Ash said. "Haven't run into him for a couple of weeks."

"Not great." Kieran wondered if he would have to explain, but no, of course Ash was already nodding. In a place like Evelyn Bay, people knew each other's business. Probably better than Kieran did himself. He hadn't seen his dad in person for more than eighteen months, when Brian had last been well enough to fly up to Sydney. Even then, Brian had been persistently confused, and Kieran's mum, Verity, had spent most of the visit patiently explaining things to him. When Audrey had been born three months ago, Verity had come alone to meet her first grandchild.

Despite this flashing-red warning, Kieran had still been shocked silent when they'd arrived earlier that day to be greeted by the void that had once been Brian Elliott. Kieran was genuinely unsure if his dad had deteriorated rapidly or if he himself had been in complete denial. Either way, at just sixty-six, the dementia had a throttlehold on him now. Even the doctors reckoned Brian had been dealt an unlucky hand.

"When's the move?" Ash glanced at Kieran's parents' place.

"Few weeks." The nursing home in Hobart was ready and waiting. "We thought Mum could do with a hand to clear stuff out."

"And what's she going to do? She's not going in as well, is she?"

"No." Kieran pictured Verity, who at sixty-four could easily pass for ten years younger and still ran or biked most days. "She's found a one-bedroom place near the nursing home."

"Right. That'll be"—Ash ran his tongue over his teeth as he searched for a word—"convenient."

"Yeah." Kieran really hoped so, because he strongly suspected Verity was going to absolutely hate it.

Ash thought for a moment. "Listen, tell Verity to let me know before the house hits the market. I'll tidy up the garden for her. For free, obviously."

"Really? Thanks, mate."

"No worries. It's a shit situation."

It was shit. Kieran had known that. He should have come home earlier.

"How long since you were last back?" Ash said, reading his mind.

"Two years?"

"Longer than that, I reckon," Ash said, even as Mia was shaking her head.

"It's been nearly three," she said, turning to Ash. "How's Olivia? I emailed her to say we'd be here for the week."

"Yeah, she's good, she definitely wants to catch up." Ash was reaching for his phone. "Let me check if she's around now actually; that's her place just up there. Fisherman's Cottage." He nodded along the row of beach houses backing onto the sand.

"Oh yeah?" Kieran could picture the low-slung weatherboard bungalow a dozen doors up from his parents' place. *Cottage* was a generously poetic name. Like pretty much every other house in the town—even a lot of the newer ones—it screamed 1960s architecture. "How long's she been renting there?"

"Eighteen months or so. Since she moved back, anyway."

As Ash dialed his girlfriend, Kieran tried to picture what Olivia Birch would look like at thirty. He hadn't seen her properly in—he tried to work it out—years, anyway, so the image in his head was firmly set at eighteen. She'd had a kind of lithe height and poise that adults described as "statuesque" and boys described as "hot." She had been a regular down at the shore, her brown curly hair tied high in a ponytail, which she pushed aside impatiently as she zipped up her wetsuit. She would still be tall, obviously, and probably still beautiful. Girls born with Olivia's looks tended to keep them.

Ash held the phone to his ear, then hung up, frowning a little at the screen. He lifted his head and, to Kieran's surprise, shouted out along the beach.

"Hey! Bronte!"

The young woman had stopped beachcombing and was now crouching at the edge of the surf, focusing a camera on something in the sand. She looked up at Ash's call, then stood, her skirt flapping in the sea breeze.

"Liv's housemate," Ash said to Kieran and Mia before pointing toward the cottage and raising his voice again. "Olivia at home?"

The girl—Bronte, Kieran gathered—shook her head, an exaggerated gesture over the distance. *No.* They saw rather than heard the word, her voice snatched away by the wind.

Ash cupped a hand around his mouth. "Where is she?"

A shrug. *Don't know.*

"Right, well." Ash turned back to his phone, the frown deepening. "I dunno. But look, she's working tonight so let's all go for drinks. She can say hello there."

"Liv's still working at the Surf and Turf?" Mia tried and failed to hide her surprise.

"Yeah," Ash said. "For now, anyway. So, what time tonight? Eightish?"

"I'm not sure, mate." Kieran pointed at Audrey in the towel, awake now underneath her sun hat. "We've got the bub, so—"

"So that's what grandmothers are for, isn't it?" Ash was already texting. "I'll let Liv know we'll be in. Get Sean along as well."

Kieran and Mia exchanged a look through which they conducted an entire silent conversation, culminating in a barely visible nod from each. They would both go.

"Okay." Texting complete, Ash picked up his backpack and slung it over his shoulder. "I'd better get back to work. I'll see you later." He leaned in to Audrey. "But not you, little one. You get to spend some quality time with Grandma."

Audrey turned her head to look at him and the wind caught the edge of her hat, ripping it off. Both Kieran and Ash lunged for it, but it was halfway down the beach before they'd moved. Ash cupped his mouth again.

"Bronte!"

The girl was now knee-deep in the water, examining a length of seaweed she held in both hands. Her canvas bag lay safely up on the sand. She raised her head at his call, the movement both impatient and indulgent.

What now?

She saw Audrey's little hat skimming along the edge of the surf and dropped the seaweed. She ran after the hat, gathering her skirt above her knees with one hand as she splashed through the water, the white crests of the waves fizzing around her legs. She nearly had it when the breeze spirited it up and away, out to sea and out of reach.

Kieran watched as Bronte stopped, recognizing a lost cause when she saw one. She dropped her skirt, the hem falling just clear of the water, and ran a hand distractedly over the back of her neck, lifting her sheet of blond hair away from her skin in a thick, messy handful. She watched the hat float away.

"What are you waiting for?" Ash was grinning. "Swim out!"

She laughed and called back something that sounded like:
You swim out.

"Don't be so bloody selfish, Bronte. You're already half in."

She let her hair fall loose again and with her free hand flashed him the finger.

Ash laughed and turned away as his phone buzzed once in his hand. He glanced down but didn't say anything.

Kieran looked out at the hat, which was doing an unnerving impression of a person as it bobbed in the surf.

"Oh well." Mia reached out and took Audrey. "I think it's gone, sweetheart. Sorry."

Audrey, unconcerned, simply lifted a chubby hand and grabbed at her mother's necklace. She yanked the silver chain in her fist as they all stood on the beach and watched as the hat dipped once, then twice, before being swallowed by the sea.

2

The Surf and Turf looked exactly the same as it had three years ago. Ten years ago, even. One whole side of the weatherboard building was still adorned by an outline of a giant crayfish, fashioned entirely from sun-bleached shells glued to the wall. A painted sign at the entrance read IN HERE FOR FISH FROM THERE, with an uneven arrow pointing to the ocean that lay a stone's throw from the outdoor dining deck.

Kieran and Mia, zipped into jackets that barely had cause to leave the closet back home in Sydney, crossed Beach Road without bothering to look either way. Evelyn Bay's main drag had the ghost-town feel that Kieran had always associated with the end of summer. Parking spaces so coveted in midseason that they sparked incidents of road rage now lay empty and unloved. Every shop, including the small supermarket, had shut for the evening, and blank windows indicated more than one business had closed its doors for good for the off-season.

It hadn't always been like that, apparently. Evelyn Bay lay sandwiched between native woodlands and the sea, and its fortunes had been driven by fishing and forestry back when Kieran's parents had been his age. Now the next generation drove dolphin-watching boats during the summer and scrabbled for work in the winter. Or they left town altogether.

The Surf and Turf was busy, which at that hour of the night and that time of the year meant a handful of people scattered across half a dozen tables. No one paid Kieran any real attention as they entered. He hadn't expected them to—twelve years was a long time in anyone's book, and the few people who'd felt the burning need to have a crack had mostly done so—but he still felt a bit relieved.

A couple of young guys Kieran didn't recognize were drinking on the outside deck, pretending not to be cold in their T-shirts in the twilight, and he was glad to see Ash had already commandeered an inside table near the back. Ash had a beer in one hand and his phone in the other, and put both down on the chipped surface as he saw them heading over.

"Verity stepped up with the babysitting duty, eh? Good on her."

Kieran nodded. His mum had, without complaint. She'd simply cleared a collection of half-filled moving boxes before settling down on the couch with her husband and grandchild for a long evening of low-verbal, high-dependency companionship. Kieran and Mia had exchanged guilty looks and hovered in the hallway, taking their time putting on their shoes and finding their phones, until Verity got up off the couch and opened the front door for them herself, rolling her eyes as they at last stepped out into the evening air.

Ash's phone buzzed on the table and he checked the screen. "Sean's on his way. He had to fix something on the boat."

"Anything serious?"

"Probably not, think he's just really busy." Ash took a sip of beer. "Even Liv was saying—"

"What was I saying?" A waitress appeared at the table, pad and pen in hand and sporting the Surf and Turf's distinctive uniform of orange T-shirt and skirt. She didn't listen to Ash's answer, instead moving around the table. "Oh my God, Mia, hello."

Olivia Birch held her arms out to Mia, who was already rising to greet her. The two women hugged, then leaned back to examine each other properly.

Kieran's guess had been right. Even more than a decade out of high school, in garish orange and with her thick curly bun already collapsing midshift, Olivia was still, by any objective measure, the most striking woman in the room.

"Hi Kieran," she said, over his girlfriend's shoulder.

"G'day, Liv."

She looked like she might say something else, but then simply let go of Mia and opened her notebook. "So, drinks?"

"Liv, thanks so much for the little outfit you sent for Audrey," Mia said, when Olivia returned with the tray. "I've got a photo—"

She pulled out her phone and Olivia put down the drinks and peered over.

"God, she is so cute. Where is she, anyway? With Verity?"

"Yeah," Mia said. "We're here all this week, though. I'll bring her in."

"Do. Or stop by my place anytime. I'm only a few doors up from you."

"Yeah," Ash said. "We kind of met your housemate earlier, actually."

"Bronte?"

Olivia glanced across the room, and for the first time Kieran noticed the girl from the beach, now also wearing the orange T-shirt and skirt. She was younger than he'd initially thought, only twenty-one or twenty-two, maybe. She was short, with a neat round face and wide eyes that made her look uncannily doll-like. Her hair was tied back now and Kieran could see that the color that had looked simply dark blond on the beach was in fact created by the kind of intricate highlights that were common on the streets of Sydney but in this context looked exotically groomed.

Bronte was carrying a glass of red wine to a corner table where a man sat alone glaring at a laptop screen. She made an inaudible remark as she placed the drink on a cardboard coaster, and the man smiled despite himself. He sat back, stretching his shoulders, and took a decent swallow of wine. He mimed tipping the rest of the glass over the keyboard in mock frustration and they both laughed. She turned away and the man put his glass down carefully, watching Bronte over his laptop screen as she threaded her way through the tables.

"She's not local, is she?" Kieran asked.

"No." Olivia shook her head. "Summer."

Ears possibly burning, Bronte let her gaze fall on Olivia, before noticing Kieran and Mia. She smiled in recognition, then held up a finger in a *wait-a-moment* gesture. She disappeared through the swinging door labeled STAFF ONLY and reemerged a few seconds later holding a battered cardboard box with LOST PROPERTY scrawled on the side.

"Not the same, I know," Bronte said as she made her way over. "But it might save you having to buy another one."

She passed the box to Mia. Inside Kieran could see dozens of sun hats of different sizes and colors, some virtually new.

"We were getting about five a day left behind at one point, so if there's anything in there for your baby, you may as well take it." Bronte picked up a small yellow floral hat still with the sales tag attached. "No one's coming back for them now."

"Thanks very much," Mia said, sifting through the box as she introduced them both. "That's so thoughtful."

"Guilty conscience." Ash grinned as he took a slug of beer. "Eh, Bronte? Least you could bloody do after letting us all down before."

"Get lost. That water was freezing." Bronte's laugh trailed off a little under Olivia's cool gaze, and she launched into the story—how she was minding her own business on the beach, and Kieran and Mia were there, and then Ash arrived—flapping the floral-patterned hat about as she spoke. The incident sounded faintly odd in the retelling.

"Ah" was all Olivia said when Bronte ran out of steam.

Bronte barely drew breath before turning to Kieran. "So Verity's your mum, is she? She's so nice. She was clearing out her shed a few weeks ago and she gave me some wire for these little sculptures I've been messing around with. I ended up giving her a hand and she let me take a few useful bits and pieces."

"Are you an artist?" Kieran said.

"Yes. Well—" Bronte paused as Olivia, who was leaning against Ash's chair, shifted. "Art *student*. I'm at uni in Canberra."

"Cool. What kind of art?"

"All kinds. I haven't decided what to focus on yet. But I want to do a big coastal series this term, so I thought this seemed a good place to, you know"—she made a sweeping gesture—"get inspired."

Even Kieran caught a flicker in Olivia's neutral expression that time. Bronte blinked, suddenly self-conscious. She was saved by a call from the kitchen hatch and, not bothering to hide her relief, hurried away.

Olivia glanced sharply at Ash, responding to something Kieran hadn't caught. "What?" she said.

Ash looked up. "Nothing."

"I didn't say a thing to her."

"I didn't say you did, Liv."

When Olivia didn't respond, Ash reached out and pulled her closer.

"Come on. Does she really matter?" Ash grinned at her until finally she smiled back. "Don't let yourself get wound up."

"No. I know." Olivia shrugged, a little embarrassed now as she turned to Kieran and Mia. "But she *is* only a student. Same as me. Or if she doesn't like that, she can say she's a waitress, same as me. But she's no more an artist than I am an urban planner. Which I'm not anymore, obviously. I just think it's disingenuous to go around saying something that's not the case."

Mia nodded sympathetically. She put a couple of baby hats on the table and pushed the box aside. "There's nothing at all around here that's more in your field, Liv?"

"Not really. I mean, at the firm in Melbourne my specialty was zoning issues for buildings over twelve stories—for which the demand around here is clearly zero—"

She was right about that, Kieran thought. The tallest building in Evelyn Bay was the former Captain's Quarters in the old colonial part of town. The heritage-listed sandstone building, now a bed-and-breakfast, had an upstairs.

"But I knew it would be like this," Olivia was saying. "When I realized I was going to have to move back, I applied to do a master's online, so at least that's something. Try to keep my hand in the industry. For whatever it's worth."

She didn't sound optimistic.

"How *is* your mum these days?" Mia asked.

Olivia shrugged. "She's fine. She's okay. Happy I'm back. She'd prefer me to be living at home with her, but there's no way. I'd go crazy in five minutes. Although—" They could see Bronte now wiping down the outside tables, her hair blowing across her face in the wind. Olivia smiled, attempting to lighten the mood. "Frying pan, fire."

Mia laughed. "Is she really that bad?"

"No, to be fair, she's not. She's just—" Olivia watched as the two young guys shivering in their T-shirts attempted small talk. Bronte smiled and shrugged and continued wiping. "*Young.* I mean, she literally didn't even know that you have to book hard-waste collections. She was dumping all this art stuff next to the wheelie bins and honestly expecting it to disappear. It's as if—"

She stopped as Ash rested his hand on her waist.

"She'll be gone soon," he said. "How long to go? Three weeks?"

"Two weeks, five days."

"There you go. Keep your eye on the prize." He grinned. "You'll be back to walking around the house naked before you know it. You'll love it."

"I'll love not having to chase up her share of whatever bill she owes me. Oh—" Olivia looked across the dining area. "Hang on, I'd better see to that."

The T-shirt boys, their arms only the faintest shade of blue, had admitted defeat and come inside to pay. Kieran watched with interest as Ash's eyes followed Olivia all the way to the cash register. He had never known Ash and Olivia as a couple. They weren't quite how he would have imagined, but then he'd never really imagined them together. Ash almost certainly had, though. Kieran would be surprised if the idea of being with Liv Birch hadn't crossed the minds of most blokes in town at one time or another.

As he reached for his drink, Kieran felt it before he saw it. The prickling sensation of being under scrutiny. He didn't move his head, instead sliding his gaze slowly around the room. It took him a second to locate the source, but when he did, it was with a sinking feeling.

The boy—man, really, these days—was standing behind the kitchen hatch. He was broad-shouldered and wearing a

grease-stained apron and an expression that made Kieran wish
he were anywhere else.

From the guy's size and stance he could have been in his
midtwenties, but Kieran knew for a fact he was nineteen. He was
wearing a name tag too small to read, but Kieran didn't need it
anyway. Liam Gilroy.

Kieran took a breath, then another, and forced himself to
make eye contact. Liam immediately pretended to be looking past
him, then turned back to his grill. Kieran waited for a feeling of
relief, but none came. There would be no real trouble, he knew—
there never was—but the room suddenly felt stifling. Kieran
checked if Mia had noticed the exchange, but she was absorbed
in picking a loose thread off one of the hats without unraveling
the whole row of stitches. He stood, a little too quickly, and his
chair squealed against the floor.

"Back in a minute."

Ash and Mia immediately looked up, both flashing an identical *don't leave me* plea with their eyes. They got along fine in
wider company but struggled with small talk one on one, Kieran
knew. Still, that couldn't be helped.

He left them to their slightly strained smiles and made a bee-
line for the restroom. There was no one else there, and he stood in
the quiet. The mirrors above the sinks were streaked, and in the
harsh lights his reflection looked a little older than his thirty years.
He was always tired these days. The lack of sleep since Audrey
had arrived had been brutal. He washed his hands slowly, debating whether he and Mia could decently leave before Sean arrived.
Probably. He and Sean went back far enough that he could get away
with it. But at the same time, it went against the grain a little.

Mia didn't really get it.

"Male friendships are so weird; you guys barely keep in
touch," she'd said to him as they were packing to come here.

"Yeah, we do. I see them every time I visit."

"In between, though. I mean, you never even speak."

That was true. Kieran had heard about Ash and Olivia getting together through Mia, who had heard it from Olivia in one of their thrice-yearly catch-up emails.

"I suppose," he'd said. "Works out, though."

And it did. Kieran was never worried about that. Partly because when the three of them did see each other they really were able to pick up where they'd left off. But mostly because if they had been going to fall apart, it would have happened twelve years ago. Kieran turned off the tap and looked away from his reflection. If they'd managed to survive that—those really dark days of blame and reckoning—they could certainly survive a couple of years of sporadic text messages.

Kieran dried his hands, checked his phone, and, unable to string things out any longer, finally pulled the door open. He'd barely stepped out into the tight vestibule separating the restroom from the dining area when he heard the familiar voice floating from the kitchen. The words were muffled by the whine of the industrial fan but were clear enough to make him stop short. Kieran stood very still, knowing with an instinct that he'd fine-tuned over the years that the conversation was about him.

"If it was up to me, he wouldn't even be allowed in here." Liam sounded very pissed off.

A girl's polite laugh. "Well, last I checked, nothing around here was up to us." It was Bronte speaking; Kieran recognized her voice now. "Anyway, he seems all right."

"And how would you know that?"

Bronte seemed taken aback. "I don't, really—"

"You don't know anything about him."

"No. I suppose not. I just—"

"What?"

"I don't get why you're giving him a hard time, that's all."

"No?"

Kieran realized he was holding his breath. He let it out. There would be no surprises in what was coming next.

"Well, whatever." Liam's voice was hard. "But the way I see it—you kill someone, you deserve all the shit that's coming your way."

3

It was lucky—or perhaps unlucky—that Sean was sitting at the table when Kieran reemerged into the bright lights of the dining area, because otherwise he would have grabbed Mia's hand, said a swift farewell to Ash, and left. He was still strongly considering this course of action when Sean stood to greet him, a broad lazy smile spreading across his face.

"Good to see you, mate. Sorry I'm late; you know what it gets like with the season change." Sean pulled his chair around next to Kieran's, and after a moment, Kieran sat down too. "I'm glad you're still here. I thought new parents would be crashed out by this time of night."

"Yeah." Kieran could feel Mia watching him closely and cleared his throat. Tried to remember what his normal voice sounded like. "Well, usually we are, but—"

"Let me guess. But Ash bullied you into coming out anyway." Sean gave a knowing nod and held up a palm. "Say no more."

Kieran's smile was genuine this time. "But we wanted to say hello, mate."

He meant it. Kieran couldn't remember a time when he and Sean hadn't been friends. Sean had always been there. There were photos of them as infants at each other's first birthday parties, and Kieran's earliest memory was of the two of them on the beach, their parents chatting while the boys dug holes in the sand and kicked water at each other.

Sean had grown from a quiet, skinny, hippie kid into a thoughtful, rangy, eco-conscious man who was at his happiest out on the water, watching the horizon rock gently from the deck of a boat. His hair was still short enough to dry with a single swipe of his hand, and he always gave the vague impression that he'd emerged moments earlier fresh from the sea and thrown on whatever clothes were at hand.

He wasn't quite the same person he'd been in the time Kieran now simply thought of as *before*, but none of them were. Mia, Ash, Olivia, Olivia's mother, Kieran's own parents. Liam. Kieran himself, obviously. No one had come through the storm unscathed.

Kieran glanced now at the kitchen hatch. At least he couldn't see Liam anymore. He sat back in his chair and tried to relax.

"Hey, hey, no one's been bullied into anything," Ash was saying. "I'm insulted by that on Kieran's behalf. He and Mia are here of their own free will."

As Ash spoke, he made eye contact with Bronte near the bar and circled his hand in a *more drinks* motion at the table. She gave him a thumbs-up and he winked. Her gaze snagged on Kieran and he tried to gauge her reaction to her conversation with Liam in the kitchen. Curiosity? Contempt? She looked away before he could tell.

"Look, I'm not claiming any different." Sean was still smiling as he pointed at Ash. "But it's funny how often people's free will turns out to coincide with exactly what you want, mate." He grinned at Kieran, who had to force himself to focus. "Happens all the time at home."

Kieran couldn't think of anything to say, and was relieved when Mia jumped in.

"Where are you two living now?" she said. "Still out by the marina?"

Ash nodded. "Yeah, same place. Got a few things that need fixing, but suits us both for work."

Kieran pictured the sprawling beach house Ash and Sean had shared for at least the past six years. It had always been a little ramshackle, but there was no criticizing the location, and it was an upgrade from the smaller and even more ramshackle place they'd shared before that.

Mia turned to Sean. "How's the business going, anyway? We saw you out there earlier. Or the boat at least."

After Ash had left them at the beach that afternoon, Kieran and Mia had looked at each other, then at his parents' house, where they knew a mountain of moving boxes awaited.

"I guess we should go back," Mia had said.

Kieran had glanced down at his baby daughter. "Or we could show Audrey the sights of Evelyn Bay. First time she's been here."

"Where were you thinking?"

"The lookout?"

Mia had shrugged. "It's up to you. You're the one who's going to have to carry her up that cliff path."

"No worries." Kieran had slipped on his T-shirt and shaken the sand off the baby sling before clipping it around him. "Too easy."

In fact, the well-worn trail winding up and away from the town had been harder going than he remembered with the extra weight against his chest. Partway up they had passed the gates leading to the rear of the town's cemetery, before the path narrowed and grew steeper. Kieran had been glad to reach the top. Twelve years ago, the former whaling lookout had been little more than a flat clearing with a single faded sign that implied, as Kieran remembered it, that it might not be the greatest idea to go clambering about on the cliffs but, hey, live and let live.

Now the lookout was a small but formal deck area, enclosed by a wire fence topped by a thick wooden railing at waist height. Next to smart laminated boards offering illustrated information about whale migratory patterns and the nesting area of crested terns, a very legible notice warned that trespassers on the cliffs risked a five-hundred-dollar fine, enforceable under local bylaw section D, amendment 16.1.

There had been no one else up there, and Kieran had sat next to Mia on a bench that had also appeared in recent years and looked out at the sea as the wind snatched at their hair. The water, which could be a thousand different sparkling colors, was that afternoon an undulating plain of dull gray green. Some way out beyond the rocks, an anchored catamaran listed gently. Sean's boat, the *Nautilus Blue*.

"Is he under?" Mia was squinting at the deck.

"Looks like it." Kieran could see the hoisted flag flapping its message. Blue and white. *Diver down*.

Kieran had scanned the water for the dark slick of a wetsuit, a head bobbing amid the waves, but the surface remained unbroken. He wasn't really expecting to see him. The wreckage of the doomed SS *Mary Minerva* lay thirty-five meters deep. Sean could be gone for a while.

The memorial commissioned in tribute to the fifty-four passengers and crew who had lost their lives nearly a century ago now stood on a rocky outcrop, facing out toward the site of the sinking.

The memorial was said to be visible from both land and

water in all weather. It wasn't, though, Kieran couldn't help but think with a sting of bitterness every time he saw it now. Not *all* weather. Still, people seemed to like it. And it was more recognition than most shipwrecks ever got. The Tasmanian waters were notorious for having claimed more than a thousand vessels, their rusting skeletal remains decaying slowly, turning the island's waters into an underwater graveyard.

"Business is good, thanks," Sean was saying now, raising his voice above the noise in the Surf and Turf. "Had a busy summer, which helps. Glad it's over now, though."

"Time for the fun stuff?" Kieran said.

"Yeah." Sean smiled. "First booking's in a couple of weeks. Got a group flying out from Norway."

"You ready for them?"

"Getting there."

This had always been a demanding time of year in the business, Kieran remembered, and nothing would have changed. Sean would have spent all summer taking tourists fishing and snorkeling and on easy shallow-water dives, making the money while it was there to be made. When autumn came and the algae that clouded the summer sea cleared, the serious cold-water divers would start flying in from around the world to take advantage of the few short months of peak underwater visibility, and Sean could do what he loved best—go deep.

The *Mary Minerva* was one of the few accessible shipwrecks in the state, but it was only for divers who knew what they were doing. And divers who knew what they were doing didn't want to waste the experience in suboptimal conditions, so the window of opportunity was limited. By July, winter sea conditions would become so treacherous that it would be impossible to reach the wreck, and the *Mary Minerva* would be left in its submerged solitude for another year.

"I was planning to be a bit further on with the safety checks by now," Sean was saying. "The Norwegians want to get into the engine room, but I dunno about it this year. I don't like the feel of that north-facing wall. I really need to get right in and have a look, but I think my good torch has gone overboard somewhere."

"I lent it to the girls." Ash didn't look up from his phone.

"My yellow torch? The waterproof one?"

"Yeah. Sorry, thought I said."

Sean blinked. "I've been looking for that for weeks, mate. I was literally about to buy another one."

Ash saw Sean's face and laughed. "Come on, don't be like that. I thought I'd said. Anyway, they needed it. They only had a small crappy one."

"It's expensive." Sean still seemed a bit annoyed. "And you're not supposed to use it for too long on land; the bulb can over-heat. Hey, Liv," he said as Olivia brought over the tray with their drinks, "are you girls finished with my torch? The yellow one?"

"Oh. Yeah, I think so." She unloaded the tray and tucked it under her arm. "It wasn't me who wanted it, anyway; it was Bronte."

Sean frowned. "What for?"

Olivia hesitated. Bronte was stacking glasses at the bar, out of earshot. "She thought she heard something out the back of the house a couple of nights."

"Really?" Mia raised her eyebrows. "What, the bit leading onto the beach?"

"Yeah," Olivia said. "I mean, if your housemate says something like that you obviously take it seriously, but—" She leaned against the table, absently running a thumb along the chain of her necklace. "Look, I'm not saying she didn't *think* she heard something. But I've been there for two years and never had any problems. Even in the summer when you've got people out on the sand at all hours." Olivia looked at Ash. "I mean, you've never heard anything either, have you, when you've stayed?"

Ash shook his head. "I had a look around, just in case, with the tourists, you know? But nothing to see. I mean, the shed's always unlocked, but nothing in there was gone. It was probably a dog or something."

Mia frowned. "Still. It's a bit creepy."

"I know," Olivia said. "It was pretty unsettling for a while. But the window in Bronte's room faces the sea, and you know what it can sound like with the wind and water. Especially if you didn't grow up with it."

They all nodded at that.

"Anyway." Olivia shrugged and turned to Sean. "She hasn't mentioned it for a couple of weeks so I think—" She broke off and turned as Bronte walked past. "Bronte, you're finished with that yellow torch, aren't you?"

"Oh." Bronte stopped, a little awkward as she realized all eyes were on her. "Yeah. I am."

"Are you sure?" Sean said. "Because if you're having trouble with noise from the beach or whatever, I've got a different one you can—"

"No, that's okay. Thanks, though. It's fine."

"Did you work out what the noise was?" Olivia asked in surprise.

"I—" Bronte's gaze flicked to Kieran and their eyes met, long enough for him to gauge her expression. Uncomfortable, definitely. Maybe a hint of pity? That wasn't unheard of, either. From the kitchen hatch came the sound of a pan being dropped and Bronte blinked. She looked back to Olivia. "Yeah, I'm pretty sure it was nothing to worry about. I'd just freaked myself out."

She turned and headed back to the kitchen. Kieran could see Liam leaning out from the serving hatch. He murmured something as she approached and they both glanced back at Kieran.

The way I see it, you kill someone, you deserve all the shit that's coming your way.

Kieran remembered Liam's words, unmistakable as they floated out from the kitchen.

There had been a silence, the industrial fan droning angrily. Kieran had tried to walk away. *Go back to the table*, he had told himself. *Go back to Mia and Ash. You don't need to hear this.* He had stayed anyway, just out of sight.

"Sorry. The guy with the baby?" Bronte had said at last. "That guy? He killed someone?"

At least she sounded doubtful, Kieran had thought. Wrongly so, but still.

"Yeah." Liam was annoyed now. "Two people actually. One of them was my dad."

"Shit. Seriously?" There was a stunned pause. "Oh my God. What happened? No, I'm sorry, you don't have to—"

"It's fine. I mean, it's not fine, obviously. But it was like twelve years ago now."

"I am so sorry, Liam." Bronte sounded like she meant it. "I was just surprised. He seems so . . . normal. Does his partner know?"

"Yeah, of course. She was at school here too when it happened. It was the day of the storm."

Kieran could hear the confusion in Bronte's silence.

"Look, it doesn't matter," Liam went on. "It was this big storm, the worst in like eighty years or something. But everyone who was here then remembers it, and they all know what he did. They could all tell you."

"What about your uncle?"

"Sean?" Liam said. "What about him?"

"I thought Olivia said Sean was coming here to meet them all for drinks, so—"

"Oh yeah." Liam gave a hard laugh. "They're all friends."

"But—" She was still confused. "Were Sean and your dad brothers, or are you related by marriage or . . . ?"

"Yeah, my dad was Sean's older brother." Kieran could imagine Liam shaking his head. "But Sean has—I dunno—*forgiven him*, or something."

"Wow."

"Yeah."

"So everyone knows?" Bronte asked.

"Most people."

"But—" A long pause. "I mean, why is everyone acting like nothing happened?"

"Same reason that Sean is still friendly with him, I guess. People feel sorry for him. Not that they should." Liam's tone was stark. "But they do. Because the other person the dickhead managed to kill was his own brother."

4

If Evelyn Bay had been quiet earlier, it was completely deserted as Kieran, Mia, and Sean stepped out into the night air. They had stayed until closing time, with Bronte systematically clearing tables around them as other customers left one by one.

At 11:00 p.m. on the dot, the manager had wiped his hands on his apron, flipped on the harsh overhead lights, and cut the music dead. He'd come out of the kitchen, clicking his long fingers toward the supply closet and calling something back through the serving hatch. Liam had emerged in response, scowling and clattering a mop and bucket in his wake. He kept his head down, his bulk hunched awkwardly as he splashed water on the floor.

It had taken Kieran a moment to realize that Liam was deliberately channeling the dirty runoff water toward his feet as he waited by the cash register to pay. It was such a strangely impotent gesture that Kieran actually felt sorry for the bloke. He didn't even bother to take a step aside, simply letting the soapy trickle seep across the tiles and pool harmlessly around the soles of his shoes. Christ, he could let the guy have this one if he needed it that badly.

Sean had observed the exchange, his gray eyes flicking from Liam to Kieran and back again, before getting to his feet. He'd strolled over to his nephew, put a palm on his back, and said something in a low, calm tone. Liam had continued splashing water on the floor until Sean had reached out a hand and simply stopped the mop. Sean was shorter and slighter than his broad-backed nephew, but right then, Liam had looked like a child. Sean leaned in again, using the same calm voice. Finally, his nephew nodded. Sean straightened and slapped Liam gently on the shoulder.

"Good man."

He'd let go of the mop handle and after a beat, Liam had carried on. Out of the corner of his eye, Kieran had seen Bronte watching, the cloth rag hanging limply in her hand.

At the door, Mia stopped to hug Olivia goodbye.

"Do you want us to wait and walk you home?" Mia said. "We're going right past your place."

"It's okay. I stay at my mum's most Saturday nights now," Olivia said. "We do Sunday-morning yoga together. I think the weekend drags for her a bit otherwise. Anyway"—Olivia brushed a stray curl off her forehead—"that's all fine. Ash'll hang around, drop me off at Mum's. But listen, let's arrange something again. One night when I'm not working."

"Definitely," Mia said, then waved a couple of baby sun hats at Bronte, who was frowning at the cash register. "Bye. Thanks again for these."

"Oh." Bronte looked up, her concentration broken. "No worries. You're welcome." Her smile faded as she dropped her eyes from Kieran and Mia to the register, the frown a little deeper now.

The road outside was dim compared with the brightness inside the Surf and Turf, only the occasional streetlamp casting a weak orange glow as Kieran, Sean, and Mia walked through the sleeping town. Kieran could hear the wash of the tide and within minutes the sea was back in view as the shops and businesses thinned out. They passed the petrol station and the small red-brick police station and, up ahead, he could see the halo of the marina's security lights cutting through the night.

"So did Liam give you a hard time?" Sean said. "Or was his revenge limited to a bucket of water?"

Kieran shook his head. "We didn't speak." That was true. In the dark, he felt Mia take his hand.

"I meant to warn him you'd be there, but I got caught up out at the wreck." Sean paused. "Shit. Maybe I should have warned you too."

"Doesn't matter. If I didn't see him there, it'd be somewhere else." The marina was close now, the vessels still and shining white under the lights. "Does Liam work at the Surf and Turf full-time now?"

"No, just casual shifts for the summer. Got him helping me on the boat the rest of the time."

"That's good."

"Yeah, well. He was at a bit of a loose end after he finished school. Anyway—" Sean had come to a stop outside a light-brown weatherboard beach house. "This is me."

Every window was dark, but as Sean opened the gate a security light tripped on to illuminate a slightly sagging veranda and an immaculately maintained front yard. A board fixed to the fence advertised the name and website of Ash's landscaping business.

"Listen." Sean stopped with one hand on the gate. "I'm sorry about Liam. I'll have a word with him."

"Don't bother, mate. I heard him talking a bit to that waitress, but he didn't even speak to me. It'll be fine."

Sean didn't reply but ran a hand over his stubble in a way that implied he knew his nephew a bit better than Kieran did. He seemed like he was about to say something else, then changed his mind. He pulled out his phone.

"I'll have to be down at the wreck most days this week." He opened a weather app and checked the forecast. "Actually, shout out if you want to come; conditions are pretty perfect tomorrow. Not as good Monday and Tuesday, but I'll still be there. Either way"—Sean raised a hand in farewell—"good to see you both. Like Liv was saying, let's do it again when she's off, yeah?"

Kieran and Mia watched him climb the wooden steps, unlock the door, and disappear inside, jangling his keys as he went. Kieran looked over at Mia. He was tired but suddenly couldn't remember the last time it had been just the two of them. It would have been only three months ago, he knew. It felt like a lot longer.

"Quick look at the beach?" he said.

Mia smiled. "Sure."

They walked hand in hand toward the sound of the ocean, turning away from the marina and to the inky night beyond. They took their shoes off as they hit sand and headed down to the water. The horizon was a jet-black line, giving way above to the bright moon and a splash of stars.

"Did Liam really not say anything earlier?" Mia said.

"Not to me. Just to that girl, Bronte. I overheard them in the kitchen."

"What did he tell her?"

"What you'd expect."

They fell quiet, not needing to say anything more. Kieran was glad. That had always been one of his favorite things about

Mia, right from the night they had met—re-met, technically—in a too-loud student bar in Sydney's city center.

He had been draining his beer and feeling, as he always had in those first couple of years, exhausted by everything. Tired of his studies, of friends that were no more than acquaintances, of the effort of opening his eyes every morning and shutting them every night. Of life in general. The fog had grown so thick, he'd become used to navigating his days half-blind.

"Yep, sounds about right," the campus doctor had said matter-of-factly when Kieran had been forced to make an appointment after repeatedly falling asleep in lectures. "Mental overload. Pretty common post-trauma. Feel like sleep's the only time you get a proper break from yourself?" He'd tapped his teeth and considered. "Maybe think about giving the counseling another crack? Fresh pair of eyes might help."

Kieran had left the clinic with a couple of numbers and reluctantly gone to the bar, where a few girls had tried to give him a couple more. What he'd really wanted was to go home and sleep, but it was someone's birthday—he couldn't remember whose—and the blokes in his class were already giving him shit for never coming out. He bought one drink and nursed it, pretending it was his third or fourth.

He'd finally reached the point where he felt he could put his empty bottle down on the counter and quietly leave without saying goodbye, when someone had stepped out of the Friday-night crowd and into his path.

"Kieran?"

He had blinked at the woman in front of him. "Yeah?"

"Hi." She touched her collarbone. "Mia Sum."

She'd had a straight blunt fringe and glasses back then that gave her a kind of pretty geek-girl vibe, and she was wearing a short black dress that he'd later learned she considered lucky.

What he'd thought was iced water in her hand turned out to be a surprisingly pleasant vodka cocktail of her own invention that years later she still referred to as Mia's Mayhem.

"I used to live in Evelyn Bay," Mia had added when the recognition was slow to dawn amid the chaos of the bar. "I was . . ." She hesitated now. "I was Gabby's friend?"

She said the name clearly, which Kieran found interesting. Most people tended to lower their voices at the mention of poor here-then-gone Gabby Birch.

Mia had seemed a little reluctant to elaborate, but she didn't need to. Kieran had placed her by then and was instead struggling to reconcile the shy girl he barely remembered with the woman standing in front of him.

He knew he was thinking of the right person, though, because there hadn't been many—or, indeed, any—other half-Singaporean girls living in Evelyn Bay when Kieran was a teenager. But the Mia Sum he remembered had been four years younger than him and always seemed to be rushing past his house to or from a piano lesson. Kieran wasn't sure he'd have recalled even that much about her except, as Mia had said, she'd been best friends with Gabby, and after the storm everyone remembered a lot more about Gabrielle Birch than they'd ever seemed to before.

He knew Mia's parents had up and moved the family to Sydney as soon as they had been given the green light by police, which had seemed like a pretty good idea to Kieran, both then and now.

Mia was still looking at him in the bar, a tiny frown forming. "Kieran, are you all right?"

"Yes," he'd said automatically.

She was jostled by someone trying to reach the bar, but held her ground. "Do you want to go somewhere else?"

"Where?"

"I don't know. Just not here."

He was sick of this place and, unexpectedly, that actually sounded good. "Yeah," he said. "Okay."

They had stepped out into the warm city air and walked a little way until Mia had pointed to a bench, where they'd sat surrounded by litter and a patch of dead grass and the sounds of Sydney after dark. They'd avoided the one old subject they had in common and instead talked about other things—city life, Kieran's internship at the physio clinic that could probably lead to a job if he managed to make it to graduation, Mia's biology degree and the subtly racist lab partner she was stuck with until the end of the year—until Mia had stretched and checked her phone.

"It's late," she'd said. "I should go."

"Already?" Kieran had glanced at his watch and been surprised by the time.

"Yeah. Besides—" Mia had looked up at him from underneath her fringe. "You've probably got an early start tomorrow, haven't you?"

"What do you mean?"

"Nothing." She smiled. "You just look like the kind of guy who hits the gym pretty hard on a Saturday morning."

"Not the gym." He'd said it before he could help himself. "I go swimming."

She had blinked. "Do you really?" The flirtatious tone dissolved in an instant and a look of sad surprise flashed across her face. She had sat back down on the bench and put a warm hand on his back. "Oh, Kieran."

Kieran sat on the beach now, years later but somehow still back in Evelyn Bay, and reached across the sand and took her hand. She'd grown out the fringe a while ago and swapped to contacts, and he wasn't sure what had happened to the black dress. She still enjoyed the occasional Mia's Mayhem, but now it was usually whipped up in their tiny kitchen and served in a tumbler from the cupboard. Life had a quieter rhythm now and he was still a little surprised how much he liked it. Nights in and not minding when the other person meant to smile but yawned instead.

"Sorry." She covered her mouth quickly as the wind blew her hair across her face. "You ready to go back? I'm so . . ." She yawned again.

"I know. Me too."

They stood, dusting off the sand. Ahead, the beach stretched out in shadow. Kieran's parents' house was only a ten-minute walk along the shoreline, but he felt Mia look into the night and hesitate.

"Go back along the road?" he said, and she nodded.

They stopped under a lamppost where the sandy path hit the tarmac of Beach Road and held the fence for balance as they put their shoes back on. There was no official pavement but no traffic either, and they walked side by side along the makeshift nature strip that lined the front of the beachside cottages. Most of the homes lay in sleeping darkness, with only the occasional glow from a front window. The houses blocked the view of the water, but Kieran could hear it lapping against the shore.

"Hey, what did you make of Liv and Ash as a couple?" Mia asked suddenly.

Kieran considered, picturing them earlier at the Surf and Turf. There was something about Ash and Olivia together that he'd found a little hard to get a read on. It could just be history, he knew. A lot of water had flowed under that bridge, for all of them. But they'd also had the faintly combative edge that some couples seemed to enjoy, but that Kieran personally found exhausting, even as a spectator.

"I don't know," he said, meaning it. "What did you think?"

"I just hope he doesn't mess her around."

He won't, Kieran was about to say, then stopped. It was Ash. He might.

"Did you notice the way—?" Mia started, then stopped, hearing the low rumble at the same time as Kieran did.

He realized what it was a split second before the car tore around the corner, the rumble becoming a roar as it careened toward them, headlights on full beam.

"Shit, watch out."

Kieran put his arm out for Mia, but she was already off the road, the small of her back pressed against someone's garden fence. He felt the rush of wind as the car shrieked past, shrill and bright in the still of the night. It hadn't come close to touching them, but Kieran's heart was pumping and his head tingled with a rush of blood. He could feel Mia's pulse pounding against his arm. He pictured Audrey sleeping in her cot at home, and thought about what could have happened, and felt faintly sick.

They watched the car race down the road, the red taillights blinking smaller until it turned another corner and disappeared completely. It had come and gone in seconds, and the only sound once more was their breathing and the gentle breaking of waves.

"Oh my God." Mia laughed with relief. "What's worth rushing for around here? There's literally nothing in this town that can't wait."

"I know. You okay?"

"Yeah, it was just a surprise."

They walked on. A few lights were glowing in Fisherman's Cottage as they passed, but Kieran's parents' house was completely dark as they crept up the driveway. He let them in, nearly tripping over the stack of moving boxes piled in the hallway. Mia went straight through to check on Audrey, who was sound asleep in her travel cot in the corner of Kieran's old bedroom. The door to his parents' room was closed, but Verity had left a note detailing how much formula Audrey had taken, which Mia glanced over while Kieran undressed.

Within ten minutes they were both in bed, the adrenaline spike from earlier having worn off, leaving behind only cloudy exhaustion. Mia was half-asleep even as she was saying good night. Outside Kieran's window, he could hear the swell of the sea.

He closed his eyes and slept, thick and heavy. He stirred only once when, somewhere deep within his dream, he heard the sound of a door slam.

5

Kieran was alone when he opened his eyes, squinting against the morning light beaming through a crack in the blind. The bedding on Mia's side had been thrown back and the sheets were cold. He raised his head and could see that Audrey's cot was empty.

The skirt and top Mia had laid out last night on the chair were gone. Kieran hadn't heard her get up. He sighed and lay back, feeling both guilty and relieved. Along with the night feedings, Audrey had been starting her day before dawn for the past month and they tried to take it in turns to get up. He was pretty sure—certain, actually—that it was his go. He checked the time. After eight. No wonder he felt unusually rested. As a father—the phrase still sounded foreign to him—that counted as a luxuriously late start.

Kieran got out of bed and pulled on his board shorts and a T-shirt. His phone showed a text from Mia, sent earlier to say she was going out to avoid waking the whole house. He texted her back. *Okay.*

Out in the hall, he stopped as his bare feet crunched against the floorboards. He looked down. A light layer of sand trailed across the wood. It had been walked through at least once, the scuff marks still visible.

Had he and Mia brought that in last night? He could see his shoes where he had left them inside the front door, but he knew how the sand got everywhere. A broom and dustpan were propped clumsily against a wall, seemingly abandoned midtask. From the kitchen, Kieran could hear his parents' muffled voices. He listened but couldn't hear Mia, or Audrey for that matter. They must still be out.

Kieran reached for the broom. It wasn't a big job, and as he emptied the dustpan into the bathroom bin a minute or two later, he grabbed an old beach towel. If he was going to swim, now was as good a time as any. He didn't like to miss a day, and rarely had in twelve years, since the very first doctor at the hospital in Hobart had issued her stark warning.

Kieran hadn't caught her name, but she'd come into his room, put down her clipboard, and pulled up the visitor's chair. She'd had short gray hair and the careworn face of someone who had seen it all before and could do without seeing it all again.

"All right. Listen close," she said. Kieran had been admitted less than twenty-four hours earlier and was still feeling shell-shocked. "Because this is important."

Kieran, lungs still heavy and aching, had tried to concentrate.

"All this"—she'd waved her pen at his body—"this will all heal. You're going to be fine. So what I need you to do is focus on your head. Because that sends people back here more often than you want to know."

The doctor had let that sink in before she spoke again.

"People can react badly when they don't know how to react to something. That's true for everyone, but men in particular can very quickly find themselves in places they don't want to be. I'm talking aggression, I'm talking family problems, heavy drinking"—she had ticked them off on her fingers—"drugs, sex stuff, prostitutes, violent porn. And you, Kieran . . ."

He had stared at her. "Me, what?"

"A guy like you, what are you, eighteen? In a situation like this? You are a prime candidate for that, my friend. *Prime.*" The doctor's tone softened. "That could be you. Easily. So I want you to make sure it isn't. Do not let yourself get sideswiped by this, all right? There's going to be a lot to deal with emotionally, so be prepared. You need some sort of release that's not going to end up with you dead or miserable or in jail. So take me seriously when I say this: Find something positive that helps."

The same day he was released from the hospital, Kieran had followed Verity into their house, dropped his bag, and walked down the hallway and straight out the back door. He had stripped down to his shorts, plunged into the sea, and swum and swum and swum.

He opened the hall cupboard now to put the broom back, and slowed as he passed the next bedroom. It had once belonged to his older brother, Finn, but at some point Kieran and his parents had simply started referring to it as the "other" room.

Other room was about right. Since Finn died, Brian and Verity had tried using the space variously as a home office and a gym. They never said it out loud, but Kieran guessed they didn't find it easy to spend time in there because for the last few years it had become essentially a storage space. It was packed full of belongings they hardly ever needed, which offered the dual benefit of keeping the room both in use and rarely visited.

The door was ajar now, though, and Kieran used a finger to push it open. It looked almost as he expected, with the addition of flat-packed cardboard boxes stacked against the walls, but he stopped when he saw that the spare bed nestled amid the clutter had been made up.

The sheets had been tucked in without much care. A dirty coffee mug stood next to the bed, along with a book spread open to mark its page and Verity's reading glasses perched on the spine. She must be sleeping there, at least some of the time. Kieran had never in his life known his parents to sleep apart. He looked at the bed now and wondered what to make of that.

In the kitchen, he found Verity leaning forward in her seat, balancing a mouthful of cereal on a spoon. She was holding it out at face height, ignoring the milk that slopped over the edge and onto the tiled floor. At the other end of the spoon, Brian Elliott opened his mouth barely wide enough to speak.

"I've had enough."

"You haven't had anything at all yet." Verity glanced up as Kieran entered and pointed him toward the fresh coffee before turning her attention back to her husband.

Kieran's parents used to compete in local triathlons together. Four years ago, Brian had come in second in the over-fifty category. Verity placed the edge of the spoon against her husband's lips, coaxing them apart. He opened his mouth like a child.

Kieran watched until eventually Verity looked over. "How was the Surf and Turf?"

He shrugged. At the table, his dad refused a second mouthful. "It was fine. Have you seen Mia this morning?"

"No. Eat please, Brian. She's not here?"

"She's taken Audrey out." Kieran checked his phone. No new messages.

He pulled out a kitchen chair and moved a box so he could sit down. The flap wasn't sealed and as he looked inside, he stopped.

In the box were some of his mother's clothes, folded neatly

next to what he could only describe as rotting household rubbish. The cream pullover Verity had knitted herself had a dark spatter across the front where a used tea bag had bled out against the wool. A browning banana peel was tucked into the pocket of a pair of trousers.

Kieran stared at the contents, then held out the box wordlessly. Verity barely glanced at it, shrugging at his silent question.

"He knows we're moving." She turned back to Brian, breakfast bowl still in her hand. "He sees me packing and he wants to help, so he puts in whatever he can find." She ran an eye over the other boxes. "He's done a few."

"This is dreadful."

Verity didn't reply, just scooped up another mouthful of cereal.

"Mum?"

"Yes?"

"You should have told me. Why didn't you tell me it was like this?"

"You have enough going on. You've got Audrey now. Work." Verity looked him calmly in the eye. "I can manage your dad. It's fine."

"It's not. Mum? This is not fine at all. This is really bad."

"I can understand why you might be feeling that way."

And there it was, like clockwork. The *active listening* that Verity was so keen on.

Kieran ignored it and tried again. "How long have you been sleeping in the other room?"

"Not long. And only sometimes." Verity gave up on the cereal and stood to put the bowl in the sink. "He gets a bit restless at night."

They were talking about Brian as though he wasn't there, Kieran realized. He wondered what Verity's current online support group—he thought it was a fairly safe bet that she was part of one—would make of that.

"It's not too late to find somewhere in Sydney, Mum," he said. "For both of you."

"It is. And we've been through this."

"I know, but—"

"Your dad would find an interstate move difficult."

"Yeah, but he'd get used to it eventually. And it'd be better for you. You wouldn't have to do this on your own. Mia and I would be around. And Audrey. It could be a new start."

Verity didn't answer, but Kieran thought he could guess what she was thinking. Verity Elliott did not want a new start. What she wanted was for things to be the way they used to be. She would never say that, though, he knew. Sure enough, she took a sip of coffee and glanced at the beach towel draped over the back of Kieran's chair.

"Are you going for a swim?"

"Can we not change the subject?"

"I wasn't trying to." Verity regarded him across the kitchen. "I was going to ask if you were coping okay."

"Oh." Kieran swallowed. "Yeah. I guess so. I mean, this whole thing with Dad is—"

He tried to find the word.

"Confronting?" Verity supplied.

"Yeah, I suppose." Kieran had been going to say *really shit*, but sure, that was close enough.

"It's . . ." Verity started, then hesitated.

Kieran waited, genuinely curious what she was going to say, here in her kitchen surrounded by half-filled boxes of rubbish-stained clothes, packed by a man who had stood by her side for forty years and now looked at her as though he couldn't quite place her. Verity stared into her coffee mug with a hint of a frown on her face. For a long moment, the only sound was the ticking of the kitchen clock, coming from a box beside the counter. Then she took a breath. When she looked up, her expression was back to neutral.

"The thing to remember, Kieran, is that feelings of uncertainty or anxiety are completely normal ahead of big—"

She broke off as Kieran stood abruptly. No. He had absolutely no interest in sitting through a *natural to fear change* session led by his mother. He'd had to do that one already, a few times in fact, with actual qualified professionals.

"If you don't want to talk about this," he said, "I may as well swim."

Verity was firmly serene. "I thought we *were* talking."

"Did you really?"

They looked at each other over the boxes. Then Verity opened her mouth.

"All right." The mask was still perfectly in place. "Be careful in the water."

Her words were as light as air. Kieran stared at his mother. She gazed back. He genuinely could not tell if she was having a dig. Slowly, he picked up his towel and walked out of the kitchen, making sure not to slam the door in case that meant something.

"Where's Finn off to?" Brian's question floated into the hall.

Verity didn't bother to correct him.

At the back door, Kieran ignored a small patch of sand he'd missed, scattering the grains as he strode out onto the veranda. He looked out at the sea, hoping to find Mia walking barefoot in the shallows or lying on a towel with their daughter.

No Mia. No Audrey. The beach behind their house was empty.

Kieran took out his phone and sent her another text. *Where are you guys?*

He walked down the thin but well-worn path through the

back gate and onto the sand. He stopped when he neared the tide line and turned, shielding his eyes.

To the north, the rolling waves fizzed white against the sand. A couple of distant boats drifted with the breeze.

To the south—Kieran froze.

To the south, just a few minutes' walk away, a small crowd had gathered. They were standing very still and close together, their heads down and dogs held tight on leashes as they watched something unfolding at the shoreline. Their distress pulsed across the sand.

Kieran would have known what it was, even without the flash of a blue uniform. Even without the police tape flapping against makeshift stakes outside what he could now see was Fisherman's Cottage. There was only one thing in Evelyn Bay that drew a crowd like that to the water's edge.

Kieran dropped his towel and started to run.

6

It wasn't them, Kieran knew, his heels sinking into the damp sand as he tried to pick up speed. It wasn't Mia and Audrey at the feet of that crowd.

It wasn't them, because someone would have knocked on his parents' door by now. Kieran would not have been allowed to sit exasperated at his mother's kitchen table while this played out a few hundred meters away.

It wasn't them, because otherwise the largely forgotten but familiar faces of neighbors that turned toward Kieran as he ran up now would surely be softened with sympathy.

It wasn't Mia or Audrey, Kieran told himself as he drew to a halt with his breath burning in his chest, because he simply could not bear it to be them.

He was right.

The small crowd shifted and parted a little, enough for him to see what it was that had drawn this silent vigil. And it wasn't them. It wasn't Mia lying still, with her hair lank against the damp sand, her bare arms mottled with an unearthly blue-white bloom of cold. It wasn't Mia sprawled lifeless at the shoreline, with the distinctive bright-orange glow of her waitress uniform darkened by the sea.

It wasn't Mia. It wasn't even Olivia, thank God, as the plastic police tape shuddered and glinted in the breeze, roping off the path leading directly to Fisherman's Cottage.

It was Bronte.

Kieran's immediate thought was a pure, shameful rush of relief. He ran both hands over his face, horrified that someone might notice. He took a deep breath.

"Do they know what happened?" he said to the woman next to him, whose name he knew he should remember. He could picture her on his parents' porch, sipping wine at barbecues. The woman shook her head, her gray hair catching the wind as her dog strained at its leash.

"They haven't said. I heard her housemate found her."

"Olivia?" Kieran could see the roped-off gate leading to Fisherman's Cottage.

The woman nodded but said no more, her eyes on the horizon. Kieran's own gaze crept back to Bronte.

She was lying on her side, lengthwise along the beach with her back to the sea. Her arms were limp and her face was pressed against the sand. The careful highlights in her hair were dull and matted. Her baby-doll eyes were closed.

Kieran had a sudden flash of her, so different from this. Running through the spray after Audrey's hat, looking out at the sea and laughing in frustration.

A single young cop Kieran didn't recognize stood near the water with his boots damp and sandy, guarding the territory between Bronte and the onlookers, who had gathered a respectful distance away. His palm was held out as though to ward off anyone attempting to get closer. No one had moved.

"Shouldn't they get her out?" someone muttered as the tail end of a heavy wave raced up the sand and threatened to lap at the edge of the girl's orange uniform.

The young cop had no idea what he should be doing; even Kieran could see that. The guy had almost certainly spent the summer dealing with lost wallets and underage drinking. The officer kept glancing desperately toward Fisherman's Cottage and looked relieved as the back door suddenly swung open and a voice shouted out.

"Oi! Bloody go around!"

A second police officer had stepped out onto the porch and was thrusting a finger in the direction of a couple of dog walkers who had broken away from the crowd and were attempting a shortcut along the cordoned-off path.

Kieran definitely recognized this cop. He used to be the young nervous one himself. Twelve years ago, the man had been Constable Chris Renn, fresh-faced and overeager to please in his first posting. Now, approaching forty and the town's sergeant, Renn looked neither fresh nor eager.

Renn's hair had been thinning prematurely even back then, and his now completely bald head shone with a light sheen of sunscreen. He had always been fit, and Kieran recognized his build as that of a fellow gym-goer, albeit one who probably had to work harder these days than he used to.

Renn watched until the cowed couple skulked off, their dog straining at the leash. He shook his head once, mouthing something that looked like *unbelievable*, then disappeared back inside. The door slammed shut and at the water's edge the young cop's face fell.

Kieran turned back to Fisherman's Cottage. A small window overlooked a sandy garden and rickety, weather-worn fence. The back bedroom, probably, if the layout of this place was anything like his parents'. Bronte's room, then. Her window looked onto the beach, Olivia had said the night before.

She thought she heard something out the back of the house a couple of nights.

Olivia had said that too.

Kieran looked at the window and imagined Bronte staring out at the dark. Listening. He glanced at the young cop, then back at the house. They'd hear all that from Olivia, he supposed, and he jumped as his phone beeped in his pocket. He pulled it out to read the message. Mia. He felt a fresh giddy rush of relief.

I'm near the Surf and Turf. Where are you? Almost immediately, a second message. *Something's happened at the beach.*

He tapped a reply. *I know, I'm here. On my way now. Talk when I get there.*

The response was quick. *What's going on? Something bad?*

Kieran looked back at Bronte. Her feet were bare and she had painted her toenails pink. A strip of seaweed was plastered to her cheek. The edge flapped in a gust of wind and settled slick and brown against her lips. She didn't move.

Yes.

Something very bad. Kieran turned and stepped away from the crowd, his legs feeling unreliable. As he crossed the sand, he thought he sensed movement in the house and gave a start. Where the bedroom window had been blank, he could now see a figure, obscured by the reflection of the glass.

Kieran took another step and the angle of the light changed, and he could see that it was only Sergeant Renn. The officer was hunched forward, his phone trapped between his shoulder and chin. He was nodding stiffly and appeared to be scribbling something in a notebook. He listened a bit longer, then ended the call and straightened up.

Renn was very still, staring out through the glass, across the sand and down to the water. Then, as Kieran watched, he lifted a hand and dragged it slowly over his face. Forget the young cop, Kieran thought. It had been a long time since Chris Renn had had to deal with anything even close to this.

Perhaps thinking the same thing, Sergeant Renn stood watching a minute longer. Then he turned abruptly and the window to Bronte's room was empty again, the glass reflecting only the sky, the sea, and the crest of white water breaking behind a lone dark shape in the sand.

7

Kieran found Mia waiting outside the Surf and Turf, with Audrey strapped in the baby sling across her chest. The restaurant doors were locked and the lights were off, but the path outside was getting busy. Small groups clustered, split, and re-formed as the morning's passersby were drawn in by the solemn faces and hushed whispers. Kieran edged through the throng and pulled Mia and Audrey into a hug hard enough to make his daughter screech.

"Sorry, little one," he said. "I'm just very glad to see you."

Kieran's hand paused as he stroked her head. She was wearing the yellow floral hat Bronte had fished out of the lost property box. From the way Mia was fiddling with the cotton rim, Kieran could tell she had heard the news.

A woman coughed. "You come from the beach, Kieran?"

Kieran looked over at a middle-aged bottle blonde who had been making faces at Audrey. She was wearing the familiar orange waitress uniform, and Kieran knew without reading the tag on her shirt that her name was Lyn. He couldn't remember a time when she hadn't worked at the Surf and Turf.

"Yeah. I was just down there."

"They're saying it's Bronte."

He nodded.

Lyn's mouth hardened into a line and she reached into her pocket and pulled out a packet of cigarettes. She took a step away from Audrey as she lit up.

"She was nice," she said. "Bronte."

"Did you know her well?"

Lyn shrugged, her shoulders tight.

"A bit, I suppose. She wasn't like some of them we get. These casuals who forget they're here to work. That wasn't Bronte. Even lately, even though she only had a couple of weeks left on the roster, she still turned up for her shifts. Good with the customers too, even the tricky ones. Especially the tricky ones, sometimes." Lyn took a short drag, her mouth falling back into its thin line as she exhaled through her nose. She flicked her cigarette ash in the vague direction of the beach. "It's too bloody dark down there, I'm always saying. It's not safe."

Kieran thought back to the night before, sitting by the water with Mia. The marina lights behind them and stretch of sand ahead disappearing into shadow. How Mia had been reluctant to walk home through the pitch black. And so they hadn't. They had gone a different way instead. He could tell from Mia's face that she was thinking the same thing.

"We've taken it up with the council," Lyn went on, her fingers twitchy. "I've told them that we need some lights along there. Twice, I've told them that. It's in the AGM minutes. But some of the residents don't like it, you know? Say it would make it hard to sleep. But I told them, you've got people coming from all over—the mainland, wherever—they don't know what the water's like. I mean, Bronte was from Canberra. She could probably barely swim—"

"They've got pools in Canberra," Mia snapped, and Kieran blinked. That was unusual for her. She was fiddling with Audrey's hat again, taking it off and putting it back on.

Lyn regarded her through a veil of cigarette smoke. She nodded toward the ocean crashing beyond the line of trees. "That's not pool water."

Kieran shook his head. "I don't think Bronte was swimming, anyway," he said, and they both looked at him. "She was wearing her work clothes."

"Oh." Lyn's whole face tightened as she absorbed that. "Well, maybe—" She blinked hard. "Maybe she . . ."

Kieran could see Lyn trying very hard to think of a good explanation. A good, perfectly plausible reason why a young woman might venture into the sea, in her uniform, late at night. A reason that would allow them all to avoid acknowledging an alternative that was suddenly hanging thick and dark and heavy in the air between them. None of them gave it life by putting it into words.

Thick, dark alternatives like that did not belong in Evelyn Bay. It wasn't fair to say Evelyn Bay was a place where nothing ever happened—things did, of course; ask anyone who had been there for the storm. But not often, and not whatever *this* was.

"She was a really lovely girl," Lyn said finally. "Really kind. She swapped with me last week so I could take my cat to the vet. And once—"

She stopped as a silver four-wheel drive pulled up, slowing to a crawl near them. The driver saw the crowd and, ignoring the empty parking space on the street right out the front, put on his indicator and made to turn into the side delivery entrance.

Kieran, Mia, and Lyn stepped back to allow the car through, the surfboard strapped to its roof juddering as the wheels crunched over the gravel. The car pulled to a stop outside the

Surf and Turf's delivery door and the engine cut dead. The driver didn't get out immediately and Kieran could make out the glow of a mobile phone pressed to his ear.

Kieran didn't recognize the car, but he knew the man. Julian Wallis, manager of the Surf and Turf. Kieran had caught sight of him the night before, cutting the music at closing time and instructing a scowling Liam to fetch the mop, and been struck by the way some people really never changed.

Julian still had the same gray buzz cut he'd had as long as Kieran had known him. He had the angular, ropey build of a distance runner, but it was water rather than road that had honed his shape. Julian had run the Nippers surf lifesaving group for kids ever since Kieran himself had been a member, and his voice had the kind of natural authority that still made Kieran feel the urge to jump into line and pay attention.

Kieran watched now as the phone screen went dark inside the car. Julian sat behind the wheel for what felt like a long minute before opening the door. When he did step out, he looked shaken. Not much, but it was disturbing to see any show of emotion on Julian's notoriously granite-like features.

Sean had once said the only difference between Julian winning the lottery and running over his dog was a tiny upward or downward inflection at the corner of his lips. There was no question which way things were going this morning. The inflection was firmly down.

He went to unlock the side door to the restaurant and for the first time noticed Lyn at the edge of the driveway, waiting in her uniform.

"Lyn. Sorry." He shook his head, distracted. "I meant to call you. You may as well head home. I'll let you all know what's happening when I know myself, okay?"

"Okay." The waitress trapped the very tip of her tongue

between her yellowing teeth and even Kieran could hear the question she was fighting not to ask. *Will we still get paid?* It wasn't unreasonable, Kieran thought, not with the slow season approaching.

Julian didn't seem to notice as he turned back to the side door, swearing under his breath as he struggled to get the lock to slide free. He tried again, successfully this time, and disappeared inside only to reemerge a minute later clutching a large bunch of keys. He slammed the door, got back into his car without another word, and reversed faster than was possibly prudent before driving back the way he had come.

"Does he still own Fisherman's Cottage?" Mia asked.

"Yeah. Gives Olivia—and Bronte, I guess—a staff discount on the rent." Lyn paused. "So I suppose Chris Renn will be needing to have a word with him."

"I saw Sergeant Renn down at the beach," Kieran said, picturing the broad police officer framed in the bedroom window. "He's in charge still?"

Lyn nodded and kicked her spent cigarette butt into the sandy ditch.

"For now, anyway—" She broke off, and before Kieran could ask what she meant, Lyn had turned her attention to the road, where a dark-haired man was approaching. He was frowning at his mobile phone, typing something furiously with his thumb as he walked.

"Oh God." Lyn rolled her eyes. "Here's another one who won't be happy. He likes his routine. He'll have to go to the library instead. George—" She raised her voice as the man, still oblivious, climbed the steps to the Surf and Turf's front entrance. He looked up in surprise when the locked door rattled in his hand. "Closed, I'm afraid, George, love."

The man blinked, and Kieran recognized him as the customer

with the laptop who Bronte had served the night before. He appeared to have his laptop with him again today, only now it was encased in a battered leather satchel slung across his chest. He had turned up the collar of his light jacket against the sea breeze and, somewhat improbably, had an actual print newspaper tucked under his arm. The fact he was no older than early forties and had the world's news on the phone in the palm of his other hand made the perfectly innocent object look like a nostalgic affectation.

"Why is it shut?" he asked Lyn, peering through the Surf and Turf's darkened windows. Kieran saw Mia watching him with a faintly puzzled look on her face.

"There's been an accident. Down at the beach," Lyn said. "Something's happened to Bronte."

The man turned at that. "Really? Is she okay?"

"No." Lyn's voice was tight. She lit another cigarette. "No. Sergeant Renn's down there now."

The man looked at her, then nodded slowly, getting her meaning. He swapped his newspaper to his other arm and pulled out his phone again, tapping with a different intent this time, his expression sober as he scrolled. Kieran watched him, then turned as Mia touched his arm and pointed across the road.

Ash, gray-faced and walking so fast that his dog had to trot to keep up with him, had his eyes down and his own phone pressed to his ear. After a silent moment, he dropped his hand and glared at the screen in frustration.

"Ash!" Kieran called, and Ash stopped. He blinked, as though he'd forgotten for a moment they were back in town, then changed direction and headed over.

"You've heard about Bronte?" he was saying before he'd even reached them. "I can't get hold of Liv."

"Renn's over at the cottage," Kieran said. "I didn't see Liv, though. Maybe she's at the station."

"Right." Ash didn't look much happier with that and raked a hand across his unshaven jaw. "I heard Liv found her."

"Found Bronte?" Mia said. "I thought she stayed at her mum's last night?"

"Yeah, she did. I dropped her off there myself." Ash shook his head and checked his phone again. The screen was still blank. "So, yeah. I don't know."

Ash looked up now and saw that the man on the steps had stopped scrolling and was listening to them.

"Jesus, do you bloody mind, George?" Ash gave the bloke the blank-eyed stare that typically made most people immediately look away. Not this guy, though, Kieran was interested to note. He held Ash's gaze before shrugging and turning back to his own phone.

"Oh my God, poor Liv," Mia said. "Can you imagine what that would be like for her? Finding her housemate like that? Especially after everything with Gabby."

"This is a lot different from Gabby though," Kieran said. "I mean . . ."

Bronte's body had been right there, for one thing. He didn't finish the thought out loud. Wished he hadn't started it.

"It's the same beach," Mia said.

That was true, Kieran thought. But it was a big stretch of sand.

"And it was around this time of year, too."

"It's a tragedy, that's what it is." Lyn had lit a fresh cigarette and inhaled with force. "Bronte was a beautiful soul. And that beach is too bloody dark. It's an accident waiting to happen."

She was still clinging to that, then, Kieran noted.

"Accident or not," the man on the steps cut in. He was reading something on his phone. "It sounds like someone was seen with her."

"How would you know that?" Ash snapped.

"Evelyn Bay Online Community Hub." The man regarded Ash. "You're not a regular on the EBOCH forum then, I take it?"

"No." Ash actually laughed. "If I want to know what my nan and her mates think about last week's bin collection, I'll pop down the retirement home and ask them."

"Fair enough. Although personally"—the man shrugged, his eyes still on Ash—"I always find it quite interesting what people care enough to bitch about."

An odd tension that Kieran couldn't even begin to read passed between the two men.

"Sorry, mate." He jumped in before Ash could respond. "You said someone was seen with Bronte? Does it say who?"

The man scanned his screen, then shook his head.

"Not yet." He dropped his phone in his pocket and headed down the steps. "But give it five minutes."

Ash looked like he was about to say something more when his own phone buzzed. He pulled it out, relief flashing across his face. Kieran watched his expression change as he read the text message.

"Shit," he breathed as he read it again.

What? Kieran wanted to ask, but all at once he found himself picturing Bronte. Standing knee-deep in the sea. Holding out the lost property box. Lying very still on the sand. And suddenly he didn't want to be the one to ask.

"Shit," Ash said again, turning the screen so Kieran could read the message. "From Sean. The person seen with her was Liam."

8

"Oh my God." Lyn broke the silence. "Liam."

She breathed out the name with a haze of smoke as they all looked at the darkened windows of the Surf and Turf, where twelve hours earlier Liam had been flipping burgers while Bronte served tables. Kieran waited for the rush of denial, the *surely-not-I-can't-believe-he-would-ever* breathless astonishment, but Lyn's lips stayed wrapped around her cigarette. She took a deep, slow drag.

Ash was staring blankly at his phone, his thumb hovering above the screen, while Mia re-tied Audrey's hat firmly under her chin, fumbling with the straps.

Kieran's own thoughts were lurching haphazardly through the night before. Through the drinks, the chat, the kind gesture from a casual waitress, before circling back to one specific moment.

You kill someone—Liam's words had floated from the kitchen hatch—*you deserve all the shit that's coming your way.*

Somewhere inside Kieran, deep beneath soft hoary layers of

guilt, a mean worm pulsated and rolled over. He breathed in and out, and opened his mouth.

"I suppose we should wait until we know more," he said out loud, because he felt someone should.

They knew plenty more soon enough. The whispers and hearsay and heated exclamations were already bouncing from mouth to ear until, in fits and starts, the story seeped out.

•   •   •

Kick-out time at the Surf and Turf was set in stone, and the night before had been no exception. At 11:00 p.m., the music was cut, customers were shown the door, and the mops and scrubbing brushes came out for the thirty-minute nightly clean and reset.

But it being the end of the summer and Julian Wallis being a reasonable man, the front-of-house and kitchen staff were one by one given the nod to head off early as they wrapped up their tasks.

At 11:13 p.m., Liam Gilroy was recorded on the main street CCTV cameras standing on the empty pavement not far from the restaurant's entrance. Two minutes and forty seconds later, Bronte Laidler appeared in the frame. She stopped a few paces away from Liam. They appeared to be talking. Liam had pointed to his car, a five-year-old white Holden. Bronte had nodded. Four minutes and six seconds after he first appeared on camera, Liam climbed behind the wheel, Bronte got into the passenger seat, and they both shut their doors. The car drove out of sight. There were no other cameras to capture what happened next.

Shortly before 11:30 p.m., the neighbor who had bought the home to the left of Fisherman's Cottage thirty-eight years earlier for a price that now sounded like pocket change, rose from her couch as the end titles of a James Bond film rolled, and moved to the window to pull closed a gap in her curtains. As she tugged the fabric together, she noted a vehicle that didn't belong to any of the nearby homes parked on the street outside. Light in color was all she could remember.

Some twenty minutes later, the same neighbor—teeth brushed and alarm clock set—opened her back door to allow her terrier-cross to stretch its legs for a final time. As she waited, she thought she heard faint voices floating from the direction of the beach.

She was unable to commit to either a male or female tone, nor comment on the topic of discussion. They had been talking, she had insisted. Nothing more. Not arguing and certainly not fighting, or as an active member of the Evelyn Bay Neighborhood Watch she would have recalled her training and summoned the police.

Either way, by the time she had called her dog inside and taken herself off to bed, she had forgotten all about it, until Sergeant Chris Renn had knocked on her door the next morning and asked how well she'd known the young waitress who had been staying in the cottage next door.

•   •   •

Ash's phone rang at last.

"Finally," he said, his features slackening with relief as Olivia's picture flashed on the screen. He turned his back on the Surf and Turf and lifted the phone to his ear. "Are you okay? Where are you?" Ash listened. "No, don't." His eyes flicked to the growing crowd. "Look, Sean's at the marina. Go there instead. I'm on my way."

He hung up and turned back to Kieran and Mia.

"Can you come? Sean didn't sound great and I'm not sure what Liv'll need."

Kieran glanced at Mia, who was trying to soothe a fractious Audrey.

"She needs feeding," she said. "You go. But tell Liv I'll call her. I'll find somewhere to sit and get this feed done and . . ."

Mia hesitated as both she and Kieran looked down the road that led home. Past Fisherman's Cottage, past the police tape. Past whatever had happened to Bronte on the shoreline.

Kieran shifted, uneasy. "Are you okay to walk back alone?" Was *he* okay with it?

"Yeah." Mia shrugged. "I mean, yes. You know, it's broad daylight. There are lots of people about. The police are probably all still over there."

"I suppose."

"Yeah." She frowned. "So I think it's fine. Right?"

They looked at each other, trying to work out exactly where the line fell between cautious and overdramatic.

"I'll walk with you," Lyn said suddenly. She finished her latest cigarette and ground it out. "I'm going that way anyway."

"Really?" Mia said. "You're happy to do that?"

"No worries at all."

She meant it too, Kieran thought. That was interesting. Lyn, who had barely said a word since Liam's name was first mentioned, was really not worried, at all.

Ash was already moving. "Let's get going," he said to Kieran. "Liv's waiting."

They headed out of town, each lost in his own thoughts. As they passed the police station, Kieran saw the few parking spots out the front and on the road were all now taken up by both patrol and unmarked vehicles. Reinforcements from Hobart, he guessed.

"Hey, is Renn getting the boot or something?" Kieran asked, remembering what Lyn had started to say earlier.

"Whole station's getting the boot," Ash said. "Budget cuts. Think the plan is to send a couple of cops over from Port Osborne in summer, but there'll be no one full-time over winter. I heard Renn was pretty pissed off about it. He could have gone to Port Osborne but decided to quit instead."

"What, altogether?"

"Well, when the station closes next month. He's moving to the mainland. Going to work for his brother's haulage business."

"That'll be different."

"Yeah. I mean, I get it. He wasn't the only one annoyed about the station closing. My mum's on the Neighborhood Watch and they petitioned and stuff, but it was a done deal. You know what it's like, though; it's only Renn and whatever sidekicks they send him for the summer. Probably costs more to keep the lights on than it's worth." Ash thought for a moment as the marina came into view up ahead, the water gleaming in the late-morning light. "Although after last night, who knows?"

The marina was close to deserted, with some of the boats already prepared for off-season storage, tarps strewn like shrouds across their decks.

Kieran spotted the *Nautilus Blue* immediately. Sean was standing by the helm, his arms crossed as he stared far out to sea. Sean's had been a close family even before the storm, Kieran knew. But afterward, seven-year-old Liam had reacted to the death of his dad by clinging hard to his uncle. Sean, barely eighteen himself at the time and reeling hard, had clung back.

It was interesting that Liam had been seen on camera with Bronte, though, Kieran thought. At the very least, it added a new edge to Julian's caginess earlier, when the man had stopped by the Surf and Turf.

Julian's gentle courtship with Liam's mother, Sarah, in the years following the storm had been one of the few positive things to emerge in the aftermath, and the *will they–won't they* green shoots of romance had kept the entire town enchanted over a long winter. They *had*, at last, in a much-celebrated happy ending, and three years after losing his dad, Liam gained a stepfather.

From what Kieran knew, Julian had embraced stepfather-hood with the same earnest dedication with which he approached any new challenge and, perhaps against the odds, he had won Liam over. It probably helped—Kieran pictured Julian hunched tensely in his car outside the Surf and Turf earlier—that Julian genuinely seemed to give a shit about his stepson.

Sean was the first to spot Kieran and Ash approaching and he said something to Olivia. She had been sitting on the dock, very still, her face down. Her head snapped up and she started to stand but Ash was already there, taking three large strides across the dock straight to her. She turned wordlessly and buried her face in his shoulder. From the heaving of her back, Kieran could tell she was crying hard. Ash put his arms around her and waited.

"What's happening with Liam?" Kieran said quietly to Sean as he climbed aboard.

"He's at the station with Sarah. Julian's got a lawyer coming from Hobart."

Kieran waited for him to say something more, but Sean turned back to the water, his eyes unseeing. On the dock, Ash murmured something to Olivia, who gave a muffled reply.

"Are you doing okay?" Kieran asked Sean.

"Yeah. I dunno." He rubbed a hand over his face. "God, this is all so wrong. What are they saying in town?"

"Nothing important."

"Yeah, right." Sean turned back to the water. "I can guess."

Kieran looked over at Olivia, who was wiping her face with a tissue. Ash was rubbing her back.

"She'd forgotten her yoga mat," Ash said to Kieran quietly, and Olivia looked up.

"That's how you found Bronte?" Kieran said to her, and she nodded.

"Mum hadn't slept well, so we were going to the early class. They usually run out of mats, though, so we stopped by my place on the way. Mum waited outside in the car—oh my God." Olivia put her hands to her eyes. "Can you *imagine* if Mum had come with me and seen her?" She looked ill at the thought. "I was only going to run in and out, but Bronte's bedroom door was open, which was a bit weird because it was still early. And I couldn't hear her in the house, so—"

She stopped. The only sounds were the water lapping against the boats and the distant call of gulls.

"I could tell from the back-door handle that it was unlocked. So I went outside, to see if she was having a coffee or something." Olivia stared at the shredded tissue. "I saw her lying near the water. She was still in her work clothes. She must have been out there on her own, all night."

A silence followed.

"Liv." Sean's voice was quiet, his eyes still on the waves. "Did Renn say what they thought had happened?"

"No." Olivia shook her head. "But at the station I overheard one of the cops from Hobart say they thought Bronte had been out on the beach for at least five or six hours, so I think that's why"—Olivia glanced at Sean, who didn't look back—"why they wanted to talk to Liam."

"Right." A shadow crossed Sean's face. "Did they ask about anything else, or was it just Liam?"

"Other things. They wanted to know if Bronte had a boyfriend. I told them about that guy she was seeing earlier in the summer." She looked at Ash. "You know, that tourist? Marco something. I couldn't remember his last name."

"That Spanish bloke who was really loud in bed?" Ash shook his head. "I wouldn't even have remembered his first name. I've managed to block him out."

The way Ash said it made Kieran think he remembered the guy quite well.

"He was Portuguese, not Spanish." Olivia looked down. "Probably doesn't matter, he's been gone for weeks anyway."

"Is there a chance that bloke had anything to do with Bronte hearing noises at night?" Kieran said. "Maybe him coming around to visit her? Bother her?"

Sean looked over at that as Olivia frowned and shook her head.

"I think he'd left before that started. The cops were very interested in why Bronte hadn't reported it, though. Or me. I mean, God." She rubbed her eyes. "I said I obviously wish we had."

Ash frowned. "You didn't do anything wrong, Liv."

"Didn't I?" A gust of wind blew through the marina and the empty masts whistled and swayed. "If I'd been there—"

Ash shook his head sharply. "No. If you'd been there last night, who knows what might have happened?"

"Maybe nothing would have happened."

"Yeah, or maybe it would."

They all fell quiet. Kieran could hear the dock creak as the boats rocked and resettled. Beyond the trees, the red brick of the police station was visible.

"Do you always stay with your mum on Saturday nights?" he asked.

"Lately I have been. If I'm not working we'll watch a movie or something. Go to yoga in the morning."

"So people might know that was a regular thing?" Kieran said. "That Bronte would be alone in the house?"

Olivia went very still. "Yeah. I suppose some people might."

"People do know that, Liv." Sean's voice was caught by the wind. He didn't look over as he spoke. "Most people who know you know that."

Olivia stared at him, her face tense. Then she blinked hard. "Oh my God, I wish I'd—"

"Stop." Ash's voice was firm. "Stop that now."

Olivia fell silent but Kieran could guess what she was thinking. The road not traveled. He had enough of those thoughts himself, and they never led anywhere good.

"Ash is right," he said, and Olivia looked up. "I know you know that, Liv, but it's true. I mean, Mia and I sat on the beach for twenty minutes last night. If we'd walked back along the sand instead of—"

Kieran stopped, remembering the walk home. Dark and still, and then, all of a sudden, not.

"What?" Sean said.

"We saw a car. Last night. Driving way too fast not far from Fisherman's Cottage."

"What kind of car?" Sean asked, but Kieran could hear the real question loud and clear. *Was it Liam's five-year-old white Holden?* Kieran didn't know what the right answer was.

"I'm not sure," he said, truthfully.

Sean frowned. He didn't know what the right answer was either, Kieran thought.

"You should tell Sergeant Renn about that." Ash's voice was oddly light and Sean's eyes flicked over. He stared at his friend, trying to gauge his tone. Ash pretended not to notice.

Kieran looked from one to the other. He couldn't read Ash either, which was a little unusual. "Yeah," he said. "I will."

Sean turned back to the horizon, his head tilted in the way Kieran knew meant he was thinking. At last, he opened his mouth. "Listen, guys, about Liam—"

He was cut off as Olivia's phone rang. They waited as she answered, listening and occasionally nodding at the voice on the other end.

"Okay. Thank you." She frowned as she hung up. "That was Chris Renn. He needs me back at the house."

Ash looked at her. "What for?"

"I don't know. He sounded . . ." Olivia shook her head. "I'm not sure. I'd better go."

"Hang on," Sean said as she got to her feet. "About Liam—"

He waited until they were all facing him.

"Liam wouldn't do this. Okay? He wouldn't."

Olivia stood hand in hand with Ash, neither quite meeting Sean's eye. The already-strange atmosphere had taken a sharp awkward turn. Sean looked to Kieran.

"You heard Liam and Bronte talking together last night, right? Not arguing or shouting. Did Liam say anything at all that sounded like a red flag?"

He waited until Kieran shook his head.

"So if Renn or someone asks," Sean said, "can you tell them that?"

Kieran hesitated. "I suppose I can tell them what I heard. But, mate, I didn't really—"

"But you did hear them. I mean, if Liam had been acting weird or aggressively or whatever, you'd have noticed, right? But you didn't. You said yourself last night that it was fine. So all I'm asking is that you tell the police that. Mate? Please?"

The wind sent the boats rocking and creaking again as Kieran looked at his friend and made himself picture Liam.

Not the Liam of last night, sullen with his grease-stained apron and the mop in his hand. But Liam of twelve years ago. Still a little boy then, dressed in a black shirt that had been bought especially for the occasion. Liam's tears had run under his chin and soaked into the stiff collar as he was handed flowers to place on his dad's coffin.

"Kieran?" Sean was pleading now. "If the police ask?"

Kieran was trying hard to think of Liam, but his mind instead kept circling back to Sean. Not Sean at the funeral, though. A few days before that. Standing in Kieran's living room, both of them eighteen and face-to-face for the first time after the storm.

It was an accident, Kieran had started to say. Somewhere in the family house that now felt too big were Verity and Brian, both so odd and strained now, even in silence. Kieran had made himself try again. He'd forced himself to speak, knowing there weren't enough words in the world to fix this. Hating it, hating himself.

Sean had stopped him.

I know, mate. It's okay.

The relief had been blinding.

Kieran looked at Sean now. His friend was still waiting.

"Listen, if the police ask—" Kieran heard the deck groan as Ash shifted his weight, but he ignored it. Ash knew how things were. Whatever his problem was, he'd get over it. "If the police ask, yeah, I can tell them that."

"Thank you." Sean's face cracked a little. "Thanks, mate. It probably won't be enough to get him out of the shit, but it might help."

Kieran doubted it would even do that. "No worries."

"And look, I know Liam can be a bit—" Sean stopped, and gave a helpless shrug. "But I appreciate you doing this for him."

I know, mate. It's okay.

It wasn't Liam he was doing it for, but Kieran didn't bother to correct him.

9

Kieran thought Ash and Olivia might want to walk alone to Fisherman's Cottage, but when he hung back to give them the chance, Ash waited for him.

"You're going this way, aren't you?"

Kieran nodded. Mia had texted to say she had got back to his parents' house safely. While he hadn't truly expected any different, he still felt relieved.

They left Sean pulling on his wetsuit.

"You're going out to the wreck?" Kieran asked in surprise, and Sean shrugged, his face grim.

"I can't see any of this putting off the Norwegians. I'm fine, seriously," he said when he saw Kieran glance at the oxygen tanks. "Check them over yourself if it makes you feel better."

Kieran had followed Ash and Olivia out of the marina and onto the road. No one suggested going the beach way.

"So, Liam," Ash said as soon as they hit the tarmac. Sand blew across the road, crunching underfoot. Behind them, Sean and the *Nautilus Blue* were well out of sight but still, Ash kept his voice low. "The thing about Liam—" Ash stopped again, choosing his words. "Look. I get it. He's Sean's nephew. They're close. But don't get sucked into saying anything about him that you don't want to."

"I'm not planning to, mate," Kieran said. "Why? Something I should know about him?"

"No," Ash said quickly, shaking his head. "I'm not saying that. I mean, I think Liam's a bit of an arsehole, that's not news. But let's be real. We were all around when the storm hit, we all know the bloody background playing out here. So yeah, Sean's probably entitled to ask for a favor and yeah, maybe he deserves to get it."

They rounded the corner and up ahead, Kieran could see the first glimpse of Fisherman's Cottage. Overhead, swooping gulls fought against the wind. Two police cars were parked on the road outside.

"But whatever happened back then is done," Ash said. "That's not going to change. So don't let it tangle you up in something you're not happy with now." A tiny pause. "Either of you, eh?"

Kieran couldn't help it. He shot a sideways glance at Olivia. She didn't react, but then she always had been better at controlling herself than he had.

It had been a very long morning. He could think of fifty good reasons off the top of his head for the tension he could see across Olivia's shoulders and neck. He didn't know her well enough now to be able to tell what she was thinking. But that hadn't always been the case. And Kieran suddenly found himself wondering, for the first time in years, how much his good friend Ash actually knew about that day of the storm.

• • •

It had been a big summer. With their final year exams done and dusted, Kieran and Sean had launched themselves headfirst into the booze-soaked celebrations. Good weather had brought a lot of tourists through that year, including plenty of bored teenage girls who could think of a few places they'd rather be than on holiday in Tasmania with their parents. Kieran considered it his personal civic duty to show these girls a good time, and whenever the beach or campgrounds or someone's rented house came alive with music playing and beer flowing, Kieran was generally there, watching the sun both set and rise through bleary eyes.

Ash had been right there beside him, of course, despite having already called it quits at school. When the students at Evelyn Bay's secondary school finished year ten, the state's education system meant anyone who wanted to complete high school had to dig out their bus pass and spend their final two years traveling to and from the nearest college.

Ash, who had coasted effortlessly in the top third of his class for his first ten academic years, had gone to visit his dad and returned with the view that trailing ninety minutes each way on a school bus was for bloody idiots with nothing better to do. He couldn't be talked around and, with that, Ash's formal education had come to an end.

It was great, though, Ash had used to say—a lot—over those next two years. He'd showed up on the first morning to wave Kieran and Sean off on the bus with a grin. Then he'd turned around and got a job at the plant nursery, worked out pretty quickly that he was pretty good at it, and started finding his own gardening work. He had money coming in. Not loads, but more than Kieran and Sean. The best bit, though, Ash reckoned, was the freedom. Being able to spend his days however he chose. Maybe so, Kieran had thought, but it still seemed that most days what Ash chose to do was hang around the bus stop in the evenings, waiting for his friends to come home from school.

For Kieran, the summer of the storm had felt almost like

a reunion, with the classroom finally behind them. They'd all been working. Ash had cooked up some idea to launch his own landscaping business and was flat-out turning his grandmother's garden into a showpiece. Kieran and Sean had worked for their older brothers, same as every year. Finn and Toby didn't muck around when it came to the diving business and it was hard work—"Minimum wage for maximum shit," Kieran used to complain to Verity, but he hadn't really meant it.

Olivia had been there too. Down at the beach in her bathers. Getting a beer from the fridge at a Friday-night house party, looking as relieved as anyone to have put the tedious bus rides to college behind her. She'd been around a lot, but not with them. Because while Kieran and Ash had a strong preference for the holiday-happy girls who stayed at sea-view cabins or the campgrounds before disappearing back to the mainland two weeks later, Olivia and her friends had a strong preference for guys who were nothing like Kieran and Ash.

She had time for Sean, though.

Kieran would sometimes glance up from whatever sagging couch he'd landed on, trying to remember the name of the girl he was talking to, and across the party he'd see Olivia and Sean leaning against the kitchen counter, chatting quietly about something Kieran could only guess at. Kieran would look over at Ash, who would also be watching and shaking his head with the same baffled look.

"I don't get it," Ash had said more than once. "Is she just really into his whole shy virgin thing, or what?"

Kieran had grinned into his drink. "I dunno, mate."

"I mean, look at him. And then look at her."

"Yeah. I'm looking."

"Then explain to me what's going on."

Kieran laughed. "I can't."

That wasn't true, though. When Kieran thought about it, which he found himself doing surprisingly often, the answer was pretty obvious. Olivia and Sean were friends. They had taken a couple of the same classes during the final school year and had been paired together on a joint project. This had once involved Sean spending a whole afternoon working from Olivia's bedroom—about which he was infuriatingly light on detail, despite an extended grilling from Ash.

"That's it," Ash had said, putting his bottle down on a sticky countertop a few weeks later and a few drinks deeper than he should have been. "I'm going to rescue her."

And he had tried, marching across the party and throwing a heavy arm around Sean before cutting him off midsentence. Olivia, to the surprise of no one but Ash himself, had blanked him until he'd been forced to slink away, red-faced, and spend the rest of the night muttering furiously into his beer.

"You and Olivia are nice and tight, mate. You're officially one of the girls now," Ash had said casually the next day, wiping the tiny hint of triumph off Sean's face.

Sean had looked to Kieran, who had checked his phone and pretended not to notice, partly because—for reasons he couldn't quite articulate—he found the whole situation a little irritating himself. After that, Sean had mostly gone back to standing alone at parties, and everyone was happy.

• • •

The police cars parked outside Fisherman's Cottage were empty, Kieran could see now as they drew closer. Caution tape had been strung between the gateposts, barring entry, and a uniformed officer Kieran didn't recognize stood watch outside. Other than that, he could see no activity at the front of the property. Whatever was happening, it was going on within the house or down on the beach, Kieran guessed.

"Do you think I'll have to go back inside?" Olivia slowed as they got nearer to the cottage.

"I don't know," Ash said. "Maybe."

They slowed with her, eventually coming to a complete stop a short distance from her home.

"Liv, hey." Ash turned to face her, his voice soft. "It's okay. Yeah? It'll be okay."

When Olivia didn't make any sign that she agreed, Ash reached out and took her hand.

•   •   •

The next time Kieran had seen Olivia properly was a few weeks later as summer was slipping away. Kieran, for once, hadn't minded too much when the heat began to dip and the tourists thinned out. His exam results had come in and were acceptable, if not overly impressive, and in a matter of weeks he'd be heading to Sydney where there was a uni place with his name on it.

It had been a warm, lazy day when Kieran had found himself climbing the cliff path to the lookout. At the top, he'd stood on the edge, peering over. Below, he could see the strip of deserted sandy beach leading to the caves. The path down was not formally marked, but it may as well have been. The worn ground showed the way as clearly as any sign.

The surface of the sea was calm above the *Mary Minerva* as Kieran picked his way down. On the edge of a rocky outcrop that was almost always underwater, the sculptural memorial to the wreck glinted in the sun, facing out toward the site.

The sea itself was empty, though. It was too early in the season for wreck diving, and even if it hadn't been, Kieran knew his brother wouldn't be out on the boat that day. Finn and Toby's request to add a cave tour to their program had languished in the council's in-box for months before unexpectedly receiving tentative approval. The news had sent them scrambling to pull together routes of varying difficulty that showcased the labyrinth of tunnels.

Kieran really wasn't sure what all the stress was about. The caves were technically off-limits, but they had all been there enough times over the years to know which of the routes led to cavernous rooms lit by internal shafts of natural light, and which led to bottlenecks and dead ends that dipped below sea level. Either way, Finn had wanted to alter the beginner route, Toby had disagreed and, when both had been summoned to a meeting by their accountant, they had dispatched Kieran with instructions to follow both courses and take photos at the turns.

Kieran got through the job in about forty minutes and, back out in the bright light of the empty beach, had dropped his towel and bag on the sand and dived into the water. He'd simply floated, staring at the vivid blue sky with no one else around. He had been enjoying the peace when he sensed rather than heard someone heading down the cliff path. Finding his feet, he wiped the salt water from his face and watched the figure descend.

Olivia.

She was wearing shorts and a T-shirt, and her hair was tied up. She was alone. She spotted him in the sea, slowed for half a step, then continued down to the beach. Kieran stood and waded toward shore, suddenly very aware as the water dripped from his bare chest that the footy off-season strength program he'd been following in the gym all summer had done him no harm at all.

Olivia thought so too, he hoped, from the tiny flicker of her eyes as she took her sunglasses off.

"Hey."

"Hey."

"I ran into Sean yesterday." She glanced around the empty beach. "He said you guys were working down here this afternoon."

"Just me now. He had to help his mum with something."

"This is working?" Olivia smiled at Kieran's towel, his wet hair. "I need to get myself a job like this."

Kieran grinned. "I've finished."

"Checking the cave routes?"

"Just the easy one. Sean told you? It's this thing our brothers are starting."

"Yeah. He said if I stopped by he'd show me. I'll be gone for uni by the time the real tours start."

"Right. Well, he's not here today."

"Oh." Olivia glanced back toward the path she'd just walked down, then hesitated. She turned her head and looked out instead at the water, then raised a hand and shielded her eyes as she studied the memorial to the *Mary Minerva*.

"They look different from this angle," she said after a moment.

Kieran followed her line of sight along the furthest rocks that snaked out from the caves and into the sea. At the very tip, the three life-size iron figures stood guard. The Survivors.

Side by side, they gazed outward, unflinching against the elements, their sculpted faces turned forever to where the *Mary Minerva* lay sunk beneath the waves.

"I can see why people like them, but they always seem kind of cold to me," Olivia said.

"Yeah?" Kieran studied the three figures. The Survivors were permanently visible from the cliffs and the sea, tall enough that even in the highest tides and the worst weather, they never fully disappeared underwater. There was no danger of that today, as they stood knee-deep and watched over the placid ocean.

"Maybe it's just their name and the wreck and everything." Olivia shrugged. "It all feels a bit sad."

"Do you know they weren't originally called that?" Kieran said, and Olivia turned to him.

"No. Really?"

"They were, like, *Trio in Iron* or something, but then someone from the council heard about them and had the bright idea to put them out there. So they paid the artist extra to change the name, point them in the right direction, and say they were a tribute to the wreck."

"Are you serious?" Olivia laughed.

"Yeah. My brother told me. He found out by accident when he was having to do heaps of paperwork for the dive permits. I guess they thought *The Survivors* was catchier."

"They thought right," she said. "No one tell the tourists, hey?"

"It's weird. I kind of like them better for knowing that, though," Kieran said. "How they nearly had this whole other life, standing around in a sunny park or something instead of stuck out there. It makes them seem more—" He shrugged, suddenly feeling like an idiot. "I don't know. Human or something."

Olivia looked at him then, something like surprise crossing her face.

"Yeah," she said finally, turning back to The Survivors. "I get what you mean."

They stood together and watched the swell of the tide.

After a minute, Olivia looked at him again. "So, Sean's not going to be here at all?"

"No." Kieran bent down and slipped on his T-shirt, the fabric sticking a little to his damp skin. When he stood up, her eyes were still on him; her hair shining in the sun, her legs long beneath her shorts. Her expression was unchanged, but there was an ember of something new sparking in that fresh sea air above the deserted beach.

Or maybe not something new, Kieran could admit to himself. Something that had been there for quite a while, on his part at least, at school and on the bus and at all those booze-soaked parties. A rush he felt whenever Olivia was nearby.

Kieran checked the cliff path. It was as empty as the beach. No one was around. No Sean. No Ash. Just him and Olivia, for once. The caves lay across the beach, cool and inviting.

"I could show you around," he said. "If you want."

Kieran waited. He realized he was holding his breath and let it out.

Olivia was still watching him. "Yeah." She smiled, slowly. "Okay, then."

10

Olivia stopped at the gate of Fisherman's Cottage and gave her name to the officer standing guard outside her own house. He motioned for her to wait and disappeared inside. A minute later, the front door opened and Sergeant Renn came out.

His bald head was hidden by his police hat, making him appear less like a nightclub bouncer than he sometimes could. Not yet forty and he looked to Kieran like a man who had absolutely had enough. It was a shame, Kieran thought. When Chris Renn had arrived in Evelyn Bay twelve years earlier, his enthusiasm for small-town policing had seemed genuine rather than simply dutiful.

He had spent all summer diligently shadowing then sergeant Geoffrey Mallott—a creaking sack of a man who preferred warnings dispensed with a grandfatherly twinkle to actual charges and paperwork. Mallott had marked off the days to his retirement on a calendar hanging in public view at the station, and been more than happy to let young Constable Renn solve any pressing cases of graffiti and littering and the occasional theft of a tourist's wallet from under a beach towel. And Renn, for his part, had been happy to oblige.

Kieran knew there was a general consensus among Evelyn Bay residents that they were lucky Chris Renn had stuck around as long as he had. He seemed competent and ambitious enough to progress elsewhere, but he had reassured them that he simply liked both the people and the place. There had been some fear they'd lose him a few years ago when he started getting serious with a woman in Launceston, but Renn was still here and she hadn't joined him, so Kieran guessed it hadn't worked out.

Now, though, Sergeant Renn simply looked tired. He saw Kieran, Ash, and Olivia at the gate of Fisherman's Cottage and lifted the police tape.

"Just you, please, Olivia. For now," Renn said, holding up a hand as Ash started to follow.

Ash looked like he was going to argue, but Olivia shook her head. "It's okay."

She ducked under the tape and Renn turned back to the house.

"Hey, Chris," Kieran called out, and the officer stopped. "I saw a car around here last night."

"Oh yeah?" Renn walked a few steps back. "Along Beach Road?"

Kieran nodded. "A bit further along. Coming from this direction toward town."

"Time?"

"About eleven thirty."

"Make and model? Color?"

"Four-wheel drive. Holden, maybe." Kieran tried to think, but what he remembered most were the lights and the noise. Renn was still waiting. "Sorry. It was driving pretty fast. Mia saw it too, though."

"Okay. Try to remember what you can. We'll grab a statement off you both when we get a chance." Renn turned back to
Olivia. "Ready?"

Renn's tone was neutral and there was nothing unusual
about the way he gestured to the front door, open and waiting
for Olivia. But somewhere deep in Kieran's primal survival in-
stincts, a warning pinged. *Tread carefully.*

Olivia herself paused, one hand still on the police tape, and
Kieran wondered if she felt it too. Then she straightened and
followed Sergeant Renn into the house where, until yesterday,
Bronte had lived.

• • •

The tide swelled in and out, slow and steady, as Kieran led Olivia
across the beach. The South Cave was the further of the two from
the cliff path, but it was his favorite.

Kieran avoided the dip at the entrance, then reached out
and offered Olivia his hand to help her over. She took it as they
crossed the threshold from the bright light into the cool dark
shadow.

"Wow," she breathed as he took out his torch and showed
her along one of the same routes he'd raced through an hour or
so earlier. The rocks arched over them, mostly above head height,
sometimes lower. The damp sand that formed the soft, wide path
repaired itself quickly, their footprints vanishing almost as soon
as they were made.

"It's really beautiful," Olivia said as they stopped and stood
side by side, examining the way the natural patterns in the rocky
walls formed strands of color, woven together over millions of
years and washed twice daily by the sea.

Kieran had to agree. It was always beautiful, even if he rarely
stopped to notice these days. He took his time leading them through,
giving Olivia a chance to absorb the caves at her own pace.

"What's down there?" Olivia asked as they came to a junction and Kieran guided her left rather than right.

"Dead end, eventually." He shone his torch down the gloomy path. From where they stood, the tunnel looked the same as the other one. "It goes pretty deep, though. You can go a fair way before you have to come back."

"You've been down it?"

"Yeah, once." By accident, when he hadn't been paying attention.

Kieran could still remember the startled leap of panic when he'd realized, too late, that he had gone wrong. Finn had warned him about exactly this, many times. Kieran knew all about the tunnels so twisty you could get lost ten steps deep. The roof over Kieran's head had instantly felt lower, hanging dark and heavy. He had checked his watch, struggling suddenly to calculate the minutes—hours, in reality—left until the tide was due to rush in.

All he could think of was Finn's warning: *If you're still in here at high tide, mate, you're not coming out.*

Kieran had made himself take a few deep breaths, all alone in that unfamiliar space, and then turned a very careful 180 degrees and started to walk, slowly. When the first sliver of daylight had reappeared—literally at the end of the tunnel—he had let himself run toward it, embarrassed by his fear even as the adrenaline still coursed through him.

"There's not much to see down there anyway," he said to Olivia now, turning the torch away. "This route's better."

They had traced the trail onward through the rocks, and eventually they could hear the sea and emerged once more near the wide-open cavern inside the mouth.

"Back again," Kieran said. "Safe and sound."

"Thank you." Olivia's cheeks were flushed and her eyes bright. "That was amazing."

"It's good, hey? You've never been down here before?"

"No, my mum says it's off-limits for a reason."

Kieran shrugged. "I mean, you don't want to be around at high tide, but it's okay now."

"Yeah." And Olivia had smiled as they stood alone in the dark cozy cave with the warm beach breeze floating in. "It's pretty good now."

And Kieran, who found it best not to overthink things, had taken that as his cue and kissed her. She had kissed him back and, after a minute or two, he had put his hand out and led her a little deeper into the cave, where a large flat rock jutted out from the wall, creating a secluded ledge.

And he had shown her, as he had shown a couple of other girls that summer, how to climb up, and they'd sat on his towel, hidden from view, and kissed some more as the afternoon light filtered in. They had stayed there, close and undisturbed, until eventually Kieran had very reluctantly checked his watch.

"We'd better go," he'd said. "The tide'll be coming in soon."

He'd helped her down and he'd been a little surprised, as they emerged, how thin and narrow the slice of beach had become. Time had slipped by faster than he'd thought. Out on the water, The Survivors were up to their waists.

Kieran and Olivia climbed up the cliff path together and at the top, she'd stopped, looking back down at the hidden beach.

"So, are you going to tell all your footy mates about this?"

"No."

"Really?"

"Not if you don't want me to," Kieran said. "I know Ash and some of the others can be dickheads sometimes, but I'm not like them."

"But—" Olivia's forehead creased.

"What?"

"Kieran—" She looked at him. "You are like them."

He opened his mouth to argue, but something in the way she'd said it stopped him.

"Well," he said, finally. "I still won't tell anyone."

And somewhat even to Kieran's own surprise, he had kept his word.

•　•　•

Kieran and Ash stood at the gatepost, behind the police tape, staring at Fisherman's Cottage. A uniformed officer had come out to fetch something from the police cars, leaving the front door open.

Kieran could see a bright hallway leading first toward what he knew would be the kitchen and living area. What little he could see of the house looked neat and cared for.

From what Olivia had said, it sounded like she hadn't noticed any signs of violence or a struggle inside. Kieran pictured the layout of the house. Bronte's bedroom window, looking over the beach. The back door, leading out to the small back-yard and the sand. What had drawn her out there?

From somewhere in the house, he heard Sergeant Renn's low voice.

There was nothing, then a short response. Olivia.

Kieran couldn't make out what either one was saying.

•　•　•

Kieran and Olivia had met at the caves for a second time seem-ingly, if not actually, by chance. Kieran had hung around the deserted beach all afternoon, eventually resorting to doing some route-mapping work for Finn and Toby as an excuse for being there. He'd sighed with relief when he'd seen Olivia's sunlit head peering over the cliffs. He'd raised a hand and she'd waved back, both smiling as she made her way down.

Two days later, he'd left Sean and Ash sitting in the Surf and Turf and jogged outside to catch her alone. He'd led her out of sight behind the community center and straight up asked when she could next meet him.

The following day, they had been on the ledge together and Olivia had looked up and spotted where Ash had used his keys to carve his name into the rock face a few months earlier. She'd run a finger over it and raised an eyebrow, and Kieran had shrugged.

The ledge was technically Ash's discovery. He'd stumbled across it the summer before in the midst of an enthusiastic campaign to convince some girl from the ice-cream shop to take her clothes off for him. It had worked, Ash had reported to Kieran later, with a grin. By mutual unspoken agreement they hadn't mentioned it to Sean, who in his own quiet way could sometimes take the shine off stuff like that.

Kieran's only real concern whenever he laid his towel out on the flat rock with Olivia was that Ash might turn up unexpectedly, a potential conquest of his own in tow. Ash had been to stay with his dad and his dad's new girlfriend—not the one he'd left Ash's mum for, another one—and been in a foul mood ever since he'd got back.

But thankfully no one ever appeared uninvited at the mouth of the cave and, for those weeks at least, Kieran and Olivia had had the place to themselves.

By the day of the storm, they had established something of a routine, and Kieran was already waiting by the time Olivia appeared on the cliff path. He was sitting by the cave entrance, glad he'd brought an extra hoodie and towel as he felt a breeze whip across the beach. The sea stretched out empty in front of him as he'd stood up to kiss her. The *Nautilus Black* was not sailing today, he knew. High winds were forecast. Finn and Toby would keep her safely in the marina.

"I can't stay too long," Olivia said when they broke apart. "It's my mum's birthday tomorrow. Gabby wants us to make her a cake."

"No worries. Looks like it might rain anyway."

Above, the earlier blue skies had given way to darkening clouds that hung low with a pregnant weight. Inside, though, the cave was oddly warm, the rocks having absorbed the heat of the midday sun.

As Kieran and Olivia climbed onto their ledge, tucked away safely from the elements, Olivia had glanced back toward the beach. The weather wasn't good.

"Maybe we should leave it today?"

"No," Kieran had said. "Stay. Please."

And he'd kissed her again and she'd kissed him back, and after that he had barely heard the rain start as they lay on the soft towels in the snug warmth of the shelter. When the lightning had begun to flash outside, it was nothing short of romantic, and Kieran had thought to himself—this almost made him laugh later—that he would remember this day.

He was surprised, when he finally sat up, to see how dark the sky was. He checked the time. It wasn't even that late. He looked over at Olivia and saw her staring down.

"Oh my God," she said.

It was the note in her voice that made him stop. He looked to where she was pointing, beneath the ledge. Across the bottom of the cave, the sand was hidden by a dark sheet of water.

•　•　•

Ash leaned on the gate outside Fisherman's Cottage and, distracted, reached over the police tape and pulled out a weed growing near the fence line.

"Sorry," he said, tossing the weed on the ground as the uniformed police officer at the door frowned. "Christ, what's taking so long?"

Kieran glanced at his watch. It hadn't really been that long, but he knew what Ash meant. It was unnerving to just stand there, not knowing what was happening.

"Bronte seemed nice," Kieran said, for something to fill the space. "From what I saw."

"Yeah, she was. All right, calm down, mate." Ash had reached over to pull out another weed but dropped it as the frowning uniformed officer looked poised to act. Ash turned his back on the house and leaned against the fence. "Bronte was good fun. Easy to be around, you know? Easygoing, I guess," he corrected himself. "I know she drove Liv a bit nuts, but it wasn't deliberate. I mean, Liv's got other things going on, stuff with her mum. It wasn't all about Bronte, even if Liv thinks it was." Ash glanced sideways. "Don't tell Olivia I said that."

Kieran shook his head with a small smile. Ash turned back to the house, his own smile fading.

"I know it's different when you live with someone, but I thought Bronte was all right." He frowned, and fell quiet for a moment. "Liam liked her. A lot. Whatever Sean reckons, that kid was into her. Bloody obvious about it too."

"And what did Bronte make of him?"

Ash reached out and ran a rough finger and thumb over the police tape looped across the gate. "Who knows, eh?"

•   •   •

Olivia pointed as the green-black water surged slick and strong across the cave floor, foaming angrily against the walls. The sight of it was Kieran's last completely clear memory of that day. Everything after that came in snatches.

He remembered sliding off the ledge feetfirst, and the shock of discovering the water he'd thought was ankle-deep was above his knees. *Come on, come on*, he had urged, watching in disbelief as Olivia took valuable seconds to reach up and snatch the water-proof bag with their phones in it.

Jesus, leave it, he must have said, because he remembered her looking at him in astonishment.

Are you kidding? No way. Her eyes were wide.

But no, Kieran was serious. Because all he could think of was Finn's warning.

If you're in here at high tide, you are not coming out.

Kieran had grabbed Olivia's arm and they'd waded through the oily blackness. The relief as they hit open air had vanished immediately when they splashed out of the cave and into daylight that was more like night. The beach had disappeared. The peak of each wave reached his chest. His skin stung in the driving rain and the sea slapped high against the rock.

The dark twin mouths of the caves inhaled huge lungfuls of water before spewing them out again, and the currents clawed at Kieran's legs, trying to knock his feet out from under him. He wiped the water from his eyes and tried to work out which way to aim to pick up the cliff path that led away from the beach and up to safety. He couldn't see it. Everything seemed different.

"Shit, Kieran, look." Olivia's voice was snatched away and he had squinted against the rain hammering down on the open sea. And it was wide open, he realized. There was nothing between them and the horizon, and all at once he knew why everything felt so wrong.

The Survivors were gone.

Where they should have been standing solid and secure with their heads always rising above the water, there was only angry ocean and a gray-black horizon. They were fully submerged, swallowed whole by the swell. Kieran had never before seen that. The fear that had been brewing inside him, strong and dark and deep, exploded to the surface.

"We have to get higher."

He'd grabbed Olivia's hand. The bottom of the cliff path was under the waves but they had forced their way, half swimming and half wading, to where it should have been. Olivia lost her footing first, and Kieran heard her gasp as she went under. He plunged in his other hand, dragging her up until she appeared, red-faced and choking. Moments later, he stumbled and the world was instantly swallowed up.

He felt himself dragged in one direction by the water and another by Olivia, and then it was his turn to burst through the surface, back into the roar of the storm. They pushed forward, Kieran counting the steps in his head until he felt the sand give way to rock under his feet. He felt light-headed with relief. They had found the path.

As the tide sucked out, gathering momentum, he put his hands around Olivia's waist and hoisted her up. She clambered higher, her bare legs leaving a bloody smear where she grazed them against the rock. She had lain flat on her stomach, shielding her face from the sheets of rain, stretching down to help him. She'd yelled something that Kieran couldn't hear over the shrieking wind.

He never reached her. The water slammed into him and next time he could see he was far away.

Olivia had untangled the waterproof bag from around her wrist and wrenched it open, using her phone to call for help. Kieran didn't know if he really remembered seeing her do that, or if he'd conjured the memory from what he'd learned afterward. He'd heard a snatch of his name being shouted into the squall and fought to swim toward her voice. He couldn't make any ground.

The waves were monstrous. He was tossed upward, then pulled so deep he couldn't tell which way to fight for the surface. He didn't know how long he was under. Long enough that his lungs were empty in a way he had never felt before.

And then, suddenly, where there had been nothing but water, there was rock. Hard and brutal, it hurtled toward him with enough force to make his teeth rattle. When the water pulled back, Kieran was still chest down, his face slick against the solid surface. Breathless and bleeding, he had raised his head and seen Olivia screaming something at him. She was pointing in a frantic gesture.

"Go up! Up! Get higher!"

Kieran had stumbled to his feet and, mustering every shred of the muscle he had worked so hard for all summer in the gym, started to climb. He hauled himself up to a craggy hole in the cliff face, buoyed at the end by the tip of a wave that a second earlier and a meter lower would have dragged him back under.

Kieran clung to that spot, sucking in ragged breaths and hearing his heart pound as he pulled himself further in. He could make out the edge of the cliff path a short way up and across, but it may as well have been a million miles away. He couldn't find the strength or courage to move. He was still lying there, with stinging eyes and aching lungs, when he saw a flash of color out on the water. It took him a long slow moment to realize what he was seeing.

It was his brother's boat.

The *Nautilus Black* was barely visible as it forged its way through the crashing waves. Past the hidden wreck and past the point where The Survivors should be standing. On, toward the caves.

Finn is here. It was Kieran's only clear thought. Finn had come for him. And, amid the pain and cold and the heavy ache in his lungs, in that single moment, Kieran had felt safe.

11

Finn had taught Kieran all the important stuff. How to swim, how to kick a footy, how to drink. How to talk to other guys. How to talk to girls. People liked Finn. They liked Kieran because he reminded them of Finn, but Finn was the real deal.

Finn Elliott brought home sporting trophies for Evelyn Bay when he was younger, and brought in tourism dollars when he was older. Finn was the kind of guy who could walk into the Surf and Turf and never have to buy a drink, but he did, often, because Finn was also the kind of guy who stood his round.

Finn had pounded the streets as a pacesetter when Verity was training for a half marathon, and he'd got out the ladder and helped Brian clear the leaves from the gutters every autumn, and he'd stood chest-deep in the freezing ocean and showed Kieran how to improve his open-water freestyle technique.

For twenty-six years, Finn was there for the people in his life, and then he wasn't there at all anymore.

Kieran couldn't remember much of the last time he saw Finn, and he was grateful for that, mostly. If Kieran's memories of leaving the cave were patchy, they shrank to almost nothing once he saw the boat. There was no medical or physical reason for this—that doctor in the Hobart hospital had been right—because his body had recovered well.

Kieran knew what had happened as he was clinging to the rocks with the waves pounding beneath him, but only because he'd asked and he'd been told. The *Nautilus Black*, a catamaran specifically chosen by Finn and Toby for its stability and maneuverability and all those things that really matter in rough seas, had been unlucky. In a literal perfect storm of events, it had crossed a breaking wave and rolled.

It still hadn't sunk, despite the sea's full fury. The catamaran's natural buoyancy had kept it on the surface, drifting drunkenly in the rolling green waves with its underside hideously exposed.

Toby had not even drowned, technically. He'd been slammed against the hull, the impact shattering part of his skull. He had died facedown in the sea without taking in a breath of water. Gone at thirty, leaving behind his wife, Sarah, and their young son, Liam, as well as his own brother, Sean.

Finn had drowned, though. He had been tangled, life jacket and all, when the boat flipped, trapping him below the surface. Finn was submerged in the end for nearly an hour, of which only the first four minutes had counted.

Kieran should be able to remember all that if he wanted to, he'd been told a few times. The lack of clarity was a defense mechanism, not a physical problem. But he didn't want to remember, so he didn't. Kieran didn't argue, but he didn't really believe it either. Because some things he remembered very clearly.

His parents' faces in the hospital corridor, for example. Kieran had seen them through the viewing window and tried not to listen to the urgent whispered conversation that ended with Verity entering Kieran's treatment room alone. Kieran had watched the open door, but Brian had never appeared.

He remembered coming home, later. The shock at the sight of the torn-apart town, still reeling from the storm damage. The strange and unsettling question now hovering around Gabrielle Birch's whereabouts. Brian retreating to his study for hours and then days. The sound of muffled crying in the house.

Kieran would have given a lot not to remember those things, and yet he did, all the time.

Ash had rung the front doorbell on Kieran's second day home, and the pair had sat in silence, watching TV with blank eyes, neither able to think of a thing to say. Ash had come back again, though, and on the fourth visit he'd brought Sean with him.

"It was an accident." Kieran had stood opposite Sean in the house that felt too big. Brian locked in his study, Verity sleeping a lot. Sean's gaze had moved around the living room he'd been in a thousand times and landed on a framed photo of Finn. Finn, smiling and happy, and just as dead as Sean's own brother, Toby.

Kieran was still struggling to find the words when Sean had stopped him.

"I know, mate. It's okay."

The relief had been blinding.

"It was an accident," Sean had repeated in a quiet voice that sounded like an attempt to convince himself. He seemed to need to hear it almost as much as Kieran. "The storm was worse than any of us thought."

Things with Sean had been different after that, but everything was. Kieran was just grateful they were still speaking.

No one knew that Olivia had also been down in the caves, Kieran had realized in the hospital. By then there seemed no point in dragging her into it too. She'd been the one to sound the alarm, but in the chaos it had been assumed she'd been up on the cliff path when she'd spotted Kieran in the water.

By the time anyone would have thought to check the finer details, the search for Gabby Birch was well into its urgent phase, and every question directed Olivia's way was focused exclusively on attempts to find her fourteen-year-old sister.

Kieran had tried a few times to call and text Olivia, but she'd never replied. Kieran hadn't been totally surprised. He wasn't sure what he would have said if she had.

A joint funeral was held for Finn and Toby on the basis that the list of mourners overlapped almost entirely. Olivia hadn't come, but Kieran hadn't been surprised about that either. After all, by then Gabby's backpack had been found.

• • •

The doorway of Fisherman's Cottage remained empty. Olivia was still inside. Ash checked the time yet again on his phone.

"Do you think there's something—" He broke off as two men came around the side of the house. Kieran was a little surprised to see that one of them was Julian Wallis, looking more composed than he had earlier at the Surf and Turf. His granite features were back in place as he pointed out security features to a police officer armed with a camera.

"Deadlocks on the exterior doors," Julian was saying.

"You installed them, or they were here when you bought the place?" the officer asked.

A pause. "They were already in."

He made a note. "How long have you owned this house?"

"Six years."

"Changed the locks at all in that time?"

"No. I mean—" Julian looked thrown. He ran a hand over his cropped silver hair. "Should I have?"

"Just confirming." The officer made a *carry on* gesture. Julian gathered himself and pointed up. "Security light up there, as well. Motion activated. I installed that."

"Your local sergeant said that bulb had blown," the officer said neutrally, snapping a photo.

Julian stared up at it, betrayal in every feature. "The girls didn't report it. I'd have put in a new one if they had."

The officer simply raised his camera again, noncommittal, and took another photo. He squinted at the screen.

"All right," he said. "Wait here. I'll check if your sergeant needs anything else."

Julian watched the man disappear through the front door of his investment property, his jaw set. He turned, seemingly noticing Kieran and Ash for the first time, and walked over, leaning heavily against the fence.

"How's Liam?" Ash said.

"You've heard, then? About him driving her home?"

"Think everyone has, mate."

"Well, that's all he did, if anyone's asking." Julian sighed. "He's not doing well. Sarah's with him. She's not too good either."

"No."

"They don't deserve this." Julian didn't exactly look at Kieran. "Neither of them. Reckon they've earned their peace and quiet."

The note of accusation was faint, but it came through on a frequency to which Kieran was highly attuned. He said nothing in response, simply letting his reaction rise and fade and pass as his last counselor had recommended.

Instead, Kieran looked up the road, where in the distance he could nearly make out his parents' house. Mia was there waiting for him, and he had the urge to be near her. He pushed himself away from the fence, then stopped as there was movement and Olivia came out of the cottage. She was clutching a few small items in her hands and had a troubled look on her face.

Sergeant Renn filled the doorway behind her. He saw Julian and beckoned.

"Quick word, please, mate."

"Of course. No worries." Julian dutifully headed up the path toward Renn. They disappeared inside, and the door shut again.

"Are you okay?" Ash reached out his hand to Olivia. "What did they want?"

"I'm not sure." She seemed a little shell-shocked. "He kept asking the same things as this morning. Stuff about Bronte. What did she talk about? What did she do when she wasn't at work? Who came to visit her at the house? But it was like he wanted something specific."

"Like what?" Ash said.

"I don't know, but I don't think I was giving it to him."

"What did you tell them?"

"Everything I could think of. That she had that boyfriend, Marco, for a while. How she was out of the house a lot getting ideas for her art. Bringing back seaweed and stuff she'd found." Olivia stopped as the shadow of an officer appeared in the front window then moved away again. "Chris asked if anything was missing."

"Was there?" Kieran said.

"All my things were okay. Bronte's purse and phone are on the counter. And the rent money's in cash on top of the fridge and that's still there. But—" She held out her hands to show a packet of birth control pills and a contact lens case and solution. "This is all they would let me take. Chris checked it over. And they're still in her room. I think they're looking for something."

Ash ran his tongue over his teeth. "And he wouldn't help you out?" He looked at his girlfriend. "Give you a clue?"

Olivia had spent much of her eighteenth year pretending not to notice that the new young constable in town had an embarrassingly obvious crush on her. She had never acknowledged it, and the then twenty-seven-year-old Chris Renn had done his very professional best to hide it, but the telltale blush that used to creep up his neck tended to betray him.

"No. He wouldn't, actually." Olivia looked at the house and seemed unsure what to make of that.

They all jumped a little as the door opened and Julian reappeared. Kieran could see Chris Renn in the hallway. He was talking into his mobile. He noticed Kieran watching and slowly reached out and tapped the door shut again.

Julian came down the path and ducked under the police tape at the gate.

"Listen, Liv, this goes without saying, but don't worry about the rent for now. If you still want to stay on afterward"—Julian jerked his head awkwardly at the police car—"we'll work something out."

"Thanks, Julian."

There was a pause. "You didn't tell me the security bulb was blown." He tried and failed to keep the note of reproach out of his voice.

"I thought Bronte mentioned it."

"She didn't."

"Oh." Olivia rubbed her eyes. "Well, I don't know what I can tell you, Julian. You know what she was like."

"Yeah. Of course." He checked himself. "Sorry. It's just been a bloody long day already. You'll be staying at Ash's for now?"

Olivia shook her head. "My mum wants me at home with her."

"Fair enough. I probably would too. All right, well, call me if you need anything, yeah? Don't hesitate, okay?"

She nodded and Ash put his arm around her.

"Let's get going," he said, and then turned back to Kieran. "Speak to you soon, mate."

"Yeah." Kieran watched them walk away together.

He had never told Ash about his meetings with Olivia at the caves, or that she had been with him on the day of the storm. Whether Olivia had told him, he supposed, depended on how close she and Ash were. Kieran couldn't guess.

He turned toward home himself, raising a hand to Julian. "See you around."

"Sure," Julian said. "And hey, is your dad okay? After last night?"

Kieran stopped. "What?"

"Hope he wasn't left too confused. It was me who found him this time." Julian noticed Kieran's own confusion and frowned. "Sorry, I thought Verity would've said. Brian was out wandering again."

"Wandering? Again?" Kieran stared at him. "How long has he been doing that?"

"I'm not sure," Julian said. "But he was doing it last night."

"Where?" But Kieran was already picturing the hallway of his parents' house that morning. The broom propped up against the wall. The sand scattered across the floorboards. He felt a sudden overwhelming urge to get home, right now.

"He was walking along the road here, a bit after midnight, when I was driving home."

"And you saw him, did you?"

"Yeah, luckily. I was doing the quarterly payroll, so it took me a while to cash up; otherwise I might have missed him. I called Verity, let her know. Your dad won't get in the car with anyone he doesn't recognize these days, so . . ." Julian shook his head. "Well, you know how he is. So I followed him along the road. Drove behind until your mum came out and got him."

"Right," Kieran said. "Thank you."

"No worries. I didn't want him getting himself into any trouble."

Through the cottage windows, Kieran could see the outline of police officers moving around. He looked back, his unspoken question of whether or not Julian had shared this information with them answered by the shadow of guilt on the man's face. He absolutely had.

"Look, I told them straight," Julian said, reading his mind, his voice low. "I've known your folks for years; I'm not looking to cause problems for them. But I've known Liam his whole life. I love that kid like my own. Sarah's devastated. We all want this sorted out. And not even for Liam, for Bronte."

When Kieran didn't reply, Julian shrugged.

"I mean it. Bronte was a good girl, the customers loved her, all the other staff too. We just want whatever bastard did this to her found before he's halfway across the mainland. If he's not already. I'm serious. The cops are wasting their time looking at Liam."

It was an echo of what Sean had said earlier and Kieran didn't reply. He could see Julian's silver four-wheel drive parked a little way along the road, surfboard still strapped to the top.

"That's the only reason I even told the cops about your dad," Julian said. "So they'd know that it was possible other people were around last night. People who weren't necessarily seen, you know?"

"I'm not sure Chris Renn needs your help reminding him what his own town's like at night," Kieran said.

"Maybe not, but it's not him running this show, is it?" Julian said. "They've got some woman over from Hobart."

Through the window, Kieran thought he could see Sergeant Renn talking to another officer. It was hard to tell from that distance, but Renn seemed to be watching them through the glass.

"And who knows?" Julian said. "Maybe your dad could tell them something that might help."

Kieran looked at him, annoyed now. "Have you seen the state of my dad lately?"

"I have, mate, yes," Julian said pointedly. "Have you?"

"Yeah, all right."

"Look. Sorry." He sounded contrite. "But the cops wasting time on Liam doesn't help any of us."

"Okay." Kieran sighed. "Renn can sort it out. I doubt my folks would've really known Bronte."

Julian said nothing but his face made Kieran stop.

"What? So she helped Mum clear out the shed once."

Julian nodded. "Your place has got a reasonable-sized shed, is all. Wasn't a one-day job."

Kieran stared at him. "You'd better tell the cops that, too."

No response. He already had.

Kieran opened his mouth again, but his phone began ringing in his pocket, quiet and insistent. He checked the screen. Mia. It went to voicemail and immediately started ringing again.

"I've got to go." Kieran started toward home.

"Give my best to your folks."

Kieran turned at that. "Seriously, mate?"

"Yes, actually." Julian's hand rested on the gate to Fisherman's Cottage. "Whatever happened here doesn't have anything to do with us, or you, or anyone from this town, I reckon."

Kieran didn't answer, just began to walk.

"We need to be looking out for each other, not at each other," the other man's voice floated behind him.

Kieran wasn't sure yet if he agreed with that or not. But he found himself thinking about it, all the way home.

12

Mia pulled open the front door before Kieran reached it, Audrey in her arms.

"The police are here." Her voice was low.

"Now? I just saw Chris Renn at the cottage."

"Not local. From Hobart."

The woman was waiting in the living room, looking out of place amid the boxes and clutter. She was wearing plain clothes and a somber expression, and had her hands clasped behind her back as she examined a framed family photo still hanging on the wall. Brian, Verity, Finn, and Kieran on the beach right outside their house, all smiles and sunlight, their arms around each other. The officer looked up as Kieran came in, and extended her hand.

"Detective Inspector Sue Pendlebury." She was tall and her dark hair was streaked with strands of gray. "I was explaining—oh, wonderful. Thank you." She broke off as Verity came into the room with a tray of coffee mugs and Brian trailing behind her. "As I'm sure you've guessed, I'm here about Bronte Laidler."

"Right," Kieran said as Verity gestured for them all to sit. They did, other than Mia, who hovered near the door, jiggling Audrey.

"Do you know what happened yet?" Kieran said as Pendlebury accepted a coffee mug.

"That's what we're trying to find out." She took a sip. "Did you know Bronte well?"

"I didn't know her at all," he said. "Mia and I met her for the first time yesterday." He hesitated. "She drowned?"

"We believe Bronte *was* drowned." Pendlebury was calm in making the distinction. "She had some bruising injuries that indicate she was held under the water."

Audrey whimpered and Mia shushed her. Verity very carefully wiped a spot of milk off the coffee table.

"That's terrible," she said quietly.

"She shouldn't have been out on the beach alone." Brian's voice rose suddenly from his armchair in the corner. They all turned and he blinked, surprised by the attention.

"I'm sorry?" Pendlebury said.

"I told her she shouldn't have been out there. Not with the storm warning."

Kieran heard Verity exhale with a sharp shake of her head.

"He's talking about someone else," she said quickly to Pendlebury who, after a beat, dragged her steady gaze back. "We were hit by a big storm here. Years ago. He's thinking of that. Sorry. He's not well. Ignore him."

Pendlebury nodded slowly. She glanced at her notes. "I hear Bronte spent a few days here. Helping you clean, was it?" Her eyes wandered over the boxes lining the walls.

"Clearing the shed," Verity said. "She was collecting a few bits and pieces for a sculpture she was working on. We had a lot of junk. I said she could help herself."

"What did she take?"

"Some wire, I think. Some sheeting from when we fixed the back decking a few years ago." Verity shook her head. "I'm not sure. It really was junk."

"And did you talk at all? Sorry—" Pendlebury's phone vibrated silently against the coffee table. A photo flashed on the screen of her smiling alongside a gray-haired man and a girl and boy in their twenties who looked a bit like both of them. She pressed a button and turned the phone facedown. "Sorry. Yes, Bronte. Did she talk to you about her life here? Boys? Work? Her impressions of the town?"

"She was very keen on her artwork. I know that," Verity said. "And her grandmother in Canberra has dementia. She talked a little about her and what that had been like. Bronte said they'd been close, you know, before."

Pendlebury looked over at Brian, still watching from his armchair, then back to Verity.

"Did Bronte show you any of the pieces she was working on?" Pendlebury said. She sounded genuinely curious to hear what Verity had to say. Kieran couldn't tell if her interest was authentic or professionally honed, but either way it was smart, he thought. Pendlebury projected the kind of natural openness that made him want to pull up a chair and tell her things. Kieran crossed his arms and sat back.

"She showed me a few drawings she'd done of places around here," Verity said. "They were lovely. Or I thought so, anyway. She was a good artist."

"She wasn't an artist." Brian was frowning. "She was still at school."

"Brian, no. We're talking about Bronte now." Verity's words were clipped, and she turned back to Pendlebury. "Sorry. It's been a bit difficult."

Pendlebury's eyes stayed on Brian. "Who does he think we're talking about?"

"No one," Verity said at the same time as Kieran said, "Gabby Birch."

They exchanged a glance.

"As in, Olivia Birch?" Pendlebury said, frowning at her notebook as they nodded. She looked up again. "I'm sorry, so who is Gabby?"

•　•　•

Who was Gabby? Gabby Birch was Olivia's younger sister and Mia's best friend and pretty much everything Kieran knew about her came from them. She was four years younger than him and shy to the point that he wasn't even sure he knew what her voice had sounded like.

On warm late evenings when Gabby was sent by her mother to fetch Olivia home from the beach or the Surf and Turf or wherever she was hanging out with her friends, Gabby would skulk up alone to deliver the message, inaudible and flush-faced.

Gabby was a girl who by rights would have slipped through her teenage years completely unnoticed, except for the fact that at age twelve she developed over one rapid summer into the spitting image of her older sister. Her face lost its babyish curves and instead became one that attracted second and third glances. She grew tall and gently rounded, and clad in their wetsuits with their long curly hair tied up, it was hard to tell Olivia and Gabby apart.

She was very easy on the eye, as Ash had pointed out in much blunter terms once when Gabby was taking off her wetsuit on the beach. Olivia, who had been within earshot, had punched him on the shoulder hard enough that Kieran could see it had hurt. *She's thirteen. Don't be disgusting.* But Ash had been right.

Kieran had never bothered to talk to Gabby, but he knew a

couple of blokes who had tried, occasionally after being rebuffed by Olivia. They were wasting their time, though. Gabby would shrink into herself as though trying to vanish and would shuffle off flustered to find Mia, her best and only friend. The pair would hole up every lunchtime in the corner of the library, where they would whisper and read and draw pencil sketches of horses.

Gabby Birch was a girl who had died in the storm. But before that, for three days, she was a girl who was missing. And before that, for fourteen years, she was a girl who was loved by her family, but did her very best to disappear around pretty much everyone else.

Kieran looked at Pendlebury and her notebook.

"Gabby was Olivia's sister," he said. "But she died twelve years ago."

"How?"

"She drowned."

"Really?" Pendlebury's eyebrow moved a fraction.

"It was during the storm." Verity frowned as Pendlebury's pen began to scratch against her notebook. "It was a freak weather event. No one was properly prepared. Our son drowned too. And another young man, Toby Gilroy."

"Liam's dad," Kieran added.

"I'm very sorry to hear that," Pendlebury said, like she meant it. She waited a respectful moment, then turned to a fresh page. Not unsympathetic, but a woman with a job to do and limited time. She looked at Verity.

"I'll get to the point. I've been told that your husband—you, Mr. Elliott—you were seen on the Beach Road area around midnight last night."

"Why are you asking this?" Brian snapped, a new edge in his voice. He turned to his wife. "Why is she asking all this again? I've already been to the station. I've told them what happened."

Kieran sensed Verity stiffen as Pendlebury leaned forward.

"Mr. Elliott—"

"No," Brian said. "I'm not having you come here to my house like this. Upsetting my wife. We've just lost our son, isn't that bad enough? I've already told you. I said hello to her. Told her to go home because the storm was coming. I've been through this down at the station—"

"He was out last night," Verity cut in. Her face had shed its helpful mask and was now tight and alert. "For a few minutes. He gets confused. He goes out walking. I can't watch him twenty-four/seven."

Pendlebury's eyes moved to her. "How long exactly was he out for?"

"Not long. I was asleep and got a call at about quarter past twelve from Julian Wallis—he owns the Surf and Turf and Fisherman's Cottage. He said Brian was on the road. I threw some clothes on and went to find them. They were only five minutes away—that way." She pointed firmly in the opposite direction to Fisherman's Cottage.

"The call woke you up? So you couldn't know exactly what time your husband let himself out?"

There was a silence. "No."

"Does he go out often?"

"It happens a few times a month."

"Has he ever been found wandering on the beach, rather than the road?"

Verity hesitated. "Last night he was on the road."

"Okay." Pendlebury sounded sympathetic. Kieran wondered again if it was a deliberate tactic. "Look, I'm not implying anything here. I know you think I am, but at this point I'm just trying to get a clear sense of what happened. There's some chance that the person who was with Bronte may have been disturbed. Maybe had to leave in a hurry."

"What makes you think that?" Verity was watchful now.

Pendlebury paused, but Kieran thought he could guess. He was pretty sure Verity could guess too. Why would anyone leave a body in plain sight on the beach when with a few short steps it could be sent floating away with the ocean currents? Given the opportunity, Kieran thought, that's what anyone in their right mind would do. Not one person in the room was looking at Brian.

"The sand pattern suggests interruption," Pendlebury said neutrally, and Verity simply nodded. Both pretending that made sense.

"Either way," Pendlebury went on, "no one's come forward so far to say they saw anything. So, if your husband's able to add something to the picture, now would be a really good time."

Kieran could sense Verity wrestling with herself.

"Well, ask him then," she said, finally. "For what it's worth."

Pendlebury attempted to look Brian in the eye. He didn't co-operate.

"Mr. Elliott," she said. "I want to ask you about last night. Do you understand? Did you see Bronte Laidler on the beach last night?"

"I've already said I did. I told her the storm was coming." Brian's wandering gaze stilled suddenly and for the first time since Kieran had come home, he had the strange sense of the cloudiness almost lifting. Brian's eyes moved again and when they settled this time, it was on Mia, still standing near the door with Audrey.

"You should talk to Mia, here," Brian said. "They'd been arguing. Mia was with her on the beach too. You should have a word with her, if you're having a word with anyone."

"Jesus, Dad—" Kieran started as Mia was already shaking her head.

"No, I wasn't—"

They both stopped. Kieran turned to Brian.

"Mia was on the beach with Gabby, Dad. Not Bronte. And that was years ago. She and I were together last night. Here. We didn't see anyone on the beach."

Pendlebury looked at Mia. "Is that right?"

Mia nodded. Audrey was squirming in her arms, thrashing her head back and forth, and Mia tightened her grip. Pendlebury flicked through her notes.

"Apologies, just to make sure I'm completely clear—" She looked up and frowned. "What exactly happened to Gabby Birch?"

13

It was a good question. It had been asked a lot over the years, and Kieran was as familiar as anyone in town with the last known movements of Gabby Birch, age fourteen.

On the day the storm would later hit Evelyn Bay, Gabby had been woken at 9:00 a.m. by her mother, Patricia, who was leaving for her Saturday nursing shift at the town's medical clinic. Gabby had promised to get up but hadn't, and was still in bed an hour later when her eighteen-year-old sister, Olivia, got home from the gym. Gabby blamed her late start on the fact that she didn't have her phone, which also served as her alarm. It had been confiscated by Trish a week earlier after a teacher had reported Gabby for texting in class. Gabby's best friend, Mia, was suffering the same punishment in her own household.

Gabby had eaten a bowl of cereal while she and Olivia briefly discussed plans for their mum's birthday the following day. In what had become something of a tradition since their parents' divorce six years earlier, the girls would bake their mother's birthday cake. They would do it that afternoon while Trish was at work, they agreed, so it would be ready for the next day. Their grandma had booked a table for lunch at the big hotel in Port Osborne.

Olivia offered to stop in at the supermarket to buy birthday cards, but Gabby said she wanted to make her own by hand. Olivia told the police later that Gabby had been very upset when her phone was taken away. She was hopeful that Trish, buoyed by the birthday celebrations, would feel inclined to return it.

Both girls knew rain was forecast.

Olivia went out at noon—to visit the shops and go for a walk along the cliff path—while Gabby was, not unusually, left home alone.

Exactly what Gabby did between noon and 2:00 p.m. was unknown. She made no phone calls from the landline and was not seen leaving the house. A birthday card that read "Happy Birthday Mum!" in glitter glue was later found drying in her bedroom. At 1:27 p.m. she used her mother's laptop to log on to the internet, which she had been expressly forbidden to do while her phone was confiscated. She had spent a furtive twenty-three minutes browsing social media sites. She then grabbed her purple-striped backpack with a kangaroo key chain attached to the zipper, filled it with library books due for return, and walked the eight minutes to her friend Mia's home.

The two girls left Mia's house together, walking another twelve minutes to the Evelyn Bay Community Library. They had taken a one-day writing workshop there that summer and wanted to work on their short stories. They returned their books, borrowed some more, and got started. After nearly an hour, the librarian heard what sounded like a muffled argument from their table behind the shelves and asked them to keep it down.

The "Asian girl," the librarian had told Sergeant Mallott and Constable Renn later, was in tears and packing her belongings, while the "tall one" appeared to be trying to convince her to stay. She was seemingly unsuccessful, as both girls left a few minutes later, together but—the librarian wasn't sure—perhaps not speaking. She had warned them as they'd left that rain was expected.

The walk home had taken them past Gabby's house, which was quiet and empty, Mia had told Mallott and Renn when it was her turn to be called into the station. They hadn't stopped, instead continuing down to the beach.

Why? Mia said Renn had asked. *Because you were arguing?*

They hadn't been arguing, Mia had insisted. Gabby had given Mia some honest feedback on her short story and Mia had taken it to heart. She hadn't wanted to stop at Gabby's house, so Gabby had followed her. It had all seemed important at the time.

By Mia's account, she and Gabby had walked a short way across the sand, watching the dark clouds gathering on the horizon. By then Mia was getting cold. She wanted to go home before the rain came. Gabby had tried to persuade her to stay a little longer, but Mia had picked up her own backpack of library books and said goodbye. She had left Gabby sitting alone on the beach.

They had parted on good terms, Mia told Mallott and Renn. This was slightly contradicted by Mia's own mother, who was later overheard confiding in a friend that she had battled her way home from a rained-out engagement party to find her daughter "upset" in her bedroom. Mia, in turn, had insisted that wasn't the case. She had simply been tired and increasingly unsettled by the storm now raging outside.

Gabby was officially sighted only once more that day, thirty minutes later, at 3:50 p.m. She was seen standing on the large flat rocks that jutted out from the beach, her hair billowing and her striped backpack over her shoulder. Then the clouds drew closer and the waves began to swell and roll in a way they rarely, if ever, did along that stretch of coast, and Gabby Birch was never seen again.

A string of storm-related injuries began flooding into Evelyn Bay's overwhelmed medical clinic shortly after 5:00 p.m. The most serious, including Kieran, were transported to the hospital in Hobart. Within ninety minutes, the phone system was down along a sixty-kilometer stretch of coast. The streets were deserted. Motorists were advised, then warned, then forced by conditions, to stay off the roads. The medical center remained overrun as treated patients, including Olivia, had no option but to stay and shelter in place. The bodies of the two local men recovered from the water near the caves lay covered by sheets in clinic room 2.

And so it wasn't until the next morning that Patricia Birch was at last able to leave the clinic after a double shift, with her daughter Olivia in tow. They returned home, both weary and battered, to discover that Gabby's bed had not been slept in.

Neighbors' doors were knocked on, school acquaintances were summoned, and when there was still no sign of the girl, a search was mounted. Volunteers helped pick through the debris of their broken town as boats scoured the water. A handful of "missing" posters were printed, but in the chaos no one managed to put up a single one. Perhaps because in their hearts no one in Evelyn Bay really thought Gabby was missing. They all knew where she was; it was just a question of whether or not the sea would give her up.

The search continued for two long days. On the third morning, Gabby's purple-striped backpack washed ashore.

•   •   •

Kieran and Verity gave Pendlebury the short version. The girl, the beach, the storm, the vanishing, the bag. The grief the town shared with her family, and the questions that inevitably lingered.

The details were all on file somewhere, if Pendlebury was that interested. Mia perched on the armchair nearest the door, holding her baby daughter. She said almost nothing.

When they had finished, Pendlebury tapped her pen against her chin. She glanced at Brian, who was watching them from his corner.

"Is there any particular reason why Mr. Elliott thinks I'm here now about Gabby rather than Bronte?"

"No." Verity's gaze was unflinching. "He's just confused."

Kieran blinked in surprise and also sensed Mia tense a little behind him. Neither corrected Verity. But Kieran felt uneasy. They'd already told Pendlebury that the details of Gabby's disappearance were all on file. If she was at all curious, it would take her two minutes to discover what Verity was now failing to mention. Kieran debated, then took a breath. Verity turned her head and met his eyes, and he closed his mouth again. Maybe Pendlebury wouldn't bother. She had enough on her plate.

The officer asked a few more questions and they told her what they could—how Bronte had chased Audrey's hat into the sea; how Kieran and Mia had seen a car driving by so fast that Mia couldn't even be sure of the color; how they both thought that Bronte had seemed "fine" at the Surf and Turf, whatever the opinion of two people who didn't know her at all was worth.

At last, Pendlebury flipped her notebook shut with a word of thanks and stood. She made her way to the door, taking out three business cards and handing one each to Kieran, Mia, and Verity. Her finger tapped on a fourth as she glanced through at Brian, still sitting in his armchair; then she returned it to her wallet.

"Call me if you think or hear of anything else," she said.

They nodded in unison as they watched her walk down the path and through the gate. Verity waited until the officer was safely back on the road before she shut the door. In the living room, Kieran could hear his dad mumbling something to himself.

Verity ignored it and went through to the kitchen. Kieran and Mia followed her, watching as she put on the kettle and leaned against the sink, staring at her reflection in the window. She reached over and opened the door of the fridge, scanning its contents. Kieran could tell she was counting her breathing, in-two-three-four and out-two-three-four. When she straightened, her face was once more as placid as a lake.

"We'll get takeout for dinner tonight." She shut the fridge door carefully.

"Why didn't you tell Pendlebury about Dad and Gabby?" Kieran said.

The kettle shrieked and Verity got out four mugs.

"I didn't think it was relevant."

"Mum—" Kieran stared. "It absolutely was."

No response.

"Mum—"

"I can hear you, Kieran."

Verity simply tilted the kettle, the water steaming as it streamed out.

"She'll find out." Mia was stroking her daughter's head. "I'm not going to be the one who tells her, Verity, but someone will. Even if she doesn't read the file, which I also think she will."

"Well, I'll deal with that as it comes. If it comes to anything at all." Verity put her mug down on the table with a soft click. "I mean, it was all sorted out at the time."

Verity was right about that, Kieran thought, which was all the more reason not to hide it.

The facts remained the facts. Among them that Brian Elliott had been Gabby's teacher. And Kieran's, and Sean's, Ash's, Olivia's,

Mia's. As the only PE teacher at the town's secondary school, he had at some point yelled instructions at every single student across the footy oval or netball court or gym.

On the day of the storm, Brian had seen Gabby at the beach. She was standing alone on the rocks and staring at the waves. A fisherman giving his dog a hasty walk as the weather drew in had spotted Brian talking to a girl whose long brown curly hair was blowing all over the place. Brian had never denied it.

Brian had been in town buying a new bike lock and was rushing home himself, he later told Sergeant Mallott and Constable Renn at the police station. He'd been walking briskly, hoping to beat the rain that was threatening to start.

Gabby caught his eye simply because the beach was otherwise deserted. He had called her name and she'd turned and given a shy wave of recognition. At that point, Brian Elliott made his way across the sand toward her.

"What did the police want to know?" Kieran had heard Verity ask later when Brian had returned from the station. Her voice floated into Kieran's bedroom, soft and low from the back veranda.

Brian's reply had been muffled, and Kieran could picture him sitting in one of the beach chairs, his head in his hands. "They asked what I'd said to her."

The rocks Gabby was standing on got slippery in bad weather. Brian told her this and warned that rain was coming. It wasn't safe. She should come back onto the beach.

Gabby had agreed, so Brian had helped her across the rocks until she was safely on the sand.

"That bloody annoying new cop—" Brian's voice was still muffled. "The young one. What's his name? Ben?"

"Chris Renn," Verity said.

"He asked if I had touched her when I helped her. Jesus."

A heavy sigh. "I said yes. Once, on her elbow, and only because she nearly bloody went in."

"What did he say to that?"

"He didn't say anything, Ver." Brian's words were clearer now. "Christ, I hope she turns up soon."

"Yes," said Verity. "I hope so too."

Both had fallen quiet.

"What else did you tell the police?" Kieran heard Verity say eventually.

Brian had asked Gabby if she was all right and she'd said she was. She seemed perhaps a little subdued, in hindsight, but not enough for him to feel concerned, as he explained to the officers. Brian told Gabby to go home before the storm hit. Gabby said she was leaving soon.

The young constable, Renn, had observed that Brian lived very nearby. Had he offered to get his car and drive her home?

Brian said he had not.

Had Brian considered it? After all, the clouds were gray and heavy.

No. It was against school policy to allow students in your car.

Even in a storm?

Even then. Besides the rain hadn't started yet, Brian had pointed out, quite rightly. And nobody knew then how bad it would be.

What happened next? Renn had asked.

Nothing.

Brian had said goodbye and left Gabby standing on the sand beside the rocks, her hair blowing and her backpack on her shoulder. He had walked the rest of the way home alone. He had seen no one, been seen by no one, let himself into an empty house, and in the process, officially become the last person to admit to seeing Gabby Birch alive.

14

If it was possible to find any kind of silver lining at all in the deaths of Finn Elliott and Toby Gilroy, it was in the timing.

When the word spread—and it had, fast—that the *Nautilus Black* had rolled, Verity and Brian Elliott were among the first to reach the cliffs. They had braced themselves against the wind, their hands pressed to their mouths and wet hair plastered to their skulls as water streamed down their faces. They had watched the boat rocking upside down in the waves and even while being treated by a first responder, Kieran could hear the pulse of their silent incantation. *Please, please, please.*

The minutes ticked on. Finn did not emerge from under the vessel.

Eventually, Verity had covered her eyes. Brian had seemed unable to look away as the rescue operation led by Julian Wallis fought its way through the swells and was almost immediately abandoned when they saw the conditions. It was already too late for this to end well, but down in the water Julian would have been able to see the desperate observers up on the cliffs.

Brian and Verity, still clinging to a hope they both knew had long passed. Toby's parents, Kevin and Anne, who had raced over from their place on the other side of town. Their other son, Sean, was there too, as was Toby's wife, Sarah. They all stood beside each other in numb disbelief. Toby's head wound was washed grotesquely clean and the high-visibility strips on his life jacket kept him in their sight the whole time as he floated facedown in the waves. In the end, both men's bodies were recovered, as was the boat, and that was more than anyone could reasonably have asked for.

In the days following Gabby's disappearance, Kieran guessed that Sergeant Mallott and Constable Renn had considered the dual fatality at the caves and decided not to push Brian Elliott too hard when they inquired about the last known sighting of the girl. Because wherever Gabby was just over an hour after she was last seen on the beach, it was not with Kieran's father as he stood on the clifftop with a dozen fellow townspeople and watched his eldest son drown.

Kieran was still thinking about that when he and Verity entered the Surf and Turf that evening. He and Mia had spent a long afternoon clearing out the hall cupboards while Verity had tried to distract Brian from helping.

"Brian. Sit. I am begging you," Kieran had heard her snap from the living room as she turned up the volume on the TV.

The Surf and Turf was quiet as Kieran pushed open the door. He could see no sign of Julian, either front of house or in the kitchen, but Lyn the waitress greeted them with a nod. She finished clearing a tray, then threaded her way through the mostly empty tables, wearing the same orange uniform and faint aura of cigarette smoke as she had that morning.

"No baby with you?" She looked disappointed at Kieran's empty arms and he shook his head.

"We weren't sure you'd be open," Verity said to Lyn as she wrote down their takeout order.

"Julian didn't want to, but I suppose he felt he should." Lyn nodded to a couple of tables filled with a handful of police officers, including one or two Kieran thought he recognized from Fisherman's Cottage earlier. They looked subdued as they ate. Sergeant Renn sat at the end of one of the tables, sipping coffee and talking to the officer next to him. Detective Inspector Pendlebury was not with them.

A third table by the window was occupied by two other men. Kieran would have recognized the better-looking of the pair even without the hint of makeup and the impractical suit that was already damp and sandy around the ankle cuffs. The reporter had been appearing on the local TV news since his hair had been that dark naturally. He was flicking through his phone. Across the table a cameraman, more comfortable in flannel and denim, yawned and checked his watch. Killing time before the 10:00 p.m. live remote, Kieran guessed.

"They were interviewing Janice Manning outside the supermarket earlier," Lyn said. "I don't know what they think she can tell them about anything; she's only been here since the late nineties. Anyway"—she punched their order in—"this'll be as quick as we can. They're short-handed in the kitchen obviously, and I'm on my own out here." She glanced at the door. Outside, the road was dark. "Julian asked me to cover. The two girls who were rostered on tonight refused to come in."

"Is that right?" said Verity. "You didn't mind, though?"

Lyn shrugged. She avoided looking at the kitchen, where Liam usually worked.

"Got my bills to pay, like everyone else. And look, I'm not saying a word—" She took a deep breath and licked her lips. "But that boy is a piece of work. Just because his stepdad owns this place, he swans around here, thinks he can get away with mur—" She stopped herself in the nick of time. "With anything. You should hear the way he speaks to me sometimes. And Julian does nothing. Spoils him, gives him chance after chance. And Liam was all over Bronte, even when she told him she wasn't interested."

"Did she?" Kieran said. "You heard her say that?"

"Not directly, but I know she would've. A girl like her wouldn't be interested in Liam. She had a boyfriend for a while anyway, foreign bloke, but still. Liam didn't like that, I can tell you." Her eyes slid to the few occupied tables. "I told the police that, as well."

Verity frowned. "It feels like you might be making a bit of a leap, Lyn."

"Sometimes you just know, though, don't you?" Lyn sucked on the end of her ballpoint pen like it was a cigarette. "Can feel it in your gut. You know what my first thought was this morning, when we heard it was him?" She paused for effect, drawing out the moment until Kieran and Verity both shook their heads. "I thought to myself, 'Yeah. That'd be right.'"

Kieran wasn't sure how to respond to that. "Right," he said, finally.

Lyn was clearly waiting for more of a reaction, and they were all saved by the sound of a bell ringing from the serving hatch. Verity blinked and shook her head as Lyn walked away.

"Back in a minute," she said, and headed in the direction of the restroom.

Kieran stepped aside to let the cameraman pass on his way out for a smoke, and wandered over to the community bulletin board. Among the usual notices for private piano lessons and sunrise yoga, a collection had been started for Bronte. Or her family at least, Kieran guessed. A grainy color printout of her staff photo was pinned to the board. She was smiling, her eyes a little too wide, as though she'd been caught off guard by the flash. A money tin sat on a small table below. A candle placed next to it had blown out, its black wick looking sad and shriveled.

Kieran fished out what little cash he had in his pockets and put it in. The box felt quite empty, but it couldn't have been there long and Lyn was right: There weren't many people about. The walk into town had been even quieter than usual. He and Verity had seen a couple of men walking their dogs in the deepening twilight. No women, though, Kieran realized now, other than Verity, who had clearly been desperate for a break from Brian.

It simply had not occurred to Kieran not to step outside. He had offered to bring Audrey with them and been surprised when Mia had looked out at the gathering gloom and hesitated.

"Do you think you should?"

"Yeah, why not?"

"I don't know. It's getting dark. Maybe it's better not to, until we know for sure what's going on."

"Maybe, but—" He shrugged. "I mean, whoever did that to Bronte, they're not after blokes and babies, are they?"

Mia wavered, then shrugged. "How can we really know that?"

"Because . . ." Because they just did, Kieran thought. He knew it for the same reasons Mia did. Because that was life. Because whatever else might come the way of grown men, they didn't wind up strangled to death in the surf. Kieran had no problem walking around Evelyn Bay now for the same reason that he didn't think twice about taking shortcuts through unlit parks, and felt no need to quicken his pace when he heard footsteps on the pavement behind him at night. For the same reason that he would have gone home along the dark beach the night before, where Mia had taken one look and balked. Kieran didn't know what had happened to Bronte, but from thirty years of lived experience he knew that whatever it was, it wasn't coming for him. Mia knew all this too. But she still made him leave Audrey at home.

Kieran looked again at the photo of Bronte. He remembered when a photo of Finn and Toby had been posted in that same spot after the storm, with a similar collection box underneath.

Kieran could still picture the exact image. It had been the one of Finn and Toby with their arms slung around each other's shoulders, an unopened bottle of champagne in hand and the *Nautilus Black* gleaming behind them as they celebrated the first day of their new diving business. Kieran had been sixteen and standing out of shot on the dock when Brian had taken the picture. It had been a good day, he remembered.

The photo had stayed on the bulletin board for nearly a year before Julian had tactfully, and after consultation with both families, removed it. Kieran wondered how long Bronte from Canberra's picture would stay up. Probably less than that, he guessed.

Kieran started heading back to Verity, who had come out of the restroom and was talking to another customer by the cash register. The man turned and Kieran recognized him as the bloke with the laptop who had tried and failed to get into the Surf and Turf that morning. The folded newspaper was gone, but the leather computer satchel was once again slung across his chest.

"Kieran," Verity said, beckoning him over. "Come and meet G. R. Barlin."

"Really?" Kieran said, the man's facial features clicking into place as they shook hands. "We briefly met this morning actually. Sorry, I didn't recognize you."

"Just George is fine. And don't worry about it." The man waved his hand. "Does anyone ever recognize authors?"

Kieran hesitated. "I don't know."

"They don't."

"Oh." But Kieran could see it now. G. R. Barlin's jaw was rather less chiseled and his gaze not nearly as piercing as the photo in the back of his books would suggest, but he had the sulky faraway look down pat.

"George has moved here from Sydney," Verity said.

"Right," Kieran said. "For the summer?"

"No." The man's tone had the hint of annoyance of someone who had been asked the question a few times. "Full-time. I'm renovating Wetherby House."

"Ah." Ash's grandmother's former home. "Garden too?"

"Whole thing. It needed it," George added, slightly defensive.

Whether it did or didn't, Kieran couldn't say, but at least that went some way to explaining Ash's unveiled hostility.

Everyone, including possibly Ash himself, had been surprised when Ash announced he was starting his own landscaping business. And no one, again possibly including Ash, had taken him too seriously at first. But he had rolled up his sleeves and spent the whole spring and summer digging and planting at his gran's place, turning the generous garden around the sandstone home into a living advertisement. Kieran and Sean had spent the same summer lounging about on the deck of the *Nautilus Black*, chatting with tourists and dipping into the cool sea, before swinging by Wetherby House to find Ash with his back hunched and sweat running down his face.

Had it been Sean, or even possibly Kieran, stuck doing grunt work in his gran's garden in the heat, they probably would have copped a bit of shit for it. But Ash simply didn't care. He did what he liked and defended it to nobody. And the property had looked great by the end. Ash's gran had baked him a cake as a thank-you for his months of labor and he, Kieran, and Sean had celebrated by getting steaming drunk by the beach.

The garden had been beautiful for three whole weeks;

then the storm had hit. Ash's work was destroyed, with plant-
ings ripped apart and uprooted bushes and trees leaving deep
trenches of exposed soil. But Ash had been back out there the
very next day, hunched and sweating again to restore the chaos.
He had succeeded, Kieran had thought, but apparently not to a
high enough standard for G. R. Barlin.

Kieran looked at the author now. Up close, he was younger
than Kieran would have guessed, given his body of work. Early
forties at the most. He was wearing a chunky knit cardigan,
which had the worn-in rustic look of something that could only
be expensive. Kieran wondered if he'd bought it especially for his
move to the Tasmanian coast. It was the kind of thing he thought
a writer might envisage himself wearing down here, searching
out to sea for his muse while the brisk salty air chapped his face.
And George Barlin wouldn't be the first creative type to have
come to Evelyn Bay seeking some sort of elusive inspiration.

"What made you choose here?" Kieran said, and George
shrugged.

"Nostalgia, really. My parents brought me on holiday a few
times when I was younger, and I visited again myself on and off
over the years. Always liked it. And it seemed like as good a place
to work from as any."

"You're writing something new?" Kieran asked.

"Yep." George tapped his laptop bag with an overstated eye
roll. "Always on the treadmill. But I prefer not to talk about my
work too much, if you don't mind."

"Not at all." Kieran suppressed a smile. He had once gone
with Mia to see G. R. Barlin appear at a literary event in Sydney.
The writer had been on a panel with two women authors and
spoken for easily half the time. "Well, my partner will be sorry
she missed you," Kieran said. "She's a big fan."

That was true, and Kieran himself liked the books too. They

were the kind of thrillers people bought in the airport, stayed glued to beside the pool, and then left in their hotel room to save on luggage weight. They sold by the shedload.

Lyn bustled back to swipe George's credit card and caught the last comment.

"I'm surprised Mia has any time for books, with that beautiful baby at home," she said. "I know I wouldn't."

"Not a big reader?" Kieran said.

Lyn scrunched up her face. "I did read a book once. Wasn't for me."

"You should try one of George's," Verity said. "They're good."

"So I've heard. Only the early ones, though." Lyn flashed an affable grin at the writer, as though expecting confirmation. "Don't bother with the rest. That's what Fiona reckons, anyway."

"Fiona?" George's voice was completely, determinedly, neutral. Lyn didn't notice.

"From the plant nursery? You know, she cuts those hedges into the shape of animals."

"Right. Yes." George returned his credit card to his wallet and closed it with a firm snap. "Well, it's a shame she feels that way. And I've always thought so highly of her creative talents."

Lyn frowned slightly, sensing something a little off behind George's smile. She was distracted by one of the police officers signaling for a water refill and bustled away.

"And yet if I were to stop by the nursery to tell Fiona her hedge animals are unrecognizable, *I'm* the arsehole," George murmured as he adjusted his laptop bag. "Anyway, nice to meet you." He shook Kieran's hand. "Give my best to your partner. Was that her you were with this morning?"

"Yes."

George nodded and looked past Kieran to the makeshift memorial to Bronte on the bulletin board. Kieran remembered seeing Bronte bring the writer a glass of wine the night before, managing to raise a smile from him as he'd glowered at his laptop.

"What a dreadful business that is," George said. "Poor Bronte. Unbelievable."

"Did you know her well?" Verity said.

"Only from in here," George said. "But I'm in here quite a lot. Did you ever see any of her drawings?"

"A couple. And she showed me a little wire sculpture creature she was working on. She seemed very good."

"I thought so too. Serious about it as well, which you don't always get in the more creative fields. She was focused. Had a professional approach to it all." George's mouth was a hard downturned line. "I would never have expected something like that to happen around here."

"It wouldn't have, a few years ago," Verity said. "I suppose that's the risk with the tourists. You never know who's in town now, with so many people coming through."

There weren't that many people though, Kieran thought. A couple of weeks earlier in the summer maybe, when two out of every three people on the street were strangers. But not at this time of year, with its empty tables and closed shops and vacant parking spots.

Kieran suspected George was thinking the same thing as the man looked around the hushed restaurant. His gaze came to rest on the table of police officers.

"I hear they're bringing Liam Gilroy in for questioning again," George said quietly. He glanced at Lyn by the serving hatch. "She'll be happy. Thinks the police have got their man."

"And what do you think?" Kieran asked, interested.

"Me?" George shrugged. "I think it's important in civilized society to respect due process." He turned his phone over in his hand. "Despite what the keyboard warriors of EBOCH may think."

"The online community page?" Verity said. "I didn't think anyone really used that."

"Well, people have found a use for it now. Still, I'm sure the police know what they're doing."

Curious, Kieran had pulled out his own phone to look up this community page, and felt a lurch as he saw the screen. Eight missed calls from Mia. He started to raise the phone to his ear, then stopped, his finger hovering over the redial button. George had gone silent and was focused on Sergeant Renn over at the police officers' table.

Kieran followed his gaze. Renn was speaking softly into his own cell phone. As Kieran watched, the officer raised his eyes and looked once, directly and unmistakably, at Verity, then away again almost as quickly. Renn ended the call. He sat for a moment, then pulled himself out of his chair and began to head across the restaurant. The TV reporter glanced up—nothing to see but Renn, slow and casual, coffee cup still in hand—and dropped his attention back down to his phone. Renn ended his stroll right next to Verity. He took a deep swallow of coffee as the cameraman returned from his smoke break. She simply waited. Renn watched until the man was safely out of earshot.

"Sorry, Verity." His voice was low. "It's about Brian."

15

It was still early when Kieran hit the cliff path the next morning. Audrey was wide awake, her dark eyes alert as she bounced along strapped to his chest, her nappy bag slung over his shoulder. Kieran's own head felt thick and heavy. It had taken a long time before he and Mia and Verity had been able to get to their beds, and even then Kieran had lain awake for what felt like hours.

He and Verity had left their order uncollected at the Surf and Turf and followed Sergeant Renn outside, where he had driven them the three minutes to Fisherman's Cottage. They had ducked under the police tape at the front gate and run down the side trail and out onto the dark beach. Kieran could hear shouts and the sound of his daughter shrieking. Mia was already on the sand, Audrey angry in her arms.

"I'm so sorry," Mia was saying. "I tried to stop him. I'm sorry."

Kieran had run to them first, then chased Verity down to the water's edge.

Brian was in the sea, neck-deep. His T-shirt broke the surface as he swam through the black water with strong, confident strokes. The police tape that had been tied to stakes on the beach where Bronte's body was found now trailed behind him like seaweed.

A pair of young officers were soaked to their armpits, their shoes and socks paired neatly on the dry sand while they floundered in the water. Kieran reached the shoreline in time to see one catch his dad. Brian bellowed and flailed his arms as the other man joined the struggle to pull him out. Brian had fought, dragging both cops and himself under the water as Verity herself had kicked off her shoes and waded in without breaking stride. Kieran was right behind her. The police officers had backed off when he and Verity managed to reach Brian. The three of them had swayed together in the freezing water while Verity held Brian's hands beneath the surface and whispered softly.

Brian eventually allowed himself to be led out. Kieran and Verity had walked him to the beach, their trio of mooncast shadows forming a grotesque echo of The Survivors against the sand. Brian had laid himself down flat on his back near the shoreline, his arms and legs stretched out as though he was enjoying the weather. Kieran had lain down next to him, his teeth chattering.

On his way into the water, Brian must have traipsed through floral tributes left on the beach for Bronte. Ribbon and cellophane were strewn about like dead sea creatures and Kieran could see Mia clutching Audrey with one arm as she tried to gather and reassemble the pile. He knew he should help her but instead had stayed next to his dad, staring up at the stars and listening as Brian's ragged breathing mingled with his own daughter's high-pitched screams. When Kieran turned his head, he could see Verity sitting some distance away, her face in her hands and her shirt stuck to her back. Kieran wasn't sure if she was shivering or crying or both.

Kieran had felt like he hadn't got the energy to move, ever again, but eventually Sergeant Renn had crouched and suggested quietly that it might be a good idea to get going before the TV guys hauled themselves out of the Surf and Turf and wandered down to set up for their bulletin.

It was only later, back at the house, that Kieran noticed the reddening around Mia's jawline and the beginnings of a bruise on her wrist. He held her arm under the lamp.

"What happened?"

"It's nothing. Let's get to bed." She was still shaken, though, her eyes bright with unshed tears.

"But—"

"It's fine. I told you. I tried to stop him. Just—" Mia let her arm slip from his grasp. "Don't leave me alone with him again, okay?"

Kieran was walking furiously now, the ocean breeze whipping across the cliff path and snatching at his clothes.

When morning had come, Kieran had told Mia to stay in bed and get some sleep. She had blinked awake.

"We didn't even offer to walk her home." Mia's eyes were swollen and Kieran wondered if she'd been crying in the night.

"Who?" Kieran scrambled to catch up. "Bronte?"

Mia nodded against her pillow. "At the Surf and Turf on Saturday night. We asked Olivia if she wanted us to wait, but we didn't ask Bronte. We were going right past her house. We could have walked her home."

They looked at each other for a long time and finally Mia rolled over. Kieran said he would take Audrey out, and this time Mia didn't protest, just closed her eyes without saying anything.

Out in the hall, Kieran had heard Verity in the kitchen. Her voice was a low murmur, and she stopped as Kieran entered. She was sitting opposite Brian, rubbing sunscreen into his arms, the way she had with Kieran when he was little. Kieran wasn't sure what Verity had been saying, but from the look on Brian's face, he wouldn't have bet on him absorbing a word of it.

"Mia has bruises from last night. She's hurt."

Verity frowned. Her palms were slick as she smoothed the cream into Brian's skin. "Badly?"

"Not badly, but she shouldn't be hurt at all."

"Of course not. I'm very sorry."

"Jesus, I'm not looking for an apology." Kieran looked at his dad. "I'm saying he's getting out of hand. Mia had Audrey with her."

"He wouldn't have meant it."

"I know that, but—"

"But what?" Verity said, her voice suddenly hard, her hands still on her husband's arm. "But what, Kieran? He didn't mean it. Look at him." She lifted Brian's hand. He held it out, obedient and childlike. "He doesn't realize he's done anything. So what is it you want? Do you think he should be punished? For something he doesn't even know he's done? Do you think that's fair?"

Verity had stared at him until he'd looked away. Brian didn't move.

Kieran hadn't given her an answer. He didn't know what he thought.

He reached a split in the cliff trail now and stopped. To the right lay the track up to the lookout, and to the left he could see the iron gates guarding the back entrance to the Evelyn Bay cemetery. Kieran felt Audrey move and settle against his chest. The walk had soothed her at least, if not him.

He wandered toward the gates. They were open, with a sign screwed to the post informing visitors the cemetery would be locked at sundown each day. Somewhat to Kieran's own surprise, he stepped inside now. The gravel path leading him forward was well cared for, with lush but tasteful shrubs planted alongside. Ash's handiwork, Kieran guessed. He'd held the maintenance contract for a while now. It all looked different from how Kieran remembered, but then again he hadn't been there since Finn and Toby's funeral. He'd meant to come, a few times. He just hadn't.

Kieran followed the pathway, realizing with a stab of shame that he couldn't remember where his brother's grave was. He could picture the funeral, parts of it at least, but if he had absorbed any specific details of the burial location, he couldn't remember them now. He wasn't even sure where to begin. The cemetery layout was disordered, with generations of Evelyn Bay residents having chosen to see out eternity right there, and all with a slightly different idea of how they'd like to lie. Kieran knew he had made the journey to Finn's burial with his parents by road, the car ride conducted in mute grief as they followed the hearses, and he turned now toward the main gates to the west.

He didn't get that far. The entrance wasn't even in sight when something flapping in the wind caught his eye. He stopped, recognizing the colors straight away.

With one hand on Audrey's back, Kieran stepped off the gravel and picked his way through the neatly mown grass until he found himself standing in front of a grave. A footy scarf in Evelyn Bay's team stripes had been carefully knotted around the headstone. It wasn't new but had the worn-clean look of something that had been machine washed regularly over the years. Kieran reached out and moved the scarf to read the name on the headstone.

Toby Gilroy.

A memory Kieran had forgotten he even possessed shot to the surface, full color and crystal clear. Liam Gilroy in his box-fresh funeral clothes, draping a football scarf across his dad's coffin. Kieran wondered now if this was that same scarf, retrieved, washed, and returned by Liam for the past twelve years. He involuntarily snatched his hand away, and Audrey whined in protest at the sudden move.

"Oh. Good. It's only you."

Kieran spun around at the sound of the voice, his fingers still tingling from the feel of the wool. It took him a second to find the speaker among the headstones.

Olivia. Her hair was tangled from the breeze and she was wearing jeans and a rust-colored pullover that Kieran suspected had been borrowed from her mum's wardrobe.

"I was looking for Ash and I heard someone." She was a little on edge and Kieran remembered the near-empty streets last night and the waitresses refusing their shifts.

"Only us," he said as Olivia came closer and leaned in to look into the baby carrier.

"So this is Audrey. Wow." Olivia's hair brushed against his shoulder and she straightened and took a small step back. "She's beautiful."

"Thank you." He looked out across the quiet cemetery. "Is Ash around?"

"I thought he said he would be. He's not answering his phone, though." A shadow crossed her face. "He must be with a client or something. What are you doing here?"

"I'm not sure."

"Not visiting Finn?"

"I actually don't know where his grave is."

"Oh." She frowned. "I'm not sure either. Ash could probably tell you. When he resurfaces."

Ash probably would know, Kieran thought, and not only because he worked there. Ash and Finn had always got along well, especially after Ash had left school and was hanging around town a lot more during the days. On weekends, Finn would sometimes wander up and he and Ash would chat about stuff that had been going on while Kieran was stuck in class. Anything from small-business tax breaks to tourist-girl arrivals. Kieran would sit and watch and try to join in when he could.

"Maybe I'll have a look around." Kieran ran his gaze over the rows of headstones. "I feel a bit bad not knowing which one's his."

"Don't feel too bad," Olivia said as they started to walk. "Visiting somewhere like this doesn't help everyone. Look at my mum. She's never let anyone put up anything for Gabby."

"Really? Nothing at all?"

"Nope. No headstone, no plaque—" Olivia nodded as they passed a memorial bench. "Not one of those. We never talk about Gabby anymore."

"Why not?"

"I don't know exactly. I thought we should, but then I've also read that rehashing the past can do more harm than good for some people. Breaks down their defenses or something. Depends on the person, I guess."

"Right." Kieran hadn't heard that specifically, but unexpectedly he thought of Verity. The way she was always doing something with her therapy books and online support groups and self-improvement homework. The brittle face of her constant, unceasing, grinding strive for inner serenity.

"So now I just let Mum lead the way," Olivia was saying. "It's not great, though. She still really struggles to accept what happened."

"Even now?"

"I think mainly because Gabby was never found."

"Yeah." Kieran hesitated. "But—"

"No, I know," Olivia said as they took a left turn, past some of the newer headstones. "It's ridiculous. I'm not saying she thinks Gabby is in her twenties and walking around some city on the mainland or anything—" There was the tiniest pause in which Kieran wondered if deep down that was exactly what Trish Birch occasionally let herself think. "But Mum used to worry about Gabby even before the storm. Because she always looked older, you know, so she'd get a bit of attention. People would forget she was only fourteen."

They turned into the next row, reading the names as they went.

"It probably doesn't help that they weren't on great terms at the end either," Olivia said, fiddling with the sleeve of her borrowed pullover. "That whole thing with Mum confiscating Gabby's phone. Gabby was really upset. And then Mum's stuck knowing that her daughter didn't have a phone with her when she went missing. It's the kind of thing that haunts you, I suppose. Oh, hey—" Olivia pointed at a simple gray headstone near the end of the line. "Is that it?"

Yep, Kieran thought as he stepped closer to read the engraving. That was it. Finn Elliott, twenty-six years old, beloved son and brother. Gone too soon.

There were no flowers or footy scarves on this plot, but it did look like someone—Ash, probably, or perhaps Verity—kept it weeded and trimmed. Kieran stood there, looking down at the earth where his brother lay buried. He had loved Finn. He still missed him. He looked up at Finn's headstone and waited to feel something. Something *more*, at least, than what he felt every day.

"Don't worry about it. My mum would agree," Olivia said, when it felt like they'd been waiting a while. She was sitting on a nearby memorial bench, watching him. "Visiting a grave doesn't do it for everyone."

He stepped away and sat down next to her, their clothes flapping in the wind. Kieran reached into his bag and mixed up a bottle of formula for Audrey.

"She tried to kill herself, actually." Olivia's voice was quiet.

"Your mum did?" Kieran looked over. "Shit, Liv. I'm sorry. That's hard."

"Yeah. That's why I had to move back. Don't spread it around." She sighed as Kieran shook his head. "I think a few people suspect anyway, though. Mum reckons it was a mistake. She said she messed up her dose, but she's been on sleeping pills for twelve years and always managed to keep track before."

"When was this?"

"A few months after the ten-year anniversary. I think it was too much of a reminder—the date coming and going and nothing having changed."

Kieran had found the ten-year mark difficult himself, and he suspected Verity had also struggled, although she hadn't admitted it. He hadn't been able to bring himself to come back to Evelyn Bay that year, or at all since, in fact.

"Bronte's parents are due to arrive today," Olivia said suddenly. She'd been staring at the headstones. "They were stuck on a cruise so have had to fly back."

"Have you met them before?"

"Once, when she first moved in. They're both civil servants in Canberra. Quite high up, I think. Her mum was involved in that committee that tightened all the restrictions around seafood export; do you remember that? It caused a backlog and a lot of the fishermen couldn't get rid of their catches for a while?"

Kieran shook his head. "Not really."

"Well, anyway. I told Bronte not to mention that too loudly around here," Olivia said. "Her mum and dad seemed nice, though. Very . . . efficient. God knows how they must be feeling now."

"Any more from the cops?"

"No." Olivia shifted uneasily. "But they were back at the house early this morning."

"Did they tell you why?"

She shook her head. "I heard they were checking the neighbors' gardens. Going through their bins."

"Looking for something?"

"Must be, but I don't know what. I asked Renn straight out when he called last night to check how many sets of keys we had. He wouldn't tell me. Just danced around it. Said it was procedure."

"Maybe it is."

"Maybe." Olivia picked at her thumbnail. "Ash says I should be careful. He reckons they think I know something I'm not telling them." She looked over. "I don't. For the record."

"I didn't think any differently."

In the silence, Kieran could hear the seagulls calling.

"If I did," Olivia said, "I would tell them. Bronte reminded me of Gabby a bit."

"Did she really?" Kieran was surprised.

"Yeah. Not physically, obviously, and not even in her mannerisms. More . . ." Olivia thought for a minute. "They were both the kind of girl who felt they had to please people. It's like this whole thing with Liam."

"What about it?"

"I mean, Sean's right." Olivia shrugged. "Liam and Bronte did get along okay. She never complained about him or anything. But she was quite sensitive to people's feelings, and Liam can be . . . intense. Other girls might have told him to get lost, but Bronte would have worried about embarrassing him. She would've let him know she wasn't interested, but it might have been pretty subtle." Olivia looked down. "And some guys don't understand anything but a loud, firm no. Some don't even understand that."

"Do you think Liam's one of those guys?"

"Yeah. I guess I do, a bit." Olivia's mouth was a hard line as she considered. "Him giving Bronte a ride home bothers me. We live so close it was unnecessary, which kind of makes me suspect he *insisted*, which never feels great—"

Olivia broke off as her phone beeped with a text message. "Shit. It's Julian again."

"What does he want?"

"I don't know. He says to call him." Olivia stood up. "I'd better get back, anyway. Ash obviously isn't here."

Kieran wiped Audrey's mouth and clipped her into the sling. "I'll get going too."

"Are you heading down?"

"No." He patted Audrey. "I'll go on a bit further. Give her a chance to settle."

"When are you and Mia going back to Sydney?"

"Next week."

"Lucky."

They started to walk. "You thinking you're going to have to settle in here for the long term?"

"I don't think I've got much choice. Not after what's happened to Bronte. I can't see that speeding up Mum's recovery."

"At least you've got Ash."

"Yeah."

When she didn't say any more, Kieran looked over and Olivia gave a small laugh at his expression.

"What?"

"Nothing." He shrugged. "You guys are good, though, aren't you?"

"Yeah. We are. It's just, if I stay here, it feels like—" Olivia stopped at the cemetery gates and sighed. "I don't know. Game over, or something. There's no point finishing my master's. Or having worked so hard in Melbourne. Not if I'm going to settle down with Ash and bang out a few kids and send them off to Nippers training with Julian every Saturday while I go waitressing. I could have done that straight out of school if I was going to." A hint of a smile. "Not that I would've had anything to do with Ash back then."

"No." Kieran could hear the rapid rise and fall of his daughter's breath. She felt warm and solid against him. "But everyone can change."

"Yeah, that's true. And Ash is . . ." Kieran waited as Olivia considered, genuinely interested what it was about Ash that had caught her eye twelve years on.

"He can be a lot of fun," she said. "More than I remember. And he's really good about Mum. I don't have to explain things to him because he already knows"—she waved her hand loosely— "about everything."

The words were vague enough to be meaningless, but Kieran could read them perfectly. *He knows about us.*

She was looking at him now. He nodded. *Got it.*

"Anyway—" Olivia's phone beeped again and she frowned. "Oh, for God's sake. Julian again. I'd better go. It was good seeing you."

"You too, Liv."

With a wave, Olivia turned and walked down the path. Kieran watched until she was out of sight, twelve years ago suddenly feeling both very distant and very near.

16

Kieran stopped when he reached the lookout, catching his breath. Audrey squirmed against his chest, irritated. She liked the comforting rhythm of a brisk pace and Kieran had obliged, all the way uphill from the cemetery to the peak of the path. Beyond the cliffs, the tide lay calm under the weak morning sun. Out on the water, the *Nautilus Blue* was anchored but Kieran could see no movement on board.

So Ash knew about him and Olivia. That was interesting, if only for the fact that he'd never mentioned it. That alone was proof of change as far as Kieran was concerned. The old Ash wouldn't have had the self-discipline to keep quiet.

Mia knew.

Kieran had told her six months after they'd met, on the night of what would have been Finn's thirty-first birthday. He'd battled through a frustrating phone call with Verity, where they had spoken for thirty minutes without really saying anything. At least his mum had come to the phone, though, which was more than could be said for Brian. Verity had said he was out. Kieran doubted it. That didn't sound like Brian. Not on his dead son's birthday.

Kieran and Mia had been lying in bed and he'd started talking and the whole story had come out.

"You and Liv," she'd said, when he'd finished speaking.

He'd lain there, listening to her breathing and feeling the warmth across the bedsheets.

"Is it a problem?" He rolled over and looked at her, already a little afraid of the answer.

"No." He'd gone slack with relief. She was still quiet, though.

"Are you sure?"

"Yeah. But—" Mia turned her face toward him on the pillow. "Gabby had guessed."

"Really?"

"I think so. She told me she thought there was something going on between you two. I told her I thought she was wrong."

"Does it matter, though?" Kieran had asked again. "It was so long ago. It doesn't matter, does it?"

"Not now. Not to me. It's just—" Mia put a hand under her head and stared at the ceiling. "I didn't believe her. So that might have mattered to Gabby."

Kieran looked back out to sea now and ran a hand over the wooden safety barrier. It had been put up within a month of the drownings and it was surprising what a difference it had made to the lookout.

The place was as isolated as it had ever been, but the sturdy bench and waist-high railing and the printed plastic information panels made the whole thing feel monitored. It wasn't, Kieran knew. Sergeant Mallott and Constable Renn had enforced the trespassing fine for just long enough to break the local habit and send teenagers seeking a quiet spot away from the caves and toward the forested hinterland instead. Psychologically, the barrier was a good deterrent. Nothing to see beyond here, it said. Stay on the right side of the line.

It was a complete illusion, though. The trail down to the beach and the caves might be overgrown, but it was still visible. Kieran looked at it, then took a step out. He didn't even need to climb over the barrier; he simply moved around the edge of the railing, brushed aside an overgrown bush, and there he was, at the top of the path.

Audrey began to whine in her sling, twisting her head back and forth and urging him to get moving again. Kieran could hear the surf below and see a thin strip of sand. The caves were hidden from sight.

He had been up to the lookout dozens of times since Finn died, but didn't often go beyond the boundary. Never when Mia was with him. But every once in a while on his own. When he found himself thinking about that day years earlier, when he'd stepped out onto this same track, with The Survivors already deeper than they should have been and storm clouds already gathering on the horizon.

Kieran steadied Audrey with one hand and began to make his way down the path now. He started slowly, but muscle memory quickly took over. As he walked he tried—the way he had a lot over the years—to think about that day differently. There were factors in his defense. He knew that. He could recite them as he walked down this trail he also knew by heart.

He had been only eighteen years old.

The tight bend at the jagged rock.

He hadn't realized how bad the storm was going to be.

The smooth rock followed by a dip.

No one had realized how bad the storm was going to be.

The first view of the caves.

He had really liked Olivia and had only wanted to see her.

The final narrow steps as the trail came to an end.

Finn and Toby were experienced enough to make their own decisions on the water.

The sand.

It had been an accident.

None of that mattered, though.

Kieran stood now on that familiar strip of beach. Out on the water, The Survivors were knee-deep. The caves were yawning black holes behind him. Maybe that was why he hadn't felt anything much at Finn's grave. Because whatever he told himself, or however many times he said it would be the last time, he always somehow ended up down here. Back in the same place. Where Finn was still dead, and it was still Kieran's fault.

He became aware of a shrieking that, for once, had nothing to do with Audrey. Around the cliffs, the seabirds were protesting his presence, swooping and circling overhead. The terns were nesting, he could see now as they hovered around their babies, anxious and agitated. The birds had rarely nested here before, back in the days when Kieran had traipsed up and down all summer. They'd become less used to visitors since the safety barrier had gone up.

Kieran moved away from them, crossing the beach to the South Cave, where he and Olivia had once lingered while the day slipped away and the tide slid in. He stepped inside now, not far, just a few paces. He could see the outline of the ledge from where he stood.

He was struck, as always, by how close it was to the entrance. He walked over. It was definitely the right ledge, though; he could make out where Ash had carved his name nearby.

Kieran reached up and ran his finger over the letters. He had almost forgotten how they all used to do that. Pull out their keys and slice their names permanently into the sea-softened rock face whenever they reckoned they'd discovered something new of interest in the caves. Only Sean had tried to talk them out of it, with predictable results. Even he had buckled in the end, and under pressure from Kieran had given in and scratched his name at the start of a route they'd mapped together in the North Cave. Sean had felt bad about it for the rest of the summer, which Kieran had thought was overkill at the time. But looking at the letters now, still legible more than a decade after they'd been made into the rock face, Kieran couldn't believe he had ever been such a dickhead. He couldn't remember how he'd convinced himself this was a good idea, or even an acceptable one.

He leaned his back against the ledge and turned to the glow seeping in from the entrance. The sea and the sky were both a brilliant blue and he could see Sean's catamaran anchored above the site of the *Mary Minerva*.

Kieran watched it for a while, the dive flag flapping. He hadn't been able to face going out there himself at all in those early years, not even to join his parents for an onboard memorial ceremony to mark the first anniversary of Finn's and Toby's deaths. But Sean had never stopped sailing out. Two years after the storm, Kieran had cracked and asked him how he coped with being on the same body of water where his brother had died.

Sean had thought about it for so long, Kieran had started to feel bad for asking.

"It's like a bubble," Sean said, just as Kieran thought he wasn't going to answer. "I sort of draw a circle around it. Keep it all in there and try to carry on like I would have if it had never happened." Sean gave a small shrug. "It feels a bit easier that way."

It was the last time they had ever talked about it, but when Sean next asked if Kieran wanted to go out on the boat, Kieran said he would. It had been about as bad as he'd feared, and he had barely said a word the whole time. But at least he'd done it, and after that it had been easier to do it again.

Kieran pushed himself away from the rock now and took a last look at the ledge. In his mind, it was always further back in the cave, buried deep. In reality, the entrance was far closer than he remembered. There was no reason he shouldn't have noticed the storm drawing in so fast. No excuse there.

He walked with his daughter back out to the beach, shielding Audrey's eyes as she squinted in the sun. Kieran dug in his bag for her cotton hat, the one Bronte had given them what felt like a long time ago now, but came up empty-handed. He must have left it at home, and Kieran suddenly thought of Mia, still back at his parents' place with Verity, and Brian.

Don't leave me alone with him again.

Kieran checked his phone. No messages and no missed calls. Still, he looked down at Audrey.

"What do you think, little one? Time to go back? See Mum?"

Audrey's baby face appeared untroubled either way, so Kieran set off across the sand. He slowed as he passed the entrance to the North Cave.

He'd never liked it as much as the southern one; there were too many twists and turns for his taste. But Finn and Toby had thought it was the better of the pair, and had spent hours mapping out routes. They'd made their mark all over the North Cave, quite literally, and even from the sand Kieran could see a couple of places where the two men had scratched their own names. As he moved forward for a closer look, Audrey decided she'd had enough. Kieran started to sing a little song she sometimes liked, but that only made things worse. His daughter scrunched up her face until it was hard and red and began to scream, the sound bouncing off the cave walls and ricocheting down into the warren of hidden tunnels.

"Okay, all right, we're going." Kieran turned, and then suddenly stopped.

For a second, in the thin slice of silence as his daughter drew breath to scream, Kieran thought he heard a strange whisper of movement.

No. He looked into the dark. Not something moving. Something going still. The frozen watchfulness of an animal. Kieran tried to listen, his palm firm on Audrey's back. He stared into the black hole. He could hear nothing but her cries and see nothing but blackness, but he had the overwhelming sense of something waiting quietly in the dark.

"Hello?"

Kieran's call echoed back to him with a hollow flatness. Sound behaved in an unusual way in the caves, he knew, sometimes drawn deep through the tunnels and sometimes muffled by dead ends and water pools. Now, though, Kieran could see and hear nothing but the two of them. No movement. No answer. Just the gaping black hole.

Still, he felt a prickle of cold that had little to do with the cool ocean air. Above the cliffs, the birds were shrieking again. Kieran turned, strode across the beach, and, arm tight around his child, climbed up the cliff path much faster than he had climbed down it.

•　•　•

When Kieran emerged a little breathless at the top of the path, he saw straight away that he and Audrey weren't alone. He sucked in some air, buying himself a minute. The other person stared back, not happy to see him either.

"Hi, mate," Kieran said cautiously.

Liam was sitting on the safety rail, his legs dangling over the edge, his broad shoulders hunched, and his face turned toward the sea.

"Were you just down there?" Liam's eyes were a little red and watery, but it could simply have been the wind and the glare.

"Yeah."

"No one's supposed to go down there."

"I know."

"The birds are nesting. You'll scare them. *What?*" he snapped, noticing Kieran's surprise. He turned back, sullen. "My dad used to show me the seabirds."

"Oh. Well . . ." Kieran stepped clear of the unofficial path and back onto the formal lookout. "Sorry."

"One rule for you, hey?"

"My baby was . . ."

Liam looked over.

"Unsettled," Kieran finished, cringing inwardly at his own excuse.

Liam rightly rolled his eyes and turned his attention back to the sea. He was sitting close enough to the edge of the rail to make Kieran feel uneasy. The cliff was a notorious suicide spot, if three in twenty-odd years was enough to earn such a reputation.

Kieran looked at Liam now, balanced on the edge, and cleared his throat.

"You walking back to town?" he said. "I'm going that way."

Liam gave a weird hollow laugh. "I'm not about to jump, if that's what you're worried about."

"I'm not," Kieran lied.

"It's not even high tide." Liam turned now and this time looked Kieran hard in the eye. "That's the real danger zone, isn't it?"

Kieran didn't reply. He made himself remember the boy aged seven, placing a footy scarf on his dad's coffin. How different would Liam be now if none of that had ever happened and he'd grown up in the family he should have had? His grandparents—Sean and

Toby's mum and dad—had always been caring in their own quiet, reserved way. They had stuck it out in Evelyn Bay for two years after Toby's death, battling with the daily reminders of their grief before they'd given in and moved far away, to Queensland, settling in a town where the seawater was so warm and flat it was unrecognizable. Kieran knew Sean had thought about joining them for a while, but by then he had reestablished the diving business and was on the cusp of it turning a profit. Sean's parents had left with promises to come back every year to visit their son and grandson, but had only managed one difficult tear-stained visit after which it was mutually decided it was better for all if they didn't make the trip to Evelyn Bay again. Kieran was still thinking about that when Liam opened his mouth.

"You got with that chick in the end, hey? That Chinese one who used to live here?"

Caught off guard by the change of topic, Kieran blinked. "Mia? She's half-Singaporean, actually."

"Nice," Liam said in such a way that made Kieran want to unclip his baby sling, place Audrey carefully down on the grass, stand up, and punch the guy full in the face. Instead, he stood completely still and took a breath.

"I'm walking back," he tried again, for a final time. *Seven years old. Footy scarf. Coffin.* "Come with me."

Liam considered, then to Kieran's surprise, he nodded. "Yeah, okay."

He swung his legs back over the railing and jumped down. They were the same height now, Kieran realized as they began to walk. Liam maybe even had the edge. He shouldn't be surprised. Toby had been tall. And Liam wasn't a kid anymore.

They walked without speaking and it was only as they passed the fork leading to the cemetery gates that Kieran felt Liam's eyes slide over.

"Aren't you going to ask me what happened on Saturday night?" he said.

"Do you want me to?" The iron gates were open, the grounds beyond them still empty.

"Everyone else seems to. I had to go in to the police station."

"I heard."

"Yeah, well." Liam kicked a rock and it bounced ahead of them down the trail. "That's what you get for trying to be nice. I didn't have to drive her home, you know. I could've left her to walk. But I didn't, did I? Not like some of the others would have."

"Which others?"

"Whoever. I don't know. The dickheads over summer. That Spanish bloke that was hanging around."

"Bronte's boyfriend, you mean?"

"He wasn't her boyfriend." Liam was dismissive. "She didn't even like him that much."

"How do you know that?"

"She said he would piss off as soon as the weather started to turn, and she was right. Same as those other bloody tourist blokes trying to impress her."

Liam had been keeping tabs on her, Kieran could tell. He would have put money on Liam knowing exactly who Bronte had been spending time with during any given week that summer.

The cemetery was well behind them now. There was no one on the track ahead or behind. The only sounds were the crunch of their feet and the waves breaking below. Kieran watched Liam as they walked. His head was tilted down, his expression dark.

"Go on, then," Kieran said. "What happened?"

Liam looked up at that. A strange tight smile crept across his face. "I knew you wanted to ask."

17

Liam squinted as a gust of sea air blew dust and dead leaves across the track. Having been invited to tell his side of the story, he now seemed oddly hesitant.

"I'd driven Bronte home before, you know." He rubbed the corner of his eye with a finger. "Loads of times."

"Like a weekly thing?"

"No. I mean, I usually offered. It's, what, two minutes out of my way? But it was so close and she mostly liked to walk." Liam shrugged. "The Saturday shift was a late one, though, so sometimes, yeah. I'd offer and she'd say okay."

One shift and not every week. Kieran wondered exactly how many times counted as "loads" to Liam.

"She said okay this Saturday?" he asked.

"Yeah. We'd been talking. About you, actually." Liam glanced over. "I didn't even know you were back and then suddenly you turn up like that."

"Right." Kieran fought the instinct to apologize. He didn't have to give notice to come back to his own hometown.

"Anyway, I was telling Bronte about what had happened back then. She was nice about it." Liam seemed suddenly embarrassed. "I dunno. So we got in my car, put some music on, drove to her place."

Kieran couldn't help noticing the cozy language. Liam made it sound like a date.

"I parked outside. She had a book she was going to lend me—something by that G. R. Barlin dickhead who's always hanging around. But she said I should read it, so I went in with her to get it."

"She invited you inside?"

"Yeah. She did." Liam sounded defensive. Either Bronte really had invited him, or he really believed she had.

"Right."

"She found the book and we talked for a couple of minutes. But then I had to get up early next morning to go to the gym, so I left."

No way. Kieran almost laughed. There was no way in this world Liam had been inside the home of the girl he liked after eleven on a Saturday night and voluntarily pulled the pin so he could be fresh for his gym session. Kieran didn't know exactly what had happened, but he knew without a shadow of a doubt it hadn't happened like that. And what was more, he was pretty sure Sergeant Chris Renn would know it too.

"So what did you guys talk about at her place?" he said instead.

"Bronte's art, mainly. She'd been working on this coastal project all summer. She said she'd got some new ideas she wanted to sketch out."

There it was, thought Kieran. The polite excuse. *I've got so much work to do.* Probably accompanied by a yawn and a faux-regretful smile while she rested one hand on the open door.

"Then what?" he said.

"I told you," Liam said. "I headed off. I had to get up for the gym."

"How long were you at her place for?"

"Hardly anything. Ten minutes or something. Then I left." Liam stopped walking now and looked at Kieran. The trail had turned to asphalt under their feet. They were nearly back in town. "But you know that. You saw me."

"When?" Kieran frowned.

"On Saturday night. You were walking along Beach Road. I drove right by you."

Kieran remembered the blinding headlights coming around the bend. The rush of air from a car passing too close and too fast in the night.

"That was you, was it?"

"Yeah, didn't you see? I saw you."

"And Mia?"

A tiny beat. "Yeah. Both of you."

Liam was staring at Kieran as he tried to cast his mind back. Could the car have been Liam's white Holden? He remembered putting his arm out toward Mia. He could hear the roar of the engine, see the taillights disappearing into the dark. He wasn't sure.

"You remember that, right?" Liam was frowning now. "I know you do. You told my uncle Sean you saw a car." He ran his hand through his hair, frustrated. "It was mine. Leaving her place."

"Sean told you I'd seen a car?"

Liam hesitated. "Only after I'd already said that I'd seen you on the road."

Kieran couldn't decide if he believed him or not. He pictured Sean's face at the marina the day before. He wasn't sure how far Sean would go to help his nephew. Pretty far, probably.

Liam was still watching him. "If the cops talk to you—"

"They already have, they've been to my parents' house."

"Oh yeah. That's right." A look flashed across Liam's face too fast for Kieran to read. "Your dad was out walking that night too, wasn't he?"

Kieran didn't answer. There was a loaded moment, then Liam took a breath.

"Look," Liam said. "I already told the cops that it was me driving, so—"

"Well, I'm not sure I can help you, mate, because I already told Chris Renn that I couldn't remember much about the car," Kieran said. "Which is the truth."

"You can tell him you've remembered now. Or get your girlfriend to tell him."

"I'm not asking Mia to do anything."

"Then you'll have to do it," Liam said. "Please."

There was a change in his voice now. The bravado had worn thin, and a layer of fear shone through, raw and exposed.

"Listen, mate," Liam tried again when Kieran didn't reply. "I didn't do anything to Bronte. Seriously. I dropped her off and I left. That's it. That neighbor heard her talking on the beach later, didn't she? So that proves it. I didn't do what they're all saying. I—" Liam was watching him intently. "I wouldn't, all right? I liked her."

They looked at each other, then Kieran shook his head. "I've got to go."

He could feel Liam's eyes still on him as he moved to leave.

"Wait," Liam said suddenly.

"What?"

"Do you still miss your brother?"

Kieran stopped. The question had a ring of sincerity and before he could help himself, he had turned back. "Yeah. I do."

"I really miss my dad." Liam was quiet now. "Sean does too. You should know that."

"I do know that."

"My mum and Julian say what happened was an accident. They reckon my dad still would have gone to help, even knowing what happened. And I know Finn died too, so no one's supposed to give you a hard time." Liam's face twisted with something both hard and soft. "But you kind of ruined my life, you know?"

"Yeah." They stood facing each other with what felt to Kieran like a rare sense of connection. "It kind of ruined my life too. If it helps."

It was one of the most honest conversations he had had in years.

Liam looked at him for a long time. "No," he said finally. "It doesn't."

He turned and walked away, leaving Kieran staring after him.

•   •   •

Kieran was still standing where Liam had left him when his phone beeped in his pocket with a text. He pulled it out. Mia.

Where are you?

He texted her back and a moment later her reply came through.

I'm coming to meet you. I need to get out for a while.

Everything okay? he wrote, but there was no reply this time.

He ran a hand over Audrey's soft head. "Let's go and find Mummy, hey?"

Kieran started walking toward town in the direction from which he knew Mia would come. The cliff trail had given way to the tarmac and residential plots of what was now the historic part of town, but back in the 1800s had been its center. The sandstone houses were set well apart and had sprawling gardens to compensate for the lack of sea views.

Kieran slowed in front of one in particular. He had passed it on the way up but now stopped to look properly. The Wetherby place. Ash's gran's former house, and now home to Evelyn Bay's current writer in residence, G. R. Barlin.

It was one of the larger houses, set back from the road. A small excavating digger was parked idle in the driveway, the company's logo obscured by mud. But its handiwork was clear. Last time Kieran had seen the house it had been surrounded by a lush sea of native trees, plants, and flowers. Now it was marked by trenches of exposed soil.

Kieran leaned on the fence and felt a stir of annoyance on Ash's behalf. George Barlin might tell himself this was a renovation, but the place looked like a bomb site. It appeared the garden was being systematically destroyed in sections. The north side had already been ripped up, and judging by the various markers attached to mature plants and bushes, they were soon to follow. No wonder Ash was pissed off.

There was sudden movement inside the house and Kieran saw the writer pace past the kitchen window. He looked to be wearing a different chunky cardigan today and was holding his phone to his ear. In his other hand, he had a sheaf of papers and was gesturing as he spoke.

While Kieran watched, George turned toward the window and stopped when he saw Kieran standing by his fence. Their eyes met over the ruined yard. They both stared, and Kieran raised his hand. George responded with a kind of reluctant salute; then, with an invisible twist of the wrist, the shutters snapped closed and he disappeared from sight.

Kieran moved away from the fence and reached for his phone. Seeing the writer had reminded him, and he pulled up a search page and typed. *Evelyn Bay Online Community Hub.*

Christ. It was worse than he'd expected. A clunky forum

staggered to life, the measures and spacing blowing out on the phone screen. Along the top, hard-to-read blue-on-gray lettering declared: *Welcome to EBOCH! Drop in for a virtual cuppa and a chat!* Pixelated steam rose from an illustration of a coffee cup.

People certainly had been dropping in; George Barlin was right about that. Over the entire previous month, the forum had attracted about a dozen comments, mainly, from what Kieran could see, about the perennial problem of tourists dumping rubbish in residential wheelie bins. In the thirty-six hours since Bronte's death, there had been more than three hundred entries.

Kieran scrolled through. The vast majority of those weighing in appeared to be brand-new members of the site. A few had uploaded a tiny thumbnail profile photo, but most hadn't bothered, lurking instead behind the default anonymous gray silhouette. Most had adopted a pseudonym, but Kieran recognized some of the names. Juliet Raymond, for example, who used to babysit Kieran some days after school, was one of many expressing dismay that "you can't even walk the streets anymore." Theresa Hartley, the former music teacher at the high school and Mia's old piano tutor, wrote that her granddaughter went to the same uni in Canberra as Bronte Laidler.

Meaghan says the students are all devastated, Theresa wrote. SurfGirl93 had liked the post, along with thirty-nine others. *Thank you*, Theresa had commented in reply to her own comment.

There were dozens of messages about Bronte. How she had covered the cost of someone's coffee in the Surf and Turf when they'd forgotten their wallet. How she had sketched a lovely picture of a daughter's new puppy on the back of a napkin and given it to her as they left. The compliments seemed sincere, Kieran thought, but superficial. No one in Evelyn Bay had really known her much beyond the orange uniform and professional smile.

There were surprisingly few references to Liam. A good handful of posts mentioned "someone" the police were talking to, but there seemed to be a general reluctance to throw the first stone. Kieran skimmed the entries as he scrolled. There was something more than loyalty to Liam going on, though, he decided. Reading through the comments in bulk, he could sense an almost collective need for it not to be the local boy. There were dozens of mentions of tourists, mainlanders, shadowy strangers. Apparently anything was better than it being one of their own.

Not everyone was so coy, though.

Liam Gilroy, wrote one anonymous gray avatar. *Is anyone seriously surprised?*

Why? several people had asked in reply.

Kieran scrolled through the whole chain, but the original commenter had remained silent.

"There you both are."

Kieran looked up. Mia gave a little wave as she walked toward them. She seemed a lot better than she had that morning, Kieran thought. As she leaned over the carrier to stroke Audrey's head, he was relieved to see the bruise on her wrist had not come up as badly as he'd feared.

"Everything okay at home?"

"I think so. Your dad seems oblivious. Calmer, though."

"That's good, I suppose."

Mia reached in and wiped a trail of drool from Audrey's mouth. "How was your morning?"

"We saw Liam."

"Really?" Mia looked up now. "Did he say anything?"

"Yeah." Kieran filled her in on Liam's account of Saturday night. "He reckons that was his car we saw racing by on Beach Road."

"Was it?" Mia frowned.

"He says so. Can you remember? It would have been a white Holden."

She thought, then shook her head. "I really don't know."

As they turned in the direction of town, Mia's eyes fell as Kieran's had on what used to be the garden of Wetherby House.

"Look at this place," she said. "What a shame. Is it still owned by Ash's family?"

"No. But you'll never guess who lives here now."

"Who?"

"G. R. Barlin."

"No. Seriously?" Mia turned back to the home, a newfound appreciation for invasive landscaping dawning on her face. "How do you know?"

"I met him. He was at the Surf and Turf yesterday morning too. The bloke with the laptop."

"Oh my God, of course," Mia breathed. "I thought he looked familiar. It was so out of context, though, I couldn't work it out." She frowned. "He doesn't look much like his photo anymore. I'm surprised anyone recognizes him."

Kieran smiled. "They don't, apparently. You'll probably get another chance, though. Mum and I ran into him last night at the Surf and Turf. And he just caught me and Audrey spying on him."

"Oh for God's sake." Mia gave Kieran a gentle slap on the arm, but she was smiling, properly now. "Now he's never going to want to be best friends with us."

Kieran had to laugh. "I'm not sure that was on the cards anyway."

"Why not? We're fun."

"We're really not. Not these days, at least."

Mia smiled and peered at the house with its closed shutters. "I should have worked out it was him yesterday. He used to come here for summers."

"Yeah, he mentioned that," Kieran said. "How did you know?"

"I took one of his writing workshops years ago. Remember? I told you."

Kieran did remember now but hadn't put two and two together. "That was here? I thought that was after you moved to Sydney."

"No, it was here. Back when he was a nobody journalist." Her smile dimmed a little. "Gabby did the workshop too. It was that one not long before the storm."

"Right. Of course." Kieran leaned on the fence next to her.

Mia's eyes were trained on the house, but the kitchen shutters remained stubbornly closed. "So what's he like now?" she said, unable to hide her curiosity.

"Dunno," Kieran said. "Seems okay. Takes himself a bit seriously maybe. Ash clearly isn't a fan."

"No, I suppose not." Mia picked a single leaf off one of the few remaining trees. It was earmarked for extraction according to the tape wrapped around its trunk. "This is actually pretty brutal. If Gabby were here she'd be so sad to see it like this."

"Really?"

"Yeah. She loved walking past this place. Even more when Ash got going with it. You could see that the garden was full of little nooks and crannies and hiding places. We called it the fairy garden. Pretended it was magic." Mia shook her head. "And that's obviously one of the many reasons we were so popular at school."

She dropped the leaf on the ground and it blew away as they turned and began to walk toward town.

"Hey, I ran into Olivia earlier as well," Kieran said as they hit the main street. The Surf and Turf was open again for business, he could see from the lights through the windows. He scanned the street, trying to spot the CCTV camera that had captured

Liam and Bronte together on Saturday night. He found it high on a lamppost.

"Was Liv okay?"

"Not really. She mentioned that Bronte reminded her a bit of Gabby."

"Oh God, did she really?"

"Both people pleasers apparently. Maybe a bit softhearted."

Mia frowned a little. "I suppose."

Kieran looked over in surprise. "You don't think so?"

"No, I do. I guess. About Gabby, at least. It's just—" Mia thought for a moment. "When someone dies, it's pretty easy to only remember the good things, don't you think? Especially if they died young. I mean, Gabby was my friend, but she could also be"—Mia hesitated this time—"a bit difficult. Like we all can be. Obviously."

"In what way?" Kieran asked.

"She could be petty." Mia sounded uncomfortable now. "Often about Olivia, really. She hated feeling left out, which she was, quite a lot. So she'd sometimes try to stop Olivia having fun or doing things without her. It wasn't mean-spirited. Just jealousy mostly."

"I didn't know that."

"Well. It wasn't easy for her having Olivia as a sister. Liv had all these friends, and Gabby was pretty much stuck with me." Mia shrugged. "Gabby didn't help herself, though. She could be really immature a lot of the time. We both could, to be fair."

They walked on and up ahead, Kieran could see the petrol station and the squat redbrick police station come into view.

"But look, it wasn't Gabby's fault." Mia sounded guilty now. "She developed physically so early and all of a sudden she had all this attention coming her way. She never really worked out how to handle it."

"Olivia mentioned that. Sounded like it happened a bit."

"A bit? Honestly, men used to stare at Gabby *all the time*. We'd be in our school uniform, we could literally be playing with toys—like a board game or something—and it wouldn't make any difference. So if she acted a bit childish and annoying, I think it was her way of trying to deal with it."

Kieran frowned. "Blokes around here used to stare at her? Which ones?"

"Looking the way she did?" Mia said. "Pretty much all of them."

She opened her mouth as though to say something else, then stopped. They had reached the police station.

Mia was looking across the street to the station's glass door. It was propped open and Sergeant Renn was speaking to Sue Pendlebury on the threshold. It wasn't clear if they were coming or going, but they both stopped talking as they saw Kieran and Mia. Renn turned to Pendlebury and said something too low for them to hear. Then both officers straightened, and Renn raised his hand and beckoned.

Kieran looked at Mia. "I'll go and see what he wants."

He had started over when Pendlebury lifted her chin.

"Both of you," she called. "Thank you."

She looked at Kieran, then past him to Mia, then turned and disappeared into the station.

18

The cardboard boxes stacked inside the glass doors of the police station reminded Kieran of his parents' house, albeit a more efficient version. Preparations for the station's closure the following month were well under way, with the cabinets behind reception standing empty and the corkboard stripped of its usual advisories about the nonemergency hotline number and warnings against leaving valuables in cars.

But the mothballing process had screeched to a sudden halt, Kieran could see as he and Mia followed Renn and Pendlebury down the hall. A large yellowing map of the Evelyn Bay township looked to have been taken down and then hastily tacked back up, presumably for the benefit of the Hobart officers. The sun-faded paint on the wall showed exactly where it had previously hung. A couple of officers Kieran didn't recognize glanced up as they passed, then turned back to their work.

"The coffee machine has already gone, I'm afraid," Renn said as he led them into his office and gestured to two battered chairs. "But we can do instant if that's of interest?"

"I don't blame you," said Pendlebury with a smile as both Kieran and Mia shook their heads. She ignored the fourth chair in the corner and stayed standing, leaning her hip against the filing cabinet from where she could see all three of them.

"Right. Hopefully we won't keep you too long." Renn sat down behind the desk that used to be the domain of Sergeant Geoff Mallott. It might quite literally be the same desk, Kieran thought, looking at the scratched surface as he unclipped Audrey and passed her to Mia.

Kieran wondered if Chris Renn was also counting off the days to retirement, semi-forced or otherwise, the way Sergeant Mallott had been that summer before the storm. Under the buzzing fluorescent lights, Renn looked older than he had yesterday morning. Kieran hoped working for his brother's haulage company would turn out better for him than Mallott's retirement had. Within six months of hanging up his uniform, Mallott had died on his sofa of a heart attack.

Renn's chair creaked as he moved a clear plastic box filled with phones, sunglasses, and watches off his desk to make room.

"The things people leave behind, eh?" he said, seeing Kieran looking at it. He opened a notebook and clicked his mouse to fire up the computer. Kieran could hear it battling as it whirred to life.

"All right. Saturday night." Renn turned to look at them. "Just want to double-check a few things. You two walked home from the Surf and Turf along Beach Road."

Kieran and Mia nodded.

"What time did you pass Fisherman's Cottage?"

"I'm not sure exactly. Would have been just after eleven thirty p.m.?" Kieran looked to Mia for confirmation. She was jiggling Audrey on her knee and gave a small nod.

"Did you see a car parked outside?"

They looked at each other again. Kieran tried to picture the beach house and the road, dim in the moonlight. In his mind, the street was empty, but he wasn't certain if he was remembering last Saturday night or one of the hundreds of other evenings he'd walked home along that same route.

"I didn't see anyone parked," Mia answered. Kieran, still a little undecided, nodded. He heard Pendlebury's ballpoint pen click and the faint scratch of words on paper.

"Lights in the cottage," Renn said. "Were they on or off, did you notice?"

On, Kieran thought, then immediately second-guessed the memory. He wasn't sure he'd glanced twice at the house.

"There were a couple of lights on, I think." Mia was frowning. "Enough that it looked like someone was still up."

More scratching of pen on paper. Renn waited patiently until Pendlebury gave him some signal so subtle that Kieran missed it.

"And you'd obviously decided to walk home along the road, not the beach," Renn said. "Bit shorter along the sand, isn't it? Any reason not to go that way?"

"It was dark. I didn't feel comfortable." Mia jiggled Audrey. "The road's better lit."

Pendlebury did not bother writing that down, seeming to find that particular answer self-evident. Renn tapped it into his computer anyway.

"All right." Renn turned back. "The car you saw driving fast along Beach Road. That was definitely coming from the direction of Fisherman's Cottage and heading toward town?"

They were both able to nod with certainty at that, at least.

"Right. Liam Gilroy says it was his. He says—" Renn tapped at his keyboard, then read from the screen. "He reckons he left

Fisherman's Cottage, was driving back toward town around eleven thirty p.m.—speeding, he admits that—and he saw you, Kieran, and put his foot down harder to give you a bit of a scare." The officer looked up. "I know we've been through this, but can either of you remember any more about that vehicle?"

Kieran hesitated. He could feel Mia's eyes on him. He tried to focus on Saturday night, and the road, but the images were being nudged out of the way. *You kind of ruined my life.*

"Look," Kieran said. "It could have been Liam's car."

He felt Mia shift in surprise next to him and Renn looked at them both.

"Yesterday you reckoned you didn't know," he said.

"No. But—" Kieran shrugged. "I mean, I'm pretty sure it was a four-wheel drive. And I'm pretty sure it was light colored. We were walking along Beach Road at around eleven thirty, like Liam said. We saw a car driving fast, like he said. So if you're asking me if it could have been Liam Gilroy's white Holden, then yes. If he says it was his, I can't say for sure that it wasn't."

There was a silence, then Pendlebury's pen began scratching again. Renn's fingers lay still on the keyboard. He turned to Mia.

"And what did you see of this car?"

Mia switched Audrey to her other arm. "I don't remember what it looked like. I couldn't say either way."

Pendlebury stopped writing and tapped her pen thoughtfully on her notebook.

"Liam said he hadn't known you two were back in town, so he was a bit upset to see you in the Surf and Turf on Saturday night," she said. "Whose idea was it to meet there?"

"Ash suggested it," Kieran said.

"And it was just a general catch-up, is that right?" She looked up at Mia, her pen hovering. "You didn't want to invite any friends along, Mia?"

"Well, Olivia was going to be there. I haven't really kept in touch with anyone else. I left when I was fourteen, and before that I only really hung around with Gabby."

"Were you and Gabby Birch very close, then?"

"Of course." Mia frowned. "We were best friends."

"Sure. It's just that, knowing teenagers, that's not always the same thing," Pendlebury said. "It's a complicated time."

That was true. Kieran thought about Ash and Sean and how their own three-way balance had shifted and resettled over the years. It had been just Kieran and Sean for a long time as kids, and then it had felt like Ash had been the one firmly by his side for those big crazy high school summers. Now it was Ash and Sean who saw each other every day and only saw Kieran every once in a long while.

"What do you do for work, Mia, by the way?" Pendlebury's question caught Kieran by surprise. For a reason he couldn't quite put his finger on, the way Pendlebury was watching Mia made him a little uneasy.

"Nothing right now." She fished out a tissue and wiped Audrey's nose. "Stay-at-home mum."

"And before that?"

A pause. "I worked in immunology research for a biotech company in Sydney."

"Impressive."

Mia shrugged. She didn't talk about it much, mainly because she missed it but felt bad admitting it, Kieran knew. He couldn't blame her. The ink had barely been dry on her employment contract when the anniversary of the storm had rolled around and, both feeling sorry for themselves, they'd taken each other out for a few too many Mia's Mayhems. Whether Mia's vomiting the next day had diluted the effects of Mia's Pill or not they were never sure, but either way, nine months later they had Audrey.

And they were happy, Kieran could say that without hesitation. They had sat down and considered their options and made a conscious decision. They loved Audrey, but it was possible to be both welcome and a surprise. With an eight-year age gap between himself and Finn, Kieran had long suspected that might in fact have been his own situation.

"And what about you?" Pendlebury turned to Kieran.

"Sports physio."

"Also impressive," she said, but he could tell she didn't mean it as much. She straightened. "All right. I think we're finished here for now." She flashed a glance at Renn, who pushed his chair away from the desk in confirmation.

Mia stood up as well, a little too fast, prompting Audrey to regurgitate down both of their fronts. "Shit."

"I'll show you to the restroom," Pendlebury said. "It's on the way out."

"I know where it is." Mia's tone was brisk. "I've been in here before."

"Of course," Pendlebury said mildly. "Still. I'll take you anyway. There are boxes and all sorts of things lying around. I don't want you to trip."

Kieran watched them go, then turned back to Renn, who was shutting down his computer.

"Let's wait outside. Get some fresh air." Renn checked his phone. "I've got to head over to Fisherman's Cottage anyway."

Kieran followed him along the hall and through the glass doors. Once outside, Renn leaned against the brickwork. He rubbed a hand over his head.

"You don't owe anyone anything, you know."

Kieran looked over in surprise. Renn wasn't looking back, instead gazing out at the service station next door. A blue car had pulled up at one of the pumps.

Kieran wasn't sure what to say, so he said nothing.

"Whatever pressure Liam might be putting on you," Renn went on. "Or your good mate Sean, for that matter, you've got no obligation to them—"

"I know that. They're not."

"Right."

Renn fell quiet, and unexpectedly Kieran found himself picturing the funeral. Not remembering Liam this time, for once, or even Finn or Toby. Instead, he could see Renn—young, newly minted Constable Renn—staring at the coffins. His uniform had been perfectly pressed, but there was now something about him that seemed weather-beaten and storm damaged, like everything else in Evelyn Bay. From what Kieran remembered, Constable Renn had barely said a word all day. But then, Kieran didn't remember much from that day at all.

"When I first started here, under Sergeant Mallott—" Renn was still looking past Kieran. "Well. Geoff had his own way of doing things, as you know. So I suppose all I'm saying—"

He broke off again. Across the service station forecourt, the woman with the blue car had finished filling her tank and gone inside to pay.

Renn's eyes followed her. "I'm saying I know what it's like to want to do the right thing. And I know sometimes it can be hard to know exactly what that is. Especially if you're being asked to support someone you trust, like your boss." Renn looked at Kieran. "Or your mate, for example."

Kieran shrugged. "You asked me about the car, I've told you what I thought."

"Yep. All right, then. Just—"

He stopped as the glass doors of the police station opened and Mia came out, followed by Sue Pendlebury. Mia was cleaned up, mostly, while Audrey looked disgruntled by the fuss.

"Okay?" Kieran said, and she nodded. He looked at the officers. "Are we right to go, then?"

"You are. Are you heading home?" Renn's tone was once again all business. "I'm walking that way—"

"Mia?"

They all stopped and turned at the sound of the voice. The call had come from the service station, and Kieran could see that the woman with the blue car was standing by the driver's door, keys in one hand. She was shielding her eyes with the other.

"Mia?" she called again. She started walking over. "It *is* you."

Mia placed her before Kieran did. "Trish. Hello. How nice to see you."

Kieran had not seen Patricia Birch up close since before Gabby's disappearance. She had never looked that much like either of her daughters, and Kieran guessed Olivia and Gabby took after their father.

Trish Birch had aged in the past twelve years, not surprisingly. But to Kieran she seemed older in a way that was hard to define. Her hair was still a neat shoulder-length bob, shiny and maybe a little lighter in color than he remembered. She had put on a bit of weight and had the faraway look of a woman who Kieran could believe relied on sleeping pills. There was something different around the eyes too. Kieran hadn't known Trish well before the storm, but he was willing to bet the heaviness he saw there now hadn't been there then. It looked to him a lot like grief, specifically old grief. The kind that left a permanent mark, like rings in a tree trunk. Brian and Verity had it as well.

"How are you, Mia?" Trish said. There was a slight pause. "And I heard about your baby. Congratulations."

"Thank you." Mia twisted her body to show Audrey in her arms.

Trish glanced down, but her gaze bounced straight back up.

She stared at Mia, who had once been the same age as Gabby. Who had shared homework notes, slept over at their house, eaten at their table. Mia, who got to grow up and have a child of her own. Live her life. Kieran could almost see the *what-ifs* swirling in the air around Trish. She turned suddenly to Pendlebury.

"You haven't worked out what happened to Bronte yet?"

"No." Pendlebury shook her head. "But we will."

Skepticism flickered on Trish's face. "You sound sure."

"I'm sure we'll do everything we possibly can."

Trish's gaze slid to Sergeant Renn. He tried his best to maintain eye contact, Kieran noticed, but seemed to be struggling. Kieran didn't blame him. He found it quite hard to look into those eyes himself.

"Because it's the same beach, isn't it." Trish's voice was steady. An observation, not a question. Gabby's name hovered unspoken.

"Mrs. Birch." Pendlebury's tone was careful. "Patricia. If you're worried there may be some connection between what happened on Saturday and what happened to your daughter, I've said I'm very happy for you to—"

Trish was already shaking her head. She gave a small, tired laugh.

"You don't need me to tell you what the connections are. Everyone knows. It's the same beach. Same time of year. The same responding officer even. So I'm sure the sergeant here can tell you all about those days. What was and wasn't done." She looked squarely at Renn. "He would know."

Pendlebury's eyes also flicked, swiftly and just once, in Renn's direction. Audrey, sensing the tension, screwed up her face and began to cry. Trish reached out and stroked the baby's head.

"Mrs. Birch," Pendlebury said. "If you want to come inside and—"

"No. I've got an appointment to get to." Trish dropped her hand. "But it's good to see you, Mia. Take care of yourself."

She turned, then paused in front of the two officers. Her mouth was pressed tight, but in the end she couldn't stop herself. "Just take it seriously this time. Please."

19

Olivia was waiting on the road outside Fisherman's Cottage, her arms crossed over her chest. Kieran could see she was staring at the small collection of bouquets laid at the gatepost, the flowers already wilting as the cellophane flapped in the breeze. She straightened as she sensed movement, looking a little surprised to see Kieran and Mia approaching with Sergeant Renn.

No one had said anything as they'd watched Trish Birch turn and walk back to the service station. She'd driven away, Renn's gaze following the car until it was well out of sight. He'd turned to Kieran.

"Let's go." He nodded at Pendlebury. "See you shortly."

"Yes," she had said simply, her eyes on his face. "See you."

Renn had not said another word all the way to Fisherman's Cottage. Now he pulled a set of keys out of his pocket, ducked under the police tape, and went to open the front door.

"They're letting you back in?" Mia said to Olivia as they stood by the gate and watched Renn find the right key. "That's good."

"Not permanently, just to get some clothes and things. And

Julian's asked me to get Bronte's work keys back. She was supposed to be on earlies this week, so she's got one of the sets for
the back door." Olivia was wearing the same borrowed outfit
she'd been in that morning and toyed with the hem of her pullover. "Chris says they'll give Bronte's parents the chance to visit
the house—if they want to, I guess—and then I might be able to
come back."

Olivia did not look at all keen on that idea, Kieran thought,
as Renn opened the front door and disappeared inside.

"If you're allowed in, do you reckon that means they've
found whatever they were looking for?" Kieran said.

"I don't know. Maybe." Olivia shook her head. "Or else
they've decided it's not in the house."

Renn reappeared in the doorway. "All yours, Liv."

Olivia rested a hand on the gatepost but went no further.
Kieran saw her glance at the dying flowers at her feet, then to the
darkened hallway.

"Do you want us to come?" Mia said, and raised her voice as
Olivia nodded. "Chris? Sorry. Is it okay if we come in with her?"

Renn saw Olivia's expression and considered. He looked at
Kieran, empty-handed other than Audrey in her sling, and Mia,
holding only the small nappy bag.

"All right," he said. "You grab what you need, Liv, but I'll
have to make a note before you take it."

Renn stepped aside to let them pass and Kieran followed
Olivia up the path and into the cool, dim hallway.

"Come through," she said. The cottage's kitchen and living
room were cozy and felt like they would be welcoming under
different circumstances, but even with Kieran's untrained eye
he could tell both areas had been searched. It looked like some
effort had been made to restore items to their rightful spots, but
even having never been there before, Kieran could tell things

were slightly off. The cushions on the couch looked somehow in the wrong order, and the entire contents of the bookshelf felt misaligned.

Even now, Kieran caught Renn casting his eye over the room. Whatever he and Pendlebury and the other officers had been looking for, they still hadn't found it, Kieran felt sure. They must be fairly certain it wasn't in the house, though, or Kieran doubted they'd have let Olivia back in, let alone him and Mia. Renn also hadn't seemed worried about them smuggling something out in their pockets or the nappy bag Mia was carrying, Kieran realized. So, probably nothing small then.

What was it? He couldn't help glancing around as well, aware he wouldn't recognize a missing item even if he tripped over it.

Olivia barely looked around, walking straight to her bedroom. Mia followed her in and sat on the edge of the bed as Olivia opened a drawer and began to pile underwear on the dresser. Kieran hovered in the hall, giving them some space.

Renn peered in to check what Olivia was doing and ducked straight back out again. He went to the back door and unlocked it, stepping out onto the veranda. He stood framed in the doorway with his arms folded and his gaze resting on the floral tributes near the shoreline. Two camera crews were down there, Kieran could see. The guys from the Surf and Turf the other night, plus a new pair. They were both interviewing a man who was pointing at something out to sea while trying to stop his dog from chewing the flowers.

Kieran turned away and came face-to-face with the last room in the hallway. The back bedroom. In his parents' house, this was his room. In Fisherman's Cottage, it had belonged to Bronte. The door was wide open. No privacy for the dead, Kieran guessed.

Bronte's room had the specific type of sparseness that suggested its occupant hadn't planned to stay long, Kieran could tell from the hallway. A double bed with a green and white duvet cover took up most of the space, along with an open clothes rack where she had hung up a single row of dresses and tops. A spare Surf and Turf uniform dangled from the end, garish against her own clothes, which were mostly black and gray. A full-length mirror was propped against the wall, with a hair straightener and a makeup bag on the floor beside it. The single window in Bronte's room looked out onto the beach, across the sand, and down to the place where her body was found.

A desk had been pushed underneath the window. Bronte's art station, Kieran thought. It was the only cluttered space in the whole room, the surface covered by different types of pencils stacked in cups, small pots of paint, and a pile of notebooks and papers. On top of a thick sketchbook lay a yellow industrial-looking torch. SEAN GILROY was printed along the side in capital letters.

Kieran looked at the torch and the desk and suddenly imagined Bronte in that room at night. Settling in with the blinds pulled down and then hearing a noise outside. Getting up from the bed or desk chair, reaching for the torch, and going to the window. Kieran tried to picture what Bronte would have done next. Would she turn off the main light and peer around the edge of the window frame, letting her night vision adjust to give her an advantage? Or would she hoist the blind up and stand there, brazen and backlit as she aimed that beam of the light out onto whatever was waiting on the dark beach? Kieran hadn't known her well enough to guess.

He turned away from the bedroom and walked across the hall and to the back door. Renn looked up as he stepped out.

"Olivia told you Bronte thought she heard noises at night a few times?" Kieran kept his voice low so as not to wake Audrey.

Renn sighed. "Yeah."

"Any idea what that was?"

"No." Renn rubbed his eyes and turned his back on the beach. "You know what it's like along here. Could have been anything at all. Dog, another animal, anything. A person. Who knows?"

He seemed very flat. Kieran wasn't sure if it was down to being here in the house, or the sight of the tributes on the sand, or the encounter outside the station with Trish Birch. *Take it seriously this time.* Perhaps simply the investigation in general. Kieran suspected having Pendlebury as a shadow would make anyone want to make sure they were doing things to the letter. Kieran looked back at Bronte's room.

"Am I okay to take Sean's torch, do you reckon?" he said. "He needs it for the wreck."

"That yellow one?" Renn said, his eyes still on the shoreline. "Yeah. You're right to grab that."

"Thanks." Kieran went back inside, blinking in the sudden darkness of the hallway. As he stepped into Bronte's room, he could hear Mia's and Olivia's voices floating from the main bedroom.

"Bronte lent me that book." Olivia sounded subdued. "She said it was her favorite of his."

"Yeah, it's one of my favorites too. They made it into a movie."

"I think I saw that. It was good."

"Yeah. The book's still better, though," Mia said, and Kieran could hear the rustle of pages. "*'For Bronte, thank you for the inspiration. Yours, George Barlin.'* Were they friends, then? The most I've ever got from him was a signature. 'All the best' once, when the signing queue was short."

"Friends? No, I don't think so," Olivia said. "George must have twenty years on her. I think he just knew her from around the Surf and Turf."

"Is his wife here with him?"

"He's not married, is he? He doesn't seem married. He's always in there alone."

"Oh." There was a pause and a muffled noise, and Kieran realized Mia was checking her phone. "No, you're right, it says here that he and his wife have split up. That's sad. Maybe that explains the sea change. I think they'd been together for a while." Mia was quiet for another moment. "They met when they were both interning as journalists at a newspaper in Sydney and have a five-year-old daughter. Separated last year. Amicable, blah blah. He's in this article going on about mutual respect and how he's never felt so creatively free."

"He should try telling his laptop that," Olivia said, and Kieran heard the sound of a drawer opening and shutting. "He seems to spend a lot of time frowning at it."

"Wow, she's already engaged again," Mia said. "Took his daughter and moved to America with her new fiancé."

"That sounds quick."

"Yeah," Mia said. "Reading between the lines of mutual respect here, I'd say he thinks so too."

Kieran went over to Bronte's desk. He reached among the art supplies for the torch and stopped. Lying near it was a small pair of wire cutters and a tiny skeletal sculpture of a crayfish spun from intricately twisted copper strands. Kieran picked it up and held it gently in his palm, looking at the wire he guessed had come from his parents' shed and that Bronte had brought to life, almost unbelievably, as this creature. He wondered how many hours she'd spent on it, and suddenly felt very sad.

"Ash can't stand George, though." Olivia's voice floated out from her own room. "It's a bit awkward at work sometimes, when they're both there."

"Because of the garden?" he heard Mia ask.

"Yeah," Olivia said. "Which I can understand. Ash tried

really hard to buy the place from his gran, but she needed a certain price to cover the retirement home, and in the end they couldn't make it work. Then George comes along, and he can afford it, fair enough. But when Ash heard he was ripping up the garden, he went to talk to George—professionally, you know—and asked him to consider keeping part of it. George didn't want to, so Ash offered to do the landscaping himself, at least have a hand in it, but George wanted to bring in some gardener from Hobart. Award-winning." Olivia sighed. "I feel bad for Ash, but there's nothing he can do, it's George's house. And George tries not to rub it in, and he's always been nice to me at work. I'm not sure this is quite what he expected when he moved here, though."

"But he would have known what he was getting himself into," Mia said. "Small-town life. It's not like he hasn't been here before. I was telling Kieran before how Gabby and I took his writing workshop that summer."

"Oh." Olivia sounded distracted. "Yeah, George mentioned something about that at work once, but Mum was there with me so I kind of shut him down. I got the sense he didn't really remember Gabby anyway. Not well, at least."

"Probably not. The groups were pretty big. They were free community things, you know? One-day workshops. So you had tourists and everyone mixed in there." Mia gave a small laugh. "And we were two fourteen-year-old girls writing stories about running a pony stable. I mean, I never *saw* G. R. Barlin roll his eyes at my work, but he may as well have."

A cupboard door slammed and Audrey started in her sleep and began to stir as Kieran heard footsteps in the hall.

"Chris?" Olivia's voice came from near the back door. "I'm done in my room. I've left my bag out if you want to check it. I just need to find Bronte's work keys, if that's okay?"

Another slam, this time the screen door. Renn coming

inside. "There were some keys in her desk, if you know which ones you're looking for."

"Thanks. Oh—" Olivia appeared at the door of Bronte's room and looked surprised to find Kieran in there. "What are you doing?"

He jiggled a now wide-awake Audrey in the sling and nodded at the torch. "Renn said it was okay."

"Right." Olivia moved over to the desk. There were three drawers and she pulled open the nearest one. Kieran could hear Mia and Renn talking in the hall but couldn't make out what they were saying over Audrey's soft grumbling.

Kieran moved the wire crayfish back to where he'd found it. Bronte had started another similar sculpture, he could see, but hadn't got far enough for him to tell what it would have been. It lay twisted and unfinished beside the large sketchbook. Still bouncing Audrey, Kieran turned the book toward him, curious now.

"You should take a look. I think she'd want people to see her work. She was really good." Olivia dropped her head as she rummaged through the drawers. "She worked hard. I don't know why I had to be such a bitch about it."

Kieran looked over. "I'm sure she didn't think that."

Olivia managed a tight smile. "I would have, if I were her." She pulled out a set of keys, examined them, then tossed them back in and shut the drawer. She moved to the next one and Kieran hesitated, then dragged over the desk chair and sat down. Audrey was writhing in the sling, so he took her out and sat her on his knee while he opened the cover of the sketchbook.

Bronte hadn't been kidding when she'd said she dabbled in different types of artwork. The book looked like the place where she had worked through her ideas and the pages were swollen with paint, glue, and pencil marks. Kieran lingered over dozens of outlines of the wire crayfish, as well as designs for a sea dragon. Over the page were watercolor paintings of the view of the coast from Bronte's window. She had taken reference photos at different times of day and slipped the printed pictures between the pages.

Bronte had definitely been into drawing, and to his eye she'd been good at it. He flipped through sketches of Evelyn Bay's town center and scenes he recognized from along the cliff path to the lookout. She had also drawn people. Kieran turned a page and Julian stared out from the paper, his face all angles. On the next page there was an outdoorsy young guy Kieran didn't recognize. A reference photo tucked into the spine showed he had dark hair and stubble and was muscular, wearing just a pair of board shorts. Bronte had focused only on his face in her drawing.

"This the Portuguese boyfriend?" Kieran said, and Olivia looked over.

"Marco? Yeah, that was him. Sean managed to dig up his last name, by the way. He and Bronte had gone snorkeling once, so it was in the payment records." Olivia shut another drawer and opened the final one. "Jesus, where are they?" She nodded at Audrey. "She's got hold of something, by the way."

Kieran looked down at his daughter, who had fallen suspiciously quiet. She had managed to grasp a black electrical cord that was snaking across the desk and was clutching it in her chubby hand, doing her best with limited coordination skills to get it into her mouth.

"No. Sorry, Audrey." Kieran reached for the cord. "What have you got here, anyway?"

The cord was a little unusual, thicker than a phone cable and with an odd-shaped attachment at the loose end. He'd seen something like it before, though, he felt. More than once, probably. He

ran his hand along its length, trying to place it as he tugged it
away from Audrey. She had a tight grip and in the end Kieran had
to pry it from her fist. Audrey shrieked in protest.

"What's she after?" Mia said, the sound bringing her to the
door.

"Nothing. A charger or something."

Kieran pushed the cord aside and swapped Audrey to the
other knee as he turned back to the book. More sketches. Lyn
the waitress wiping a table. George Barlin, looking much more
candid and realistic than in his author photo. Olivia with her
head down.

Kieran was about to point out the drawing to Olivia when
he stopped. A pair of familiar eyes gazed out from the opposite page. Verity. She was staring into the middle distance, her
chin tilted up, and had been caught seemingly unaware in the
pose. Kieran looked at his mother. It was a little unnerving to
see her in this setting, in this dead girl's rented room. It was an
excellent likeness. It was impossible to ignore the hollow look
in Verity's eyes.

When had it been drawn, Kieran wondered, and under what
circumstances? He couldn't imagine Verity posing willingly, but
when he flipped through to the handful of loose reference photos
tucked inside the back cover, they were only of scenery. He leafed
through them. The beach, the town, the lookout. No faces.

Maybe Bronte had drawn people from memory, or maybe
she'd got rid of the photos when she was finished. She had kept
the photo of the Portuguese boyfriend though, Kieran thought,
whatever could be made of that.

He turned another few pages and the portraits gave way to
watercolors of the coast and seascapes, with more reference photos tucked in alongside. He looked at the paintings of the beach
and thought about the first time he'd ever seen Bronte, down at

the water's edge. She had obviously been looking for ideas then, he realized now. He remembered her holding a length of seaweed in her hands. Crouching down by the shore.

Audrey was grizzling again on his knee, still trying to reach the black electrical charger.

"For God's sake, Audrey."

Kieran tried to wind the cord out of the way, but it was plugged in under the desk. He began to push it out of sight instead, then stopped. Something was edging its way into his thoughts. After a moment, he slowly reached down to the skirting board and pulled the plug free.

Beside him, Olivia extracted a set of keys from a drawer with a noise of relief.

"Finally." She held them up in faint triumph, then looked over to see Kieran holding the charger. "Everything okay?"

"Yeah," he said but, curious now, he stood and ran his eye once more over Bronte's minimal belongings. The bed, the clothes rack, a small chest of drawers, the desk, the mirror propped against the wall, a small bookshelf. Not many places to put something, and yet the whole room had that same rummaged-through feel as the rest of the house. More so, in fact, which was not surprising. The police would have been particularly thorough in here, he guessed.

Kieran wound the cable around his hand, still keeping it out of reach of Audrey, much to her disappointment. He could see no sign of what he was looking for, but that didn't necessarily mean anything. For the sake of completeness, he put Audrey over his shoulder and leaned down to check under the bed. A few pairs of shoes were lined up beneath, along with a battered suitcase. Streaks in the dust suggested the police had already checked there, and more than once.

"What are you doing?" Olivia's voice had an edge to it and

Kieran looked up. The daylight streaming through the window cast her face into shadow.

Mia appeared at the doorway. "What's going on?"

Kieran stood again and frowned. He held out his hand, dusty now from where he'd pressed it against the floor. The black charger dangled from his palm.

"That first day we saw Bronte on the beach," he said. "Didn't she have a camera?"

20

Kieran held out the camera charger. Olivia looked at it, then over to Bronte's desk, where the black length of cord had been plugged into the wall at one end and into nothing at the other. Finally, she reached out and took it from Kieran, winding the cord slowly around her palm.

"Excuse me." Olivia's voice was strangely calm as she edged past Mia in the doorway, walking down the hall to the living room, where Sergeant Renn had her overnight bag open and was writing down the contents in his notebook. It was very difficult not to look furtive carrying out a task like that, Kieran thought, and Renn was no exception, straightening quickly as they came in.

Olivia went up to him, the cord in her outstretched hand.

"Is it her camera, Chris? Is that what you're looking for?"

Renn's eyes went to the charger, then to Olivia's face. He didn't reply out loud, but at last his head inclined a fraction. *Yeah.*

"Do you think someone took it?" Olivia's voice was very quiet. "The person who hurt her?"

A small shrug this time, perhaps involuntary. *Possibly.*

"Why, though?" she said. Renn didn't react at all to that one, Kieran noticed.

Olivia was staring up at him. "Why didn't you feel you could ask me? Chris? You could have just asked me if I knew where it was."

"We did, Liv," Renn said finally.

"No. No, you asked if anything was missing." Olivia sounded like she wanted to be angry but didn't have the energy to be anything but sad. "That is a very broad question, isn't it? I mean, Bronte kept all her stuff in her own room." She looked down at the charger in her hand. "She had to keep all her stuff in her own room because I had a go at her in her first week for leaving things lying around the house."

Olivia squeezed her eyes shut at the memory.

"I answered everything you asked me, Chris, the best I could," she said when she finally opened them again. "If I missed something, it was because I'd come home to pick up my mat on the way to yoga with my mum and found Bronte was dead."

Sergeant Renn looked at her, and Kieran remembered the hot flush that used to creep up his neck. There was no sign of that now, but his expression had softened a notch.

"Yeah. All right," he said quietly. He nodded at her overnight bag. "Look, I'll help you carry this to the station. Get someone to give you a lift to your mum's."

"I was going to stop by Ash's place."

Renn stroked his chin, almost certainly thinking of Trish Birch outside the police station. "Not really any of my business, Liv, but I reckon your mum might need to see you more."

Fresh anguish crossed Olivia's face, and she bent down to zip up her bag.

A figure was trudging along the road as they all stepped out through the front gate. Sean, Kieran could see. He turned his head as he passed Renn and Olivia setting off together toward town and slowed his pace. They acknowledged him but didn't stop.

"What's happened? Is Liv okay?" Sean asked as he reached Kieran and Mia outside Fisherman's Cottage. He looked fresh from the sea, his skin still damp where it met his shirt. The *Nautilus Blue* must be back in the marina. Sean saw his own torch in Kieran's hand, then looked up, confused. "What's going on?"

"The good news is that you get this back." Kieran handed over the torch and explained about the missing camera. Sean's face creased as he listened.

"Do they think something's on the camera?"

Kieran shrugged. "Renn didn't say. It looked to me like Bronte was more into drawing than photography, anyway."

"Yeah. That's what I heard." Sean stared at the house. "So what does this mean for everything?"

Kieran could see the concern but, behind the flicker of the eyes, something else. A calculation. *What does this mean for Liam?*

"I don't know, mate," Kieran said, honestly.

"Did Renn say anything else?"

"He barely said anything at all," Mia said, and Sean looked over. "I'm pretty sure he only confirmed the camera thing for Liv because he felt bad about what her mum said earlier. Trish cornered him outside the station. Was going on about how they need to take things seriously this time. I guess she still thinks he and Sergeant Mallott didn't do enough for Gabby."

Sean turned his torch over in his hands, his face troubled. "I thought they did take things with Gabby seriously. It all felt pretty thorough considering—" He stopped awkwardly. Didn't glance at Kieran. "Considering everything else going on during the storm."

"Yeah, they did take it seriously," Mia said, her voice hard and flat. "I had to go into the police station with my parents three times in those days before Gabby's bag was found."

"That many?" Sean looked surprised. "What for?"

"Because the librarian told them Gabby and I had been arguing."

"Were you? What about?"

"Nothing," Mia lied. "We weren't."

She didn't look at Kieran, and he didn't look at her. They had already had this conversation, within the first year they'd been together, on what was the anniversary of the storm and of Gabby's disappearance. They had been in Kieran's student flat, trying to go about things as normal but both becoming increasingly withdrawn as the day stretched out. Mia had been making dinner and finally dropped the knife she'd been using on the cutting board with a clatter.

"I didn't tell the police the truth," she said. "Back then, when they asked what Gabby and I were fighting about."

The words seemed to come out of nowhere, but Kieran could tell they had been brewing all day. Longer. For years, probably. He looked up from the couch and waited. Surprised, but at the same time, strangely not. The day of the storm had been so surreal, he felt there was nothing about it that could surprise him now.

Mia breathed out. "We were arguing about you."

"Me?" So Kieran could still be surprised, he was interested to find.

"I had this stupid—" Mia rolled her eyes. "God, I don't know. Schoolgirl crush. On you. It was ridiculous. You didn't even notice I was alive back—"

"Mia, I did—"

"No." She held up a hand to cut him off. "You didn't. And that's exactly how it should've been. I was fourteen, you were eighteen. So it's fine. But all the girls in our year knew you—you and Ash anyway—and I'd told Gabby that I had this *thing* for you. Then on the day of the storm, in the library—"

Mia fiddled with the partially chopped vegetables in front of her.

"Gabby said she'd found out you and Olivia were sneaking around together. And I was so jealous, which was so stupid, because it's not like I was even on your radar." She sighed. "But it was partly the way Gabby told me as well. We were supposed to be best friends but she was so *gleeful*. Like she knew it would hurt me but she couldn't wait to tell me anyway."

Mia began chopping again.

"Anyway, I told her I didn't believe her, even though I kind of did really. She got upset, I got upset. I wanted to go home. She followed me. It was obvious I was annoyed and she spent half the time trying to convince me she was telling the truth and the other half apologizing. And after all that, she was right. You told me yourself, you really were meeting up with Olivia."

Kieran had stood up and gone over to her. "I'm sorry."

Mia had wiped her eyes with the back of her wrist. "No, it's not your fault. And it wasn't Gabby's fault. I'm just sad that that was the last time I ever saw her. I wish it had been different."

"Why didn't you tell the police this when they asked?"

"Because I was fourteen. And both my parents were in the room with me the whole time I was being interviewed, and I was too embarrassed. And I knew if I'd told the truth my mum would have been worried because, you know—" Mia shrugged. "None of the mums in Evelyn Bay were the biggest fans of you and Ash back then."

Kieran had pictured Mia's mum. Regal, soft-spoken, very kind. "I thought Nina liked me?"

"She does," Mia said. "Now."

Kieran thought about this as he looked at Mia standing in front of Fisherman's Cottage. The cellophane around the flowers rustled. The house looked lifeless once more.

"But the police spoke to heaps of people in those days when we were all searching for Gabby," Sean was saying. "I mean, how many times was your dad called in, Kieran?"

"A couple, I think," Kieran said quickly, not wanting to get into that again. "Liv said her mum had had a bit of trouble coming to terms with things. Maybe that's all Trish really meant."

"Okay, but Jesus." Sean's face darkened. "I know she's been through a lot, but join the bloody club. We've all had to come to terms with stuff we didn't want to." He took a breath. "Sorry. I'm sorry. That sounded really harsh." He shook his head as though to clear it and looked at Kieran. "Are you guys going home? I was actually on my way to your place."

"Oh really?" Kieran said. They started walking.

"Your mum called me. Said she's clearing stuff out and has a couple of life jackets she's getting rid of."

Kieran pictured the cupboards still filled with all the trash and treasure that no one had yet begun to tackle. "Yeah, not long left now until the move."

Sean didn't answer. He was distracted, staring hard at the road in front of them as they walked. Finally he took a breath.

"Listen, mate, I'm sorry to ask, but did Renn say anything else at all about this camera thing back there? Or Liam?"

Kieran hesitated. "They asked us about Liam. Earlier at the station. Renn and Pendlebury."

Sean looked up. *And?* The unspoken question hung in the air.

"I said I thought it could have been his car we saw on Saturday night." Kieran could feel Mia's eyes on him. "Driving toward town, like he said."

"And that was it? That's all they asked about?"

Kieran didn't look over. "Pretty much."

"Okay. Thanks, mate," Sean said quietly. It seemed like he wanted to add something more, but stopped as they reached Kieran's parents' house.

Verity was on her knees in front of a kitchen cupboard when they arrived, sweeping things into boxes.

"Oh good, I'll get those life jackets," she said when she saw Sean. She disappeared outside and returned holding them over her arm.

"Thanks," Sean said. "I've got a few on their last legs after the summer, so this is great."

"It's good you've been busy," Verity said. "It must be nearly time to open the wreck, isn't it?"

"Yeah, getting close," Sean said. "Got the first clients in a couple of weeks."

"God, I used to love it down there when I was younger," Verity said. "Brian as well. That's kind of how we met."

"Really?" Sean said, and Mia also looked over in interest. Kieran just waited. He and Finn had heard the stories plenty of times over the years.

"Yeah." Verity's smile changed her face, and Kieran realized how long it had been since he'd seen that. "I mean, I knew who Brian was, I'd seen him around. But then a group of us began going out to the *Mary Minerva* on someone's dad's boat, and it was out there where I really got to know him. We started talking, and then we started diving together, and then we started meeting up back on shore." Verity smiled to herself. "We used to go out there all the time together. Even when we weren't diving. We'd anchor a boat near the wreck, swim over to the caves, and spend the day on the beach."

Kieran remembered standing in that kitchen with Finn and hearing that very same story.

"Oh God, please, I'm begging you. Just stop there." Finn had rolled his eyes good-naturedly as Verity and Brian exchanged intimate smiles across the table. "None of us needs to hear that I was conceived on that beach or anything, thanks very much."

"Not you, mate," Brian had said with a grin, throwing his arm around Kieran, who had groaned while Finn laughed.

Verity looked at the old life jackets now in Sean's hands.

"Brian used to love it out on the water," she was saying. "We used to free dive. Not around the wreck, obviously, but in the shallows."

"Seriously?" Sean laughed. "That's pretty hard-core. Even I don't do that."

"No." Verity's smile faded and she touched one of the packing boxes with the toe of her shoe. "Well. It was a different time."

A muffled thump came from Brian's study, followed by a barked swear word. Verity watched the door. When she turned back, her face seemed ten years older.

"You should come," Sean said suddenly, and they all looked at him. "Tomorrow. Come for a dive. Conditions will be okay. I'll be going out anyway, it'd be good to take a couple of people down. Do a practice run. Come. All of you."

Kieran saw Mia, who had never taken to breathing underwater, already shaking her head. Sean looked back to him and Verity. "Or both of you, then. See it again before you leave."

"Well—" Verity glanced again at the study door. "I suppose I could check if the respite carer is available but . . ." She was tempted, Kieran could tell. There was another small thump from the study, and what was becoming a familiar shadow crossed her face. "But it's probably not a good idea. Thank you, though."

"Yeah, no worries." Sean shrugged. "Let me know if you change—"

He broke off as the study door squeaked open. As though

feeling the heat of their collective attention, Brian stepped out. He stopped in the kitchen doorway when he saw them all standing there. His features folded with bewilderment, annoyance, and something that looked very much to Kieran like fear. His dad didn't know who they were or what was going on, and he was scared. Brian's uncertain gaze darted around the room before fixing suddenly on Audrey, who stared back from Mia's arms, unsure whether or not to burst into tears.

"Everything all right, love?" Verity aimed for light and airy but fell some way short.

Brian pointed. "Who's that baby?"

"That's Audrey, our—"

"No. I meant, what's it doing here?"

"Brian—"

"I don't understand." His eyes clouded with confusion. "I thought that girl of Finn's decided not to go ahead with it in the end."

Verity looked like she'd been slapped. Her mouth hardened, and she shook her head, stiff and tight.

"Audrey is Kieran and Mia's baby. Our granddaughter. She's visiting."

Brian stared at Audrey a moment longer, then made an irritated noise in the back of his throat. He dismissed her with a flick of his hand and, without another word, turned and shuffled back into his study. The soft click of the door echoed through the kitchen.

•   •   •

The water was cold, Kieran knew, but he had stopped feeling it a while ago. He was neck-deep, his toes just able to scrape the sand during the dip between waves. The light was fading fast as the evening drew in. Kieran let the next wave lift him, treading water as it surged and passed. He had swum, long fast laps, and was tired now. But he couldn't seem to make himself get out of the water.

After Brian had returned to his study, Sean had gathered his life jackets and torch and made to leave.

Verity, who had been staring glassy-eyed at the kitchen table, blinked. "Oh Sean, I'm sorry. He's very—"

"Come diving, Verity." Sean had stopped her. "Before you move. Anytime you want. You know what it's like down there. Focus, breathing, all that good stuff." He gave her a small smile. "Doesn't leave too much space to worry about anything else."

"Thank you. I'll think about it," she'd said, in a way that suggested she actually might.

Kieran had left Mia in their bedroom, rereading a G. R. Barlin novel she'd found on his bookshelf while trying to persuade Audrey to sleep. He'd grabbed some empty packing boxes and started systematically stripping the clutter from every cupboard and shelf in the living room. After a little while, he'd heard Verity clattering with boxes of her own in the kitchen. He could hear nothing from his dad's study.

Kieran worked fast, making the decisions on first sight—*box or bin, box or bin*. He skimmed entirely over paperwork, boxing it blindly without reading it. He had made the mistake of looking too closely once before, two years after Finn had died, when Kieran had been searching for his own birth certificate. He'd instead stumbled across a worksheet that Brian had half completed during what could only have been a counseling session.

Kieran's immediate reaction had been utter astonishment that Brian had engaged with any kind of therapy at all. He wondered if Verity had bullied him into it or, more likely, Kieran suspected, Brian's grief had manifested itself physically. It had happened to Kieran too for a while, with persistent headaches and stomach problems that seemed to have no real cause or cure. Brian Elliott would never have sought help to get his head straight, Kieran knew, but he might have if his body was letting him down.

The worksheet had been marked CONFIDENTIAL across the top, so Kieran had of course read it in its entirety. He wasn't sure what the task had been, but Brian had filed his thoughts into two columns.

Kieran was only eighteen, Brian had written. *Kieran was old enough to have known better. Kieran made an honest mistake. Kieran put his brother in danger.*

The argument continued all the way down the page.

Finn could make his own choices. Kieran should never have put him in that position. Finn would have done everything he could to save Kieran. Kieran needed his help.

At the very bottom of the page, a conclusion: *Kieran is*

Brian hadn't finished. Kieran had spent the rest of that week ransacking the house trying to find a second page or another worksheet, but if Brian had ever completed his thought, it had not been on paper.

Kieran is . . . what?

He'd returned to that question a lot over the years.

Kieran had turned back to the task at hand and was about to shove another folder of documents into a shoebox when he'd heard movement in the doorway.

"Thanks for doing this." Verity was running her eyes over the near-empty shelves. "You've made good progress."

"No worries. Can I do anything to help with Dad?"

Verity gave a bleak smile. "I think that's a bit beyond both of us, unfortunately."

She picked up one of the stacks of papers and leafed through them. A corner of a photo stuck out and she pulled it free.

"That was a nice day," she said, turning the image so Kieran could see. "I remember that being taken."

Finn, Toby, and the *Nautilus Black*. It wasn't exactly the same photo as the one that had been pinned up on the Surf and Turf bulletin board for a year after their deaths, but it was a close variation. The composition was essentially the same—the two men, their arms around each other, the champagne, the new paint shining on the boat in the background—but it had been taken a few seconds earlier or later and the overall effect was weaker. The men's smiles were a little less natural, and Finn's eyes were hooded on the cusp of a blink. It didn't have the buoyancy of the original but somehow seemed a little more real. Verity ran her thumb across Finn's face.

"We've got the better version in an album somewhere," she said, almost to herself.

"Hey," Kieran hesitated. "What was Dad talking about earlier? About Finn and a baby?"

He could tell that Verity was considering bluffing, but either the inclination or the energy fell away and she shook her head.

"I honestly don't know. Finn was always closer to your dad than he was to me."

She broke off as there was a clatter from Brian's study. She closed her eyes and took several deep breaths. When she opened them, her face was tight.

"Do you think you could call Sean?" she said. "Ask if we can go diving tomorrow after all?"

"Sure. If you want to."

Verity, ignoring another ominous thump, put the photo of Finn back on the pile, facedown. "Yes," she said. "I think I do."

Kieran drifted up to his neck in the sea now, still thinking about Verity and Brian and Finn as he watched the twilight creep in. He had gone out deep and swum a few more laps back and forth between his parents' house and Fisherman's Cottage, and was now treading water somewhere in the middle.

He had seen only two dog walkers—both male—on the

beach the whole time he'd been out, but as he bobbed in the growing gloom now, he caught a sudden flash of movement of someone cutting down one of the side paths. Kieran stilled in the water as he watched. Not coming after blokes and babies, he told himself. He believed it, but he was still a little relieved when the figure came into view. Olivia's mum, Trish Birch.

She was wearing the same dress as earlier in the day when she'd confronted Sergeant Renn at the police station, but now she was holding something gray and bulky under one arm.

The beach was deserted as she checked both ways along the sand, her gaze skimming right over Kieran, submerged to his chin in the waves under the darkening sky.

He watched as Trish crossed the beach and picked her way over the flat rocks that cut out into the sea. The same rocks where Gabby was last seen by Brian Elliott, twelve years earlier as the storm clouds grew. The rocks were slippery then and would be slippery now, Kieran thought as he watched the woman edge her way out, still clutching the bulky object. He frowned. What was she doing?

Trish reached the tip of the rocks and Kieran was about to call out—a warning or something, he wasn't sure—when to his astonishment, she took the bulk in both hands and, with some effort, swung her arms through a graceful arc and hurled it straight into the sea.

Kieran's mouth opened, letting in salt water. Locals never threw things into their ocean. He couldn't remember the last time he had ever seen someone toss something in. Even the floral tributes to Bronte had been placed well above the tide line so the plastic wrapping wouldn't float away. Trish watched the gray shape bob once or twice and then, with Kieran still wondering if it had somehow been an accident, she stepped away from the brink, picked her way back over the rocks, and walked straight across the beach to disappear the way she'd come. The whole thing had taken less than a minute from start to finish and the beach was deserted once again. It was like she had never been there.

Except—Kieran swiveled now in the water, turning back to the outcrop. The gray object was still visible, floating out to sea. He'd made the decision before he'd even fully formed the question and was cutting through the water with long freestyle strokes. He could feel the current pulling him and did a quick check, head up, wiping the water from his eyes. The shape had drifted even farther, well into the deep water. All around Kieran, the light was fading and the horizon to the east was a silvery line. He thought about Mia and Audrey and slowed.

He could see the object was taking on water fast now, its air pockets leaking. It hung low and heavy in the water, barely breaking the surface. One try, Kieran decided. He put his face down and kicked hard.

It was gone by the time he reached the spot. He drew in a full breath, upended his body, and dived, fingers outstretched, eyes open but blind in the black water. His lungs were tight from the effort of the swim, and he knew as soon as he was under that he hadn't got enough air to go deep. He was on the verge of kicking up—back to the surface and the air, back to Mia and Audrey— when his fingers grazed fabric.

A bag. Kieran swung his arm and caught a strap, clamping it tightly in his fist. He pulled. The bag was heavy and it jerked his arm, dragging him deeper. He tightened his grip, turned his face upward, and kicked.

He gasped as he broke through to the air, treading water for a minute as he caught his breath. He ran his free hand over the bag. Some sort of backpack, he could tell now. It felt like it was growing heavier by the second and at last, worried he would drop it, Kieran began battling his way back to shore.

He carried the bag out, dumping it faceup in the sand, and flopped down next to it, his heart pounding. It was an ordinary gray backpack, from what he could see in the dying light. It appeared in good condition other than being soaking wet. Possibly even brand-new. Kieran kneeled next to it. He hesitated, but only for a second. He reached out, unzipped the flap, and looked in.

Kieran blinked, not understanding what he was seeing. The bag was filled with rocks. He put his hand in and pulled out the top one. It was definitely a rock, the kind that lay around every garden or pathway in Evelyn Bay. He turned it over in his hand. It seemed completely unremarkable. He put it down on the sand, then reached in again and again. Soon he had a small pile of rocks and a completely empty backpack. Kieran felt around inside, checking for anything caught in the lining or an inside pocket. There was nothing else in there.

He sat back on the sand and picked up the bag itself. There was no name tag, nothing to indicate who it belonged to, but as he turned it over he stopped. Across the back, and hard to make out in what was left of the light, he saw something. The writing had been made on the pale gray canvas in permanent black marker. It had survived the water unscathed.

A phone number, and two words: *Please call.*

21

Kieran stared at the two words until the letters started to lose meaning. Then he replaced each rock in the bag and carried the whole thing back along the beach to where his towel, clothes, and phone were still waiting for him on the sand beyond his parents' veranda. He picked up his phone, turned the bag over, and dialed the number. He listened without speaking, then slowly hung up.

Kieran slipped his hoodie on and, at a loss as to what to do next, sat on his towel with the backpack at his feet and the clear starry sky above him. He stared out at the perfect straight line where the inky sky met the blackness of the water, thinking. He didn't know how long he stayed like that, but his board shorts had almost dried when his phone pinged in his hand.

Kieran wasn't sure what he'd been expecting, but when he checked the screen it was simply an alert that reminded him to stop for two minutes and be fully aware and present in his surroundings. He was supposed to do it every day but hadn't managed once since he'd been back in Evelyn Bay. He was still gazing at his phone and debating whether or not he could face doing it now when a noise made him jump.

"G'day," a voice called. "What's got you so engrossed?"

"Hard-core porn." Kieran swiped the screen closed as he turned to see Ash shut the gate behind him and approach across the sand, a six-pack of beer dangling from his hand. "What's up?"

"In that case, you've probably got time for at least one," Ash said, offering him a bottle. "Mia said you were out here."

"Thanks." Kieran took the beer and Ash kicked out a corner of Kieran's towel and sat down. They both looked out at the water, drinks in hand, the way they had a hundred times before.

"Been swimming?"

Kieran nodded. "Weirdest bloody thing happened."

"Oh yeah?" Ash lifted the bottle to his lips.

"Yeah." Kieran pulled Trish Birch's wet backpack closer and told him what he'd seen.

Ash was quiet when he'd finished. "Right."

"God knows what she's doing." Kieran moved the bag so they could see the writing, hard to make out now in the dark. *Please call.* "That's Trish's own cell number. I rang it, went through to her voicemail." He sat back. "So, what do you reckon? Do I tell someone? Renn?"

"Well—" Ash stroked his stubble. He did not seem as surprised by all this as he might be. "Maybe don't. If you don't mind. Trish does this sometimes."

Kieran stared. "Sorry, does what exactly?"

"This." Ash pointed at the backpack. "Chucks a bag of rocks in—yeah, I know, mate, it's insane—" He grinned despite himself at Kieran's expression. "Sorry, no, it's not funny at all. And I shouldn't say 'insane,' that's not fair." Ash's smile faded. "I didn't know Trish had started again, though. Liv hasn't said anything, so maybe she doesn't know either."

"What is it she's doing, though?"

Ash took a long pull on his beer and swallowed. "It's something to do with Gabby's backpack, and where it was found after she went missing. The bag washing ashore three days later, right by the place Gabby was last seen?" Ash shrugged. "Trish has got it into her head that there's no way it could have happened like that."

"But it did," Kieran said. "That's where it was found."

"Yeah, Trish reckons it was dumped."

There was a long silence.

"She thinks Gabby's bag was dumped?"

"Yep," Ash said. "Deliberately. I guess so it would be found in the water and the search called off, whatever. I don't know."

"Are you kidding?"

"No."

Kieran looked down the dark beach. He could no longer make out the spot where he had watched Trish Birch. The same spot where Gabby had last been seen by Brian twelve years earlier, and where her purple-striped backpack full of library books had been found sandy and sea drenched on the shore, after three days of searching. Kieran turned back to Ash.

"Dumped by who?"

"Who knows?" Ash shrugged. "That'd be the big question, I guess."

"Has Trish talked to Renn about it?"

"Yeah, she has. I mean, I only know all this through Liv. But it started a while ago, around the ten-year anniversary mark—" Kieran remembered Olivia mentioning the anniversary in the cemetery. What had she said? *Mum found it hard.* Clearly.

"And I guess Trish felt Renn wasn't taking her seriously enough," Ash was saying. "So she started testing it out. Throwing backpacks in, seeing what happened to them."

"And what did happen?"

Ash shrugged. "I think most disappeared without a trace, so God knows how many she chucked in. But one was pulled up in a fishing net, and then another got caught around Mike Tate's boat propeller. Did a fair bit of damage, so Trish had to come clean. Renn managed to smooth things over, kind of made it go away—"

"That wouldn't have been too easy. Expensive mistake to fix."

"Yeah, well, you know." Ash drained his bottle and shrugged. "Renn's always had a bit of a thing for Liv. Or maybe he felt guilty for not listening to Trish in the first place, who knows? Anyway . . ." Ash reached for another beer. "Whatever. He made Trish promise not to do it anymore, but that was around the time she got a bit heavy-handed with the old sleeping pills, so that's when Liv moved back to keep an eye on her."

Kieran looked at the backpack. "Do you think Trish has secretly been doing this the whole time or just started again?"

"Hard to say." Ash shook his head. "Best guess would be she's started again. This whole thing with Bronte has sent everyone a bit crazy. Have you seen that online forum? It's going nuts."

"EBOCH? Yeah."

Kieran had ventured back into the pixelated world of the Evelyn Bay Online Community Hub that afternoon to find things were getting heated. The dam had broken and Liam's name was being bandied about freely now. Division lines were emerging between those who wanted this whole mess resolved so they could feel comfortable forgetting to lock their doors once more, and those who couldn't believe the cops were wasting their time looking at a local. Bronte herself, Kieran noticed, was barely mentioned at all.

He turned back to Ash. "I can see what happened to Bronte

would feel pretty bloody close to home for Trish. But what's she hoping for with this backpack thing? That she'll throw enough of these in to be able to prove some point about Gabby?"

"I have no idea. I suppose so."

"How many have washed up in that spot?"

"To be fair, not many, as far as I know." Ash kicked the bag with his toe. "But we're not exactly talking hard scientific conditions, are we?" He sighed. "Liv won't be pleased. She was saying before all this that she thought Trish might be turning a corner. Think she was hoping she might be able to head back to Melbourne."

"Would you go with her?"

"Think I'd be invited?" Ash's tone was light, but Kieran could detect the hint of a genuine question in there.

"I dunno, mate," he said, honestly.

Ash didn't reply straight away. "Liv's a bit pissed off I wasn't around earlier, when you guys were at her place with Renn. She says she's fine but that thing about Bronte's camera has left her shaken up."

"Yeah, that was weird. Makes you wonder what's on it."

"Or who, eh?" Ash rubbed his eyes. He sounded tired. "I would've been there with Liv if I could, but I had clients. I couldn't just drop them, they've got three rental places. I'll need the business over winter."

"Work going okay?"

"It's okay," Ash said, but a flat note in his tone suggested it was going no better than that.

"I walked by Wetherby House earlier."

Ash looked up at that. "Saw G. R. Barlin's handiwork on the garden?"

"Yeah."

Ash took a swallow of beer, a long one this time. "Yeah," he said finally. "I'm not sure what I'm going to do about that."

"There's not much you can do, is there? Not if he owns the place."

Ash didn't reply and, after a moment, shrugged. The moon had moved across the sky and Kieran was at the bottom of his second bottle when he stifled a yawn.

"I should let you go." Ash made to stand up and brushed the sand off his shorts. "You've probably got baby duties to attend to."

"You going home now?" Kieran said.

"In a while."

Kieran looked at him. "Avoiding Sean?"

Ash gave a half smile. "Maybe. He hasn't been around much himself, though. He's out at the wreck all day every day, then I think he goes to Sarah and Julian's place to see Liam. Things are weird now. The atmosphere in the house is shit. Sean's been—" Ash paused. "I don't even know how to describe it."

"I suppose he's worried about Liam."

"It's a bit of that. But I think he also knows if it comes down to it, I wouldn't defend Liam."

Any warmth the sand had captured during the day had slipped away now and Kieran felt cold as he stood up. "Why not?"

"No inside knowledge or anything." Ash took his time draining the last of his beer. "Liam just reminds me a bit too much of us."

"Seriously?" Kieran thought about the sullen boy and felt almost insulted.

"Yeah. You don't think so?"

"No—" Kieran started, then stopped. Maybe.

"It's a few things. The footy stuff, the boozing, the girls—it's all the same as it was then. You know what it was like. I suppose it was all good fun, but—" Ash frowned and examined his empty bottle.

"Right."

Because it must have been good fun, Kieran thought, otherwise why did they do it every weekend? But it was interesting looking back how the good fun had sometimes felt a lot like hard work. Like the time Finn had congratulated Ash for successfully talking some girl into taking him back to her accommodation. On hearing this, Kieran had rolled up his sleeves, gone to a party at the beach that very night, and determinedly cast off his virginity in such a joylessly transactional exercise that the best bit had been being able to tell Ash and Finn it had happened.

Or all the other times he'd found himself standing in the sticky kitchen of yet another crusty holiday rental, shouting over the music at a girl he was barely interested in. Hoping she didn't wander off, though, because then Ash would laugh and Kieran would have no choice but to join Sean, who was inevitably standing awkward and alone in some corner, flushing red every time any girl even looked his way.

It had all seemed so important at the time, Kieran thought as he stood on the beach now. Life and death.

"Well"—Kieran looked over at Ash—"even if Liam is a bit of a dickhead, it doesn't mean he did something to Bronte."

"No." Ash sighed. "And I'm not saying he did. But there's always been something a bit off about him. Like the way he looks at Liv in the Surf and Turf when he thinks I'm not watching. Stuff he says to her. I dunno. Sean can't see it. He still thinks of Liam as this messed-up little kid who's struggling to make his way in the world, and whatever Liam is"—Ash shook his head—"he's not that."

A thin shaft of light broke over the sand. Across the beach and the back fence, Kieran could see Mia silhouetted in the doorway. She held a hand up to shield her eyes and was scanning the darkness for them. She didn't step out, though, Kieran noticed. Even knowing they were there somewhere, she still wasn't willing to be on that beach at night.

"I'll let you go, mate." Ash looked down at Trish Birch's backpack. "Do you want me to take that?"

"It's all right. I'll do something with it. You'll tell Liv about it?"

"Yeah, I'll have to. She won't be happy, though."

Kieran picked up the bag and weighed it in his hand. He remembered swimming after it, drawing in his breath as he dived down to chase it. It had been sinking fast. If he hadn't caught it, would it have washed up on the sand a few days later?

"What do you reckon about all this?" He couldn't read the writing on the bag anymore. "Do you reckon there's any chance Trish might be right?"

Ash ran a hand over his head. "God, who knows? I try not to get involved. Just help out Liv wherever I can. All I know is, that was a crazy day. A storm like that?" He shrugged. "A lot of things happened that day that'll never happen again."

Their eyes met this time, and something Kieran couldn't quite put his finger on passed between them. Then Ash looked at the house, and at Mia, who was still waiting.

"All right. I'd better be off." Ash turned to leave. He looked out into the night ahead of him. "Christ, they actually should do something about this beach. You can barely see a bloody thing out there."

Kieran watched as Ash raised a hand and walked away. Within a few steps, he was gone.

22

One of Kieran's favorite things about living in Sydney was no longer needing a cold-water wetsuit. He stood among the racks of rental equipment in Sean's shed at the marina, fighting his way into the thick material, and wondered how he had ever used to find this easy.

Verity had slipped into her borrowed suit with no trouble, and her voice now floated in from outside the shed, where she was standing in the sun talking to George Barlin.

"Is it okay if he comes too?" Sean had asked when Kieran had called to say they would like to see the wreck after all. "He's been hoping to go down for weeks."

"No worries. He's certified, is he?" Kieran wasn't sure why he was surprised.

"For around the outside, yeah. We'd all better stick to that anyway. I'm still not sure if anyone's going in this year." Sean had paused. "And listen, Liam'll be there as well."

"Right."

"He's part of the business. He needs to be ready when the Norwegians arrive."

"I didn't say anything, mate," Kieran said. "It's your decision who you take down."

"Yeah, sorry." Sean had sighed. "He needs something to keep him busy. Julian reckons he can't have him back in the Surf and Turf for a while. And Liam said something the other day that made me think people are giving him a hard time when he's out. He says they're not, but now he just sits at home all day with his mum."

Kieran had duly expected Liam to be subdued, but had still been taken aback when they'd approached the *Nautilus Blue* that morning. Liam's head hung down and his movements were overthought and slow. He'd barely glanced up from loading the oxygen tanks as they walked over, and even then his eyes had such a faraway look that Kieran had immediately decided to double-check every piece of equipment Liam handed them.

George Barlin, at least, was in good spirits.

"I've been waiting for this all summer," Kieran could hear him saying to Verity now. "I've wanted to go down to the wreck for years, but I wasn't qualified for the depth."

"I haven't been down there in a good while," Verity said.

"How long?"

"I don't know. Long enough that if the certification could expire, it would have. I've done a lot of shallower dives, though. My husband used to really enjoy it too. Have you been out to the *Mary Minerva* site at all?"

"On a boat? No, but I've seen it from land. Went up to the lookout to see The Survivors. Interesting piece of art."

"It is. It looks different from the water. Brian and I used to sail out to that spot about once a year—"

Kieran stopped, one arm in his wetsuit, listening. He was a little surprised. He hadn't known that.

"Well, actually, we used to go exactly once a year," Verity

was saying. "For the anniversary of our older son's death. He drowned, sadly."

"I know. I'm sorry," George said. "Finn, right? It was tragic."

"Yes." Verity sounded a little surprised that George knew his name. "Thank you."

"I was here myself that summer, running a writing course. I've never seen anything like that storm in my life," George said. "I've been reading around it a bit at the library since I got back. Having a look at the old photos and things. But I remember it myself. It was terrible. Very difficult if you're caught out on the water in that. Liam's father was on the same boat, wasn't he?"

"Toby." Verity's voice was so soft Kieran had to strain to hear. "They weren't caught out on the water, though. They were responding to an emergency call for Kieran."

"That's what they were doing?" George's words were also close to inaudible. "I knew Kieran had an accident, but I hadn't realized the two were connected."

"Yeah. Finn and Toby went out on the boat to try to save him."

"Oh." George paused. "But, sorry Verity, I thought—"

Kieran couldn't listen to any more. He forced his other arm into the wetsuit, zipped it up, and shut the shed door behind him, loudly enough to make the voices outside fall silent.

• • •

The rush of the wind and waves made it hard to talk on board the *Nautilus Blue*, but as they rounded the point and the caves came into view in the distance, George shifted from where he was sitting.

"Amazing," he said as The Survivors came into sight. The trio stood strong and straight, the water lapping at their waists.

Struggling under the weight of his gear, George scrabbled to the other side of the boat and pulled his phone out of his backpack. His arm lurched as he tried to line it up straight with the horizon and take a photo.

"How many actually survived the shipwreck?" he said to no one in particular.

"It's not known exactly," Verity said. She was also watching the sculpture as they drew nearer. "Officially twelve, but they think there might have been a few more than that."

"The records aren't great?"

"There were a couple of men with various charges pending." Verity gave a small smile. "They didn't manage to make it to shore to have their day in court. And a few others who probably had mistresses they preferred to their wives and kids."

"Is that right?" George said. "So, what? They disappeared into the water and resurfaced as someone else?"

"Maybe. Who knows?"

"That's why you can't trust anyone in Evelyn Bay," Liam said suddenly. He'd been staring out at the water with his chin in his hand. If he'd meant it as a joke, it fell flat.

Sean cleared his throat.

"Not to endorse what Liam's saying," he said with forced levity. "But if you want to lock your bag away in the dry box, George, I'll secure it before we go under."

"Phone too?"

"Yeah, best place. The box is watertight, it'll be fine in there."

George snapped a couple more photos, then handed his things over. He turned back to the shore.

"I wonder what the passengers on the *Mary Minerva* made of that sight?" George said. "One of the last things most of them would have seen, I guess."

Kieran followed his gaze to the caves, their gaping mouths opening onto the thin strip of beach that flashed white with each breaking wave. The Survivors stared back at him, impassive. A particularly large wave crashed into the sculpture, and the woman at the edge of the trio disappeared completely for a second. Kieran looked away.

Sean was squinting into the water as he guided the boat.

"Right." He cut the engine. "We're here."

They took turns jumping from the catamaran into the water, and as Kieran submerged he was immediately grateful for his cold-water suit. The waves that had been rough at the surface became calm once the water closed over Kieran's head, and the weight of his equipment dissolved.

They descended in single file, following the anchor line down. Liam led the way, disappearing first into the murky green. George followed, and then it was Kieran's turn. He traced the line with his gloved fist, listening to the inward hiss and outward roar of his own breathing. Somewhere above Kieran was Verity, with Sean the last on the line. Kieran inhaled and exhaled as he let himself sink deeper, to the wreckage waiting below.

He peered through the cloudy green water, watching for the Mary Minerva to take form. The skeletal outline emerged first, like a crude bird's-eye sketch of a boat. It almost looked intact for a few moments, through that dense watery filter, but as Kieran descended farther a tangled nest of fallen beams and collapsed walls sharpened into detail. The remains of the ship lay silent and still on a clear bed of sand, too deep for seaweed to grow.

Kieran let go of the line and floated, watching fish drift in and out as he saw Verity appear. She glided down next to him, almost anonymous in her suit and mask.

"Verity, you pair with Kieran," Sean had said back up on the surface. "And George—" Sean had hesitated and glanced at Liam, whose expression had been dark. "You stick with Liam, and I'll go between you all."

Neither Liam nor George had looked particularly happy with

this arrangement, but now Kieran could see the two men moving together up ahead. The pair swam slowly along the side of the wreck, thick white clouds bubbling from their masks in regular bursts. George may have been certified, but he'd done his training in warm water, Kieran could tell. He had the upright swimming style of divers used to better visibility, and rather than sticking to a frog kick, he kept lapsing into a flipper kick that stirred up sediment in cold water, making it hard to see.

Kieran and Verity exchanged a look as best they could through their masks and turned and swam in the other direction. They passed Sean hovering in the midst of the tangled mess as he examined something with his torch. He raised his hand, thumb and finger forming a circle. *Okay?* They reflected the gesture. *Okay.*

Kieran let Verity lead the way, floating alongside her as they moved around the ship's bow, still tall and towering. Verity kicked—with the correct frog-like motion—and swam up the length of the metal, tracing its curve. She turned back to Kieran and gestured for him to join her.

This had been a good idea of Sean's, Kieran thought now. The breathing, the buoyancy. Everything about it was otherworldly. No wonder Verity liked it. It felt as though they were in a different reality. He liked it too.

They swam side by side, stopping for a few minutes by the ship's anchor, now thick and swollen with rust. Verity reached out and touched Kieran's arm as a fish whipped out from the wreck and flashed by. Kieran felt the mild sway of current as she moved.

Gabby's backpack.

The thought came to him with the flow of water. Kieran had never really stopped to consider that bag before, beyond the tragically obvious implication. But he thought about it now. The search had ground to a halt after the bag was found washed up on the beach by a group of dog walkers. The soaked purple mass had been pulled out of the water within sight of the rocks where Gabby had last been seen before the storm hit; the same storm that had torn up trees and destroyed homes and roared into the caves and swallowed The Survivors whole. The same storm that had flipped a boat and dragged two strong local men to their deaths.

Kieran paused beside the wreck and felt the weight of the underwater currents press against his wetsuit. A push and pull, firm and persistent. The water did what it wanted. So it was lucky—perhaps he'd even go so far as to say conveniently lucky—that Gabby's bag had been found at all. Kieran thought about this now as he floated, and felt a strange coldness seep through him that had nothing to do with the ocean.

He swam on, distracted enough by his thoughts that it took him a second to realize that Verity had pulled up short. She was pointing at something through the water, and Kieran looked over to see George swimming toward them, very fast, his legs flipper-kicking up a cloud of sediment. Immediately on high alert, Kieran surged forward to meet him, one hand ready to grab his backup respirator line in case George reached up with that terrible cut-throat slashing signal. *No air.*

But no, Kieran could see now as they came face-to-face. George still had his primary respirator in his mouth, the bursts of bubbles flowing normally, if a little fast.

Kieran put his finger and thumb together. *Okay?*

George's expression was distorted by his mask but his hand immediately went out flat, palm down, twisting back and forth at the wrist. *Something wrong.*

Kieran pointed, trying to work out what. *Mask? Oxygen?* George was shaking his head. He raised a hand, his thumb and first finger forming an L shape with his glove, and suddenly Kieran realized what was right in front of him. George was all alone. Kieran twisted around. Near the stern, he could make out only the beam of Sean's torch as it bounced and swept over the twisted wreckage. He could see no other diver. No Liam.

George was making an L shape again and a frantic thumbs-up motion.

Kieran repeated it back to make sure he'd understood. *Liam has gone to the surface?*

George started nodding behind his mask.

Kieran put out his flat palm and twisted his wrist. *Something wrong?*

Yes. A mirrored reply. *Something wrong.*

23

The ascent to the surface felt like the longest one Kieran could remember. They had found Sean and immediately begun the slow crawl upward. Kieran could tell Sean was considering pulling ahead, calculating how far he could push the safety standards. He was starting to drift up, and Kieran had reached out and caught his wrist. *Don't. Stay.* Kieran could see the effort it took him to slow down, but he did, and the four of them moved toward the surface together. Another minute, another nine meters.

Liam was on the boat.

He was sitting cross-legged, hunched over as he stared across the sea to the caves on the shore. He had stripped off all his equipment including his wetsuit and was shivering in just his shorts, a towel draped around his shoulders. He looked up as they emerged.

"What happened?" Sean was the first on board, his fear visibly waning at the sight of his nephew alive, if perhaps not completely well. Sean waited, but Liam wouldn't meet his eye.

"I dunno."

"You don't know?"

Kieran had not often seen Sean angry, but he was fast getting there now.

"Liam?" Sean tried again. "Oi. Hey. You listening? What's going on?"

"I said. Nothing."

"Nothing?"

"I'd had enough, all right?"

Sean stared at his nephew. "Are you serious? So, what, you just decided to come up? Didn't bother telling anyone?"

"George saw me." He didn't glance at the writer, who was watching Liam closely, his brow creased.

"That's not what I bloody meant," Sean said. "And leaving George is a whole other thing for you and me to have a very long chat about, by the way."

"Yeah, okay. I can hear." Liam shook his head. "I don't know what I can tell you. I'd had enough of being down there so I came up."

Sean looked at him, shivering on the deck. "Did you even ascend properly?"

A small nod. The only sound was the water lapping against the boat.

"All right," Sean said, finally. "Let's get back. We'll talk about this later. You got anything you want to say to everyone?"

No answer.

"Liam? Jesus, you're still not even listening—"

"I am. Sorry. It's just—" Liam was frowning now, his eyes focused on the shore.

"What? What's going on, mate?"

"There's something wrong out there, you know."

Sean blinked. "Down at the wreck?"

"No. Out there." They all turned to follow Liam's gaze, toward The Survivors and the cliffs and caves beyond.

"What are you on about?" Sean frowned.

"The birds have been all riled up lately." Liam's voice was still flat. "On and off. Something's been scaring them."

George tilted his head, squinting. Above the cliffs, the sky was mostly still and clear. "They look fine now."

"And what would you know about how things are around here, mate?" Liam snapped. "You don't even know how to kick properly." He sighed, his energy spent. "They're fine right now, but they've been getting worked up about something." He jerked his head in Kieran's direction. "It happened the other day when he and his baby were messing around down there, and the day before that."

"You went down to the caves?" Verity said sharply, fixing Kieran with a gaze that made him squirm. "With Audrey?"

"Yeah. Only once, though. And not for long."

His mother did not look away. "Why would you do that?"

"I hadn't planned to, I—" Kieran stopped. He couldn't explain. "The tide was out. It was fine."

Verity didn't answer but continued to stare at him in a way that set him on edge.

"What, Mum?" he said. "For God's sake, she's my child."

Verity still didn't reply. Kieran could feel the others watching and he turned away, annoyed.

"Perhaps it was a sea eagle," George said out of nowhere, and they all looked over. He shrugged at Liam. "Upsetting the birds. Could there have been a sea eagle around? Trying to get at the babies?"

Liam blinked at him. "I don't know." He looked very tired. "Yeah. Maybe."

There was a roar as Sean fired up the engine. "Christ. Let's just get back to land."

•   •   •

If the journey out to the wreck had been quiet, the journey back was silent in a different way. The mood was still somber as they disembarked.

George was off the boat as soon as they docked. He stripped out of his wetsuit, pulled on a T-shirt from his bag, and with a thank-you that managed to sound at least partly sincere, he disappeared through the marina gate, shaking his head.

As Liam took the wetsuit away to rinse it down, Sean turned to Kieran and Verity.

"I'm so sorry," he said, rubbing a hand over his face. "If you want to go out again another time—"

"It's fine, Sean. I wanted to see the wreck once more, and I did," Verity said as they headed to the shed to get changed. "So, thank you. Really."

Kieran had less trouble getting out of his wetsuit than he'd had getting into it, and this time it was him waiting outside the shed for Verity. Still a little cold from the water, he moved around to stand in the sun and leaned against the wall, feeling tired suddenly. Over the sound of equipment being hosed down around the back, he could hear Sean's voice.

"—know you're not having an easy time but—"

Liam gave a short hollow laugh at that. Sean ignored it.

"—but you can't leave people in the water. It's bad enough now, but you do that with the real clients and I could lose this business. Or something worse happens."

No answer.

"I mean it, mate. Liam? It's a serious safety issue. You know that. You can't—"

"I had to come up because I couldn't stay down there anymore." Liam's reply was so low Kieran barely caught the words.

"What do you mean?" Sean said.

"I got water in my mask and I was clearing it but I sucked some in and—" Liam stopped.

"That's nothing new, though." Sean's voice was soft now. "How many times has that happened? Hundreds."

"Yeah, I know. But this time—" It seemed for a second like Liam might not say any more. "When the water was in my nose and mouth I felt like I couldn't breathe. I mean, I could—the air was coming through and everything—but I felt like I couldn't, you know? I couldn't stand it. Being down there. So that's what happened. All right? I needed to breathe, so I came up."

There was a silence.

"Okay," Sean said. "All right, mate. You should have come and found me, though. Or anyone. Not disappeared like that."

"I know. But—" Liam sounded embarrassed now. "I didn't know how long I had. I was scared I was going to rip my mask off."

Neither of them spoke for another moment.

"Is it that bad?" Sean said.

"People thinking I killed a girl? Yeah, it's pretty bad."

Kieran heard movement around the front. Verity was ready. Still, he stayed where he was.

"All right." Sean's words were almost inaudible. "Maybe—" A pause. "Maybe don't mention this to anyone else for now, mate."

Verity's head appeared around the corner.

"Ready?" she said, and Liam's reply was lost.

"Yeah." Kieran stepped away from the shed, and he and Verity walked together out of the marina. As they hit the road, they both opened their mouths at the same time.

"Sorry," Kieran said. "You go."

"I was just going to say I'm going to get a coffee to take home to your dad." Verity's voice was light but still frosty. "Apparently the Surf and Turf could do with the business. Do you want to come?"

"I suppose," Kieran said. "You know it was Julian who told the cops about Dad wandering, don't you?"

"I do. It was also Julian who kept him safe until I got there. Not for the first time, either."

"Right," Kieran said as they started to walk. "Listen, though, I'm sorry about taking Audrey to the caves. You're completely right. I was on the lookout and I could see the tide was out and—" He looked over.

"Okay," Verity said simply. Ahead, the Surf and Turf's sign was lit up.

"I won't take her down again."

"That's up to you."

"Mum—"

"Like you said, Kieran, she's your child." Verity's voice was steely calm. "But you'd be very sorry if anything happened to her."

Kieran stopped walking. After a few paces, Verity relented and stopped as well. She turned and they stood on the street and looked at each other.

"Is there something you want to say to me, Mum?"

"No, Kieran."

"Are you sure? About Finn, maybe?"

"No."

"Because I'm sensing a little passive aggression here." He was goading her now, using the same placid tone Verity was so fond of.

"Well." She looked him in the eye. "I'm sorry you feel that way."

"Mum—"

"Kieran." Verity sighed heavily. "Let's not. Okay? You're right. Audrey is your child. But if something happened to her, you would be sorry. And that's all I want to say."

It wasn't, of course, but she was already turning away. "I'm getting coffee. You're welcome to come, or not."

Kieran watched her for a few moments longer, then followed.

●   ●   ●

The large screen normally reserved for sports was lit up with the local news bulletin as they pushed open the door to the Surf and

Turf. The sound was off and images flickered as piped eighties music filtered from the speakers into the room.

Lyn was again back in uniform, frowning as she pointed a remote at the screen and stabbed at the buttons.

"They had the news crew here this morning," she said to Kieran and Verity as they came in. "Wanted to see what they got."

"Have Bronte's parents arrived?" Verity said as she placed their order.

"Yeah, Chris Renn brought them in here. They only stayed for a minute. Didn't say much." Lyn nodded at the bulletin board where a printed sheet had been pinned up next to the photo of Bronte. "There's a community meeting being set up for tonight, though. Reckon they'll be there then."

Kieran walked over. The notice announced details of the meeting at the Evelyn Bay library. Sergeant Renn's photocopied signature was at the bottom. Kieran looked at Bronte's face, then touched the collection tin on the table below. It barely moved, heavy now.

"Here we go," Lyn said, pointing at the TV news. She tried once more with the remote, then gave up and resigned herself to watching without sound.

The dark-haired reporter was standing on the familiar stretch of beach outside Fisherman's Cottage, speaking into a microphone. The camera panned out, capturing from a respectful distance two people standing by the shallows, their faces ashen. Kieran didn't need the caption to know who they were. Bronte's father had cropped graying hair and was wearing a smart wool coat over jeans. The woman was short, like Bronte, and the same shade of blond, cut to a crisp line at her shoulders. They were both dressed in navy. Not quite a funeral color, but close. Bronte's dad pressed a crumpled tissue to his eyes as his wife placed a huge bunch of pink roses on the pile that had collected near the water's edge.

The wind caught the cellophane and toppled the bouquet onto its side as soon as she let go. Bronte's parents didn't move, simply staring at the heap of decaying flowers as though it might hold some answers.

The footage was replaced by a smiling photo of Bronte, a new one Kieran hadn't seen before. She was beaming in front of a framed painting Kieran guessed was one of her own.

The image disappeared and Sergeant Renn filled the screen. He spoke into the camera, formal and stone-faced. Kieran couldn't read his lips, but he could guess what he was saying. *If anyone has any information . . .*

"Are you going to this community meeting, then?" Kieran said.

"Absolutely." Lyn looked away from the television as a close-up of Bronte's pink flowers flashed up on the screen. Her eyes fell instead on the kitchen where Liam had until recently worked. "Wouldn't miss it."

24

They were early, but others were even earlier and the library was already busy.

Ash's dog, Shifty, was tethered by his leash to the bike rack outside, and Kieran rubbed his head as they passed. He remembered the day Ash had found the dog, lost or abandoned and lurking in a shifty manner around the delivery entrance of the Surf and Turf. Ash had felt bad and taken him home, where both the dog and the name had stuck.

Kieran looked past Shifty now to a notice taped above the returns chute informing visitors that the community meeting was to be held in the function room. It was unnecessary. The thick hum of chatter drifted out through the bookshelves, and the room was already near capacity as Kieran edged his way in with Mia. Verity and Brian were behind them. Mia took one look at the standing room only and turned the bulky stroller around.

"I'll park it in the lobby," she said as Kieran lifted Audrey out. She wheeled the stroller away, disappearing past the audio-book stand.

Kieran surveyed the room. Someone had offered Brian a seat and Verity was trying to convince him to take it. Eventually, the person in the next chair stood and gestured to Verity, who looked embarrassed but sat them both down gratefully, her grip tight on Brian's wrist. Kieran swapped Audrey to his other arm and found a place to stand near the door.

The rows of seating faced a raised area at the front of the room, where four chairs sat empty behind a table. A laptop was open and Bronte smiled out from two large photos projected onto a presentation screen. She was dressed like she was going somewhere in the first image, smiling like it was a special occasion. In the other, she was sitting on a wall in a garden in jeans and bare feet, her arm around a large sleepy-looking golden retriever.

Liam was not there; Kieran could tell simply from the atmosphere. Sean had come though, as had Julian. They stood together in the far corner, their backs against the wall and arms folded across their chests. The weather-beaten man to Julian's left was leaning toward him confidentially, chatting away while stabbing at the air with his folded sunglasses to make a point. The next couple along were looking anywhere else as they pretended not to have noticed either Julian or Sean.

Julian seemed to be trying his best to ignore everyone, staring straight ahead with a fixed gaze and nodding only occasionally as the man rambled on. Sean had his head down as he rubbed the bridge of his nose. Kieran tried to make eye contact, but Sean didn't look up. The room was too busy for Kieran to fight his way over and, to his shame, he felt a faint stirring of relief that he didn't have to make the choice.

Kieran noticed movement and saw Ash raising a hand to him through the crowd. He was seated in the second row, his other arm slung over the back of Olivia's chair, rubbing her shoulder blade with his thumb. Olivia's mum, Trish, sat on her other side, her back perfectly straight. They watched silently as a camera crew set up near the lectern.

"Hey, guess what? I finally met G. R. Barlin," Mia whispered as she slid in next to Kieran. "I caught him signing his own books in the recent returns section. We both pretended he wasn't, though."

Kieran smiled. "I'm sure you were very tactful."

"I went for gushingly complimentary. I meant to say I loved his books and accidentally said I loved him. He was very gracious." Mia looked around the room herself for the first time, her smile fading now. "No Liam?"

"No."

Kieran could see Lyn sitting a few rows over. Her eyes flicked to Julian, then she leaned over and murmured something to the woman sitting beside her, who looked similar enough to be a sister. The second woman's face tightened.

Kieran heard a voice behind him.

"Sorry. Could I—?"

He turned to see George Barlin squeezing in and took a step sideways to make room.

"Thanks." George looked grateful. He was wearing yet another chunky cardigan. Kieran wondered exactly how many he owned. George smiled at Mia. "And hello again."

If he was at all embarrassed, he hid it better than she did. George took stock of the rows of chairs filled with people packed shoulder to shoulder.

"Be here or be square, hey?" George said without humor. "At least people are more civil to each other in real life than they are online."

Kieran nodded. "I see that community forum's been taking off."

"It really has." George's face was serious. "People need to

watch themselves, actually. A lot of defamatory comments are being hurled around in there. Especially as no one's been charged yet." He glanced toward Sean and Julian, who had barely moved.

"Is anyone moderating it?" Mia asked, reaching out to take Audrey from Kieran as the baby started to grizzle.

"There used to be a couple of people. Volunteers, I'm guessing, but that was back when it was mostly rates and rubbish complaints. If anyone's doing it now, they're overwhelmed. There've been posts on there for days that should never have been allowed up in the first place."

"About Liam?" Mia asked.

"Some," George said. "Not all—"

He broke off, taking a step back as Detective Inspector Pendlebury attempted to edge her way in through the door.

"Excuse me," she said, her words suddenly very audible as a hush of anticipation fell over the room.

Pendlebury ignored it and threaded her way through the crowd to where Olivia was seated. She stepped in and leaned over Ash's chair, bending in close to murmur something to Olivia. Kieran watched, along with the rest of the room, as Pendlebury tilted her head toward the waiting stage and then the door, possibly explaining procedure as a courtesy to Bronte's housemate. Olivia sat very still while she listened, as did Ash next to her. It was interesting, Kieran thought, how no one seemed particularly comfortable being seen by their friends and neighbors *helping the police with their inquiries*, no matter how innocent the exchange. Kieran looked over to Sean, who was watching them like everyone else.

"The police are monitoring it now, though," George said quietly, his eyes on Pendlebury.

"The forum?" Kieran said.

"Yeah. I think so. Occasionally a post will just disappear.

But there's a mountain of libelous stuff left up there, so my guess is they're focusing on pulling things they think have some connection with the investigation."

"Stuff they don't want people to know?" Kieran said.

"Or talk about, maybe?" George shrugged. "Who knows? I've been trying to keep an eye on it. Work out what's getting deleted, but it's moving too fast for me to keep up."

Kieran pulled out his phone, unable to help himself, and saw Mia do the same. *Welcome to EBOCH! Drop in for a virtual cuppa and a chat!*

People were doing a lot more than that, Kieran could see. An argument over whether or not to boycott the Surf and Turf ran over three pages. Kieran looked up and saw Julian's eyes trained on Pendlebury. The Surf and Turf would survive, surely, he thought. People needed somewhere to eat or, more crucially, drink. Still, the fact that anyone was even suggesting avoiding the place was troubling. Kieran turned back to his screen.

Bronte liked to have sex on the beach at night. An anonymous gray avatar insisted so. He—she?—knew someone at the gym who had seen her down there with a guy last month. Kieran had no idea if that were true. Judging by the responses, no one else did either. He looked around the crowded room, trying to match faces with some of the comments. He didn't know where to start.

One reply had been deleted.

The gray avatar still remained but the comment box was shaded out. *This comment by Blainey82 has been removed for violating EBOCH guidelines.*

Kieran looked at it for a minute, then moved on. Directly below, Mia's old music teacher, Theresa Hartley, had chosen to weigh in again, commenting on the original post.

I don't believe for a minute Bronte was like that. My granddaughter says she was one of the nicest girls at university. You can tell from this, she had written, and posted a website link. Her comment had in turn prompted a string of responses ranging from patient to furious, informing Theresa that it was entirely possible to be a nice girl while also enjoying consensual sex in a semi-secluded place.

Curious, Kieran clicked on Theresa's link. It went through to a page on a social media site that Kieran had heard of but had felt too old and jaded to get to grips with every time he'd tried to check it out. It was an online tribute to Bronte where visitors—mostly her fellow art students in Canberra from what Kieran could tell—had put up pictures and video messages. Some had shared sketches and paintings of Bronte, and quite a few had posted pictures Bronte had drawn for them. *I can't believe she's gone,* one girl had written. Theresa's granddaughter, Kieran guessed by the surname.

Kieran felt Mia touch his arm. She was still looking at the EBOCH page. She twisted her screen so only he could see and subtly tapped a post with her nail.

Brian Elliott was seen on the beach the night Bronte Laidler was killed. Kieran felt his chest go tight. He checked the avatar. Anonymous and gray, of course. Not even a proper nickname, just a string of numbers. *He walks around at night.*

Don't, a reply said. *He's got dementia.*

He was also the last one seen with Gabby Birch. Remember that?

Kieran felt sick. Across the room, he could see Julian was now looking at his own phone, tapping at the screen.

"It could have been anyone," Mia whispered, reading his mind. "Liam will have told people about your dad wandering. Anyone could have written that."

"That doesn't exactly make it better," Kieran said, glancing over to where Verity appeared to be trying to talk Brian into staying seated.

"No, but—" Mia broke off as there was a movement behind them and the collective attention of the room was immediately focused on the door.

Sergeant Renn came in first and nodded to Pendlebury, their faces identically hard. There was a hush and a stillness in which it seemed for a moment like no one else was coming. Renn half turned, then Bronte's parents appeared at the door. Pendlebury had cleared a route and every eye in the place followed them on the long journey from the back of the room to the front.

They were civil servants up in Canberra, Kieran remembered Olivia saying, and they dressed like it. They had changed clothes since the news bulletin and both looked as though they could be on their way to a business breakfast meeting, in crisp shirts and suit material. Kieran imagined them in their hotel room, trying to decide what to wear. Silently taking turns to use the wobbly ironing board. What was appropriate for speaking on behalf of their dead daughter? Nothing, was the answer. Or anything. Kieran guessed they had fallen back on the familiar clothes that at least in their normal lives offered some sense of being in control.

Sergeant Renn remained standing as the other three took their seats. He picked up the microphone from the table and fiddled with the button.

"Can everyone hear me all right?" There was an affirmative murmur in the room. "Right. Well, thanks for coming, everyone. I think most of you know me. I'm Sergeant Chris Renn, I've worked here in Evelyn Bay for close to thirteen years. And this is my colleague from Hobart"—he gestured down the table—"Detective Inspector Sue Pendlebury, who some of you will have seen around with her team these past few days."

Renn checked his notes on the table.

"You're all aware of the tragic event on Saturday night involving Bronte Laidler, who a lot of us had come to know through her job at the Surf and Turf. Bronte hadn't been with us long but had quickly become a popular face around here, and I know how shaken we've all been by what's happened. Tonight we have with us Bronte's parents, Nick and Andrea Laidler, who join us from Canberra." Renn turned to the couple, who had both been staring out at the sea of faces. They blinked to hear their names mentioned. "We're very sorry you're here under such sad circumstances, but our community welcomes you."

Bronte's father inclined his head, short and sharp, while her mother mouthed something, tight-lipped. *Thank you.*

Renn turned back to the crowd. "We know this is a difficult time and naturally raises a lot of questions, but we want to assure you that we are out there speaking to a lot of you, pursuing a number of lines of—"

There was an indistinct murmur from somewhere to the left of the room and Renn frowned and stumbled, his train of thought broken.

"Ah—" He checked his notes. "Yeah. We're pursuing a number—"

"I said, why are you harassing the locals, Chris, mate?" There was nothing indistinct about the words this time, and every face turned to look. Kieran could see the speaker now. A bloke in his forties, with the body of a surfer under his collared checked shirt. His hand was resting on the shoulder of a boy of about thirteen who could only have been his son. Kieran recognized the man. Heath something. He ran the Nippers lifesaving program with Julian.

"We're not taking questions now, Heath, mate." Renn's voice was firm. "Talk to me later."

"Yeah, okay, but I'm just asking why you're wasting all this time talking to us, when we all know whoever did this has been back on the mainland for days." Heath nodded to Bronte's parents, whose faces were frozen. "Look, I'm very sorry for what happened to your daughter. Believe me, I am. I've got kids of my own." Heath lifted his hand on his son's shoulder. "But we—us, here—we didn't do this to you. And I want to know, Chris, what I'm supposed to tell my boy when he comes home asking why his mate's dads are being hassled by the police?"

"How about you tell him that's what happens when someone is harmed? People get hassled." Renn didn't bother to use the microphone this time. He held Heath's gaze, then looked around the gathering. "Now, this is your community. Mine too. And I am happy for you all to sit here and listen to what's being said. But let's have some basic respect, yeah?" He waited, then turned back to his notes. "Right."

The rest of Renn's introductory wrap-up was brisk and, Kieran suspected, even shorter than he'd planned, and then it was Pendlebury's turn. She stood and tapped the keyboard of the laptop and the photos of Bronte disappeared.

"Please take a look at the screen." She tapped the keys again and two fresh images came up.

A camera. And a laptop.

Kieran's eyes snapped to Mia's—*Laptop, too?* she mouthed— and they both immediately glanced over at Olivia. The back of her head was perfectly still. Ash, partly in profile, was staring at the screen, his hand slack now against the back of her chair.

"These are two items of interest," Pendlebury continued, pointing to the pictures. The images were catalog shots, with close-up inserts of the branding. Pendlebury tapped the relevant identifiers on each, holding her finger against the screen until she was sure she had the audience's attention. "Take note, please, of the make, here and here, and the model numbers— here, here. There will be flyers at the door on your way out with this information. I ask that you please take one or more and pass them on to your neighbors who aren't here tonight."

Pendlebury turned back to the screen. Bronte's parents were both staring at the table.

"We believe these two items belonged to Bronte Laidler," Pendlebury said. "We have not been able to trace them, and believe they may have been discarded locally. We are asking you to check your properties, your bins, your sheds, your gardens, your walking trails. Anywhere that these items could have been disposed of hastily."

There was a muted muttering at that, which Pendlebury chose to ignore. But Kieran guessed she knew it as well as every person in that room. To get rid of something in Evelyn Bay, all you had to do was step out of your back door and there were a million liters of water waiting to take it off your hands. Although—Kieran couldn't help but glance at Trish Birch—not always. Sometimes things came back, apparently.

Pendlebury pointed out some distinct features of both the camera and the laptop, leaving the pictures up so the TV cameraman could get his shot while the journalist scribbled the details. She repeated the hotline number, tapped the keyboard once more, and the images of Bronte returned.

She made eye contact with Renn, and they both looked at the Laidlers. Pendlebury leaned in and exchanged a few whispered words with them, then straightened.

"Bronte's parents, Nick and Andrea, will now make a statement. They will not be taking any questions tonight. Please direct queries or information to me or to Sergeant Renn afterward."

Pendlebury passed the microphone to Bronte's parents, who were getting to their feet. They stood straight-backed and grim-faced in their sharp suits, Bronte's father handling the microphone with more ease than either Renn or Pendlebury had. He was wearing a tie, which made it the only one in the room.

Kieran looked at them standing side by side in the library's tired function room, in front of photos of their late daughter. They looked out of place, he thought. Quite literally, as though they didn't belong here. This wasn't their life, he could almost see them thinking. This wasn't happening to them.

Nick Laidler put his phone on the table and tapped the screen once. His head was bowed and he took a deep breath before looking up.

"Bronte was our only child," he said. His volume was perfectly calibrated for the microphone and the size of the room, and he spoke with the clear measured pace of someone used to addressing groups. He referred briefly to the notes on his phone. "She was a joyous, much-loved little girl who grew into a beautiful, talented woman. Bronte was a keen artist and a friend to many. She was—"

Nick paused as his wife suddenly reached out and lightly touched her fingers to his suit sleeve. He glanced down at her hand, then up at her face. Andrea Laidler had been standing perfectly still as her husband spoke, but her eyes had been moving. She was looking, Kieran realized now, at every face in the crowd in turn. At one, then the next, then the next, then the next.

She turned toward her husband and beckoned for him to pass her the microphone. Kieran saw Pendlebury and Renn exchange a look.

Nick lowered his head and whispered something to his wife. Her reply was inaudible as she motioned again for the microphone. This time he passed it over, then slid his phone along the table so she could read the notes.

Andrea ignored it. She raised the microphone with the

practiced movement of someone also accustomed to public speaking. She fixed her eyes on the crowd.

"Who did this?"

Bronte's mother's words cut through the air. She waited. No one made a sound. Her gaze continued its slow crawl. Every single person was staring back, but Kieran saw more than one drop their eyes as the woman turned their way.

"Who did this?" she said again. Her husband reached out and tapped the screen of his phone firmly, turning it squarely in front of her, but Andrea stayed focused on the room, her scrutiny clear and cold.

Kieran knew he couldn't have been the only one expecting tearful, wet, messy grief. He could feel the atmosphere thicken as he and everyone else scrambled to catch up, all reaching the same conclusion at more or less the same time. Bronte's mother was not sad. Or, at least, not just sad. She was furious.

Andrea's hand was trembling as she raised the microphone again, but her voice didn't waver.

"We weren't sure why our daughter wanted to come here for the summer. Why she would choose to spend months here—" A small bristle from the crowd, and her husband frowned. Andrea ignored them both. "But we loved Bronte. She said it was important for her art, so we supported her. We always tried to do that. And when Bronte came here, she did her best to fit in and she was welcomed, mostly—"

The last comment was delivered pointedly in the direction of Olivia, who was staring down into her lap. Ash tightened his arm around her and Trish simply looked stunned. Kieran saw Renn shoot an unspoken question at Pendlebury, who hesitated then shook her head in an almost invisible response.

"Bronte came here with an open mind," Andrea was saying, her voice tight. "Curious about life here. Interested. Trusting."

She stopped, her gaze still stealing across the room. To George, then Mia, then to Kieran himself. He looked back and as their eyes met he thought, suddenly, of Verity. He could see his mother leaning forward in her chair, her lips parted as she watched the other woman speak.

"My child's last moments would have been horrific." Both Andrea's voice and hands were shaking now. "I can't let myself think about how scared she must have been. Can you imagine what that would have been like for her? In the water? She couldn't breathe."

She swallowed and her words hung in the air. Kieran felt George shift next to him. Across the room, Julian was staring back at Bronte's mother, his defiance almost convincing. Sean had a hand over his face.

"I know you're waiting for me to ask for your help," Andrea said at last. "So I will. Please. I'm begging you, if you know anything about what happened to my daughter, please tell us." She took a breath. "But you should also know this: I will find out either way. I'm not going to pretend I know where to start, but I'll pay people who do. Investigators. I'll drain our bank accounts. I'll mortgage our houses. Whatever I need to do. Because I think this man—" Andrea pointed at Heath, who looked like he wished he could disappear. "I think he's wrong. I think the person responsible is probably in this room. I think it's one of you." There was a silence. "But maybe not. I don't care, I just want the truth. So either way, no stone left unturned. If you're out there—" She scanned the room again, not so slow and steady now. "If you're hoping this will go away, you're going to be waiting a long time. Someone hurt Bronte. I want to know who. So unless you want every secret in this place dragged to the surface, I recommend everybody in this room opens their mouths and starts talking."

There was more than a murmur at that, and Renn got to his feet.

Andrea held up a palm, stopping him. She looked around the room once more, then shook her head.

"Never mind." She put the microphone down and spoke in her normal voice. "I've said what I wanted to say."

25

The water at dawn was as cold as it ever was. Kieran ducked his head under, his breath catching in his chest. He started to swim, pulling himself through the surf, raising his head every ten strokes to check on Audrey, who was tucked in her sleeping bag on his towel on the deserted beach.

Kieran had woken up in the dark, alerted by the stuttering warning cry from the cot, and had crawled reluctantly out of bed. He had fed Audrey and read to her from a picture book that hinted heavily on its front cover that it would unlock her genius potential. Instead, it had sent her back to sleep, which in that moment seemed like an even better result. They should have put that on the cover. By then, the sky was starting to lighten but the house was still sleeping, so Kieran had wrapped her up, grabbed his towel, and taken them both out into the crisp morning cold.

His head was still full of the community meeting as he swam. Renn had moved fast after Bronte's mother's speech, Kieran had to give him that. Her words had barely landed before the sergeant had taken two swift strides across the stage and, hands firmly on their backs, shepherded Andrea and Nick through the crowd and out of the door.

It had taken everyone else a little longer to react, the response swelling from a rumble to a low roar. Mia had been quick off the mark, darting out with Audrey to reclaim the stroller, leaving Kieran and George pressed closer than was comfortable as they and several hundred of their neighbors attempted to squeeze through the bottleneck at the door. A pair of uniformed officers were passing out fistfuls of flyers as they spilled out through the main library and into the cool night air. When there was space to stop, Kieran craned his neck back over the crowd, trying to see Verity and Brian.

"Well, I have to admit, I did not expect that." George examined his leaflet with the printed images of Bronte's camera and laptop. He frowned. "These have to be long gone, surely?"

"I would think so."

"I wonder if the police know what was on them. I mean, stuff gets backed up, doesn't it? It seems to happen to me whether I like it or not, sometimes."

"I suppose," Kieran said. "Depends what kind of setup she had in place."

Kieran spied the top of Brian's head and could see him being steered by Verity, who was holding his arm. Pendlebury had slowed to help and was subtly clearing a path through. As they passed an officer handing out flyers, Pendlebury took a couple. She folded one in half lengthwise, creating a crisp edge, which she presented to Verity. *Take this.* It was an unremarkable gesture, but there was something insistent about it that put Kieran on edge.

"Well, either the police don't know what was on them"— George looked up from the flyer and over to Pendlebury—"or they do know and haven't managed to work out the significance yet."

Perhaps sensing the scrutiny, Pendlebury turned her head their way. Her eyes moved between Kieran and George, and something passed across her face. It was gone almost immediately as she was forced to bring her attention back to Brian. Pendlebury had barely helped him down the last step when she was accosted by an angry woman in a pink fleece.

"I'm going to head off," George said, then hesitated. He turned back to Kieran. "Listen, mate, now's not the time or place, but there was something—"

He was stopped short by movement over Kieran's shoulder, and Kieran turned to see Ash approaching, dog leash in hand, his large frame backlit by the glow from the library. George made to leave.

"Catch you another time," he said, raising a hand.

"You seen Sean anywhere?" Ash said, lightly shoulder-barging the writer as he passed but otherwise ignoring him completely.

"No. Think he and Julian must have made a quick exit."

"Don't blame them, that was bloody intense." Ash shook his head. "I'd better go too, then. Liv's waiting. She's pretty upset." He lowered his voice. "Not going to be the only one, I reckon. People look freaked out, don't you think? All that stuff Bronte's mum was saying about things coming out?"

"Yeah." Kieran could see people snatching glances at each other. The atmosphere outside the library felt loaded. "They do."

"Makes you wonder, hey?"

"It does."

Kieran finished swimming his lap in the sea now and lifted his head, wiping the water from his eyes. He could tell Audrey was still asleep, snug in her blanket beneath the red-gold morning sky. Kieran plunged under the surface once more, feeling the burn of the cold. He swam several fast strokes, his muscles loosening as he found his rhythm. He stayed under longer this time, and when he lifted his head again, he almost breathed in a lungful of water. Audrey was where he had left her, but the beach was no longer empty. Kieran could see a figure on the sand, their shadow falling over his daughter as she slept.

Kieran had found his feet in seconds, driving his way through the water to the shore, ignoring the frigid air stinging his wet skin.

"Oi!"

The figure turned at his shout. Kieran swiped the salt water from his eyes, blinking as the face took shape. Trish Birch.

He slowed, just a little. Trish straightened and raised her hand. She took a step away from his daughter, and Kieran stopped running and started wading instead. *It's okay*, he told himself, while his heart still pounded.

"Hello," she called as he hit the sand. "I'm so sorry. I was—"

"No, I'm sorry." Kieran reached them and bent down for his towel, a little unsure why he still felt the urge to position himself between Trish and his baby as he dried off. Audrey was asleep, peaceful and oblivious. "I just got a surprise."

"Of course," Trish said. "I was only—" She faltered, a tiny frown on her face as she glanced around. "I mean, do you think it's safe to leave her on the beach?"

Not blokes or babies, Kieran thought, although from the way his blood was still pumping, he wasn't sure he believed it himself. He picked up Audrey and she stirred in his cold arms.

"I didn't think anyone else was here," he said.

"No. Plus it's absolutely none of my business." Trish gave him a small smile. "I used to hate people telling me how to parent. I'm sorry. Don't let me disturb your swim."

"Probably time I finished up anyway."

Trish's face had a healthy glow from the morning air, but

also a pinched look that made him wonder if she had been crying. The ocean had soaked up the reddish tinge of the morning
sky, and her eyes followed the movement of the tide as she looked
out at the water. No, Kieran realized. Not just looking. *Scouring.*
He hesitated.

"Trish, I have your backpack. If that's what you're searching
for. I'm sorry, I pulled it out of the sea after you threw it in. I
didn't know what it was."

"Oh. Olivia said you'd found it." Trish looked embarrassed, but
still her gaze crept past him once again to the waves. Kieran wondered if there was another bag out there yet to turn up. Maybe
more than one.

"Do you want it back?" he said. "It's in our shed. I can get it."

"No." She looked uncertain, then rallied. "No. I promised
Olivia." She gave a self-conscious laugh. "I can't imagine what
you're thinking. It must seem completely crazy."

"No." Kieran shook his head. It didn't, actually. When Kieran
felt his daughter's weight in his arms and imagined himself in
Trish Birch's position, it didn't seem that crazy at all.

"Well. I'm not sure most people would agree with you,
but thanks for saying it anyway." Trish reached out and gently
moved Audrey's blanket aside to better see her face. "It never
changes, you know. Even when they're older. You'd take a bul-
let for someone who won't even wave to you at the school gate.
Then suddenly they're ripped away and—" Trish shrugged.
"Well, you were there last night, I'm guessing? Heard Bronte's
mum?"

Kieran nodded.

"I used to be like that," Trish said. "Not as articulate or well
resourced. Angry, though. Behind closed doors at least. I never
had the courage to do it in public. I felt I had to be polite and nice,
give people a reason to want to help me." Her face hardened. "It

didn't make any difference. My daughter's still gone. Maybe I should have let it all out, like Bronte's mum."

She looked so unsettled by the thought that Kieran felt worried for her. Beyond his parents' back fence, he noticed a light burning in the hallway. Someone was awake.

"Why don't you come in for a coffee, Trish? Have a chat with Mia. My mum's in too. You can hold the baby."

Trish was already shaking her head. "No. Thank you, though—"

"It's no trouble."

"It's honestly better if I keep walking. Truly. Thanks anyway." Trish glanced at the house, a little awkward. "Does Verity know about the backpacks?"

"No," Kieran said. "I won't tell her, if you don't want me to."

"Thank you." Trish looked relieved. "I'm sure your mum would understand, but she's always been so—" She considered. "*Together.* Even after everything."

Kieran thought about his mother and her brittle calm and did not reply. Trish's eyes were on Audrey.

"She'll burn out," she said out of nowhere. "Bronte's mum. She doesn't think she will, but she will. You can't maintain it forever. She'll end up—" Trish sighed. "I don't know. Doing her own secret crazy things like the rest of us."

She looked up from the baby and out along the still deserted beach.

"I've kept you out of the water long enough," she said. "You must be freezing."

Kieran was, a bit. The sky was fully light now. The glow from the house was still visible.

"You sure you won't come in?"

"No. I'm going to keep walking." She gave Audrey a last smile and turned.

Kieran watched her for a few paces.

"Hey, Trish, wait," he called, and she looked back. "How many times have you done that? With the backpacks?"

"I'm not doing it anymore. I promised Olivia."

"But so far?"

A long pause. "Dozens. I'm not sure, exactly."

"And how many washed up at that spot near the rocks?"

"Two."

"Two."

"Or three." She shrugged. "Depending on whether or not you count Gabby's."

"Right. Do you count it?"

"Some days yes. Some days no." Trish looked away now, embarrassed and exposed by her grief. "Anyway, enjoy your time with your little one. They grow up fast." *If you're lucky.*

The words hung in the air, but she didn't say them, just raised a hand in farewell. Kieran watched as she walked away along the beach, her face turned yet again toward the ocean and the relentless push-pull of the tide rushing in and out.

26

Mia hadn't stirred when Kieran had crept out of the bedroom earlier, but she was up now. He found her sitting alone at the kitchen table, staring into the light of her phone screen.

"Hello," she whispered as he looked in from the hall. The house had a heavy stillness, but he had the sense that behind closed doors, his parents were awake. It had been hard work convincing Brian to come home with them after the meeting, and an exhausted Verity had steered him straight to the bedroom as soon as they'd got into the house. Mia had sat down to feed Audrey, and Kieran had laid down just to rest his eyes. When he'd next opened them, it had been the early dark of morning.

"Did you get some sleep?" he said.

"On and off. I kept waking up and couldn't stop thinking about things."

"What kind of things?"

Mia turned her phone so he could see the screen. A girl smiled out from a news piece on the screen. Not Bronte, as Kieran had maybe expected, but Gabby.

"The article's an old one. From the tenth anniversary," she said in answer to his surprise. She stood to take Audrey. "Nothing new. I don't know. It was just everything last night, listening to Bronte's mum."

"I saw Trish Birch out walking just now," Kieran said.

"Really? She didn't have another backpack, did she?"

"No. But it sounds like she's thrown loads of them in over the years. She wasn't even sure how many." Kieran mixed up a bottle of formula for Audrey and handed it to Mia as she sat back down. "She reckons two of them have washed back, like Gabby's did."

"Two."

"Yeah," he said. "So, not many."

"Not zero, though."

"No, that's true."

Mia was quiet.

"What's up?" he said.

"Nothing. I was just thinking." Mia began to feed Audrey. "God, I was so relieved when Gabby's bag was found washed up. I thought they were going to keep calling me and my parents into the police station every day until—well, who knows when? When I heard they'd found her bag"—she looked back at the girl's picture—"I was glad, honestly. I was happy it was over, more than I was sad about what had happened to her." Mia's gaze slid to her daughter. "I mean, what does that say about me? She was my best friend."

"Nothing." Kieran sat down next to her. "You were fourteen years old. It doesn't say anything."

"Maybe." Mia didn't sound convinced. "But—"

She stopped as they both heard the hall floorboards creak. The kitchen door opened and Verity came in, dark circles under her eyes. Mia reached out and swiped her thumb across her phone screen and Gabby disappeared.

"Morning," Verity said, putting on the kettle.

"Dad okay?"

"About the same." Verity reached for a mug and cleared a space on the counter to set it down. She picked up her reading glasses and a creased piece of paper. It was one of the leaflets from the meeting, Kieran could see. He watched as she turned it over in her hand, looking at Bronte's missing camera and laptop. The kettle boiled, and she set the leaflet aside.

"Hey, did Pendlebury say anything to you last night?" Kieran asked as Verity poured boiling water into her mug.

"When?"

"When she was helping you with Dad after the meeting. I thought you were talking."

Verity found a spoon and stirred. "She just asked how the packing for the move was going."

"That was it?"

"It was a thirty-second conversation, Kieran."

Kieran looked around the kitchen at the stacks of half-filled boxes. Someone—Brian, he very much hoped—appeared to have packed a glass of milk in a box by Kieran's feet. He could see the glass lying on its side now against the bottom, the yellowing stain soaking the cardboard. He looked back at the leaflet on the counter, the line where Pendlebury had folded the paper still visible.

"Do you think there's any reason she asked that, Mum?"

"Like what?" Verity's face was firmly placid. "I hear she's been asking a lot of people all sorts of things."

"I suppose," Kieran said. "But—"

Verity simply waited.

Kieran shrugged. "After that meeting, a lot of people were trying to talk to her. But she found time to ask you about the move?"

"Or she found time to help a confused man on the steps and make a few seconds' worth of small talk while she did it." Verity picked up her coffee. "I'm going to take my yoga mat outside, if either of you need anything."

Kieran and Mia watched her leave.

"She needs to be careful," he said as they heard the back door close. He stood up to head to the shower. "We don't want Pendlebury to start thinking things about Dad."

Mia turned back to her phone screen. "For what it's worth, I think your mum's smart enough to know that."

The morning sun was brighter by the time they got both themselves and Audrey organized enough to leave the house. They walked through town toward the cliff path, slowing as they approached Wetherby House. The ruined garden looked even worse than Kieran remembered, if that were possible. A couple more trees had been felled, he thought, and the soil in the exposed trenches looked cakey and dry.

Mia's gaze landed on a dirty white pickup parked directly on the street outside, taking up what could have been two spots. Gardening equipment was stacked in the tray at the back.

"Is that Ash's?" she said, squinting at the logo on the side. "Trying to piss off G. R. Barlin?"

"Yeah, looks like it," Kieran said, although he couldn't see Ash or his dog anywhere. He and Mia stopped and leaned on the fence of Wetherby House. Kieran couldn't be sure, but it had a settled stillness that made him feel no one was home.

"Lucky George can write better than he landscapes," Mia said, then sighed as a cry of protest rose from the stationary stroller. "Let's keep moving. What did George make of last night?"

"Surprised, I think, same as everyone. But Trish Birch was interesting. She reckons whatever Bronte's mum said at the meeting, she'll run out of steam sooner or later."

"Really?" Mia said. "I wonder if that's true. It's almost impossible to know, isn't it? How you'd react. I think people would be relieved if this was resolved soon, though. Not just for the obvious reason. Have you been on EBOCH today?"

Kieran shook his head as they reached the cliff path, and he began pushing the stroller up the slope.

"It's going mad on there," Mia said as they walked. "It's all anyone's talking about. And people are already getting on the front foot, outing each other over all kinds of stuff. Apparently Paul Holland and Natalie Whatshername who used to work at the school have been having an affair for *four years*. There's some suggestion her youngest might be his."

"Wow."

"I know. I never would have picked that."

Kieran slowed when they neared the cemetery. Shifty was tied up at the entrance and whined as they approached. Kieran stopped to stroke his back. Through the gates, what he could see of the grounds lay deserted. No sign of Ash.

"Any more mentions of my dad online?" Kieran said as they carried on walking.

"Not that I've seen. So that's good at least." Mia's dark hair blew across her face as they turned an exposed corner. "Hopefully it all calms down soon. People get hurt when old stuff gets dragged up. I mean, look at your mum when Brian let that thing slip about Finn getting a girl pregnant. I caught her in the kitchen in the middle of the night afterward and I think she'd been crying."

"Yeah," Kieran said. "I'm surprised she took it quite so hard, though. I mean—" They both looked at Audrey at the same time. Kieran smiled and Mia shrugged. "Anyone can mess up their birth control. It doesn't make him a bad person or anything."

"No. Of course not," Mia said. "But it seemed like a shock

for Verity. I guess it was just an unexpected reminder that Finn wasn't perfect."

"I don't think any of us thinks Finn was perfect."

Mia looked over in surprise. "You kind of do, though."

"No, we don't."

"Yes, you do. You really can't see it?" Mia looked genuinely curious. "What about all those photos that are usually everywhere at your house? Finn the footy star, Finn the businessman, Finn the all-round great guy."

"Yeah, so? He was a great guy. What's wrong with that?"

"Nothing," Mia said quickly. "Nothing at all. And I didn't even really know him. I'm just saying, your folks' place is a bit of a shrine. Plus the way you all talk about him. And that's fine, if it helps. But—" She saw Kieran's expression and her tone softened. "I'm sorry, I'm not trying to argue about this."

"No, I know. Me neither," Kieran said, panting a little now under the weight of the stroller as they approached the top. "But Finn really was a good guy."

Even as he said the words, a memory Kieran had almost forgotten tumbled off a dusty shelf in his mind. He couldn't remember exactly when it was from, but it must have been a couple of years before Finn died, not long after he and Toby had started the diving business.

What had happened? Kieran tried to dredge up the details. Finn and Toby had got themselves into a dispute with a local tradesman. Something about shoddy work on the boat, which he'd then refused to repair or refund. Finn and Toby had asked, Kieran remembered now, then argued, then pleaded, but the bloke had refused to budge.

Kieran could picture Finn, relaxing down at the beach outside the caves one warm day a couple of weeks after he and Toby had decided they hadn't got much choice but to cut their losses.

Kieran had been sixteen and lying on his towel, feeling a little light-headed from the beer and the sun and not looking forward to swimming back to the boat. Toby had been there too, of course, and Sean. And Ash as well, Kieran thought, as he pictured Finn standing there, golden in the afternoon sun. Bare-chested, beer in hand, and a grin on his face as he'd made them laugh with his story of what had played out the night before. How he'd put on his best shirt, gone to the Surf and Turf where the tradie's girl-friend was letting her hair down with a few mates and, without even breaking a sweat, had swept her off her feet and straight into the spare bed at her friend's place.

By the next day, anyone who was interested had heard about it. The tradie had been suitably pissed off, and everyone else—Finn, Toby, Ash, perhaps not Sean, but even Brian—had laughed and agreed it was no more than the dickhead deserved.

Kieran slowed as he walked along the cliff path with Mia and their baby daughter and wondered—for the first time ever, he realized with a flush of shame—what the girl herself had made of it all.

Ahead on the path, Mia was saying something. "I mean, Finn was your brother, obviously you're going to miss him. It's just what I was talking about the other day, how grieving people nat-urally focus on the good bits. You're not the only ones, though. Olivia does it too, Trish Birch definitely. Sean about Toby. Liam too, of course. Bronte's parents, I would imagine—"

Mia stopped as they hit the lookout. Even from up there, they could hear the shrieks echoing below. The birds were screaming again.

"What is going on?" Mia put a hand against the safety rail and leaned over. "I've never seen them like this."

"They were riled up the other day when I went down there—" He stopped as Mia looked up sharply.

"I didn't know you went down there."

"Oh," he said. "Yeah."

"I thought you'd stopped doing that."

He shrugged.

"Why didn't you tell me?" Mia was watching him now.

"I don't know," he said. "I'm sorry. But it was low tide. I had my phone if anything happened."

"It's not the safety stuff. Or not only that." Mia looked out, beyond The Survivors to where the *Nautilus Blue* was bobbing in the waves above the site of the *Mary Minerva*, dive flag raised. She turned back to Kieran. "I mean, are you okay? Being back here?"

"Yeah," he said. "I am. It wasn't—"

He stopped and they both turned again as another chorus of shrieks bounced off the rocks, echoing and discordant. Kieran hoisted himself up onto the barrier and leaned over at the waist, looking straight down, beyond the overhang to the sliver of beach that was visible.

"Can you see—?" Kieran started as Mia held up a hand.

She was craning her neck at an angle, listening, but all he could hear beneath the screech of birds was the wash of the sea. Neither spoke, then suddenly Mia pointed.

Kieran leaned over the barrier again. At first, he could see nothing. Then, all at once, he caught it. A shadow flickering dark against the sand. From the angle and the position of the sun, it had to be thrown by the scramble of movement from one place. Kieran watched. The shadow was gone, but only from sight. He looked at Mia. Someone was at the mouth of the caves.

27

Kieran could hear Audrey's cries growing fainter as he edged down the overgrown path. Mia had tried to stop him.

"Don't. Please, Kieran. Seriously. It doesn't matter who's down there."

He had leaned over the safety rail as far as he could. "What if they don't know how deep the tunnels run? Or about the tide?"

Mia had leaned out again as well, squinting into the wind. They could see no one. She had pushed her hair out of her eyes, exasperated.

"Oh God, I don't know. Is it bad if I say I don't care? Please, don't go. I know you think what happened to Bronte can't happen—"

Another flicker of shadow and they both stopped.

"Tell you what," he said. "I'll go down halfway and stay on the path. See if I can spot anyone from there."

Mia had eventually agreed. Kieran had left her and Audrey at the top, looking down over the water. The gust of wind caught Audrey's wail, mournful and pleading, and Kieran almost stopped walking. He was no longer quite sure why this had seemed like a good idea.

He made himself go to the halfway point, where his view of the caves was completely obscured by a jutting rock. Kieran debated, then went a few steps lower. He stopped as the path rounded the curve, revealing the water below, gray-blue and glistening. The shadow had disappeared and the stretch of empty beach lay before him. The birds circled warily overhead.

"Who's down here?" Kieran called, his voice bouncing off the rocks.

The faint echo was swallowed by the sea. No one replied.

"I saw you." His words repeated, tumbling over themselves before fading away. "You're not supposed to be down here."

The only response was the roll of the water, leaving a foamy residue as it chased itself in and out. Then the birds collectively seemed to bristle, and Kieran felt himself tense a split second before he registered the flash of movement.

A shadow, tight and black in the sun, emerged from the hidden gloom of the South Cave. Someone stepped out, blinking as the darkness gave way to daylight.

Kieran squinted as the figure became clear, then he sighed and pulled out his phone. He sent a text to Mia.

It's fine. It's Sue Pendlebury. I'm going down.

"Kieran." Pendlebury raised a hand as she saw him. She looked a little windswept and damp as she headed across the beach, a fine dusting of sand in her hair. She had a computer tablet tucked under her arm.

"Was that you I heard?" She looked back at the cave and frowned. "The sound's unusual in there. It seems to get swallowed up somehow."

"Yeah, it does." Kieran met her near the tide line. "It's the tunnels. Makes it hard to tell where it's coming from." He looked around. "Is Renn here?"

"Just me. Sergeant Renn is with Bronte's parents."

"How are they?"

"Hopeful we can give them the answer they need," Pendlebury said. "As am I."

"Right." Kieran could see that the cuffs of Pendlebury's trousers were damp and he wondered how far she'd gone into the caves. The routes were strewn with pools, some shallow, some deceptively deep. "Is there something you wanted down here? Because the tide's still pretty high. Some of the cave tunnels are below sea level. If you get lost, you can drown. It's not safe."

"Understood." Pendlebury nodded out to sea. "It was really them I wanted to look at."

"The Survivors?"

"Yeah." She tilted her head as she scrutinized the three figures. Kieran waited, watching the salt water wash against the sculpture.

"Are they supposed to be happy or sad?" Pendlebury said suddenly. "I mean, is it a celebration of the people who made it, or a memorial to the ones who didn't?"

"I don't know," Kieran said. "I think it could be either."

"Open to interpretation?" she said as he shrugged. "To be honest, I don't really get art. It's more my husband's thing."

Kieran watched as she took the computer tablet out from under her arm and turned it on. She held it at about shoulder height, her eyes going from screen to sculpture and back again. It was deliberately tilted at such an angle that he couldn't see what she was looking at. Pendlebury glanced over at him.

"Your mum really should have told me about your dad's connection with the Gabby Birch case, you know," she said, her gaze now back on the statue. "Or you should have. Last person to see the girl before she disappeared? I had to find that out for myself, and when I have to find things out for myself"—she reached up and swiped the screen—"it makes me wonder why."

Kieran blinked at the sudden change of topic. "Yeah, I know that. And Mum does too. There's nothing in it, though."

"I'm very glad to hear it," Pendlebury said, still staring at The Survivors.

Kieran pictured Verity in the kitchen that morning, the milk-stained packing box where Brian had again attempted to help her, and he felt a powerful need to protect them.

"Listen, if you're thinking my parents had something to do with Bronte—or Gabby for that matter—you're wrong."

"Am I?" Pendlebury's voice was neutral.

"Yes. I mean, obviously. Look, I know it's not great that my dad was out on Saturday night—I get that, we all do—but you can't spend five minutes with him and seriously believe he'd have the presence of mind to steal a laptop and camera."

"I didn't say he did, Kieran."

"No, okay. But were you hinting at it? Last night at the meeting when you were talking to my mum?"

Pendlebury clicked the tablet screen off. "It sounds like you've been thinking about this a bit."

"About the consequences of my father's irreversibly deteriorating mental health? Yeah, surprisingly, I think about it quite a lot."

"Fair enough." Pendlebury looked at him, her hair catching in the wind as she considered. "So tell me this. You're a local. If you were me, where would you be searching for Bronte's missing laptop and camera?"

"I really have no idea." Kieran met her gaze. "Although George Barlin reckons you might already know what was on them anyway."

"Does he, now?"

"Yes." Kieran nodded pointedly at the computer tablet she had been scrutinizing. "He does."

Pendlebury turned back to The Survivors. A cloud cleared overhead and the water sparkled again.

"Has George Barlin been saying anything else, out of interest?"

Kieran remembered George outside the library the previous night, their conversation interrupted by Ash's arrival. He frowned. "Like what?"

"Anything. Just curious," Pendlebury said, and Kieran had the odd sense she was weighing something up.

He waited, but when she didn't say any more, he looked toward the path. "I should get back. Mia's waiting. You probably shouldn't stay down here alone."

Pendlebury nodded, and they turned and together began to walk across the sand.

"Do you come down here much yourself?" Pendlebury asked. "Think about your brother?"

"Not really. I can think about him in other places."

"That's true. Were you two close as siblings?"

"Of course. He came out in a storm to save my life."

Pendlebury looked at Kieran, again with that expression he couldn't read, then glanced back out to where the *Nautilus Blue* bobbed on the gentle current.

"Liam spends a bit of time out there, though, doesn't he? Helping Sean with the business. They don't find it hard after what happened to Toby?"

"You'd have to ask them." Kieran shrugged. "Look, they probably do. But the wreck is where it is, so there's not much they can do about that."

"And it seems you all enjoyed some good times down here as well once," Pendlebury said, as they approached the North Cave. Even from across the sand Kieran could make out the scratched letters in the rock, and as they drew closer he could see his own name clearly. Finn's was above it and Ash's some-where beyond that, he knew. Years later, still there, still per-fectly visible. He felt a fresh burst of irritation at his younger self.

"Marking territory, was it? Whose idea was this?" Pendle-bury walked right up to the cave entrance and ran her finger over the lettering.

"We all did it. I can't remember."

It had been Finn's idea. Stuff like that usually was. Kieran's phone beeped in his pocket and he checked it. Mia.

"I'm going back up," he said. "You should come too."

Pendlebury didn't say anything. She was staring deep into the cave, unmoving. Kieran followed her gaze and for a moment, less than that even, Kieran again had the uneasy sensation of some-thing waiting in the dark, holding its breath. He realized his own lungs were tight and he exhaled. Pendlebury turned suddenly, and the feeling was gone. Kieran had no idea if she'd felt it too.

"Don't keep Mia waiting," she said. "I'll be a few more min-utes yet—" She held up a hand before he could protest. "Liter-ally, a few minutes. I'm not going exploring on my own, don't worry."

"Are you sure?"

"Absolutely. You go."

She wanted to get rid of him, Kieran thought as his phone rang this time.

"All right," he said. "Be careful, though."

"Always," Pendlebury said with a smile. He could feel her watching as he trudged over the sand and started up the cliff path. As he neared the halfway point, just before the beach dis-appeared from view, he stopped and looked back.

Pendlebury had turned away from the caves. She was holding up her tablet once more, standing very still as she stared out at The Survivors.

28

Kieran could tell something was different as soon as he unlocked the front door. He and Mia had dissected his conversation with Pendlebury all the way back down the cliff path, pausing only to give Shifty another pat on the head as they passed the cemetery gates. The Surf and Turf had looked close to empty as they walked by, so they had stopped and ordered two coffees to go from a waiter Kieran didn't know.

Now, as Kieran used his free hand to push open the door to his parents' place, it immediately felt odd. The door swung free and unimpeded, a shaft of daylight illuminating the hallway. Kieran's footsteps rang out with a strange hollow echo as he walked inside. Mia was right behind him.

"Oh," she breathed.

The hallway was completely clear.

Every sagging half-packed box was gone. Kieran could see the dust streaks where they had stood, and loose sand crunched under their shoes. He had grown used to the front door opening only three-quarters of the way, and to having to edge around a tower of cardboard every time he went in or out. Now he walked straight through, his steps sounding too loud against the bare floorboards.

"It's the same in here," Mia said, and Kieran looked past her into the living room. The couch and coffee table were still there, but the small mountain of boxes that he had helped part fill himself was gone. Brian was sitting in his armchair by the window. He had been gazing out but lifted his head as he saw Kieran. He frowned as though trying to grasp a thought.

"Are you all right, Dad?" No reply. Kieran turned back to Mia. "What's—?"

He stopped and they both turned as Verity came out of the kitchen, drying her hands on a tea towel. Her face was mottled pink and she had half-moon sweat stains under the arms of her T-shirt.

"Oh," she said. "Hello. Good walk?"

Kieran stared at her. "Where are all the boxes?"

"Some are in the other room. Some are stacked out on the back veranda."

Kieran waited but she said no more, just folded the tea towel into a square. "For God's sake, Mum," he said. "What are you doing?"

"What does it look like? Getting organized." Verity went back into the kitchen and they followed her. She had started but not yet finished the process in there. "The clutter was getting ridiculous."

"You moved those boxes all by yourself, Verity?" Mia said. "You should have waited until we were back."

"Most of them weren't heavy. Cushions and ornaments." Verity put the kettle on. "I could slide the ones that were."

Neither Kieran nor Mia said anything. As the kettle rumbled, Verity stared at the sink. At last, she turned and looked at them properly.

"I've been trying to pretend this move isn't happening. But

it is. And ignoring it and putting things off isn't helping. It's bad enough having to leave here without half my clothes and belongings getting destroyed in the process by your dad trying to help. I need to accept this and make the best of it." She reached for the kettle. "So that's what I'm doing from now on."

Kieran took a breath. What she said seemed genuine, but it was hard to tell with Verity these days. He looked at Mia, who gave a tiny nod.

"I'll get Audrey settled," Mia said. "Then we'll give you a hand in here, Verity."

"You don't have to. I can manage."

"We want to, Mum," Kieran said. "That's why we came back. So you don't have to do it all on your own."

It was a long afternoon, but by the end at least they could see the main surfaces and floors again. As evening rolled around, Kieran was ready to do nothing more than flop into bed and he could tell Mia felt the same way. He groaned when his phone beeped with a text. Sean.

"He's asked if we'll go for drinks tonight at the Surf and Turf," he said to Mia. "He says it's been dead. Julian's worried."

"Is he? I know it was pretty empty earlier, but I didn't realize it was that bad." Mia stifled a yawn. "Are Liv and Ash going?"

"Sounds like it."

They looked at each other. Audrey, fractious all day, had at last settled. The bed was right there. Mia closed her eyes but stayed standing.

"We should go," she said, "if Verity feels up to babysitting." She still had traces of dust from the packing boxes in her hair. "Besides, once your mum and dad move, this might be the last time we're here."

Kieran hadn't considered that, he realized with a jolt. While he texted Sean back, he wondered if it were true. When his parents left, would there still be enough here to bring him back again? Maybe, he thought as he hit the send button. Or maybe not. He honestly didn't know.

Kieran and Mia didn't talk much as they walked into town. The evening had an echo of that awful Saturday night that was impossible to ignore, and as they passed Fisherman's Cottage, Mia looked away. A single large fresh bouquet had been placed among the wilting ones. From Bronte's parents, Kieran guessed, but didn't slow down to check.

The Surf and Turf was empty in a way he had never seen it before. There wasn't a single person on the outside deck as they approached, and through the lit windows he could see most of the tables were unused. Kieran was about to climb the steps when he felt Mia touch his elbow. She made a subtle gesture and Kieran turned to look.

Julian was standing by the side of the road a little farther along, a short way past the CCTV camera. His short silver hair was tinged yellow from the streetlight as he leaned into the driver's side window of a white Holden four-wheel drive.

Liam's car, Kieran recognized straight away. Was that the car he had seen on Saturday night? he wondered again. Strangely, as he looked at it now, he could picture it almost clearly, speeding around the corner out of the blackness, a little too close for comfort. Whether the memory was real or manufactured, Kieran really wasn't sure.

He could make out Liam now sitting in the driver's seat, mostly in silhouette. Liam held the steering wheel with one hand and was rubbing his eyes with the other.

"Is he crying?" Mia whispered.

"I don't know." He could be, Kieran thought as he watched Julian reach in through the open window and place a palm on his stepson's shoulder. Julian was saying something now, leaning in further until his face was almost hidden.

Liam dropped his hand from his eyes and must have spotted them through the windshield, because suddenly Julian turned their way. He straightened and both men looked directly at them before Julian nodded in greeting.

"Thanks for coming by," he called. He shrugged in an attempt at humor. "Kept the best tables for you."

Kieran nodded back in response and, as they climbed the steps to go in, he saw Julian lean back into the car.

He heard Ash well before he saw him.

"Seems to be taking you a very long time," Ash was saying. "Writing this book. You've been at it for months. Poking your nose into people's business."

"It's called a research phase." George Barlin was already half on his feet, staring at his laptop screen as he clicked the keyboard to shut it down. A mostly full glass of red wine stood abandoned on the table. "I was a journo for fifteen years. I like to look into things that interest me."

Ash made a dismissive noise. He was leaning against George's table, arms folded across his chest, and barely glanced over as Kieran and Mia came in.

"Haven't got writer's block, I hope?"

"Nope. Thanks for the concern."

"Just want to make sure you can keep up the mortgage payments on that beautiful house of yours."

"Writer's block is for amateurs, mate." George didn't bother to look at Ash as he snapped his laptop shut. "I do this for a living."

Kieran shot a look across the room to where Sean was seated by the window. He was watching the exchange openmouthed, a couple of half-empty beer glasses in front of him.

"Still." Ash was fully focused on the author. "Be a real shame to turn in a dud."

George didn't reply as he got out his satchel.

Ash leaned in a little. "I'm just saying, letting those super-high standards of yours slip would be—"

"Ash, mate." Kieran tried to jump in, but George held up a hand.

"It's fine. The thing is, Ash, I only take criticism from people I'd go to for advice." George's tone was light but cut straight through. "And when it comes to writing, do you know how many people are in that group? About three, my friend. And not one of them is you."

"Hey, I'm not implying anything, mate. I don't even read them." Ash took a half-step forward as George moved out from the table. "But I heard reviews for your last one were—what's the polite term?—mixed."

"Well." George looked faintly amused. "That book let me buy your nan's treasured family home for cash. So I reckon I must be doing something right."

Ash opened his mouth, then closed it again in such a way that Kieran almost had to smile. The door to the restroom swung open and Olivia appeared. She looked tired and her head was down. She started toward Sean's table when she noticed Ash and George in the other corner and stopped in her tracks.

"But you seem to be struggling to understand what all this means, Ash," George was saying. His voice was flat and slow, like he was talking to a child. "It means I own that house now. And the garden. It also means you'd better stop hanging around my property at all hours with that look on your face. You think I didn't see you out there again this morning?"

"I've been keeping an eye on the cops for you, mate. You know how they've been stopping by your place the last few days?

Yep." Ash's voice was hard. "I've seen them in there talking to you. Why are they asking you so many questions, anyway?"

George looked at him closely before giving a small shrug. "Who knows, eh? Who knows what they've uncovered?"

"Liv says you wrote a pretty personal message in Bronte's book."

"Hey, Ash. Don't," Olivia said, but George simply frowned.

"Did I?" he said. "Probably. Bronte was trying to make it in a creative industry. I know what that's like. She enjoyed my books. I thought her pictures were good. Her plans for making a living in an artistic field seemed professional and realistic, which is rare. You don't see that a lot. So, yeah—" George nodded. "If it surprises you that Bronte and I had enough in common to have some sort of loose friendship, then that says a lot more about you, Ash, than it does about me."

"I don't know about that, mate. Not with her ending up like she did."

"Ash!" Olivia was angry now. "Enough!"

His eyes met hers and for the first time he hesitated. In the corner, Sean was on his feet. The sole waiter at the cash register kept looking anxiously at the door, probably wishing Julian would hurry up and return. Ash turned back to George, not quite ready to let go yet, but George had already taken a step toward the exit.

"The thing is, mate," George said as he put his satchel strap over his shoulder, "you can try to make this about Bronte—bit ghoulish and tacky, if you ask me—but we both know that's not what's driving this. It's not even really about me ripping up that garden. Which, once again, I own."

"I don't know what you're on about." Ash was frowning.

"No?" George's voice was steady and soft. "It's not about the fact that it annoys you that I make more money than you doing a creative job that you don't respect? Or how you think you could have done a lot more with your life, but have realized lately that you'll probably never leave here?" He glanced at Olivia, her face stormy. "Or how you suspect your girlfriend is too good for you? Which she absolutely is, by the way. You're right to be worried. What?—" George gave a hard laugh at Ash's expression. "It's not magic, mate. It's called paying attention to your surroundings. I mean, I know literally nothing about your father, other than the fact you clearly have a very poor relationship with him—"

"Stop tearing up the bloody garden!" Ash shouted. "Jesus, it's not about any of that stuff. Just stop destroying my garden, all right?"

There was a long silence. Ash rubbed his hands over his face and held them there, breathing in and out. Finally, he dropped them.

"Forget it," he said, his voice quiet now. He looked defeated. "It's too bloody late anyway."

No one moved, then Ash shoved a chair out of his way with a clatter.

"I need some air."

He let the door slam. Olivia was a few paces behind, looking upset. Through the windows, Kieran saw her follow Ash around to the side of the building. George waited only until they were clear, then adjusted his bag and walked out himself without a word, shaking his head.

Kieran and Mia watched him go, then looked over at Sean, who had sat down again in the corner.

"Maybe we check if Ash is okay then call it a night, hey?" Mia murmured.

"Yeah, I think so."

"I just want to put some money in Bronte's collection box. Thanks," she said as Kieran handed her some cash to add to what she was fishing out of her own purse. "I'll see you at the table."

Kieran could hear the faint sounds of Ash and Olivia talking outside as he sat down opposite Sean. He couldn't make out the words, but the tone floating through the closed window had the feel of an argument.

"What do you reckon?" Kieran said as Sean looked up. "Try again tomorrow?"

"I don't know. Maybe." Sean raised his eyes to the window as the voices outside grew a little louder, then died away again.

"Should one of us go out?" Kieran said, but Sean just shrugged.

"Wait until they come in. They do this sometimes. It runs its course, they make up."

"Even after what George said?"

Sean managed a thin smile. "Was any of that news to you? Was there anything said over there that you didn't already know about Ash?"

Kieran thought, then shook his head.

"No," Sean said. "Me neither. Or Liv, I reckon."

"It might have been news to Ash, though."

Sean sighed. "God, you'd hope not, by now." He looked up as the door opened, and Julian came in, along with Sergeant Renn. They were talking, but both fell quiet as they seemed to sense the lingering atmosphere in the room. Julian recovered first and beckoned the waiter to the coffee station to take Renn's order. Renn took a seat to wait, seeming almost as surprised as Kieran had been to find the place so empty. He leaned back heavily in his chair. He looked like he'd had a hard day with Bronte's parents.

"What did you make of the meeting at the library?" Kieran asked, and Sean rubbed his face with his hand.

"Liam didn't do it," he said, his voice smothered. "I know him. I'm not sure what more I can say."

Kieran didn't reply, and eventually Sean looked up.

"You too, hey?" He sounded resigned. "Throw away the key?"

"Mate, no." Kieran shook his head. "I honestly have no idea. You know Liam better than I do. And the cops haven't made a move on him, have they? So that's something."

They both looked over to Renn, who had taken a computer tablet out of his bag and was looking at the screen, flicking through in a way that was unremarkable but suddenly felt very familiar to Kieran.

"Pendlebury was down at the caves earlier," Sean said, reading Kieran's mind. "I saw her from the boat."

"Yeah, I saw her too. Mia and I were—" Kieran saw Mia heading toward them, and moved over to make room for her. "I was just saying to Sean that we saw Pendlebury at the caves."

"Did she say what she was doing?" Sean said. "Seemed like she was there for a while."

"No. She was looking at The Survivors."

"Oh." Sean frowned. "Why from the beach? Why not the lookout? Or the water, even?"

"Don't know, mate."

Sean shook his head and drained the last of one of the beer glasses. Outside, Ash and Olivia seemed to have fallen quiet. Kieran was wondering if they were still there when he heard Olivia say something. Her tone was blunt. The restaurant was so empty, it was hard not to feel like they were eavesdropping.

"I can't believe people have abandoned this place," Mia said. "After how many years?"

"Yeah," Sean said. "Julian says they'll come back, once this is all over. But who knows how long it'll go on?" He sighed. "Have you been on that local chat forum? There was something a few days ago about a boycott of this place, I think."

"There was," Kieran said. "A lot of people weren't in favor, though."

"No? I can't face going on there. Some of the stuff people were writing was unbelievable. Listen—" Sean stood up. "I need another drink. Do you want anything? While we're waiting for Ash?"

Kieran looked at Mia and they had a silent conversation.

"Thanks, mate," Kieran said. "We'll have one with you while we wait."

Mia watched him leave, then turned to Kieran.

"Listen, I meant to say, there was something else about your dad on the forum," she said in a low voice. "I saw it before. It's nothing to worry about—"

Kieran had already got out his phone and was pulling up the EBOCH site.

"It was someone saying he looked frail at the meeting," Mia said. "Here—"

She leaned over and touched his screen, scrolling until she found the comment. She was right, it was nothing more than that, but still Kieran's heart constricted a little in his chest at the sight of anonymous strangers gossiping about his dad's health.

"Maybe we could ask Renn if he could get it deleted," Mia said. "I mean, like George said they were doing. If they're deleting some posts, how hard is it to delete that?"

"He thought it was only stuff to do with the investigation, though."

"I know, but still."

Kieran scrolled through, scanning the comments for any further mention of Brian. He couldn't see any immediately, but there was an ocean to wade through now. Mia had been right, the people of Evelyn Bay were absolutely spilling their guts about each other. It made him feel depressed to look at it. Kieran was about to close the screen when his gaze snagged on a rare deleted entry.

This comment by Theresa Hartley has been removed for violating EBOCH guidelines.

Kieran frowned. Theresa Hartley, Mia's music teacher with the granddaughter at Bronte's uni in Canberra. What had she managed to stumble across, Kieran wondered, that was deemed by the police too hot to share? He located the search function on the site. Theresa had been reasonably active, he saw now, with several dozen posts to her name. Several dozen, but only two deleted ones.

Kieran tapped on her earliest deleted comment and the thread claiming Bronte had been caught on the beach having sex popped up. Of all the lurid remarks on that topic, Theresa's had been removed. Kieran tried to think. What had she said originally? The replies to her post were still visible. *Having sex doesn't mean she wasn't a nice girl*, someone had responded to her.

That was it. He remembered now. Bronte was a nice girl, Theresa had written. Her granddaughter said so. And then she'd posted a link. Kieran pulled up his own browsing history. The link to the social media site he felt too old for was still there. He clicked through and the tribute page to Bronte popped up.

Kieran looked through the latest posts. There were some sketches, a poem that struggled to rhyme the name Bronte with anything useful, a few drawings. He scrolled down to one image and paused as he felt a stir of recognition.

It was a photo. Not of Bronte, but of a beach. Evelyn Bay's beach, specifically. Kieran could see Fisherman's Cottage in the corner. It was the first photo in a gallery simply entitled "Summer Scenes."

Kieran opened the gallery. More ocean shots. All local, he could tell. A streetscape of the town itself. An artfully taken shot of the outside of the Surf and Turf. The Survivors, as seen from the lookout.

Had Bronte taken these photos? She had, Kieran felt sure. Not only from the fact the images were posted on her own tribute site, but because the photos had the familiar style he'd seen in the art book in her bedroom.

He scrolled on. A few pictures of the cliff path, then they were back to the seascapes. The pictures had clearly been taken recently but—Kieran stopped again, his thumb hovering above the screen.

He was staring at another photo of the beach. This one had been taken down low, near the sand as the waves rushed in. Kieran ignored the close-up sight of a thick cord of seaweed, his eyes instead drawn to the background. In the distance, small but recognizable, three people stood near the surf. A man in board shorts holding a baby, a dark-haired woman, and a big guy with a big dog.

Kieran, Mia, and Ash, on the beach on Saturday afternoon in Evelyn Bay.

Kieran stared at the photo and tried to process what that meant. He and Mia had flown in, Bronte had captured them in this photo, she had chased Audrey's hat, and less than twenty-four hours later, she was dead. He touched Mia's arm and held out his screen.

"The link to these was deleted from the forum," he said under his breath.

"Really?" Mia glanced over toward Renn as she took the phone.

Kieran watched her face as she scrolled through, waiting to see if she would come to the same conclusion. Like him, she froze at the beach shot, leaning in close to the screen.

"Wait. We saw her take this one. Didn't we?" Mia's voice was hard to hear. "When was that? Was it the same day her camera went missing?"

Kieran nodded.

"But—" Mia looked worried. "If her camera went missing that night, are these the photos from it?" She was staring at the pictures. "How are they online?"

"I don't know," he said.

Kieran sensed movement behind him and turned. Olivia.

"Listen, we're going to head off," she said as she approached, with Ash half a pace behind. They came to a stop at the table, both wearing identical blank expressions. Kieran couldn't tell if their argument was concluded or continuing.

"No worries." He looked at Ash, whose eyes were raw in a way Kieran had never seen them before. "Listen, mate—"

"What's that?" Ash cut him off. He was looking at the photo on the screen in Mia's hand. When she didn't answer, he reached out and took the phone without asking. He stared at the image. The seaweed and, in the background, the figures in the surf. "What is this?" he said again.

Olivia leaned in, trying to see, as Sean appeared behind them with three glasses in his hands.

"What's going on?" he said, looking from Kieran to Ash.

Ash didn't answer, just touched the screen to enlarge the image.

Sean slid the drinks onto the table and wiped his hands on his shorts and tried again. "What's on the phone?" He looked at Kieran. "It's yours, isn't it?"

Kieran glanced at Mia. She had her eyes on Renn, who was talking to the waiter.

"There are some photos online." Kieran spoke very quietly. "We think they might be from Bronte's missing camera."

"Are you serious?" Olivia stared for a second, then her hand darted out toward the phone. Ash simply turned his shoulder slightly, blocking her.

"Wait, is that you in that picture?" Her eyes snapped from Ash to Kieran and Mia. "You as well?"

Ash held the screen close to his face as he scrolled. Sean was crowding into his other side, trying to see, but Ash kept his body twisted and the phone out of reach.

"I don't understand," Olivia was saying. "What's going on? Why are you in those photos?"

Ash stopped suddenly, his thumb hovering over the screen, his mouth a downturned line. He blinked once, slowly, as though he would be surprised if he could find the energy.

"Well," he said, his voice flat. "At least we're not the only ones."

He dropped the phone onto the table, faceup, and Kieran crowded in, feeling the other three do the same. A fresh photo was on the screen and Kieran scrambled to register what he was seeing.

It was a rock pool, craggy and deep. The water collecting in its crevices looked slick and almost oily, reflecting a naturally filtered image of the sky and the clouds. And something else.

Someone was standing by the pool, a little way behind the photographer, possibly unseen by her. The mirror image of his face was captured in the pool, the expression warped by soft ripples, but the identity clear.

"Liam." Olivia drew in a breath.

"Wait—" Sean said, but it was no good. In a collective, instinctive reaction, they all looked toward Renn.

"Wait," Sean said again. His hand shot out and landed on Kieran's, which was already covering the phone. "Guys, listen. Please. Just wait a second—"

"It's too late," Kieran said.

Renn was watching them now, coffee cup forgotten. Computer tablet still open in front of him, finger poised mid-swipe. He looked at their faces, and at the phone they were crowding around, and his hand twitched against the tablet screen. If Kieran hadn't been sure before, he was now.

"It's too late, mate," he said. Sean's palm was heavy on his wrist. "They've already seen them."

29

Kieran opened his eyes in the night to find Mia already awake, her face lit up by her phone. They lay side by side and went through Bronte's photos together, slowly examining each one. The beach, the shops, the seaweed, Liam, themselves. Each time they reached the end of the gallery, they scrolled back to the start and went through again. The process didn't take long; there were only fifteen shots.

"This can't be all of them," Mia whispered at last. "They're so . . . mundane."

Kieran shook his head against the pillow. He'd been thinking the same thing. Mia stared into her phone, then clicked a button and the screen went blank.

"I don't like it that we're in there," she said into the darkness.

She finally fell back into an uneasy sleep but Kieran lay awake for hours, closing his eyes at last only to be woken what felt like moments later by Audrey.

Ash had simply walked out of the Surf and Turf the night

before without saying goodbye. He had stood apart while the rest of them pored over their screens, and the next time Kieran looked up he had gone. Olivia had tried calling, and eventually her phone had beeped with a text.

"He's at home." She reached for her bag and was gone, the door slamming behind her. Through the window, Kieran saw her turn in the direction of Ash's place. Sean had barely said anything, other than to ask once more that they not show Renn the photos. Kieran and Mia had agreed, mainly because Kieran felt sure it made no difference either way. They had sat there for a bit longer, all glued to their phones, until eventually Sean had looked up, his face heavy.

"You guys go, if you want to. I'm just going to sit here for a while."

Their offers to stay had been turned down until it had become awkward, and at last they'd left him sitting alone with his thoughts in the near-empty Surf and Turf.

The morning had dawned with a flat blue sky, and Mia was yawning as Kieran settled a fractious Audrey into the stroller. Brian sat in his chair and watched them put their shoes on. Kieran could hear Verity tackling the remaining boxes in the kitchen.

"Still nothing from Ash?" Mia said, and Kieran checked his phone. He shook his head. He'd left a few messages. All had gone unanswered and Mia eventually texted Olivia.

"Okay, she says Ash let her in last night, but didn't come to bed," Mia said, reading the reply as they stepped outside. "When she woke up this morning, he'd slept on the couch and had already gone out."

"To work?"

"I guess so."

"Right," Kieran said, starting down the road now. He stopped as he realized Mia wasn't following. She was looking the other way, shading her eyes.

"Let's go the beach way," she said.

"We've got the stroller."

"We'll carry her down then. Just a little way."

"Why?" It would be the first time Mia had set foot properly on the sand since Saturday night, as far as he was aware.

"I don't know, really. I want to see the spot where Bronte took our photo. And the others."

"I'm pretty sure the cops have already done this," he said, nodding at the phone in her hand. "Traced her movements, or whatever. That's got to be why Pendlebury was looking at The Survivors the other day, hasn't it?"

"Still." Mia shrugged. "Do you mind?"

"No," he said. "But I'm not sure there'll be anything to see that we haven't seen before."

He was right, at least about the beach. They identified as accurately as they could where they had first seen Bronte, beachcombing and crouching in the surf to look at seaweed. Now there was nothing at all to distinguish that spot from the long stretch of sand on either side. Farther along, though, above the tide line outside Fisherman's Cottage, Kieran could still make out a shimmer as the wind ran through the plastic-wrapped bouquets. Mia stood near the surf, holding her hair in a fist as she followed his gaze.

"Let's go back to the road" was all she said.

Kieran couldn't see the *Nautilus Blue* in dock as they neared the marina. On the off chance, he knocked at the door of Ash and Sean's beach house, but it was clear no one was home.

"Hopefully he's at work at the cemetery or somewhere, licking his wounds," Mia said, but she was frowning.

"Probably," Kieran said. "Knowing Ash."

Although, really knowing Ash, Kieran thought, it was unlike him not to bounce straight back from something.

They walked on, past Lyn having a cigarette beside the delivery entrance of the Surf and Turf. Mia slowed a little further along as they compared their position with the angle on Bronte's photo of the streetscape.

"Maybe this is stupid," Mia said as she found herself edging up against the dusty window of the newsstand to get the right line of sight.

"Maybe." Kieran nodded up the street toward the residential end. "But at least we're in good company."

Pendlebury was leaning against a low wall, her computer tablet out again. She had been squinting from the screen to a sandstone cottage but was now watching Mia hold her own phone out. They all looked at each other, then Pendlebury raised a hand and beckoned. A polite order, rather than an invitation.

"Great minds," she said lightly as they approached. "Sergeant Renn said he was in the Surf and Turf last night, thought that link had leaked." Pendlebury looked a little put out, but not particularly troubled. "So, if you're following those photos, I'm guessing you'll be heading up the cliff path to the lookout?" She pushed herself away from the wall. "I'll walk with you. I'm going that way myself."

"So we're right, then? These photos are from Bronte's camera?" Kieran said as they started walking through the old part of town.

Pendlebury reached out a hand for Mia's phone. Her thumb moved over the screen rapidly as they walked, checking the images, and after a few paces, she handed it back with a nod. "They're some of them."

"How did they get online?" he asked.

"Bronte's uni provided online storage space as part of her

course," Pendlebury said. "Art students have a lot of high-res files, I'm guessing. Bronte uploaded her stuff most days." She nodded at Mia's phone. "Ideally they wouldn't have gone on that social media site, but at some point she'd allowed other students shared access to some of her folders. Group projects, apparently."

"You couldn't block them?" Kieran said.

"We could, but then people start to wonder why and that's not always—" Pendlebury stopped short. Her pace slowed and she made a noise of frustration. "For God's sake."

They were approaching George Barlin's house, ripped-up garden and all. Parked on the road outside was Ash's dirty pickup.

Kieran could see Ash through the windshield, sitting in the driver's seat, engine off, arms crossed against the steering wheel. Shifty was next to him on the passenger's side, head out of the window and tongue lolling.

"He's been warned about this." Pendlebury glanced at Kieran. "He has to move on. I am very happy to—"

"No, it's okay." Kieran put the brake on the stroller. "I'll talk to him."

Ash had already fired up the engine by the time Kieran had crossed the road.

"It's all right, I'm going. I had something to see to but—" Ash leaned out of his open window and raised his voice in Pendlebury's direction. "I'm leaving now, okay? You don't need to call your mates, I'm going."

Ash sat back heavily in the seat and reached for the gears. Kieran put a hand on the door.

"Hey, wait a sec," he said.

"What, mate? I've got work to do."

"I messaged you."

"Yep." Ash sighed. "I'm at work, mate."

"Yeah, okay, but—"

Ash finally looked over. His face still carried a hint of the exposed nerve Kieran had seen the night before, but today he simply seemed tired.

"What?" Ash said again.

"Are you all right? After last night?"

"Fine."

"Right." Kieran still didn't move his hand off the door. "Because that stuff George was saying—"

"Oh." A tiny crease appeared around Ash's eyes. "Yeah, no, that's fine. Look, mate"—he put the truck into gear—"I've got to keep moving."

"Well, give me a call if you—"

But Ash was already raising an arm out the window in pointed farewell to Pendlebury. Kieran dropped his hand and took a step back as the truck moved away. They all watched until the vehicle was out of sight, then Kieran returned to the stroller. They started walking again.

"What did that garden look like before, out of interest?" Pendlebury said as they hit the cliff path.

"Beautiful," Mia replied.

They covered most of the hike up in silence, each lost in their own thoughts. As they neared the top, Mia jogged a few paces and caught up to Pendlebury.

"Do you think whoever took Bronte's camera and computer knew she was uploading the pictures somewhere?" she asked.

"I couldn't say." Pendlebury had her eyes on the ocean as they walked. "It depends who it was and why they did it."

"And you said these photos we can see online aren't all the ones she'd saved to her student folders?"

"That's right."

Mia was scrolling through her phone again as they walked,

her thumb moving up and down. "But would you say these ones are"—she hesitated—"a reflective sample?"

They had reached the top of the cliffs and stopped at the lookout. Out on the water, The Survivors stood tall. The *Nautilus Blue* rocked in the waves beyond, the blue-and-white dive flag visible. Pendlebury ignored the view, looking instead at Mia.

"All right," she said. "I can see you're worried because you and Kieran appear in one of the photos, so let me put your mind partly at ease. You are not the only ones."

"Really?"

"Not by a long way."

Kieran wasn't sure why he didn't feel more relieved.

Pendlebury turned back to the safety rail, her eyes on The Survivors.

"How's that tide looking, Kieran?" she said. "Low enough for a trip down?"

"Now?"

Pendlebury tucked her computer tablet under her arm. "Now would be good."

•   •   •

Mia didn't look happy but she didn't argue. Kieran passed her the stroller, and he and Pendlebury stepped around the barrier and made their way alone down the unmarked trail. When Pendlebury hit the sand at the bottom, she stopped, ignoring the birds that had risen into the air almost as one. She took in the gaping voids of the caves, then raised her face and squinted back up the steep cliff face to where they'd been. She took out the tablet again, frowning as she moved her index finger across the screen.

"All right," she said. "Now, I want you to bear in mind that Bronte was a twenty-one-year-old girl with a digital camera. So I'm not kidding when I tell you she took a lot of photos. Having said that—" Pendlebury held the screen so Kieran could see it.

"Can you identify the locations of any of these images? Take your time."

Kieran took the tablet and began to flick through Bronte's photos slowly, unsure what he was about to see. Many of the pictures were cropped so close they were essentially anonymous. Grains of sand, a tight photo of seaweed plastered green and jewel-like against a dark surface. He flipped back and forth, feeling Pendlebury's eyes on him.

"Sorry, I'm try—" Kieran started, then stopped, because all of a sudden he did recognize something.

A craggy surface with sand dusted across the face and crevasses carved deep by the water. A sharp line of contrast where daylight met permanent shade. The mouth of the North Cave, Kieran knew. There was no doubt, none at all, because in that tight-cropped photo, among the crevasses and the sand and the shade, his own name was carved into the rock.

Kieran looked at the casual scars of those letters that he had left years ago, captured now on a dead girl's camera, and felt a dash of fear.

He was still staring at the picture when Pendlebury reached across and swiped the screen again. A similar shot appeared, but this time it was Ash's name cutting through the corner of the frame. Another swipe and Ash's name was visible again. A different carving this time, the angle making it harder to read. Kieran couldn't tell where that one had been taken.

Pendlebury reached over and even before she swiped, Kieran could already half guess what was coming. Finn, then Finn again. The *R-A-N* tail end of another Kieran. Toby.

Kieran made himself look up and meet Pendlebury's eye.

"These are barely in shot," he said. And it was true. He looked down again, this time at the *S-E-A* of Sean. The image was very tight, with the letters out of focus and distorted by the shadows from a harsh flash. Kieran pointed to a piece of flowering lichen blossoming next to the *S*.

"Bronte was clearly taking close-ups of the rock," he said. "These don't mean anything."

"I didn't say they meant anything." Pendlebury's face was perfectly neutral. "I was asking if you knew where they were located."

"Some of them. I suppose."

"All right," she said. "Show me."

Kieran led her across the sand to the mouth of the North Cave. It was cool and dark in the shadows, and it took a minute for Kieran's eyes to adjust. He could see Pendlebury blinking as she gazed around.

"Here." He pointed to the wall. "These ones you saw yesterday. And there are a few more over here."

Pendlebury flipped open her tablet and scrutinized the screen, then the rock face. She took a few steps one way, then pulled out her own phone and took a photo. Then a few more steps and another photo. Kieran watched as she repeated that several times, trying to re-create the angle. She stared at the tablet and shook her head.

"I don't think this one is right. The space between the lettering isn't the same." She turned the tablet screen so Kieran could see. He could make out Ash's name in the corner of the photo.

"It might not be." Kieran shrugged. "There are a few around."

"Can we find them all? I'd really like to get these locations marked off."

The cave stretched out before them, deep and meandering. "They could be anywhere. I wouldn't even know where to start."

"There was no system to it?"

"Not really. Originally we did it when we'd mapped a new route." Kieran found he didn't have the energy to defend it. "But a lot of the time it was just because we were bored. Not Sean so much, he thought it was a shit thing to do. He did it once because I made him, but me and Ash would do it all the time. And Toby. And Finn, obviously."

"Anyone else? Mia?"

Kieran stopped. He felt cold in the shadows. "No. Why?" He glanced up, although the lookout was completely invisible from where he stood. "She's never been down here. Why are you even asking?"

"What about Gabby Birch?"

"No." Kieran stared at her, confused. "What does she have to do with anything? Or Mia?"

"I'm just asking questions, Kieran. Trying to build a picture." Pendlebury paused. "How about Olivia?"

Kieran couldn't tell if she knew, or if she was fishing. He couldn't tell if it mattered. "Yeah, Olivia's been here."

Pendlebury was peering into the cave. The birds had settled and Kieran could hear the waves breaking on the shore.

"Can we go in further?" she said. "See what we can see?"

"No," Kieran said. "Not with me. It gets like a maze. I don't know it well enough."

"You used to."

Kieran nodded at the names scratched into the wall. "I used to do a lot of things I don't do anymore."

"Fair enough." Pendlebury flipped the tablet around so Kieran could see the photos once more. "Take a look at these, then. Is anything else familiar enough to pinpoint?"

Kieran flicked through more of Bronte's photos, dreading each new shot.

"The Survivors, obviously," he said. "And that's the edge of the path at low tide. North Cave again." He was strangely aware of a faint niggle burrowing somewhere deep as he looked through the images, but he couldn't dig it out. Something felt a little off. He skimmed through a few shots too closely cropped to recognize, then came to a halt at the sight of a familiar corner he had seen many times. The ledge in the South Cave, where he and Olivia used to meet. Kieran could feel Pendlebury watching him.

"I know where that is."

"Show me, please?"

They both squinted in the light as Kieran led the way back out across the beach, this time to the mouth of the South Cave. As they plunged once more into the gloom, Kieran pointed at the photo on Pendlebury's screen and then to the ledge.

"Those shots were taken around here."

Pendlebury walked over to the rock and ran her fingers over it. She dropped her hand and took out her phone, firing off a few shots of her own before frowning at the screen. She looked up again, noticing Ash's name scratched into the rock above the ledge. She raised an eyebrow at Kieran, who shrugged.

"Like I said, there are a few."

His voice bounced off the walls before being absorbed and deadened by the sand. Pendlebury cocked her head, listening.

"I can't get used to the sound in here," she said, turning back to the ledge.

Kieran waited, feeling uneasy. Outside, through the arch of the cave's entrance, he could see a wide strip of beach lying between them and the sea. Under his feet, the sand was firm. It wasn't wet, it wasn't covered with water. Everything was fine, he told himself. The tide was out, not in. They had plenty of time.

"What's wrong?" Pendlebury was looking at him.

"Nothing."

"Are you sure?"

"Yes." Kieran pushed back against a rare wave of claustrophobia. The roof suddenly felt unusually low and he put a hand up to check it was still out of reach. "Sorry. I used to come to this spot a bit when I was younger."

"Before the storm?" Pendlebury was still watching him. "On the day of the storm?"

"Both." Kieran shrugged.

She was quiet for a moment and ran her hand thoughtfully over the cave's rocky wall.

"I had a friend. *Have* a friend, technically, although—" She sighed and started again. "A couple of years ago my friend and her husband were having a few quiet drinks at home on a Friday night. After dinner, they went for a dip in their own backyard pool. By the time she realized he wasn't messing around, he was in serious trouble." Pendlebury shook her head. "Didn't make it. She's struggled badly ever since."

"I'm sorry," Kieran said. He meant it.

"Thanks. It's been hard. For her, obviously. But also watching her slowly self-destruct, you know?"

Kieran did know. He remembered it well, those first years after Finn's death. Trying different ways to cope. Some worked, a lot didn't. He remembered the keen sliver of hope followed by the overwhelming frustration of disappointment. The secret fear he was running out of things to try. And then, in the midst of it all, suddenly there was Mia. Appearing in front of him unexpectedly, a longed-for oasis of calm in a shabby student bar.

"Mia helps a lot," he said. "And Audrey."

"And things with your folks?"

"Well, they love me, obviously. But they also loved Finn. So—" He wasn't sure what else he could say about that.

Pendlebury had a curious look on her face. A mix of sympathy and something else he couldn't place.

"Kieran," she said. "I have to ask. What do you think happened here that day of the storm?"

"What do I *think* happened? I was here. I know what happened."

"Of course." There was an odd pause. "So I'd be interested to
hear it from you."

Kieran stared at the ledge, and then he opened his mouth
and he told her. The real version. About Olivia and how they
used to meet up and lay their towels out in this spot. How one
day the weather was bad, and she'd suggested they leave but he'd
asked her to stay. So they had, but they'd let time slip away until the sand had disappeared under the water and all at once it
was too late. He hadn't been able to find the path. The sea had
been stronger than he was. Kieran's brother and his best friend's
brother had come to save him. They had died. And he had survived.

Pendlebury listened without interruption.

"That must have been very hard for you," she said when he
finished.

Kieran didn't reply. Sometimes sharing the story was almost
a release of tension, but other times, like now, he felt nothing but
shame. Either way, reliving it always left him feeling drained.

Pendlebury pressed her lips together and Kieran had the
strange sense that she was arguing with herself.

"I can't imagine what that must be like to live with," Pendlebury said at last.

"It's not great."

"No. I saw what guilt did to that friend I mentioned." A
shadow crossed Pendlebury's features. "We used to be very close,
but she's like a different person now. Kieran—" She turned her
head in the vague direction of where the town lay, well out of
sight beyond cliffs and water. "There are a lot of people dragging up all kinds of things right now. A lot of chatter being flung
around, and not all of it true or helpful."

Kieran wasn't sure what to say to that. He could hear water dripping somewhere in the cave.

"I would really hate for you to stumble across a half-baked version of this," Pendlebury said.

Kieran felt a prickle of warning at the base of his neck. "Half-baked version of what?"

Pendlebury's internal struggle flickered again in her eyes. She stared deep into the cave, then back out to where the seawater was foaming blue and white against the sand. At last, she took a deep breath and looked him in the eye. Decision made.

"Kieran, there's something you deserve to know."

30

Pendlebury started toward the mouth of the cave. "Let's get out of here first. I think it would be helpful for Mia to hear this too."

This time, it was Kieran following as she led them back out into the daylight, blinking.

"What—?" he started, but she held up a hand.

"At the lookout. Then we'll talk."

They found Mia sitting on the bench, rocking the stroller back and forth as they emerged at the top of the overgrown path. She looked up, her worried expression turning into relief.

"Finished?" She went to stand, stopping when she saw Kieran's face. "What's going on?"

"Something's come to my attention recently that I think Kieran should be aware of," Pendlebury said, taking a seat on the bench. Mia looked wary but slowly sat back down too.

Kieran remained standing. In the pale summer light, the sea was sparkling. Above the wreck he could see the *Nautilus Blue* listing gently.

"All right." Pendlebury's voice was calm. "I'm here in Evelyn

Bay to find out what happened to Bronte Laidler. That's it. That's my whole job. This storm of yours, Gabby Birch's disappearance, all this local gossip that's getting put about online—none of that is why I'm here." She paused. "But part of asking questions means you tend to get answers. Things that aren't necessarily relevant to me, but it doesn't mean they're not relevant at all."

Kieran shifted impatiently. Mia was looking back and forth between them.

"I've spoken to George Barlin a couple of times," Pendlebury said. "You know he's a former journalist?"

"Yeah."

"You've read his books?"

"Most of them," Kieran said, and Mia nodded.

"Me too," Pendlebury said. "Not my usual taste, but not bad at all. Anyway, since he moved here, he's been doing a bit of research around the storm."

"For a book?" Mia said.

"He says mostly for his own interest. He was in town that year. He said experiencing that storm was something he's never forgotten." Pendlebury shrugged. "Personally, it's none of my business if he's planning to write about it or not. And at first, I wasn't too interested in what happened back then. Like I said, I'm here to worry about what took place a few days ago, not twelve years ago." She stared out at the water, tapping a finger absently on her knee. "But then George mentioned something that did strike me as interesting."

"What?" Kieran said.

"The accident that happened out here? With you and your brother and Toby Gilroy?" Pendlebury turned to him now. "The timing doesn't work."

Kieran frowned and saw Mia do the same.

"What do you mean?" she said. "What timing?"

"The events on that day of the storm. You getting into trouble in the water, Kieran. The distress call, the attempted rescue. The drownings. It can't have happened the way you think it happened."

"Of course it did." Kieran gave a laugh that sounded odd to his ears. "I was literally there."

Pendlebury shook her head. "No. It didn't."

She opened her computer tablet again, squinting as she shielded the screen from the sun. Kieran waited, suddenly disoriented, like when a wave dropped out from under a boat. Momentarily airborne, followed by a jarring slam.

"Are you going to tell us what you mean?" Mia was saying. She got to her feet and came to stand next to Kieran.

Pendlebury held up a finger, nodding as she searched for something. Finally, she made a noise of satisfaction and looked up.

"Right. So the accepted version of the accident—by you, Kieran, by everyone, essentially—is that you were here at the caves doing some route mapping work for your brother, the storm came in faster than you realized, and you were swept into the sea. You've told me Olivia Birch was with you—"

Pendlebury stopped suddenly and glanced at Mia, who rolled her eyes. Of course she knew.

"But as far as anyone else is concerned," the officer continued, "Olivia was on the cliff path, hurrying to get home in the rain when she saw you in trouble in the water. She made an emergency call, the word got patched through to Julian Wallis as head of the local search and rescue operations, and he put out an alert that was picked up by Finn and Toby. They confirmed they would respond, they raced out on the *Nautilus Black* from the marina, rounded the point here by the caves, and were hit by a freak wave. The boat sent out a distress signal of its own, but nothing could be done and they drowned."

Kieran gave a tight nod. "That's about it."

"Right. The thing is, the time of every one of those calls and alerts was noted. They're right there—fair enough, they're spread all over the place across various official records—but they're backed up by phone data, emergency signals. The individual times are correct, they've never been in dispute." Pendlebury looked over at Kieran. "The problem George Barlin picked up when he sat down with all those separate documents in one place and looked at them properly with his notebook and writer's quill or whatever, is that the story doesn't work."

"In what possible way does all that not work?" Kieran said. He felt Mia shift next to him.

"The only way the timing fits is if Finn and Toby were already out on the water in their boat when they got the radio message that you were in trouble."

Kieran stared at Pendlebury, but she was looking past him now, out to the *Nautilus Blue*.

"It takes, what, fifteen minutes—absolute minimum—to sail out here from the marina, correct?" she said. "That's what I understand."

"Yeah." Fifteen was pushing it, actually; twenty was much more typical.

"Right. Well, from the time Olivia's first emergency call was made—confirmed by phone records—to the time your brother responded on the *Nautilus Black* radio, just under four minutes had elapsed. Less than three minutes after that, the *Nautilus Black*'s distress signal was activated, with the GPS positioning them out there on the water beyond the caves."

Pendlebury looked at Kieran now.

"From when you were swept away to when your brother and Toby arrived, not even ten minutes had gone by. They can't have been at the marina when the emergency call came in; they were already out on their boat."

Kieran shook his head. "No. That's—"

"See for yourself." Pendlebury handed him the tablet. "The important bits are highlighted."

Kieran took it, and Mia leaned in to see, her face close to his. He could hear her breathing as he tapped the screen. A phone record appeared, and another, then a string of official reports and records. Kieran flicked back and forth, again and again, trying to absorb what he was seeing while Mia read over his shoulder.

Not trusting his own eyes, he glanced at her.

"What do you think?" He was surprised to find himself whispering.

She pointed at the screen. There, and there. And there.

The emergency call made by Olivia, the log report filed by Julian, the response by the *Nautilus Black*, the activation of the boat's distress call.

Kieran tried to concentrate. How long had he been in the water before he was thrown onto the rock and caught that first glimpse of the *Nautilus Black*? It had felt like hours, but—Kieran made himself focus. But he had survived, so it could only have been minutes, at most. How many? He looked down at the screen. Less than ten, according to the black-and-white text in front of him.

Kieran opened his mouth. "If these timings are right—"

"They are."

"Okay, but—" He couldn't think of a single thing to say.

"Why has no one picked up on this before?" Mia said, but from her tone Kieran could tell she had also guessed the answer almost as soon as she'd asked. Because with everything else that had happened that day, the minutiae simply hadn't mattered. Not to the traumatized crowd who'd gathered on the clifftop to watch two men drown. Not to townspeople faced with damaged homes and destroyed businesses. Not to the family of the missing girl, last seen on the beach with her backpack and then never again. Ash's voice rang in his head. *It was a crazy day.*

"So if those timings are accurate, that would mean Finn and Toby—" Kieran was still not quite there yet.

"That Finn and Toby were out on their boat and headed in this general direction before they even knew you were in the water, yes," Pendlebury said. "So whatever went wrong that day, Kieran, it wasn't your fault in the way you think it was."

Kieran opened his mouth but felt like he couldn't draw breath. He felt Mia's palm on his back, rubbing in circles. He bent forward and buried his face in his hands.

He could almost see it, and felt sick with giddiness. He'd been carrying this weight for so many years, he couldn't imagine what it might feel like to be able to set it down. The lightness and the freedom. He could tell Verity. He could try to tell Brian. The thought of that flashed so tempting and bright it was almost painful.

But beneath the dazzle he felt something sliding and flickering. A question. Kieran tried to ignore it, but it turned over in his mind. Prodding at him, soft but insistent. He raised his head and thought from Mia's face that she was wondering the same thing. The same question Verity would arrive at after the initial rush had ebbed away. The same one everyone in Evelyn Bay would eventually gossip about over their coffees and keyboards. Kieran knew what they would all ask, because he was already asking it himself.

Kieran could feel Pendlebury's eyes on him. She seemed to know what he was going to ask even as he opened his mouth.

"What were Finn and Toby doing out on their boat in the middle of the storm?"

31

Pendlebury didn't answer. Kieran waited but she simply gazed back, a faint hint of regret or apology or both in the air.

"Why were Finn and Toby out on their boat?" he tried again.

"I don't know that, I'm afraid."

Kieran wasn't sure if the dull rushing he could hear was the ocean or the blood pounding in his ears.

"Finn knew the storm would be dangerous," he said. "He and Toby were two of the only people who realized how bad it could get. They were the ones warning us the day before to stay off the water."

"I understand that. But I still can't tell you why they were out there." Underneath Pendlebury's neutral tone, there was a note Kieran couldn't place.

Mia was watching her. "Can't or won't?"

"Can't. I would be speculating. I'm sorry," she said to Kieran, who was leaning heavily against the safety rail. "This is obviously a lot for you to process. I hope I've done the right thing in telling you, but I feel in the end the truth's usually the best—"

Pendlebury broke off and pulled her phone out of her pocket. Kieran hadn't heard it ring, but she frowned at the lit-up screen.

"I'm so sorry, I really have to take this." Pendlebury lifted the phone to her ear. "Just a minute, please," she said into it, then lowered it again. "Thanks for showing me around down there, Kieran. I'll make my own way back to town. And, listen—" Her full attention was on them and she was silent for a long moment. "If you have any questions, you know where the station is."

Pendlebury raised the phone, dropped her head, and turned away. Kieran didn't move, unsure if this was her way of avoiding further discussion. He felt Mia touch his arm.

"Let's go," she said firmly, and clicked the brake off the stroller.

The lookout was out of sight behind them before either of them spoke again.

"She knows why they were out there." Mia's voice was low.

"I think so too," Kieran said. "Or has an idea. There was something in the way she was talking, right? So why won't she say?"

"I don't know."

Their footsteps crunched along the trail as they passed the cemetery gates. Kieran marched on, barely registering the path in front of him. He kept trying to take a breath but was finding it hard to fill his lungs. After a few more paces, he felt Mia slow.

"Stop. Take a minute." She parked the stroller. The path was deserted in both directions. From where they stood, the ocean was an unbroken flat plain.

Kieran turned to her, his chest still tight. "What did you make of that stuff she showed us?"

"About the timings? I'd want to check it properly, but—" Mia nodded. "What she was saying looked right to me."

"Me too. And also George Barlin, yeah? He spotted it on his own." Kieran ran his hands over his head. His heart was hammering like he'd been swimming for hours. "So—" He was struggling to form his thoughts. "Is that it? Just like that? It's suddenly not my fault anymore?"

"I'm not sure," Mia said. "Yes. Maybe."

"So what now?"

"I don't know."

"I don't know either. Oh God, Mia. I am so *tired*." He covered his eyes. They were hot and prickling. "I am so tired of feeling guilty."

"I know." She put her arms around him. "It's okay."

"But this means I don't have to feel that anymore, right? That's what this means?"

A pause. "That's right."

He pulled back. "So why don't I feel any better about it?"

Mia looked at him, her hands still warm against his arms. She didn't say anything, and he almost had the urge to smile.

"I know you're thinking the same thing as me," Kieran said.

"And what's that?"

"You're thinking that I don't feel better because it's bothering me why Finn was on the water."

"Okay, yes," she conceded. "That is what I was thinking."

Kieran's almost-smile faded. "And that if Pendlebury knows but wouldn't tell me—" He breathed out. "There's a reason for it. So what's the reason?"

"It could be a lot of things," Mia said. "I don't think you can draw any conclusions from that."

"Can't I?"

"No. You can't." Mia fell quiet, then looked back along the path. "I was actually thinking something else too."

"What?"

"That if Pendlebury does know why Finn was on the water, that's some pretty impressive inside knowledge," she said.

"Especially for a woman who's not a local. She might be a good cop, I don't know either way, but she's definitely an outsider. She wasn't here for the storm, she doesn't remember it the way we all do. If Pendlebury knows something about what happened here twelve years ago—something that specific—it's because some-one's told her. Someone who was here. It has to be."

Kieran stared at her, the possibilities lining up like cogs on a wheel. Mia was right. If Pendlebury knew, someone else knew too.

"Who?" He felt deep down he had the answer to this, but his head was spinning too fast to focus.

But Mia was already nodding.

"Well, it's like Pendlebury told us herself, isn't it?" she said. "If we have any questions about this, we know where the police station is."

• • •

Sergeant Chris Renn was dragging an empty filing cabinet out-side when Kieran and Mia walked up to the station.

Kieran held the glass door open for him as Renn edged the cabinet out.

"Thanks," Renn grunted. A corner caught on the door hinges and he gave it a whack to wrench it free. He picked the cabinet up without any trouble and slid it in against the brick wall, next to four others. "Someone from the school's coming to collect them this afternoon."

The sergeant dug a tissue out of his pocket and wiped the shine from his forehead.

"What can I do for you two?" He glanced down at the stroller. "Three."

"Why were Finn and Toby out on the water that day?" Kieran said, and he sensed rather than saw Mia roll her eyes. They had rehearsed this on the way down, but now that he was here the subtleties had deserted him.

Renn didn't ask what Kieran meant. He looked at them both for a long minute, then turned back to the station. He straightened one of the filing cabinets and reached for the glass door.

"Come in."

The station felt even emptier than last time as they followed Renn through. The remaining desks were still cluttered, and Kieran saw one of the uniformed officers from the community meeting nudging someone's laptop precariously close to the edge to make space for his own. He stopped when he saw Kieran watching him. The map of Evelyn Bay had fallen down and stood on the corridor floor, propped up against the wall, its laminated corners curling inward.

Renn showed Kieran and Mia into the same office as before. There was only one chair in front of the battered desk now, and they waited while he fetched another. When he came back, he put his hand over a small pile of photos stacked by the computer and turned them facedown. Pictures of Bronte supplied by her parents, Kieran realized belatedly.

"Right, then," Renn said when they were all settled. "What's all this about?"

"Finn and Toby. On the day of the storm." Kieran crossed his arms over his chest and tucked in his hands to stop them shaking. "They were already out in the *Nautilus Black* before the call came in to say I was in trouble."

Renn looked slowly from Kieran to Mia. "Who've you been chatting to? George Barlin?"

They shook their heads and Kieran saw a shadow of surprise cross Renn's face. *Pendlebury, then*, Kieran could almost see him thinking. Whatever Renn made of that, he masked it well. He was such a far cry from the flushed constable who had followed Sergeant Mallott around town, jumping in fear and obedience at his every word. It was hard to believe he was the same man.

This Renn, older and in the boss's seat now, squared his keyboard against the edge of his desk, buying himself a moment.

"So what are you getting at, Kieran, mate?" he said.

"Finn and Toby didn't go out on the water for me. The timing doesn't work."

A statement, not a question. Kieran braced himself for a straight denial, but Renn held his gaze.

"Well, I'd have to double-check the records—" Renn's tone was measured, but Kieran saw a flicker in the sergeant's face. It was as good as a confirmation.

Mia had caught it too. "I don't think you need to check anything, Chris. If that's how it happened, you would know."

"Okay," Renn said, still calm. "Well, if that's the case, then what exactly is it you want from me?"

"Why did you bury that?" Kieran leaned in. "How about we start right there?"

"Me?" Renn stiffened a little at that. "Mate, I wasn't in charge back then."

"Sergeant Mallott, then. And that's a bullshit excuse. You were both on duty. Whatever went on in the storm, you'd both know about it. You two were the ones who dealt with everything."

"Yeah," Renn said. He sat back in his chair so heavily the wheels squeaked. He sounded suddenly very tired. "We did, didn't we? Every single thing that happened in that storm. He and I had to deal with it."

"So you did know, then? And what? Never mentioned it?"

There was a silence. Kieran braced himself for the order to leave but it didn't come. The muted rattle of a photocopier firing up floated in from the hallway.

"What happened to Bronte has been really hard."

Kieran, who had been about to launch in again, stopped in

surprise at his words. Renn turned over the stack of photos on his desk. The dead woman smiled out and his face tightened.

"It's been hard for everyone, I know that. But in all my years in this job, I never thought I'd see something like this happen here. I keep thinking about what I've done—or haven't done, maybe?—for that to happen on my watch. When did Evelyn Bay become a place where a girl who comes for summer work ends up dead?" Renn turned the photos facedown again and Bronte disappeared once more. "I want it cleared up. I had her mum and dad in here again earlier and I want to be able to give them an answer. I can't leave here with this on my conscience, but they won't keep the station open indefinitely—"

He surveyed his half-empty office and took a breath.

"George Barlin told me and Pendlebury something looked off with the storm timings when we went round to his place to get him to sign a statement about Bronte. He thought he'd messed up his research and kept asking about it. Wouldn't let it go."

There was a clatter from out in the hallway, and they all looked at the door. A muffled swear word floated in, followed by the sound of a box being repacked. Renn turned back to Kieran.

"And this is at the same time as Pendlebury was getting very interested, mate, in the fact that your dad was the last person seen with Gabby Birch, and then also found wandering around when Bronte was killed. I'd already got Trish Birch talking up a connection, and then suddenly there's George Barlin picking holes in a timeline concerning your family that day, Kieran."

Kieran felt like he could hardly breathe. The stroller creaked as Mia rocked it back and forth.

"That storm—" The phone on Renn's desk started to ring. He checked the number, then waited until it stopped before he spoke again. "The storm has done its damage. There's nothing to be gained from letting that wound fester. I really believed that. I still do. Things were done and decisions were made at the time, rightly or wrongly, and as a community we got through it and we moved on. But Pendlebury wants answers about Bronte as much as I do, so she's asking questions." Renn dropped his chin. "And she's looking years into the past and then she's looking at Brian, and so I have to tell her about some of those decisions made back in the storm. Because I want this resolved for Bronte and for her mum and dad, and we're not going to be able to do that if I've got key officers wasting time looking in the wrong direction."

Kieran swallowed. "Thank you, Chris."

"Don't thank me yet."

The office was so quiet, they could hear someone's mobile ringing in another room. And suddenly, in what felt like a blinding premonition, Kieran had the urge to turn back the clock. Refuse to take Pendlebury down to the caves, tell her he'd made his peace with the storm and wasn't interested in dredging it up again. He wished he and Mia had gone home instead of coming here to this police station, where he suddenly found himself very afraid of what Sergeant Renn was going to say next. He felt Mia stir. She looked worried too.

"Finn and Toby were already out on the water that day," Renn said. "You're right about that. Despite all the warnings and whatever, they'd got on their boat as the storm came in and by the time we got word you were in trouble out at the caves, they'd already left the marina. And I didn't know exactly why then, and I still don't." Renn looked Kieran in the eye. "And that's the truth."

He took a breath, and Kieran had to fight the urge to tell him to stop talking. He'd heard enough. That was all he needed to know.

"But this is what I can tell you. After Finn and Toby drowned, we worked hard to bring their boat back in, to show your families we cared about those blokes. We said we'd look it over, me and Sergeant Mallott. Try to help your families by giving them the best information we could about what'd happened."

Renn shifted again in his chair. There was no disguising his uneasiness now.

"And as it was, Sergeant Mallott did find something on the *Nautilus Black*."

"What?" Kieran couldn't stop himself. "What did he find?"

"Gabby Birch's backpack."

32

There was a rustle from inside the stroller, the soft thrash of limbs, and Audrey began to cry. Kieran barely registered the sound. Mia had curled herself forward with her elbows on her knees and her face in her palms. Audrey's wails bounced off the office walls until finally Sergeant Renn moved to stand.

"I've got her." Kieran got up and reached into the stroller. "Don't touch her."

Renn held up his hands and sat down again.

"The bag was locked in the dry box—" Renn realized Kieran had stayed standing. "Sorry, do you still want to hear this?"

Kieran felt a lot like he was shaking, but Audrey was steady in his arms as he soothed her. Did he want to hear? *Gabby Birch's backpack*. What he really wanted was for that not to be true.

Mia said something, her voice muffled. She lowered her hands and tried again. "Just tell us."

Renn glanced at the door. There was no sound from the hall now.

"Me and Geoff Mallott were working flat out from the minute

that storm passed through. The town was a wreck. We had people injured. We'd been organizing the search crews for Gabby, getting word out. Circulating her description, what she'd been wearing. Her bag. Purple stripes with a kangaroo key ring." Renn rubbed his neck, remembering. "Looking over the *Nautilus Black* was a courtesy. We didn't have the time really, wouldn't have done it for tourists. But with it being two local men, local families—"

Renn looked up at Kieran, still on his feet.

"We wanted to make sure you all felt like we'd taken care of them. But we were busy, and I'd been held up at the station dealing with things still coming in and I was rushing down to the marina to meet Mallott. I was nearly at the gate, you know, that one where you can look straight across the docks?"

He paused, as Kieran nodded.

"I was still a fair way away but I could see Mallott already on the boat. He had the bolt cutters out and was working on the padlock on the dry box. My phone rang; it was the medical center with some crisis, and I had to stop at the gate to take the call. I was annoyed, I remember, pacing up and down because I needed to get them off the phone so I could get on with things. I looked out across the docks and I could see Sergeant Mallott. He'd got the box open and was reaching inside"—Renn stared at his desk, his gaze somewhere far away and long ago—"and he pulled something out. And it looked to me a whole lot like purple-striped fabric."

Kieran held Audrey tight as Renn opened his mouth again.

"And I remember feeling completely blindsided. I didn't know what to make of it, and I couldn't work it out, because I was stuck on that bloody call." Renn breathed out. "It took ages, and I'm having to search my bag for notes I made hours earlier, and I'm being transferred by the medical center to a doctor at the hospital, and then at last I can hang up.

"So I'm rushing into the marina, apologizing, stressed-out,

and I'm expecting Mallott to call me over to the dry box to cor-
roborate, take some photos, but he doesn't. He's just standing on
the deck—as normal as you like—and he says he's all finished.
He asks me to call the relief coordinators and tell them we'll be
coming around to do checks and updates."

Mia made a small noise in her throat. She was staring at
him, her hands clasped tight in her lap.

"So I asked Mallott straight-out what was in the dry box."
Renn's mouth pressed into a hard line. "And he said there was
nothing much. Those were the words he used. Nothing much.
Charts and things. The lid was wide open by then. I had a look
inside. There was no bag in there."

Kieran felt a stirring of hope. "Maybe you were wrong."

"Yeah, I wondered that too. I mean, it had been chaos, and
I must've repeated that description of Gabby a hundred times. I
thought maybe I was so tired I'd got confused. So I said to Mallott that I thought I'd seen him lift something out of the box. He
looked me in the eye and he said no." Renn shook his head. "And
I knew that he was lying to me. I could tell. It was the first time
I'd ever known him to do that. I couldn't think what to do."

The faint sounds of chatter rose and fell as someone passed
in the corridor. Mia took a breath. "So what did you do?"

"Geoff and I stood there looking at each other, and then he
got on his radio like nothing had happened. He ordered me to
follow him to the cars and we went and did our relief checks. We
were at it until the early hours. When we finally finished, I went
home but I couldn't sleep. I kept running it over in my mind, and
the next morning I felt sure I knew what I'd seen." Renn gave a
hard smile. "Mallott was already here at the station when I got
in. Early—earlier than I'd ever known him to get here—like he
was waiting for me. So I put it to him straight, said I thought I'd
seen Gabby's bag in the box. He sat me down. Here in this room."

Renn nodded to where Kieran and Mia were sitting on the other side of the battered desk. "And he told me I was wrong."

"He denied it?" Kieran said.

"Well, he wouldn't admit it," Renn said. "Which isn't quite the same thing. But he brought me in here, gave me a coffee, talked in that matter-of-fact way of his about how we had three families grieving. Did I really want to go stirring things up when we had no answers, only more questions? He kept going on about how before I went upsetting families, I'd really want to have proof of something, like the bag itself. Did I have the bag? Did I have anything like that?"

Renn leaned back and his chair groaned.

"We argued. Me and him. I wanted to call in the families, starting with Trish and Olivia. Tell them what I'd seen. Mallott kept repeating himself. Really calm. We had two men dead. A lot of people to think about. Your parents, Kieran, worried about your recovery. Toby's wife was filled up to her eyes with prescription meds, she was so upset by what had happened. His boy, Liam, was only young. And wherever Gabby was, she wasn't on that boat anymore. So we were no further forward."

Renn closed his eyes, frowning.

"So yeah, we argued. As much as that was possible. I was young, brand-new. Mallott was my sergeant. I know—" He held up a hand as Kieran opened his mouth. "I know that's no excuse, but that's how it was. I went back to the *Nautilus Black* myself, but there was no sign of any backpack by then, so the chain of evidence was already destroyed. Next thing, I hear some dog walkers have found the bag on the beach. Pretty bloody convenient, like Trish has always said."

Kieran pictured Trish Birch. The way she scoured the sea. He felt his chest clench.

"When I heard the bag had washed up," Renn said, "I reckon I had about five seconds to open my mouth and tell everyone what I thought had really happened. But it had been such a bloody hard time and I'd been running on empty for days, working nonstop. I could barely think straight. And the funerals were around the corner and everyone was still shaken up and vulnerable and—" He stopped. "I didn't say anything. And then after that, I couldn't, could I? I felt like my hands were tied. The funerals were dreadful. The families were devastated and it was obvious how much Finn and Toby had meant to everyone, and I thought—"

Renn looked up at the ceiling, blinking.

"I don't know, honestly. I suppose I started to think maybe Geoff Mallott was right. Finding that backpack on the boat only gave us more questions than answers about Gabby. It didn't clear anything up, and it would definitely cause a lot more confusion and pain. Mallott reckoned we'd all had enough of that. I wondered if maybe he had a point."

"This is bullshit." Kieran surprised himself. He saw Mia look up. "It is. So what if the bag was on the boat? Gabby fell in the water. Finn and Toby must have fished out her backpack. That's all."

"No." Renn was already shaking his head. "No, mate. That bag hadn't been in the sea. There was a bit of damage to the boat itself, yeah, but that dry box was watertight. You know what it's like. Nothing gets in there. I could see it for myself, even while Mallott stood there lying to me. There was no water in there. You could still read the handwriting on the charts. The bag can't have been wet when it was put inside, or it would have leaked and dripped all over the place. But it was bone dry in that box. Someone carried that backpack on board."

Mia fixed her eyes on Renn. "Who?"

"Who knows?" he said. "Gabby herself? Finn? Toby? Someone else? But if Gabby Birch was on that boat that day, it wasn't because she was pulled out of the sea."

33

Mia was the first to react.

"We have to tell Olivia," she said, pushing back her chair. "And Trish."

"Wait," Kieran started, but she was already standing up. "Mia, okay, just—"

"No." She slowed, though, and took a step closer. She touched his arm. "No, Kieran. We're not going to do this. This is not the kind of thing you want to keep to yourself. Do you hear me? It would be unbearable." She didn't need to look at Renn, who had his elbows on the desk and his head in his hands. "I can't do it, and I can't watch you do it."

"But—" Kieran felt Audrey twist in his arms and his head was suddenly full of Trish Birch. Her backpacks. Her slow walks up and down the shoreline, searching for a sign from someone so long gone. How would Kieran measure up against the nightmare of his own child lost? He thought about Trish, and Bronte's parents, and—his heart constricted in a familiar way—Brian and Verity. He could feel the flutter of Audrey's pulse. He didn't know how any of them got through a single day. He couldn't bring himself to imagine what it took.

"I'll tell Trish and Olivia," Renn said, into his hands.

Mia turned. "You've had twelve years to tell them."

"I know." He raised his head. "I have wanted to, though. Every single time I see Trish, I think about telling her. Every time. When I see her on that beach. When I hear that she's thrown another one of those bags of hers into the ocean. How much longer can I stand back and let her keep doing that?" He rubbed his face in frustration. "I've wanted to tell Olivia, whenever I can see that she's sad or worried. Which is a lot. So yeah, I'm very aware of what it's done to that family, don't you worry about that. The thing that's stopped me, for what it's worth—" There was a long pause. "The truth hurts a lot of people. That was the case then, and it's the case now. And it still doesn't bring Gabby back. Trish and Olivia stay hurt anyway."

Mia wavered, then opened her mouth. "But Trish—"

"Yeah, I know." Renn stopped her. "I do know. I'll talk to them. And Toby's family. With everything going on, it's going to come out anyway. Sue Pendlebury knows now, and I can't see George Barlin letting his questions about the timings drop. But I'd like to tell Trish myself. So I can tell her I'm sorry." Renn looked like a man lost. "And I'd like Olivia to hear it from me."

Mia was already reaching to put Audrey in the stroller, but Kieran stayed where he was.

"Wait," he said.

"Kieran," she said. "You know they have to be told. Whether Chris does it or we do, they have to hear it."

"I know that." Kieran held on tight to his daughter and looked at Renn. "But you have to give me the chance to tell my mum first."

•　　•　　•

Verity was in the ocean. She was standing waist-deep with her head moving slowly back and forth as she watched Brian swim laps. Brian drove through the water with a smooth freestyle stroke. His technique was still very good, Kieran thought. He hadn't forgotten that, at least. Verity shielded her eyes and waved as she saw them approaching.

"He loves this. And it's easier than trying to persuade him to have a shower," Verity said, her smile fading as she noticed their faces. "What's wrong?"

They took her to sit among the boxes on the back veranda. Brian lay on his towel in a patch of sunlight with his eyes closed, letting the heat dry his board shorts.

Kieran didn't know how to begin. After a few false starts Verity frowned—"For God's sake, Kieran, just say it"—and Mia had to step in. She faltered as well, as Verity's face slowly began to change, hardening around the eyes first and then the mouth and jaw. Kieran took over once more and eventually, with Mia's help, they followed Verity's advice and just came out with it. Verity sat with her hands in her lap and her head tilted forward as she listened to them explain what Pendlebury had said, and then Renn. The timings, the boat, the box, the backpack. Kieran didn't finish speaking as much as trail off as Verity suddenly stood up.

"Right," she said. "Well, I'd better get your dad dried and dressed."

"But—" Kieran watched in disbelief as she walked across the veranda. "Mum, wait. Just, stop, okay? Are you going to say anything?"

"What can I possibly say to all that?" She didn't look at them. "Obviously, it's not true."

"But Sergeant Renn—"

"Chris Renn is wrong."

Mia shifted. "He sounded sure, Verity. From the way he was talking, he's obviously thought about this a lot."

"Then he's lying."

"Mum—" Kieran blinked. "Are you serious? Why would he make this up?"

Verity was attempting to get a resistant and sleepy Brian to his feet. "I have no idea why, Kieran. Although"—she gave Brian a tiny shove of frustration—"I am quite curious to know why you've decided now is a good time to rewrite history."

Kieran stared at her. "That's not what I'm doing."

"No? Going to the station specifically to ask leading questions about things that happened years ago? About Finn and his boat and what time he was on the water and all kinds of rubbish—"

"I—"

"Because it sounds like classic deflection—"

"Bullshit. Mum, that's not—"

"Not what?" Verity pulled at Brian's arm, her voice trembling with the effort to control it. "Not an attempt to channel blame away from yourself and onto your late brother? I'd be very interested, Kieran, to explore what has triggered this—"

"That's not what he's doing, Verity—" Mia was cut off with a sharp look.

"You stay out of this, Mia. This is family business—"

"Hey, don't speak to her like that."

"She is not part of this," Verity snapped. She paused, her hands still on an unwilling Brian, then flicked her eyes back to Mia. "Or are you? Is it you who's been encouraging all this? Stirring up trouble with some story about Finn and that girl's bag? Because it's always struck me as pretty lucky for you, Mia, that my husband came along when he did to take the heat. Otherwise the last person to see that girl alive was you."

"Hey! Watch it. This has nothing to do with her." Kieran was on his feet now. Mia didn't move. "This is about me. I wanted to ask Renn. Because I wanted to know—"

"What?" Verity had given up on Brian, leaving him sprawled on his towel. She was staring at Kieran. "What was so important that you just had to know?"

"I wanted to know if it was true that Finn and Toby were out on the water already. Mum? You get that, don't you? I needed to know if the accident was my fault."

Verity was very still, breathing in and out through her nose. "What does that matter now? It was so long ago. Finn's dead. I have accepted that. Nothing can—"

"It matters to me," Kieran said. "Of course it matters to me. It should matter to you too."

"Finn's not here. That's all that matters to me. Blame is not healthy or productive."

"Yeah." Kieran gave a hard laugh. "I realize that. I'm not sure you do, though."

"What's that supposed to mean?"

"You think somehow I'm too blind or stupid to see what this has done to you? Both you and Dad? That I don't feel what you feel about Finn being gone? That I don't think about him all the time? That I don't look at Audrey and have at least some idea what you've been through? That I don't regret what happened *every day*?" Kieran almost laughed. "Do you think I haven't noticed that you and I can't have a straight conversation where you don't try to pretend that everything is fine?" Kieran could feel the blood pounding in his ears as he looked at his mother. "Not very convincingly, by the way."

He felt Mia touch his arm but ignored it.

"I know how hard it was losing Finn, Mum. I get that. I really do. You can admit it." Kieran could hear himself pleading. "Please. I—"

"All right." She stopped him short. "All right. You want to know how I really feel about all this?" Verity straightened. "I feel that trying to accuse your brother of something, when he's no longer here to defend himself, is despicable. Finn is dead. You're the one who is still here, and you're the one still causing problems for us all."

"Me?" Kieran blinked. A strange and unpleasant sensation washed over him. A sudden dizzy adrenaline rush of free-falling. He felt it dislodge something sharp inside him. "I'm not the one with a dead girl's bag on my boat."

Verity slapped him.

He hadn't seen it coming and the impact was hard enough to make his vision flash white. Kieran's mother had never in his entire life raised a hand to him. The sound seemed to echo off the empty house.

"You really want to hear it, Kieran?" Verity's tone was strange and soft now.

He put his fingers to his face. The skin was hot and he could feel the sting of the blow. "I think you really want to say it."

"Finn died because of you. It was your fault."

There was a thick silence. They looked at each other, properly, for what felt like the first time in years.

Kieran lowered his hand from his face. It still hurt. "Feel better now?"

"Yes, actually. I do." Verity inhaled, and exhaled. "Wish I'd told you that twelve years ago."

Without another word, she turned her back on him, stepped straight over Brian, and walked into the house. Kieran heard her footsteps disappear down the hall, then nothing but the sound of the door to Finn's room clicking open and shut again.

34

Kieran lay next to his daughter on the bed, jangling his keys over her face to make her laugh while Mia turned a page of a dog-eared G. R. Barlin novel.

"Maybe we should just book those flights," Kieran said. "Go home tomorrow."

Mia looked up. "Do you want to?"

"I don't want to leave things like this, but—"

They both turned their heads at the sound of Finn's door opening across the hall. The floorboards creaked, then, farther down, Brian's bedroom door squeaked open and gently closed shut.

Mia frowned. "She'll probably be more willing to talk in the morning."

"I'm sorry for how she spoke to you," he said, not for the first time that afternoon.

"It's okay. None of this is about me."

Kieran didn't say anything, just shook his keys gently and watched his daughter smile. It had been hours since the argument.

After Verity had locked herself away, Brian had thankfully let himself be led to bed, where Kieran had tucked him in like a child. He had closed his eyes and slept, tired from his swim. When Verity still did not emerge, Kieran and Mia had taken Audrey down to the beach to give her some space. They had returned, much later, to find her still shut in Finn's room. Kieran had been able to hear her moving about, but his knocks on the door had gone unanswered. At last, he and Mia had holed up in his own room, trying and failing—on Kieran's part, at least—to make sense of the events of the day.

Mia closed the book and reached over to check the time on her phone. The light was fading outside. "Should we make dinner? We could go and get something from the supermarket."

"Peace offering?"

She smiled. "Worth a try. Either way, we all have to eat."

"Yeah. I suppose." Kieran pulled himself up. "If we're going, we should go now. They probably still shut early."

They walked to town along the road, Audrey snoozing in the carrier against Kieran's chest. Fisherman's Cottage was in darkness as they passed, the police tape still fluttering at the gate. Someone had removed the flowers and the space looked oddly bare. They walked on and as they reached the spot where they had seen the car blast past all those days ago—Liam's car, allegedly—Kieran reached out and took Mia's hand. There were no cars tonight.

"It feels—" Mia started, then hesitated. "This week has felt like the days after the storm."

"I don't remember that too well."

"Oh yeah, of course. It was weird, though, people were out and about when they had to be, but it was like everyone kind of disappeared into themselves for a while. Self-preservation instinct kicking in or something."

She fell quiet for a way.

"What are you thinking?" Kieran said as the lights of the marina came into view up ahead, a bright halo in the twilight.

"Same as you, probably." Mia shrugged. "Trying to think of a good reason why Gabby's bag was on your brother's boat."

"Yeah?" Kieran looked over. Mia had known Gabby as well as anyone. He waited as she breathed out, his flash of hope slipping away as the seconds drifted by. Eventually she shook her head.

"I don't know, Kieran, I'm sorry. The best I can come up with is a chance encounter, like they found it or something. But that doesn't make sense either, because you'd just hand it in, wouldn't you?" She sounded sad. "All I can tell you is that Gabby didn't really know your brother or Toby. I've been trying to think of something I might have forgotten, but I can't. We were fourteen, they were grown men. We didn't know them as mentors or diving instructors or anything like that, and definitely not as friends. She'd seen them around, and"—Mia paused for a fraction of a beat—"I guess they would have seen her, obviously. But no more than that, as far as I knew."

"Right." Kieran listened to the sound of their footsteps for a while. "The thing is—" He couldn't help himself. "Something feels really off. I mean, yeah, Finn was my brother and yeah, you've probably got a point that we only remember the good things. But he could be an arsehole at times, I really do know that. He wasn't at heart, though. He was just a normal bloke, with good points and bad points. I genuinely believe that. So maybe I'm kidding myself, but it feels like a big jump from that to—" He shrugged. "Whatever some backpack on his boat suggests."

"I couldn't say, Kieran." Mia's eyes were on the marina. The gentle creak and groan of the boats filled the evening air. "I honestly didn't know Finn or Toby at all."

The lights were on in the Surf and Turf as they walked past, but the place was again virtually deserted, with nearly every table empty. Through the window, Kieran could spot the grainy picture of Bronte still smiling out from the bulletin board. He wondered if the collection tin had been passed on to her parents yet. He presumed it still would be, despite what had been aired at the community meeting. He wondered what Nick and Andrea Laidler would make of it. A kind gesture from those who cared, or a case of far too little, far too late, from people who had let their daughter down?

By the time they reached the small supermarket, it was nearly closing time. Audrey was stirring a little in the sling.

"I'll go in," Mia whispered. "You keep walking."

The streets were dark and mostly empty. A few lights burned behind blinds in front windows, but Kieran saw only the odd dog walker. Still all men, he noticed. He wondered how long that would last. He couldn't guess. Audrey fidgeted, unsettled, and he was pacing the roads on autopilot when he slowed in front of Wetherby House. He had come this way without fully realizing it.

Kieran stood on the grassy verge and stared at the wrecked garden. The lights from the house threw sharp shadows across the upturned earth, but other than that it looked exactly the same as it had earlier that day, when he'd seen Ash parked outside. There was no sign of him now. Kieran jumped a little as he sensed movement, and looked around. He half expected to see Ash loitering in what was left of the greenery, but instead, the front door creaked open and G. R. Barlin appeared in the frame.

"Sorry," Kieran called, raising a hand. "Just us."

"Hang on." George disappeared back inside, then returned, holding something under his arm as he pulled the door shut behind him. "When I saw you, I thought your mate was back for a second."

"No."

"You have the same build in the dark." George smiled at Audrey. "Baby's a bit of a giveaway, though." He held a bag of books over the fence. "For Mia. Some of mine, some others that she might like."

"Oh." Surprised, Kieran reached for the bag. "Thank you."

"Kind of an apology on my part as well." George shook his head. "Pendlebury stopped by earlier. I didn't realize I was stirring up trouble with those storm timings. I thought it was interesting, that was all."

"Interesting is definitely one way to put it," Kieran said. He managed a smile. "I'm grateful to you, though. Knowing makes a big difference. For me, anyway."

"Good to hear."

"Why were you looking into it anyway? You're not writing about that, are you?"

"God, no." George frowned. "The new one's about biological warfare in a near-futuristic dystopia."

"Ah."

"Yeah." George shrugged. "The storm was just something I was reading about on the side." He was quiet as he glanced down at baby Audrey. "I'm having some custody issues. Personal stuff. My wife—ex-wife—is overseas. It makes things complicated. Legally, and otherwise."

"I'm sorry."

"It is what it is. I don't really like to go into it. But it's a bit like the landscaping, and the diving; sometimes I need a distraction. Then this terrible thing happened to Bronte." George shook his head. "I don't know. It's not how I expected things to be down here."

He leaned on the fence as they both surveyed the black upturned soil. Kieran remembered Bronte's photos and imagined her, alive and vibrant, walking past this very spot, camera in hand as she headed toward the cliff trail. All at once, something itched in the back of his mind, hazy and elusive. He frowned and looked back at the garden. "What's the plan for all this, anyway?"

George scratched his chin. "You know, I'm honestly not too sure. The landscaper gives me an invoice every few weeks and I pay it. I should probably ask him. It seemed like a good idea when I moved in, modernize it a bit, make it my own, you know? But now—" He shrugged. "If I'd realized it was going to be such a pain in the arse, I would have left it alone. It's been more trouble than it's worth."

Kieran looked up the street toward the cliff path. Ash's dirty white pickup was nowhere to be seen. The neighboring houses stood silent, set back from the road with their blinds shut. The niggling feeling remained. He turned back to the excavated garden, its destruction nearly complete. Kieran hesitated, then opened his mouth.

"You found anything interesting in there?" His voice was oddly light, even to his own ears.

George's eyes flicked over in the dark. "Like what?"

"I don't know," Kieran said. "Anything."

"The body of Gabby Birch buried in the flower beds your mate dug all alone by hand twelve years ago?"

The only sound was the purr of a single passing car.

"No," Kieran said quickly as the road fell quiet again. "That's not what I meant."

"Wasn't it?" The writer looked a tiny bit amused. "This whole time you never once thought that might be what was going on here?"

Kieran didn't answer.

"Don't worry." George gave him a knowing smile. "I won't

tell anyone." He paused. "Ash was here this morning, actually. He apologized."

"Really?" Kieran couldn't hide his surprise.

"Yeah. Or at least I think that's what he was getting at. I did too." George surveyed the patch of the garden still to be dug up. "I've been wondering if maybe he and I could work something out with this. I suspect Ash might actually know what he's doing more than my current guy."

"I don't think you'd be sorry," Kieran said. "You two would probably get along pretty well if you gave each other a chance. Ash is a good bloke when he wants to be."

"Yeah. Well, we'll see." George shivered in the crisp air. "I'll get back inside. If Mia wants any of her books signed, tell her to shout out."

"Thanks. I'm not sure how much longer we'll be around, though."

"Is that right? I hope not because of anything I've stirred up with the storm?"

"No. Not just that, anyway. It's a few things."

"I can't say I blame you. I really hoped I'd stay here long-term, but now—" George looked tired. "I'm not so sure. Places like this, they need to be tight-knit to work. Once the trust is broken, they're stuffed. Whether people see it or not, the writing's on the wall." George turned back to his big house, with its torn-up grounds and its sprawling, empty feel. "Anyway, it was good to meet you both. Hopefully we'll cross paths again."

He raised a hand and Kieran watched him open the front door and disappear into the blazing light. The door closed and the street was dark and sleepy once more.

Kieran stood there alone with Audrey. The writer had gone, Ash's pickup was not there, the road to the cliff path was empty. Except suddenly, something new snagged deep in Kieran's mind.

No. Not new. Different. A dogged feeling that he was missing something tugged at him. Kieran stared into the night and forced himself to think. It was the same sensation he'd had earlier that day, down on the beach with Pendlebury. He closed his eyes and tried to focus, but the idea was like water, slipping through his fingers.

Finally, Audrey stirred and his phone buzzed with a message from Mia. Kieran blinked and began to walk, the elusive thought creeping alongside him, always just out of reach. He chased it, without success, the whole way back.

35

The house was quiet as Kieran and Mia let themselves in. Kieran heard the door to Finn's room click shut again as they stepped into the hall, and he walked through to find Brian sitting alone on the back veranda.

Where once there would have been a cold beer in his hand, Brian instead held a glass of tap water, still fizzing a little with dissolved medication. He didn't seem to mind, though, and was gazing peacefully out at the dark waves breaking white against the sand. The night air was crisp and the tide sounded strong and refreshed.

Kieran went in to get Audrey's bottle and came back out to find Mia had pulled up a spare chair next to his dad. Brian had a cushion across his lap and Audrey lay on it, cradled in his arms. Kieran looked to Mia, who shrugged.

"He wanted to hold her. He's doing a good job."

Kieran watched Brian stroke Audrey's fine baby hair with his large palm. She reached for his thumb. Brian gazed down at her and smiled.

"He's strong," he said. "From the day he was born he was like this. A little champion. Aren't you? My little mate."

"He thinks she's you," Mia whispered.

"Or Finn."

She shook her head, smiling. "He said your name before. It's you."

Kieran looked at Mia as she turned back to his dad and daughter. He wasn't sure if he believed her, but it didn't really matter. He loved that she'd said it.

"I'll go and start dinner," he said at last.

"I'll go." Mia got up and gave him her seat. "You supervise this."

Kieran pulled up the chair and sat down beside Brian and Audrey, listening to the sounds floating down the hall from the kitchen and the gentle wash of the tide.

"I'm sorry," Kieran said quietly. "I'm sorry about what happened to Finn. I really hope you know that."

Brian glanced up, then back down at Audrey, the faint smile on his face never changing. It was impossible to know if he understood. Kieran searched his milky eyes for any sign of lucidity, something more than a confused man lost to illness. He could see nothing.

Kieran opened his mouth to say more, then stopped. His dad looked happy. Relaxing in his family home, a cold drink of sorts on the table next to him, his granddaughter in his arms, listening to his beloved ocean.

Could this be enough? Kieran wondered. If this was all that was possible? If Brian didn't remember what he thought Kieran had done, didn't remember those black days when they lost Finn? If what had happened was gone forever, was that the same as forgiveness? Kieran wasn't sure, but he thought about it, as they sat there together, looking out at the moon on the water.

After a while, the back door opened and Mia put her head out. She saw Audrey dozing again and dropped her voice to a whisper.

"Dinner's nearly ready."

"Thanks."

Mia looked at Brian, who hadn't even turned his head. "I guess we'll offer him some? See if he'll take it?"

"Yeah." Kieran gave her a small smile. "He still seems quite out of it. He missed his perfect cue to blink to life and tell me that nothing that happened to Finn was my fault and he loves me and forgives me."

"That's annoying." Mia trailed her fingers over Kieran's hand as she moved past. "I still love you, for what it's worth. And Audrey does, I'm pretty sure."

"Thank you. Me too." Kieran looked at her, leaning against the railing. The night sky was big behind her. "We should get married, Mia. You and me."

"Yeah—" She started to smile but was forced to stifle a yawn, covering her mouth as they both laughed. "God, I'm sorry. I am so tired. But yes, definitely." She smiled at him, for real this time. "I think we should too."

"We could do it soon, when we get home. Don't you reckon? This autumn or something, before it gets too cold."

"That sounds nice. Get Audrey a little bridesmaid's outfit." Mia leaned in, put her hands on either side of his face, and kissed him gently. "Let's do it. It'd be really good. I'd love it."

"I would too," Kieran said. "It'd be great."

They looked at each other for a long minute, grinning. Even Brian looked happy.

"Do you think anyone would come?" Kieran said, looking from his dad to the quiet house.

"You mean your mum? She'll come."

"Really?"

"She will," Mia said. "She's hurt right now. And maybe she hasn't handled all this as well as she could have, but if she didn't love you, you'd have found out for sure twelve years ago."

Kieran sat for a moment, thinking about that.

"It's so weird, isn't it? How one thing can change so much," he said. "If that storm had fizzled out at sea, or hit a few kilometers further up the coast, who knows what would have happened? Or wouldn't? Finn would probably still be here. Dad would still be like this, I guess, but these last few years wouldn't have been the same at all. Change that one day and everything would have been different."

"That's true." Mia's voice was soft in the night. "But maybe not all the changes were for the worse. Sometimes I think what happened to Finn—" She paused. "I'm not for a minute saying that was a good thing, of course not. But you're right. It did change your life, but I'm not sure it was in the way you sometimes think it was." She was lit up by the glow spilling from the house. "Honestly, Kieran, I think it made you a better person. Kinder, definitely. More aware of other people, more conscious of your actions."

Kieran looked at her and she shrugged.

"You have changed since back then." Mia nodded at their sleeping daughter. "Because if you hadn't, if you were the same person now as you were when the storm hit, there's no way the three of us would be together."

Audrey snuffled and stirred a little in Brian's arms. Kieran watched her, imagining for a second that different world and a different life. He reached out for Mia.

"That would be no good at all."

"Honestly?" Mia reached back. "The old you wouldn't even care."

•   •   •

Kieran woke up in the middle of the night instantly certain of something, but something that vanished as soon as he opened his eyes. He lay there staring at the ceiling, listening for the summoning cry from the cot, but for once all he could hear was the gentle wheeze of Audrey's breath as she slept on. He could feel Mia warm and still beside him.

Kieran closed his eyes again, waiting for either the thought or sleep to return. Neither did, and as the pre-dawn blue seeped in and Audrey's breaths grew less steady and more alert, he scooped her out of her cot, grabbed his towel and board shorts, and crept through to the kitchen.

Verity was already there.

She was sitting at the table with a single light on and a photo album open in front of her. She hadn't joined them for dinner the night before, despite both Kieran and Mia knocking on the bedroom door. In the end they had left a plate of food outside in the hall, which had remained untouched until they went to bed. Brian, though, perhaps sensing his moment to rise to the occasion, had been surprisingly compliant and all four, including Audrey, had sat and eaten together for what Kieran thought could be the last time in that house. A little hushed, a little different from how any of them had expected their family to be, but together none-theless. Kieran had watched Audrey with Brian, the two of them smiling at each other in an instinctive and reflexive display of love. Life going on, like it or not.

Verity looked up from that same kitchen table now as Kieran hovered in the doorway.

"Mum—"

"Kieran, I am so sorry." Her voice was quiet.

"Me too."

Verity's eyes dropped back to the photo album. The page was open to the instantly recognizable image of Finn and Toby, taken on the day they launched the *Nautilus Black*, champagne and smiles on the dock.

"I felt so angry," she said. "With you."

"I know. I am sorry."

"I don't feel that way now." Verity lifted her head to face him. "Whatever I said yesterday. I really don't. What happened to Finn wasn't your fault. Timings or no timings, I've always known that. They would have gone out there for anyone in the water when that emergency call came in. In the same situation, Finn would always have made that choice."

"It wasn't anyone in the water, though," Kieran said. "It was me."

"It happened to be you, but that still doesn't make it your fault."

Verity beckoned for him to sit down and Kieran pulled out a chair. He could see the photo in front of her. The scene was familiar, but up close he could tell it wasn't the same shot that had hung as a memorial in the Surf and Turf all those years ago, or even the one that he'd found while he was cleaning out the living room. It was yet a third variation, Finn and Toby turned a little more one way or the other, their smiles caught a split second earlier or later. Minor details, Kieran thought. Not enough to make a real difference. The picture still captured Finn at his happiest.

"And I don't know what I can say about that backpack," Verity said quietly. "Other than that Finn was a good man. I know he was. But us losing him wasn't your fault, Kieran, and I should have said that years ago. It was a terrible accident, and that's all it ever was." She raised her eyes. "I hoped you understood that, but I should have made sure you did."

"Thank you."

"Actually, no. Even that's not completely true," Verity said suddenly. She ran her thumb over Finn's photo. "I knew you felt responsible. And I let you. There's no excuse for that. But God, I was just so sad, Kieran. And I was angry with Brian for not coping. I felt like I couldn't say how hard I was finding it, because he was always struggling enough for the both of us. But we never really blamed you, Kieran. You should know that. We just wanted Finn back."

"I am really sorry, though." Kieran's throat and chest felt tight. "I wish things had been different."

"They could have been different." Verity looked down at the photo once more, then turned the page. "We could have lost both of you that afternoon. But you're here, with Mia and Audrey. I still have you, instead of just memories of both my sons stuck in a photo album. And I'm grateful for that every day."

Kieran leaned over and hugged her, Audrey's little body solid and warm between them. Verity hugged him back and for the first time in a long time he felt like she meant it.

"I heard you talking before about leaving early," she said as he pulled away. "Please don't. Not if you don't want to."

"Thanks. I'll talk to Mia. Either way, it's good to be here now." He could feel the boxes by his feet under the table. He hesitated. It was worth one more try. "Move to Sydney, Mum. We can find somewhere up there for Dad. It will make no real difference to him, and it would make a big difference to you. And to us."

He braced himself for the standard barrage of excuses, but to his surprise Verity reached out and stroked Audrey's hand. "You don't think I've left everything too late?"

"I really don't." Kieran shook his head. "It's not too late."

"No?" Verity let Audrey's fingers wrap around her own. "Well, maybe it's not, then."

Twenty minutes later, Kieran was out on the beach as the sun crept up over the horizon. Audrey lay fed and warm in her sleeping bag on the sand while Kieran plowed through the waves. For once, he found he was simply enjoying it.

When he got out, his mind felt clearer than it had in a while. He sat on the beach next to Audrey and together they watched the early-morning sunlight glint gold on the water. Audrey smiled as a seagull waddled closer and Kieran took out his phone from under his towel and snapped a couple of photos.

He shielded the screen from the growing glare and scrolled between the pictures, trying to decide which was the better one to send to Mia. Back and forth, back and forth. It didn't matter. They were almost identical.

Kieran's thumb stopped against an image. The nagging feeling was back. The subtle, slippery one that had plagued him yesterday at the beach and last night as he spoke to George Barlin. The one that had woken him. The same one, he realized now, that had hovered almost imperceptibly in the early-morning dark of the kitchen as he'd joined Verity at the table.

Kieran almost had it. For a single moment, he had almost caught it as he sat there on the beach. What was it? He made himself concentrate. Verity at the table. The photo of Finn and Toby and the *Nautilus Black*. That felt close somehow. What was it about those photos? Variations he had seen so many times over the years. Similar, but not the same.

And, all of a sudden, there it was.

Kieran stood up abruptly, startling Audrey.

"Sorry," he said as her face crumpled. "Sorry."

He picked her up and held her in his arms. He rocked her gently as the thought that had been bothering him—the fluid, flowing pull at the edge of his consciousness—grew solid and took shape. At last, Kieran could grasp it and examine it, as he stood on the beach and looked out at the ocean, a realization dawning with the light.

36

Kieran stopped on the back veranda just long enough to brush the sand off himself and Audrey. He let them into the hallway, hurrying now, but paused at the bedroom door. He looked in. Mia's side of the bed was already empty, the covers thrown back.

In the kitchen, Verity's coffee mug was rinsed and drying on the rack and the door to his parents' room was shut. Kieran stood in the hall, debating. From the bathroom opposite he could hear the sound of the shower running. He knocked on the door and waited. When there was no answer, he checked the time and tried again. The water continued to run.

Kieran looked at Audrey. "All right, little one." He took her back through to the bedroom and laid her carefully in her cot. "I've got to go, but someone will be out soon. Shout if you need anything."

Audrey looked very much like she was planning to do exactly that as Kieran scribbled a note and left it on the kitchen table. He grabbed his shirt and shoes from the hall and pulled the back door closed behind him.

He went the beach way, which had always been the fastest. There was no movement around Fisherman's Cottage now, but the house still had a different feel as he passed. A dull emptiness. Bronte's window, where Kieran could picture her standing as she listened for noises in the night, was blank. The foreshore was bare now. Someone had removed the decaying flowers from near the shallows where her body had been found. The sea had washed clean any sign she had ever been there.

Kieran walked on, past the marina, where he could make out the *Nautilus Blue* in the dock. He slowed his pace, wondering what would happen to the business when word spread about Gabby's bag having been found on board the near-namesake boat. The Norwegians might not care, but the locals would.

Kieran turned and kept moving toward town, past the police station. He thought about Sergeant Renn and his promise to have those painful and long-overdue conversations with two families today, and Kieran very nearly stopped. He spent a minute in silent debate and then, checking the time, pressed on.

The lure of caffeine had attracted a few early risers through the doors of the Surf and Turf that morning, at least. Kieran could see Lyn through the window, carrying a tray. There was no sign of Julian or Liam. No Olivia either, although he hadn't expected to see her. Kieran remembered the strain on her face in the Surf and Turf the night before last and wondered whether she'd woken up that morning at her mother's house or at Ash's place. Kieran guessed it depended where she felt more secure. Anywhere was probably better than the hollow loneliness of Fisherman's Cottage now.

Kieran continued on, not slowing outside George Barlin's house this time. In daylight, the garden looked even worse than it had at night. Kieran glanced at the windows, but he could see no movement inside. The niggling sensation started up again, but

Kieran knew now what it had been trying to tell him. What had George said, as he'd leaned against his own fence the night before, his expression hard to read in the dark?

The writing's on the wall.

Kieran did not stop until he reached the top of the cliff path. There, he paused at the lookout, leaning against the safety rail as he had so many times before, feeling the wind rushing over the sea and rocks. There was no one in sight.

Below, the ocean was large and empty, all the way to the perfect horizon. He leaned over, craning his neck. The beach below was a thin strip, small enough that Kieran immediately felt uneasy. Out to sea, the waves lapped high against The Survivors. All around him, the birds bristled and flapped.

Kieran looked out at the water, to the spot where he had last seen Finn. The guilt was still there, like a scar, but now it felt different. What Kieran had always believed, and what had really happened that day, were not one and the same. He understood that, even if he hadn't quite accepted it yet. Still, he repeated it to himself silently, turning the information over and over in his mind. What it had meant then; what it meant now.

Kieran stepped past the barrier and started to make his way down. At the bottom of the cliff, the water was washing up high over the sand and he checked the time again. The tide was coming in. But it was not there yet.

Kieran ignored the South Cave, where he and Olivia had met on that strange day as the sea and storm moved in. Instead, he stood at the mouth of the North Cave. As the edge of the water nudged his shoes, he looked at the names that had been carved into the rock. The marks left behind by him and his brother and their friends. And he thought of Pendlebury. What had she asked him as she stood there, so deliberate and precise, in this very spot?

Can we find them all?

They could be anywhere.

Kieran stared into the yawning mouth of the cave, and the blackness inside. The eerie sensation of something watching and waiting trickled through him once more. He stood on high alert, but he could hear nothing but the heartbeat pulse of the ocean.

He could go in, step through the entrance and into the gloom. He could speed this up. But he had already spent too long mentally navigating the dark of those caves, wandering exhausted over the same old ground. Battling to change something that couldn't be changed, instead of trying to find his way out to the light.

Enough, Kieran thought. It was time to stop.

He stepped away. The seawater was creeping around his feet. He didn't need to go in. High tide had a way of washing everything out.

Kieran turned. He walked the few steps across the sand back to the path, then went up a short way, settling for a point just out of sight of the cave and well out of reach of the lick of the tide. He sat, and he watched the water slither in. Above him, the cliff path remained deserted. Below, the beach slowly disappeared.

Kieran waited as the birds circled overhead, watchful and wary, calling to him that he was right. But as the sea crept closer and time ticked on, he slowly began to wonder. He was still arguing with himself when he sensed rather than heard it. A splash of movement.

Kieran stayed very still and stared at the edge of the cave, holding his breath as the seconds trickled by. He thought he might have imagined it and then, all at once from the blackness, a figure appeared. He watched as the figure waded out, knee-deep in water, bag over shoulder.

Kieran breathed out. It was what he'd expected, but it was

still a shock. The figure turned toward the path, saw him, and froze.

Kieran stood, a little unsteady on his feet. For a long moment, the only sound was the slap of waves hitting the rock, then he opened his mouth.

"Did you find it yet?" Kieran's voice echoed off the cliffs.

A silence. Deliberate and calculating. "Find what?"

"The message Gabby Birch scratched into the rock on the day she died."

37

Kieran waited, the blood rushing fast and loud in his ears.

Knee-deep in the water, Sean stared back at him.

Sean's hair was damp and the seawater had soaked his clothes, darkening the colors. He didn't speak, but his head tilted in a familiar way that Kieran knew meant he was thinking. Kieran pointed at the bag over his shoulder.

"What've you got in there? Chisel? File? You'd need it." Kieran took a few steps down the path until he could see the mouth of the North Cave, where the names casually carved more than twelve years ago still scarred the rock face. "Those markings stick around forever."

Kieran looked at Sean, who had been his friend for as long as he could remember. *Deny it*, he wanted to say. *Please, mate. Tell me I'm wrong.*

Sean's face flickered and Kieran felt a surge of hope. Then, as he watched, Sean's gaze slid past him. Across the deserted beach. Up the empty cliff path.

They were alone.

When Sean's eyes met his again, Kieran could feel that fact being closely considered. He took a breath.

"Pendlebury knows." Kieran managed to sound more confident than he felt. "She's worked it out. Close enough, anyway. I could tell, the other day when she was down here. She's got Bronte's photos. She's got a picture of your name carved in the rock. The letters are blurred, so I didn't notice at first. And it looks pretty similar, but it's not the same. It's your name, mate, but I know you didn't write it."

Kieran could see the salt water rushing into the North Cave, disappearing into the hole.

"You were right about damaging the caves. It was bloody stupid and I know you tried to tell us, and we wouldn't listen. You were right and we were idiots." Kieran saw Sean's mouth tighten. "But you did do it once. Because I pushed you into it. And I know you felt bad afterward. You felt so bad that I feel really sure—knowing you, mate—that you wouldn't have done it again. So if your name is somewhere else in this cave, who scratched it there?" Kieran looked at his friend. "And what else did they write?"

Sean had turned his head and was now staring at the sea, past The Survivors and out to where his beloved wreck lay invisible under the waves. The water foamed and swirled around him.

"Pendlebury will find it," Kieran said. "Sean? She'll work it out and then she'll bring in all the backup she needs and they'll search this whole place until they find it."

As he said the words, he remembered Pendlebury's face as they had stood at the mouth of the cave, and felt instinctively that what he was saying was true. If she wasn't there yet, it was only lack of local knowledge that was keeping her half a step behind. That wouldn't last long, he knew. Kieran looked at Sean and could tell, from the slack weariness in his eyes, that he knew it too.

"Had Bronte guessed?" Kieran said.

Sean's face creased and he gave a tiny shake of his head.

"But she would have?" Kieran said. "Or you were worried she'd tell someone else who would?"

No shake of the head this time. No denial. Kieran looked at the man he had known for so many years, and it was like looking in a mirror. Kieran knew what he was seeing, because he knew it well. He had lived with it every day. Guilt.

He took another single step down the path. Just one step closer to the water and then he stopped. That was far enough.

"What happened here, mate?" he said.

"It wasn't how you think."

"How was it, then?"

The only sound was the sea rushing between them. Then Sean opened his mouth and began to speak.

38

Toby and Finn were late.

Sean lay flat on his back on the deck of the *Nautilus Black* and felt the dip of the waves as he watched the sky. There were still patches of blue above, but if he turned his head he could see a darkness gathering in the distance. He zipped his fleece up to his chin and checked his watch. He'd give them another five minutes, no more. Toby wanted help unloading some equipment into the boat shed before the weather turned. Sean probably wasn't going to get paid for it. There was no way he was going to get wet for it.

He heard the marina gate squeak open and propped himself up on one elbow in hope. Not Toby or Finn. Better, though. Olivia. Sean sat up properly now, feeling a familiar nervous thrill. Her curly ponytail was blowing and her skirt flapped in the breeze as she shut the gate behind her. Then the girl turned toward him and Sean felt a mild stab of disappointment.

Not Olivia. Her little sister, Gabby.

Gabby hoisted her backpack higher on her shoulder as she

walked over. Her face was uncertain as she cast her eyes around the empty dock, answering her own question before she asked it. She stopped in front of the boat, looked up at the older boy, and seemed to completely lose her nerve. Sean felt a bit sorry for her.

"Hey," he said.

"Hi." Her voice was hard to hear.

"Looking for Liv? She's not here."

"Oh," Gabby said, disappointed. "Has she been by?"

"No, I haven't seen her all day. You tried calling her?"

"My mum took my phone." She seemed embarrassed. "I need to find her, though. It's our mum's birthday tomorrow. We won't have time to make her cake otherwise."

"Fair enough. I suppose ignoring your mum's birthday won't get your phone back any faster," Sean said, and Gabby gave an unexpected smile. He hadn't seen her do that often; she was normally so solemn. She looked back down, still smiling at her shoes, and for a second she looked even more like her sister than usual. Sean took out his own phone and tried Olivia's number. They waited as it rang out.

"Sorry." He shrugged. "I'm sure she'll turn up."

"It's okay," Gabby said, her forehead creasing. "If she's not here, I think she's probably at the caves."

It was Sean's turn to frown. "Why would she be there?"

Gabby looked up at him as though trying to work out whether it was a genuine question. Deciding it was, she reddened and dropped her eyes again.

"Because she meets Kieran there."

"Olivia meets Kieran at the caves?"

"Sometimes."

"Why?"

"To . . ." Gabby shrugged, her face flushed, her eyes anywhere else. "Do things."

Sean stared. "What things?"

"I don't know."

But she clearly did know, and suddenly Sean did as well, and all at once he felt a hot rush of mortification at having to learn about it like this.

"Didn't Kieran tell you?" Gabby was looking at him now, her curiosity overcoming her shyness.

"Yeah. Of course."

Gabby nodded, but she didn't believe him, Sean could tell. She was—God help him—throwing him a rope. He looked at this girl and at her expression tinged with the faintest hint of pity and felt a fresh sting of humiliation.

Sean thought about Kieran, or specifically, the way Kieran would watch Olivia at parties but never quite make the effort to talk to her. Except on the odd occasion when Sean would be chatting to her. Then bloody Kieran seemed to be everywhere, with drinks and jokes and lots to say.

"Anyway," Gabby said, glancing at the sky. The blue had given way to a dirty gray and the wind was whistling through the empty masts. "I'd better go."

Sean blinked. He'd almost forgotten she was there. "You're not going to the caves now, are you?"

Did Ash know, he wondered suddenly, about Kieran and Liv? Probably. Kieran had probably told Ash. He and Ash told each other things like that. Stuff they didn't tell him.

Down on the dock, Gabby shifted her backpack from one shoulder to the other. The kangaroo key chain rattled against the purple zipper. "I'll go and check quickly. I really need to find her."

Sean shook his head. "Have you ever been down to the caves?"

"No, but—"

"Because you can't just go wandering around down there, especially if you don't know what you're doing. It's not safe. And the weather's not good."

"Well—" Gabby seemed torn. "Could you maybe take me?"

Sean felt the first drop of rain. He looked along the dock. Still no sign of Toby or Finn. There was no one around at all.

"Please?" The wind caught Gabby's hair and she swept it away from her face. She looked up at him, and Sean was momentarily disarmed. "Our mum will be home in a few hours."

"You need your phone back that badly?"

"She's had it for nearly a week."

Sean hesitated. Her eyes were so hopeful. He checked the sky once more. "Okay. But we'll have to be fast. Tide's on its way in."

"Really?" Gabby smiled then, right at him. "Thank you."

Sean shrugged. His brother was late. His friends were occupied with activities that clearly did not involve him. He was getting cold waiting out there. He felt a second spot of rain. Sean pointed to her backpack. It looked heavy.

"Leave that here. I'll lock it in the dry box."

Gabby shrugged the bag off her shoulders and Sean pulled it on board. It was solid and unwieldy with books. He dropped it in the box and scrabbled around until he found Toby's spare key. It was hanging from a lanyard with a small pocket torch attached. Sean locked the box and put the lanyard in his pocket as he grabbed a pen and a piece of scrap paper. He checked the time.

4:15 p.m., he scribbled. *You were late. Gone to caves.*

He stuck the note where Toby would be sure to see it, grabbed his own torch, and climbed off the boat and onto the deck, where Gabby smiled in a way that lit up her face.

•   •   •

The cliff path was empty. Sean and Gabby walked side by side, leaning forward a little into the wind. It was stronger than Sean could remember it being before. He half hoped they would see Kieran and Olivia appear around a corner. Then at least they could all turn back. But the trail stayed empty.

Sean glanced sideways at Gabby. She was as tall as her sister, and almost as tall as Sean himself. The wind snatched at their clothes as they walked, and she kept having to brush her hair out of her face.

"Nearly there," he said.

"Great." She gave him a shy smile, and Sean found himself suddenly hoping that, in fact, they wouldn't see anyone else.

They stopped at the top of the cliffs. The sea was angry and green, foaming as it raced toward the sand. The thin beach looked deserted below.

"Can we go down?" Gabby said.

Sean frowned. "Your sister might not welcome us just turning up, you know."

Gabby's smooth face took on a faintly pious air. "That's her own fault. She was supposed to come home and help me."

Sean couldn't help but laugh, and she smiled back.

"Yeah, all right," he said. "Come on, then."

Her smile broadened as Sean showed her the path. He led them down, hearing her footsteps behind him the whole way. At one point, she stumbled and he reached back to help her.

"Sorry," she said. "Thanks."

The beach was thinner than Sean liked to see. There was no one down there.

Gabby stood on the strip of sand and Sean watched her spin in a curious circle, soaking up the sight of the towering cliffs, the gaping dark mouths of the caves, the sea as it roared in and out.

"Wow." Gabby turned to him. "I can't believe I've never been down here before."

Sean grinned. "Pretty good, hey?"

"Really good." Gabby circled again, her head tilted back as she looked up at the cliff face.

"Should we find Olivia?" Sean said, and Gabby blinked, refocused.

"Oh. Yeah. Where would she be?"

"You tell me." Sean shrugged. "I guess in one of the caves?"

"Olivia!" Gabby called across the empty beach, the sound snatched away by the wind almost before it left her mouth.

"She won't hear you. You often can't hear anything properly inside there, even on a good day."

"Oh." Gabby peered with interest into the North Cave. "Maybe we should go in?"

"You want to?" Sean glanced at the sea. The Survivors stood solid amid the swells but deeper than he thought they perhaps should be. He looked away. "Okay, really quickly, though."

"Okay." Gabby smiled at him again and he felt a warm surge.

Sean went first, the sky low as they stepped over the threshold into the North Cave. Sean lit the path with his own torch, then fished around in his pocket and pulled out the small spare one attached to the dry box lanyard.

"Here. You can use this."

"Thanks." Gabby took the torch from him and switched it on. They moved deeper. She followed close enough that Sean could feel the heat from her body.

"Oh, look. Kieran," she said suddenly, and Sean felt a wave of disappointment. He turned, expecting to see his mate silhouetted in the dwindling daylight at the mouth of the cave. But Gabby was pointing her light at the wall, where Kieran's name was scratched alongside some others. Ash, Finn, Toby.

"What is this?" she said.

"It's this thing they do," Sean said. "It's not hard, you just need a fishing knife or your keys or something." He pointed at the lanyard dangling from her hand. "It's easy enough."

Gabby ran a finger over the damp surface. "But what does it mean?"

"Nothing, really." Sean shook his head. "When one of them worked out a new route or was the first to visit a part of the cave or something, they'd mark it. Except for Ash—he does whatever he wants."

"But your name's not here." Gabby turned to him. "You don't find new routes?"

"Yeah, I do," Sean said truthfully. "Just—" He looked at the names of his friends and brother. "I dunno. Doesn't seem much point sometimes. The others seem to get to a lot of stuff first." He felt suddenly embarrassed and shrugged, but Gabby nodded.

"Yeah," she said, her voice quiet. "I get that."

Their eyes met. Through the slice of daylight still visible from the mouth of the cave, Sean could see that it had started to rain outside. He could hear the gentle rhythmic tap of water on rock. They stood there for a moment, Gabby's features soft in the dim light.

"I don't think my sister's in here."

"No, I guess not." Sean glanced over his shoulder. "Do you want to go a little further in? Or head back?"

Gabby lifted her chin to see beyond him, curious.

"Maybe a bit further?" she said. "Who knows? Maybe us two will discover somewhere new."

"I don't think today's the day for that." He smiled. "But let's see what we can see. This way."

The sandy floor was already soft and saturated under his feet.

"Your shoes might get wet," he said.

"That's okay, they'll dry."

He led her in, stopping when they reached a junction where

the path split in six directions. Sean shone his light down the first tunnel. The ground dropped quickly below sea level and the sand was already waterlogged. The roof of the second one was lower, but after an initial dip, he thought the way through should be visible and clear.

"Are you okay to wait here for a minute?" he said. "I need to check the path ahead. You've got your torch?"

"Yep." Gabby held up the key lanyard, the beam reflected by the damp rock.

"Okay, I'll be as quick as I can."

Sean shone his own light in front of him. The path was one of the wider ones and good for beginners, at the start at least. Deeper down—deeper than Sean planned to take them—he knew the tunnel split along ways he hadn't been. The main route was fine, though; Sean had mapped this for Toby himself. He moved along until he was satisfied they could get through, having to go a little further than expected before he felt certain enough to turn and head back.

The six-way junction was empty as he stepped into it again.

Sean blinked in the gloom, his torch throwing shadows against the rocks. Where was Gabby? Had she seriously got herself lost in those few minutes or—Sean felt a lurch—had he? He twisted around. No, this was the spot.

"Gabby?" he called.

"Yeah?"

He saw a beam of light bounce off the wall opposite and heard the quick splash of steps from one of the tunnels behind him, and as he turned she was back in the clearing. She was smiling.

"I'm here," she said. "Hey, look. I was just—"

"Jesus, please don't go wandering off."

"Oh. I'm sorry."

She looked crestfallen and Sean felt bad.

"It's okay," he said, and then they both started speaking at the same time.

"Sorry," Gabby said again. "You go."

"I was going to say we can get through, but we'll have to be quick. If you still want to?"

"Yeah." Her smile was back. "Please. If you don't mind."

"I don't mind."

Sean led the way to the second tunnel, shining the light ahead of them.

"Watch your head as you come through here," he said, and almost without thinking reached out to guide her over the dip. He felt Gabby's palm slide into his and he gripped it.

"It's so dark," she said. A beat passed, then two, and only then did she drop his hand. He could still feel the warm spots where her fingers had been.

"Follow the light, you'll be okay."

"Where do all these tunnels go?" she said as he led them past a first fork and took the second one, turning again a few steps later.

"Everywhere," Sean said.

They moved along until the walls opened wider and the roof rose to create a small clearing. Sean stopped there. He could feel the water lapping at his feet now.

"We probably shouldn't go any further. The weather's really coming in."

"No, that's okay." In the soft light, Gabby's face glowed. "This is really cool. Thanks for showing me."

"You're welcome."

The rock circled them as they stood close together in the center. The sound of the rain and sea floated in from outside and bounced around, the peaceful rhythm amplified and then dulled by the complex honeycomb of caves. Gabby walked a few paces, examining something on the near wall as Sean watched.

She could—almost—have been one of The Survivors. Standing there, outlined by the weak light, her back turned and the salt water lapping at her feet. Then she moved. Just a small shift in weight and the in-out of breath, but enough to break the illusion before it was fully formed.

Gabby was still looking away, focused on something he couldn't make out in the dark. Somewhere, a wave broke and the sea surged, fresh and cold against Sean's own legs as it fizzed white around Gabby's bare calves. Sean watched as she reached down with her free hand and gathered her skirt hem above her knees. The air was filled with a fine haze and her T-shirt clung to her back and her waist.

The sea swelled again, and this time the drag of the undertow was strong enough that he took a step toward her. She didn't notice. Her face was tilted down, the silver chain of her necklace glinting against her collarbone as she leaned forward to examine something in the water. She dropped her skirt hem as the tide rushed out again, and lifted a hand to sweep aside her ponytail, which had fallen over one shoulder. It was heavy from the sea spray. A single strand of hair had caught in the corner of her mouth and she brushed it free, her fingertips running across her lips.

Sean felt a tightness spread across his chest and shoulders.

If you're going to do it—

The thought whispered beneath the rush of a wave. The undertow pulled again. He fought it, briefly, then took another step. She heard him now, or sensed him at least. Some disruption in the natural rhythm flowing around her.

If you're going to do it—

She looked up. He sucked in a breath of salt-soaked air.

Do it now.

Sean steeled himself, then all at once stepped in, took her warm hand in his, and closed his eyes.

His lips brushed hers and the sensation was there and then immediately gone. She had pulled clean away before he even realized it. He looked down, his lips still tingling, his palm holding nothing but cool air. He could still hear her breathing, but it sounded different now.

Time stretched out, long and tortuous. Sean simply couldn't look up. When she still didn't say anything, he forced himself to lift his head and meet her eyes. She was no longer smiling in the glow of the torch.

Her expression was one of shock and something else. It took him longer than it should have to place it, and as soon as he did, he immediately wished he hadn't. Embarrassment. And not entirely for herself, he realized with a hot flush of shame. Gabby was embarrassed for him. Sean scrambled to think of something to say, anything at all, but his throat burned with humiliation. He stood there, in the raw and excruciating silence, and felt something barbed slowly unfurl inside him.

"Sean—"

"What?" The word sounded hard to his own ears and he could hear the note of attack in it. He was relieved. For an awful moment, he thought his voice might crack.

"Nothing. I'm really sorry—" Gabby started.

"What for? I don't care." That hard note again. Sean tried to laugh it off, but it came out wrong. He saw Gabby take a small step back and the tiny movement infuriated him.

"I'm sorry." She raised her finger and touched her lips, nervous and exploratory. "I didn't realize you were going to—" She swallowed. "I've never actually—"

She suddenly looked so young, Sean realized, the clarity slicing sharp and deep.

"For God's sake," he said, because he couldn't find the words he wanted. "Don't be such a baby."

Gabby blinked, hurt. She took another small step away from him.

"I mean, you're the one who asked me to bring you here," he said.

"I wanted to find my sister."

"Bullshit. Don't give me that."

"It's true."

"Really? That's not why you wanted to come here? To 'do things'?" He mimicked Gabby with such accuracy that she flinched.

"No, I just wanted to see the caves and find my sister."

And from the way she said it, Sean knew it was true. The humiliation of even thinking that she had wanted anything else left him breathless.

"I need to find Olivia," Gabby said again. She took a ragged breath. "Olivia!" Her voice wavered as she called out. She started crying now, rolling childish tears. There was no answer. "Olivia!" She turned to Sean. "I have to go home now. Please."

Sean stared at her, and in his mind flashed a terrible image of Olivia and Kieran emerging from one of the dark passages to see him here, alone with this crying girl. The thought was followed instantly by another realization.

They would find out.

A cold horror washed over him. Whatever he did now, or didn't do, they would hear about this. And Ash would too. And all of Olivia's friends, and then everyone else. Everyone they'd gone to school with, everyone they saw around town. They'd all hear how Sean had made a pass at Olivia's little sister and how it had all gone really badly wrong.

"Please." Gabby's face was shiny with tears.

"Just shut up a minute. Let me think." But he couldn't. He couldn't think of any way to avoid what was coming to him.

Kieran and Ash would be brutal. They would absolutely rip him apart, laughing themselves sick the whole time. They would never, in his whole life, let him forget this. Olivia wouldn't talk to him anymore. His parents would find out, and Toby as well. Toby would laugh too.

"Please. I want to go home."

"Jesus." Sean shook his head, his heart pounding with the knowledge of what was waiting for him outside that cave. "So just bloody go, Gabby."

"I don't know the way."

Maybe he could leave Evelyn Bay. The thought unraveled in front of Sean like a lifeline. Maybe he could move somewhere interstate. He felt a tiny burst of hope. Maybe he could do that. Could he? He tried to think.

"The floor's wet. My legs are getting wet. The water's coming in. Please."

"Bloody hell, Gabby." But she was right. Sean looked down and felt the water pulse higher against his own skin and the sensation brought him crashing back to the present.

"Christ. Yeah, okay, follow me." Sean pushed past her, the back of his hand brushing hers. He snatched it away as though he'd been burned. "Hurry up."

That's what he would do. He would leave Evelyn Bay. He would pack his stuff and book a flight and move somewhere else. And he'd make new friends, and meet new people, and everyone would forget all about this eventually.

The thoughts ran through his head on a chattering loop as he felt his way through the tunnels. The water was higher than he had realized. He held his torch with one hand and felt the roof with the other as it dipped and lowered. At the junction, the water was thigh-deep now and he had to duck his head to get through the opening.

"Wait." He heard splashing behind him. "Sean. Wait." Gab-by's voice had a muffled directionless quality.

"This way," he called, but didn't stop. He couldn't look at her. He could just hear her splashing over the sound of the rain now hammering down outside.

The water was pouring from the sky in sheets as he emerged into a daylight that was more like night, and he was relieved as the rain hit his face, disguising the first few stinging tears that threatened to slip out. Sean slowed when he hit the spot where the beach usually lay and, against his better judgment, looked back.

"This way," he called again into the entrance of the cave.

And he heard—he was sure he heard, above the howl of the wind and the driving rain and the rush of the ocean bearing down—the splash of movement in the dark. Gabby was right be-hind him, somewhere.

He couldn't face her. Not out here in the open, no matter how rapidly the light was fading. He couldn't stand the thought of that awful long walk back to the marina together, every step agonizing and shameful.

"This way," Sean called again.

Then he turned and waded through the water to the path and the cliffs. He didn't look back as the greedy sea lapped against the rock. He started climbing. He needed to hurry. The storm was coming in.

39

Kieran stared at Sean, his head pounding. The seawater rushed in and out of the North Cave, foaming white against the rock. Kieran looked into its empty mouth and felt sick.

"I thought she was behind me." Sean's voice was quiet. The waves were swirling around his legs now. "She had a torch. I thought she was following me out."

Kieran couldn't tell whether Sean was telling the truth or had managed to convince himself it was the truth. Kieran's own thoughts were clamoring, falling over each other as he tried to make sense of things. He said the first thing that rang true.

"Did Ash and I really give you that much shit?"

Sean just shook his head. "It's not your fault."

Kieran stared at him across the water. "Sean? Mate? I'm sorry. I really am. You didn't deserve that. Not from Ash, and definitely not from me."

Sean rubbed a hand over his eyes. At last, he opened his mouth. "I'm pretty sure Toby and Finn found my note."

Kieran thought of the message scribbled in haste by Sean as Gabby waited on the dock.

4:15 p.m. You were late. Gone to caves.

"After I left here, I went straight back to the marina," Sean said. "I thought Gabby would follow me there, to get her backpack from the boat. But the boat was gone. I had a couple of missed calls from Toby on my phone, but the signal was already patchy by then. The weather was—" He broke off. "It was bad."

Kieran didn't say anything. He knew how bad the weather had been. He remembered it very well.

Sean was also silent for a moment. "The storm was so much worse than I'd expected. I know Toby would have been worried about me out here. Finn too." He breathed out. "I think they came looking for me."

Kieran took another step closer. "They might have gone out looking for you," he found himself saying, "but the emergency call came in for me."

Sean shook his head. "They didn't head out here because of you."

The water was lapping at Sean's thighs now but he still didn't move, simply staring into the gray-green sea with an odd look on his face.

"What did you think when Gabby's bag washed up?" Kieran said.

"I was relieved. I didn't know how badly the boat was damaged, so I was worried they'd find her bag still in the box, but I guess it got washed away in the accident."

It hadn't, Kieran knew now, but looking at Sean standing deep in the water, he didn't want to get into it.

"Gabby's name was all around town when Trish realized she was gone," Sean went on. "I was so scared when she didn't come back. Then I was scared that she would, and that she'd tell everyone what I'd done. But when her bag washed up, it all kind of stopped. Everyone was so worried about other things. Toby and Finn were still dead and you were back from the hospital and we had the funerals, and after all that was over, the whole thing with Gabby—" Sean opened his hands in the empty air. "It was weird. It felt in some ways like it had never happened."

"Until Bronte?"

Sean closed his eyes as though in pain. "Yeah. Until then."

40

The beach outside Fisherman's Cottage was dark, even in the moonlight. The warmth of the day had disappeared with the sun hours earlier and that stretch of shoreline was empty, the day-time visitors all long gone.

Sean stopped outside the cottage, relieved to see lights still burning through the windows. It was late, after eleven thirty already according to his phone, but he could tell from the shadow of movement inside that someone was still up. He dusted the sand off his feet and pulled his shoes back on before walking up the side path to the front door. He thought that was better than knocking on the back. He didn't want to give Bronte a heart attack.

Sean rang the bell and heard the sound of footsteps in the hall. The front door opened, sending a shaft of light onto the path. Bronte's face appeared in the gap. Her look of mild suspicion turned to surprise when she saw Sean standing there.

"Oh, hello. I thought—" Bronte started.

"Sorry—" he said at the same time.

They both stopped.

"Sorry to turn up like this so late," Sean tried again.

"No, it's okay." The door opened wider. "I thought you were Liam. He just left." Bronte glanced over Sean's shoulder, as though perhaps half expecting to see his nephew still loitering. She looked a little relieved that he wasn't. The road was empty. "What brings you here?"

"I wondered if I could grab my torch back? That yellow waterproof one that Ash gave you?"

"Oh. Sure." The door opened all the way and Bronte stepped aside to let him in. She was still wearing her orange waitress uniform but had taken her hair down. "Sorry to have kept it so long. I hadn't realized you needed it."

"It's okay. But I was checking the weather and it looks like tomorrow might be my last chance for a while to get right down inside the wreck." Sean followed her in. The house smelled cool and fresh. "I've got this group from Norway coming soon, so I need to get in while I can."

"No worries. It's in here." Bronte led him down the hall toward the glow spilling out from her bedroom. "Olivia was going on again about stuff lying around, so I put it away." She flashed a smile at him. "Do not tell her I said that; it'll make things worse."

"You guys not getting along?"

"Oh. We're okay." Bronte shrugged. "It's not really me she's annoyed with."

"No?"

She laughed. "Well, that's what I tell myself, anyway. But I know she hates work. And I'm not sure what's wrong with her mum, but there's some issue there. Maybe when I'm gone she'll let Ash move in here. She'd be happier with him around."

"Maybe. I'm not sure they're thinking about that, though."

Bronte looked at him in surprise. "Ash is. For sure."

"Has he said something?"

"No, but he's obviously crazy in love with her," she said with a smile. "He's dying to get serious if Liv would let herself admit how much she really likes him."

Sean couldn't help but smile himself at her enthusiasm. "So you reckon I'll be looking for a new housemate of my own before too long?"

"I'm afraid so. That is a solid prediction. I mean, I get that Ash might not be Liv's usual type in Melbourne or whatever, but they're actually really lovely together when they just relax."

Bronte moved around the bed to her desk, which was crammed with art supplies. Sean hovered in the doorway and she waved him in with one hand while rummaging through a drawer with the other. "Take a seat," she said. "It's in one of these."

The bed was the only option, so Sean moved her open laptop closer to the pillow and sat on the edge. He looked past Bronte to the window above her desk. The blind was open and he could see the black ocean beyond. He frowned.

"Hey, listen, are you sure you don't need that torch any-more? I really could do with that waterproof one back, but I've got a different one at home you could—"

"No, honestly, it's fine."

"What about those noises you heard? Do you feel safe enough without it, or—?"

"Yeah. I do. But thank you." Bronte glanced at the window, a little awkward now. "I'm pretty sure it was just that man from up the road. You know, Brian? The one with dementia. I was help-ing his wife go through some stuff in their shed the other day and she let slip that he'd been wandering. Maybe don't spread that around. I think she was a bit embarrassed. She shouldn't be, though." Bronte pushed her hair off her forehead as she turned back to the drawer. "My grandma was ill with the same thing. I didn't like to say anything earlier in the Surf and Turf in front of your friend, because Brian's his dad, right? It felt a bit personal— oh—" She straightened with a smile on her face and the torch in her hand. "Here it is. How's everything going with the wreck, anyway?"

"Yeah, good. Nearly ready for the season." Sean reached across the bed for the torch. "Thanks. This'll help, at least."

"No, thank you for lending it. And for letting me tag along on that boat trip the other week, by the way. The photos came out really well."

"Which ones? The Survivors?"

"Yeah. You want to see quickly?" Bronte was already sitting down. The bedsprings creaked as she moved closer and she shuffled her laptop around so they could both see. The back of her hand brushed his as she reached for the keyboard. "Here. These ones."

"Yeah. Wow." Sean leaned in. He had seen The Survivors from the water thousands of times, but even so, the images were still striking. They were crisp and full of color. "These are really good."

"Thanks, I was pretty happy." Bronte examined the picture on screen. "I couldn't have got them if you hadn't taken me along."

She shifted a little on the bed as she clicked the keyboard and the photos moved on to the next sequence. Now Sean could see The Survivors on screen again, but different this time. Ankle-deep in water in front of a blue sky, with a thin slice of beach in the foreground of the shot. He recognized the angle immediately.

"You've been down to the caves?" he said.

"Yeah. I wanted to get both sides." Bronte tapped the keyboard again and another image appeared. "Liam told me once that he'd gone down there with you a couple of times as a kid before the barrier went up, so I thought it couldn't be that hard to get down. And it's not, is it?" She wrinkled her nose. "The path's still pretty clear."

Sean frowned. "You've got to be careful down there. The tide can come in fast."

"Yeah, I know." Her eyes were on the laptop. "I only go at low tide. It's worth it, though. Look at the good stuff I got."

The mouth of the North Cave flashed up, the screen growing progressively darker as the images took them deeper and deeper. Sean could follow the first few turns, then the route became less distinct. He could see why she was happy with the photos. She had captured the feel of being right inside.

"Look." Bronte was pointing. "Isn't that amazing? That's one of my favorites."

He looked at a close-up photo of lichen on rock. It was surprisingly beautiful.

"Nice," he said. "Where was that?"

"I can't remember exactly." Bronte frowned. "Near that big central bit in the first cave. Where a few tunnels all break off at the same time. You don't recognize it?"

Sean shook his head. "I know the junction but I don't think I know that bit."

"You must've been there at some point, though." Her eyes were locked on the screen. "Your name's on the wall. See?"

She clicked, then pointed, and Sean looked. And there, in a hazy and unfocused photo of a part of a tunnel that Sean did not recognize, carved in capital letters that he knew were not his own, was the beginning of his name.

"You don't know this spot?" Bronte glanced sideways with a small smile. "I hope it was more memorable for your girlfriend."

The room seemed suddenly both huge and small, and Sean felt the bed listing like a boat. He closed his eyes for a count of two and when he opened them again the movement, at least, had stopped.

"Which girl is that, then?" he said, shocked by how normal his voice sounded. His tongue felt heavy and dry.

"Wow, you really don't remember?" Bronte laughed. She didn't sound unhappy, though. "Abigail or something? Anyway, it was like 'Sean and whoever,' and I thought there was a date as well—" Sean held his breath as Bronte clicked forward. Nothing but rock and lichen. She sat back. "Yeah, it was pretty dark. Looks like I didn't catch that."

"Do you know what the date was?" His words sounded thick to his own ears.

"No. I think it was quite old, though. Maybe ten years or so?" She shrugged. "I'll bring a better flash next time."

Sean was looking at the screen but all he could see was Gabby Birch. Gabby, as he left her waiting safely in the middle of the junction while he went ahead to check the route. The key dangling from the torch in her hand as she soaked up her surroundings, exploring this territory that was—for her, at least—uncharted. Gabby, happy to wait for him, feeling grateful to be there. Gabby, surrounded by tunnels of clean fresh rock, with a key in her palm and an idea forming. Gabby, finding a spot and carving her name, the way she'd been told others had done before her. Carving Sean's name. Perhaps to mark the day they explored the cave together. Perhaps as a thank-you. Perhaps because in that moment she'd believed, in some small way, they were almost friends.

It was all Sean could do not to bury his face in his hands. Instead, he sat completely still and didn't let himself move. "You're going to that spot again?"

"Yeah, definitely." Bronte was nodding. "It's really eerie. I'll get an exhibition out of it, for sure."

"You reckon you'll be able to find it, though?"

"Yeah, I will. Not off the top of my head, but once I'm in there."

She looked on through the shots. Sean sat next to her, his eyes unseeing. Finally, he spoke.

"You probably shouldn't go back down there. You could get fined."

She smiled. "I'll risk it. I'm trying to get into this art school in New York. It's so competitive; they only take a few people a year. I need something really good for my exhibition topic."

"And this is it?" Sean looked at her art desk with the boxes of pencils. His voice sounded odd to him but she didn't seem to notice. "I thought you were mainly into drawing?"

"I am, but this is for my advanced photo module next term. We all get some temporary space in the state gallery, plus there's a bunch of national competitions I'll probably enter." She tapped the keyboard. "This interior life of the caves stuff will work. It's the kind of thing that gets attention."

In the darkened window, Sean could see himself reflected on the bed, his shape distorted in the glass. He could hear the sea outside.

"Please don't go back down there, Bronte."

"Why?" She turned to him, her face close to his. She was—he could hardly bear it—touched by his concern.

"It's dangerous."

"I'll be careful." She smiled at him. "Anyway, you obviously got in and out alive."

The ocean was calm, but when Sean spoke again he could barely hear himself over the sound of the waves.

"That's true."

He looked back to the window. He couldn't believe it when he felt himself put his feet on the floor. The bed creaked as he stood up. *Sit down.* The thought was hard to hear over the noise of the ocean. *Please sit down.* Sean remained standing. He went over to the window. Placed his torch back down on the desk, next to a little wire sculpture of a crayfish.

"The moon's great tonight." His voice wasn't his own. His mouth was forming words that came from a place so deep inside him that he hadn't known it existed. "The light was making these really beautiful patterns over the water. Did you notice?"

He couldn't bring himself to turn around, but he saw Bronte's reflection watching him.

"Really?" she said. "No. I didn't see."

"You can't really tell from in here." Sean stared out at the waves for what felt like a very long time, but he knew wasn't. Because he really didn't need that long to decide. Some part of him had already decided, the instant he saw the photo. "Do you want to go out to the beach? I'll show you."

Bronte looked up from the bed. He turned and could see the duvet creased from where he'd been sitting next to her. She was still there, her fingertips resting lightly against the bed where he'd just been. Waiting, maybe. When he didn't move, she shrugged and smiled.

"Sure. Let's go and see."

Was that a tiny hint of disappointment in her voice? Sean still couldn't hear properly; the sea was loud enough now to drown her out. She stood up, right in front of him, and he moved past her and walked to the door before he could stop himself.

"Great," he said. "Bring your camera."

41

A thousand thoughts were crowding Kieran's head, but the only thing he could see clearly was the way the water was circling Sean. The swell was waist-high and rising. His friend still didn't move. Kieran took another step down the cliff path, stopping at the point where dry land disappeared.

"Come out."

Sean had both hands over his face and Kieran could see he was crying.

"Come out, mate."

No response. The water surged.

"I can't find Gabby's carving," Sean said at last. "I've been looking, but I don't know which tunnel she was in. The police will find it, though. Or someone else will one day."

"Sean, mate. That's okay. All right?" Kieran tried hard to keep his voice calm but he was struggling. "You can explain. A decent lawyer will—"

"That doesn't matter." Sean almost laughed. "Everyone will know, won't they? Liam. And Olivia. And Trish. You." His voice dropped. "*I* know."

"Okay. I get that, mate. But come out of the water. Please. Now. I know you can feel the tide, Sean." Kieran was afraid to look too closely out to sea, scared to see how high the water was lapping against The Survivors. "You know what that means out here."

Sean wiped a rough palm over his eyes. When he dropped his hands, he wasn't looking at Kieran or the path. He was staring at the caves. "I knew what high tide meant back then, too."

"No, mate, just—" Kieran was already punching in the emergency number on his phone. He took another step and was in the water now. He blurted his location to whoever answered and turned back to Sean, who was standing very still. Kieran's heart lurched with every wave rolling in. "Sean. Come out."

No answer.

"Sean. Please." The tide felt like it was moving very fast and Kieran shouted to make sure he was heard. "If you go in now, you won't come out again."

Still no reply, only the swell of the water and the screams of the birds circling overhead. The Survivors continued to look away. Kieran made himself check. They were deep now.

"I can't follow you, Sean." Even as Kieran spoke, he took another step into the water. "I'm not going to come in there and try and stop you. Someone's coming but it's not going to be me." The freezing waves washed against his legs and he had to brace himself to keep his balance. "I can't do it to Mia and Audrey."

Sean didn't react. His distress had given way to a cold calm that made Kieran feel very afraid.

"Sean?"

His friend at last dragged his gaze away from the caves, steadying himself against the pull of the tide as he turned to look at Kieran.

"How did you do it, mate?" Sean's voice was almost lost

beneath the crash of the surf and the call of the birds. "Live with that guilt after the storm?"

"How? I don't know, I—" Kieran's thoughts were racing but even in the midst of them, he knew the answer. Of course he knew. Mia and Audrey. He looked at Sean through the spray. "I was lucky. I found something that mattered to me more."

Sean seemed to accept that. He turned back to the caves, still horribly calm.

"Listen, you can do that thing you talked about," Kieran tried, desperate now. "Can't you? Just draw a circle around it all and pretend—"

"Not this."

At last, Sean moved. He drew in a breath, then took a step toward the North Cave.

"Wait."

Sean didn't stop. He didn't look back.

"Please wait." Kieran was well in the water now. He wouldn't follow, he promised himself, even as he waded deeper, the sand soft and shifting under his feet. "Please—"

Sean ignored him. He was moving fast now, forcing his way through the water.

"Wait!"

He didn't, instead driving forward, pulling himself onward as the breakers rolled alongside. He seemed to stop for a single moment, at the very mouth of the cave, then dropped his head and followed the rush of the water from daylight into the darkness.

"Please—"

The surf swelled, almost knocking Kieran's feet out from under him, and he had to fight not to get dragged in. He heard the smash of water hitting a wall of rock inside the cave, and when he'd found his footing and the wave retreated he couldn't see Sean at all anymore. Kieran's eyes raced over the surface as he splashed through the water, waist-deep himself before he realized it. The freezing ocean pulled at him. The mouths of the caves yawned open and empty.

Sean—who had always been there, who had been Kieran's friend for all of his life—was gone.

Kieran felt like he couldn't breathe. He couldn't think what he should do. He could see the waves lapping high against The Survivors and suddenly it was twelve years ago and he was lost all over again. He scrambled in the water, his head twisting from the caves to the cliff path, trying to find his way out. He couldn't see the bottom of the trail. It was submerged, he realized, and his world lurched until he wasn't sure what was sky and what was sea.

"Kieran?"

The shout bounced off the rocks. He tried to steady himself, focusing on the mouth of the cave. It remained dark and hollow. No one was there.

"Kieran! Up here!"

The voice wasn't coming from the caves. Kieran blinked. He wiped the water from his face and squinted up against the bright sky.

Mia.

She was edging her way down the cliff path, Audrey strapped to her chest. She rounded the jagged rock from where she could see the vanished beach clearly for the first time. Her face collapsed at the sight of him in the waves.

"Kieran!" A flurry of rushed steps, her voice nearly lost over the sound of the water hitting the rock. "I saw your note. What are you doing? Oh my God!" She looked ahead. "Where's the rest of the path?"

"Wait, don't!" The sight of her snapped him back into himself.

He held up his hand as another wave nearly knocked him off his feet. He stumbled but held firm this time. "It's not safe."

"Jesus, yes, thank you, I can see that!" Mia shouted back, but at least she stayed where she was. Kieran started wading toward her, pushing through the sea until he heard another smack of water on rock. He stopped, fighting against the drag of the current. The black void of the cave entrance gaped wide as Mia turned to look too.

"Has something happened?" she called, but her voice was quieter now.

Kieran nodded. He couldn't find the words.

"I'll get help." She was already reaching for her phone.

He shook his head. "It's on its way."

Mia hesitated, then took another couple of steps down. The noise of the sea and the cries of the birds were deafening. She stopped clear of the edge of the water.

"Then you've done everything you can do, Kieran." Her voice cut through, firm and clear. Her feet were dry, out of reach of the waves. He could see Audrey moving against her chest. "You can come out of there."

Kieran could still hear the sea thundering in and out of the tunnels. He dragged his eyes away from the caves and back to Mia.

"Whatever's happened here,"—her voice was still calm—"it's done now. It's over."

She stretched out her hand to him.

"I can't come any further," she said. "You have to come to us."

Kieran looked at her. He had loved Finn. He still missed him and wished he were here, and he guessed he always would. But as he saw Mia standing there, something he realized he'd known for a long time shone through like a beacon, small but clear and bright. Finn was gone, and he wasn't coming back. But Kieran still had others in his life. Other people he loved. Mia, reaching out for him, and Audrey, small but with so much ahead. Kieran thought about Verity and Brian, waiting for him at home. He thought about his friends and couldn't help but look one last time at the caves.

Then he turned away. He looked toward Mia and began pushing his way forward through the water to her and Audrey. He kept moving, not letting himself stop until he felt the sand give way to firm path under his feet. When he was close enough, Mia reached down and he stretched up and she helped pull him clear of the sea.

Kieran was shivering hard but she was warm as she steadied him on the path. He wasn't sure what else to do, so he put his wet arms around her and Audrey and held them both until he felt himself begin to breathe again. He wasn't sure how long they stood there together, their heads close, Mia's hands on his back.

Finally, he straightened. "Let's go. Let's go up."

"Are you sure?" Mia looked at him. "Are you ready?"

"Yeah." He nodded. "I'm ready."

They turned toward the path, winding clear and dry ahead. Kieran didn't look back at the lifeless caves or the angry sea or the lonely gaze of The Survivors. He reached out instead and took Mia's hand as she held their daughter and they made their way together, up to higher ground.

ACKNOWLEDGMENTS

This book took me to a beautiful part of Australia and my thanks go to the many people in Tasmania who were kind enough to share their stories and experiences with me. Thank you to the staff at the Eaglehawk Dive Centre in Eaglehawk Neck for guiding me through such a fascinating experience underwater, and patiently answering my many questions about diving in Tasmania.

I am grateful to Grant Blashki, Lead Clinical Advisor for Beyond Blue, for sharing his professional insights around the impact of grief as well as the research and treatments available.

Any mistakes or artistic liberties throughout the book are my own.

My sincere gratitude to the real Sue Pendlebury and George Barlin who successfully bid for the chance to name a character at the Peter Pan Committee's Literary Lunch to raise funds for Barnardos. Thank you so much for your generous donation to this important cause and for lending your names to two of my favorite characters.

Thank you to the many people who worked so hard on this

book: my editors Christine Kopprasch at Flatiron Books, Cate Paterson and Georgia Douglas at Pan Macmillan, and Clare Smith at Little, Brown; my agents Daniel Lazar at Writers House, Clare Forster at Curtis Brown Australia, Alice Lutyens and Kate Cooper at Curtis Brown UK, and Jerry Kalajian at the Intellectual Property Group; and my publicists Clare Keighery at Pan Macmillan, Amelia Possanza at Flatiron Books, and Grace Vincent at Little, Brown.

Thank you to my friend and former publicist Charlotte Ree from Pan Macmillan, whose promotion has rightly taken her onward and upward, but whose dedication and wisdom have been a driving force in the success of my books.

Thank you to my brother Michael Harper for Shifty the dog's name and backstory, and as always to Mike Harper, Helen Harper, Ellie Harper, Susan Davenport, and Ivy and Ava Harper for their support.

A big welcome to the two new arrivals who in no small way helped inform the character of baby Audrey: my son Ted Strachan and niece Isabel Harper.

And, as always, my love and gratitude to my husband Peter Strachan, our wonderful daughter Charlotte, and beautiful baby Ted. I couldn't do it without you.

ABOUT THE AUTHOR

Jane Harper is the *New York Times* bestselling author of the #1 international bestseller *The Dry*, *Force of Nature*, and *The Lost Man*. *The Survivors* is her fourth novel. Jane previously worked as a print journalist in Australia and the UK and now lives in Melbourne with her husband, daughter, and son.

janeharper.com.au